T0193929

Reviews of "From Moses to Moses"

"Taylor's command of the details of Maimonides' life, as well as the cultural and political features of the historical period, is simply magisterial."

"His account of his subject's valiant attempt to preserve the Jewish culture and its ancient repository of biblical teachings is as engaging as it is moving."

"A rigorously researched and lucidly presented account of a philosopher's extraordinary journey."

"The prose is unfailingly clear throughout."

Kirkus Reviews

"This is a work of fiction that aims to fill in the blanks related to one of the most influential Jewish philosophers, Moses ben Maimon, also known as Maimonides."

"Irving Taylor's speculative historical novel From Moses to Moses chronicles the eventful life of Maimonides."

"The storytelling is cohesive, its pace set by the few events of Maimonides's life that are known."

Clarion review

"*Taylor shows a keen grasp of the historical period and its complexity and fills in some unknowns about Maimonides.*"

"*The book will be appreciated by those familiar with Maimonides' teachings or fascinated by the historical period, laden as it was with factors—political, religious, ethical— that still plague the Middle East today.* "

"*......doesn't shrink from exploring the many criticisms aimed at Maimonides back then but keeps the overall portrait positive, emphasizing the philosopher's unusually liberal views on women's rights and citing cases showing him making open-minded judgments based on his best understanding of God, science and scripture.*"

Blueink review

FROM
MOSES
TO
MOSES

IRVING TAYLOR

authorHOUSE®

AuthorHouse™ UK
1663 Liberty Drive
Bloomington, IN 47403 USA
www.authorhouse.co.uk
Phone: 0800 047 8203 (Domestic TFN)
*   +44 1908 723714 (International)*

Published by AuthorHouse 08/09/2019

ISBN: 978-1-5462-9755-0 (sc)
ISBN: 978-1-5462-9754-3 (e)

ABOUT THE AUTHOR

Irving Taylor is Emeritus Professor of Surgery at University College London. Prior to this he was Head of Departments of Surgery in Southampton (1981-1993) and University College London (1993-2008). He was Vice Dean for Professional Affairs at UCL between 2008-2015, an elected member of Council of the Royal College of Surgeons of England for ten years and a Case Examiner on the UK General Medical Council for eleven years. He has written or edited 35 textbooks in surgery but "From Moses to Moses" is his first attempt at an historical novel. He is married to Berry and they have three daughters and seven grandchildren.

Whatsoever thy hand findeth to do, do it with thy might; for there is no work, nor device, nor knowledge, nor wisdom, in the grave withest thou goest.

Ecclesiastes 9:10

Dedicated to four fabulous females, Berry, Justine, Tammy, and Gabi, and to my dear departed parents, Sam and Fay Taylor.

GLOSSARY

A glossary providing definitions of terms which the reader might be unfamiliar with is provided here.

Arabic mile approximately 2.2 km

Baruch Hashem Bless the Lord

Beth Din rabbinical court

bimaristan medieval Islamic hospital

chometz leavened bread

dayan rabbinical judge

dvar Torah a Torah discussion

eshet chayil woman of worth

gaon Talmudic leader

Halacha Jewish law

Kaddish prayer recited by mourners

ketuba marriage certificate

legua (league) approximately 4.2 km

maariv evening prayer

madrasa Arabic educational institution

mazel tov congratulations

meyaledet midwife

mezuzah scroll affixed to doorpost

minyan quorum of ten men for prayer

mikva ritual bath

mishna oral law

mitzvah Torah commandment

nagid religious leader

Nisan Hebrew month

Passover/Pesach holiday remembering the exodus from Egypt

rebbetzin rabbi's wife

Rosh Hashanah Jewish New Year

shacharit morning prayers

Shavuot Pentecost

shechitah ritual slaughter of animals

shidduch marriage arrangement

shiva seven days of mourning following a death

sifra; sifre commentaries on books of the Torah

talmid chacham Torah scholar of repute

Tevet Hebrew month

tefillin phyllacteries

tosefta compilation of Jewish oral law

tzadik righteous religious person

yeshiva school of Torah studies

PART I

CORDOBA, SPAIN

1135–1148

1

It was a false alarm. The contractions were regular but not particularly intense. Hannah, the *meyaledet* (midwife), accompanied by her helper, had been called but was not concerned.

"Please let my husband know," requested Sarah. "He has been most anxious in recent days and is immersed in prayer."

"I will inform your husband. But do not worry. It will be at least another two days. Just think, you could have a Passover baby." Hannah had a reputation for accuracy in predicting delivery times.

Sarah was reassured and smiled benignly. This was a novel experience for her.

"I will leave you these balms to be rubbed into your belly three times a day," Hannah instructed. "You must eat lots of nutritious foods and drink fresh milk with honey." She then left with her helper.

As Sarah lay on the bed, alone with her thoughts and anxious about the baby to come, she thought about her marriage, how she'd only been nineteen on their wedding day. Her husband, Rabbi Maimon ben Yosef, was thirty-two. She knew not everyone thought she was a good match for Maimon, but he didn't seem to care what other people thought, and neither did she. Sarah was a butcher's daughter, and her father had no background of Torah study.

"What kind of *shidduch* is this?" was a refrain whispered amongst the more critical members of her husband's congregation.

She was so proud that her husband was considered the most respected and erudite rabbi in Cordoba. He had been a judge, a dayan, for seven years, and when he was first appointed, he was the youngest in living memory.

Sarah also knew that Maimon was very conscious of his illustrious heritage. He was a direct descendant of Rabbi Judah ha-Nasi, one of the greatest names in rabbinic Judaism, who was the second-century editor of the important legal text called *The Mishna*. She was also aware that his lineage went back as far as to King David himself. Rabbi Maimon reassured her frequently that their marriage was appropriate irrespective of what others thought. Not long before they were married, Maimon told her that he had a vivid dream in which God commanded him to marry the daughter of a butcher. Prophetic dreams of this type were highly regarded by members of the community. The decision to marry was therefore accepted.

She remembered how kind and considerate Maimon had been when they first met in the presence of a chaperone. They had decided to marry soon after this first and only meeting. In accordance with Jewish religious practice, they did not have a prolonged engagement.

The wedding took place a week after the festival of Shavuot. The entire community were invited to the festivities, as were many colleagues and friends from as far away as Tudela. Maimon's own rabbi, Joseph ibn Migash from Lucena, who was also his close friend and confidante, officiated. The traditional wedding canopy was erected in the central square in La Juderia, the main Jewish quarter.

The wedding was an occasion filled with joy. Sarah could

not remember a time when she'd been so happy. The flamboyant dancing of men, separated from women by an opaque barrier, continued well into the night. Vast quantities of food and drink were consumed. Blessings to both her and Maimon were delivered in melodic style.

She smiled to herself as she remembered how, following the festivities, she was left alone with her husband for the very first time and they made their way to the bridal suite. Prior to the wedding, she had immersed herself in the ritual bath (the mikva) to achieve purity, and her mother had provided her with relevant information for her conduct on the wedding night to conform with accepted modesty. Neither bride nor bridegroom was entirely relaxed, but with patience and gentle coaxing the marriage was consummated. Sarah was grateful that they were both comfortable in their lovemaking.

The subsequent seven days were taken up with social gatherings, much rejoicing, and celebratory dinners at different houses, the couple surrounded by friends and relatives.

She was conscious that her husband was physically attracted to her and that their lovemaking had become increasingly more passionate. He frequently told her how much he admired her resolute personality. She was reserved and modest in company and yet had strong views that she was unafraid of expressing to her husband in private. Rabbi Maimon was pleased to apply his deep Talmudic knowledge to contemporary issues that she raised and which he had never previously considered.

They enjoyed a comfortable life in Cordoba. He was well supported by his community, and his position as dayan and head of the Beth Din resulted in a degree of wealthy respectability. In addition, her parents' butchery business was extremely profitable, and since she was an only child, they were generous with both money and gifts. The couple's house was large and well-furnished. It was a two-storey house roofed with broad, flat tiles. The top storey had a covered balcony. Rabbi Maimon was often seen reading on the balcony in the early evening. Each room had carpets from Persia or Egypt. Numerous tapestries covered the walls, many with biblical themes. Beautiful textiles purchased locally from merchants and some from India were arranged tastefully around the rooms. The hall and rooms were tiled with glazed alternating colours in the form of decorative mosaics.

Sarah prided herself on her appearance. Both she and her husband were always dressed in the manner that would be expected of a rabbi and his wife. She was modestly attired, very often with colourful silks, especially on the Sabbath and the festivals, with a headscarf in the form of a turban or a shoulder-length veil and a floor-length tunic with long sleeves in accordance with the Jewish custom for married women. She insisted on attractive clothes which made her appearance more elegant and mature. Maimon was invariably robed in a long tunic with wide sleeves, his head covered with a turban that was almost indistinguishable from his Muslim neighbours', although he wore an embroidered skullcap when indoors.

Sarah had introduced her own style into the previously drab, male-dominated religious surroundings. She loved the appearance and feel of ceramics obtained locally but also from abroad. She purchased ivory carvings and lead crystal, all greatly appreciated by her numerous visitors and approved by her husband.

Maimon spent a significant proportion of each day immersed in study of Torah and the oral laws. He had an extensive library. His books included not only standard religious texts but also collections of works on philosophy, medicine, theology, and science. He often commented on how unrewarding life would have been without the widespread production of paper, which for the last two hundred years had been freely available throughout the Islamic world after being introduced by the Chinese. Books had become more available and more plentiful than in the Latin West, where they continued to be written on expensive parchment. The Arabs had paper, and the Latin West did not.

The major paper factory in Spain was in Xàtiva, a town close to Valencia.

Sarah stretched, yawned, and then smiled as she propped herself up in bed. Yes, her life with Maimon was full indeed, and that was the way she liked it. Between his studies in his grand library and the time he spent in the synagogue, times she knew were a great comfort to him, there sometimes were spells of loneliness for her. A wave of contentment washed over her as she felt her stomach. She could deal with a little loneliness. She rubbed some of the balm onto her stomach and appreciated the warming sensation.

There were several synagogues within Cordoba, but her husband's was the most popular and prestigious. It was situated on Calleja del Panuelo, an irregular cobbled street in the nicest part of the Jewish quarter. The décor in the synagogue was elaborate with marble and the finest timber. Even the women's gallery was comfortable and easy to access, unlike in other synagogues. The women, although unable to be seen by the men, were able to feel the full spiritual force of the surroundings. Sarah invariably sat in the front row and welcomed visitors with a smile, which gained her the respect and admiration of all the congregants.

"What a capable woman, and so young" was a frequent comment, even from people who were initially so condescending of her status before marriage.

"Always with a smile, the rebbetzin is so welcoming. Rabbi Maimon has done well."

Sarah was content, enjoyed her life as a rabbi's wife, and felt fulfilled. Her hospitality became legendary. Whenever a stranger entered the synagogue, she greeted the person with a friendly smile and, in partnership with her husband, extended an invitation to their home for a meal. She provided constant support to her husband and relieved the burdens of his responsibility for pastoral care to his congregants whenever possible.

Three months after the wedding, Sarah proudly announced

to her husband that she was pregnant. Maimon was overwhelmed. Tears welled in his eyes as he recited prayers to thank God and to ask for a safe birth.

The pregnancy was uneventful. Maimon was overtly emotional and insisted on pampering his wife, ensuring regular rest with good food as recommended by Hannah. Sarah's parents were delighted. They provided large quantities of the finest roasted meat on a regular basis. Members of the community offered assistance as the pregnancy progressed. Hannah visited regularly and provided constant reassurance and advice.

The birth was predicted to take place around the time of the festival of Passover, an extremely busy time. Much work around the house was required to ensure that the house was spotless and all signs of leavened bread, *chometz*, were removed. Sarah tried to assist in these endeavours with some difficulty and left much to her maid, Dina, and her husband when he was available.

"Please relax, Sarah. We will manage. Should the baby be born on Pesach, it will be a great mitzvah and a sign of a great future," remarked Maimon, who was happy to provide constant reassurance.

Suddenly, on the day after the false alarm, Sarah felt a stab of pain that told her the contractions had returned. This time they were more acute and frequent. Hannah had been summoned and the doctor warned. Sarah groaned and looked towards Hannah, who returned her look with a nod.

"Your wife is progressing well," she told Rabbi Maimon. "It will not be very long. Go to the synagogue."

Sarah lay on a large divan surrounded by embroidered pillows. She was in obvious pain and was sweating. She was comforted by Dina and Hannah. Oil was rubbed into her flanks.

Hannah raised Sarah's legs to examine.

"You're nearly there now. Try gentle pushing."

Sarah's face contorted. She grabbed hold of Hannah's hand and squeezed hard.

Boiled water was prepared, lavender water was liberally sprayed, and childbirth commenced.

Rabbi Maimon had initially gone to the synagogue, but whilst there he remained anxious and decided to return home to be with his wife. He took a shortcut, across the Guadalquivir bridge and then through the market where Muslim merchants were laying out their grains, beans, seeds, and nuts. He prayed in an undertone as he approached his house. His calm, however, was shattered by the screams emanating from the bedroom.

He sat down on a settee in the patio and anxiously fidgeted with his prayer shawl. His friend Yaacov, who had accompanied him from the synagogue for support and was himself the father of five children, told him to relax.

"Don't worry. This is normal."

Maimon was not convinced. He continued to recite psalms. Men were not allowed to enter the birthing room. He estimated that Sarah had been in labour for at least six hours. Surely this was not normal. He began to pray with almost fervent intensity. The screams continued. He could hear frantic shouts as Hannah barked orders. The doctor, who had arrived soon after Hannah, was audibly agitated. Maimon paced the room. What was happening? Why all the shouting? He tried to relax, but it was impossible as he feared for his wife and child. His anxiety reached a crescendo.

"What is happening, Yaacov?" He was perspiring, and his hands were shaking. "How much longer? I can stand it no more." And then a brief period of quiet was followed by the gentle cry of an infant.

"Baruch Hashem." Yaacov hugged him. "Mazel tov!" Yaacov shouted with joy.

Dina appeared on the patio. She smiled, but her almond eyes revealed a tear. "Rabbi, you may come in to see your son."

Maimon was concerned. Dina seemed reluctant and far from jubilant.

Maimon followed Dina into the room. He was horrified by what he saw. He was sure the scene would remain lodged in his mind for years to come. Sarah was lying on the divan clutching a tiny new-born baby. Hannah had positioned herself between Sarah's legs and was pushing into the pelvis, struggling with linen towels and trying to stem the bleeding. There were large spreading bloodstains on the marble floor and divan. Hannah acknowledged Rabbi Maimon's presence but looked fearful. Sarah was pale and dishevelled. Rabbi Maimon sat by her side and held her hand.

"Dear husband, we have a beautiful boy. Baruch Hashem." She seemed to have difficulty speaking, and her voice was hardly audible. Maimon kissed her forehead tenderly. The baby was crying with his head against Sarah's chest. He was a good colour, but his forehead appeared wrinkled and his face squashed. The doctor looked anxious. He shook his head. He was rubbing an herbal remedy consisting of fennel and mashed garlic into Sarah's abdomen, but to no avail. The bleeding continued relentlessly. Sarah put the child to her breast, and he sucked voraciously. She smiled and looked content. For almost two hours she slipped in and out of consciousness but throughout insisted on clutching the baby against her breast. Fear and foreboding gripped Rabbi Maimon.

Slowly, life slipped away from Sarah, and it pained Maimon more than he could have imagined. On the eve of Passover, Sarah died peacefully, still holding her baby. Sadness overwhelmed Maimon. He knew he would forever loathe 30 March 1135 (14 Nisan 4895). He knew he would never forget the love of his life, the butcher's beautiful daughter, his Sarah. His beloved beautiful Sarah.

A distraught Hannah handed the baby to Maimon to hold. With tears in his eyes, he kissed the tiny forehead.

"Your wife is no longer in pain. May her soul rest in peace."

Hannah washed the baby's tongue with water to ensure that he would speak properly. Honey was rubbed on his palate to give him a good appetite. He was then bathed in warm water and milk.

The baby, soon to be named Moses, was then taken for routine after-birth care.

2

Rabbi Maimon had lived in Cordoba all his life but still had difficulty in coping with the unbearably hot summer months. This summer had been particularly oppressive. There was no cooling breeze to provide relief, and his long flowing coat and turban seemed inappropriate in the circumstances. He was nevertheless conscious of the facilities which were made available to the population, especially for managing the long periods of summer heat. There were numerous public baths and drinking water fountains, and many houses, including his own, had indoor plumbing and internal running water.

Cordoba was surrounded by a Roman wall with thirteen gates, but the one through which he preferred to enter the city was the Puerta del Puente, which allowed him to pass by the large plaza and be cooled by the spray from the central sparkling fountain. If time permitted, he would sit for a while and contemplate in the well-tended garden.

Spain was experiencing a "golden age". As Rabbi Maimon wandered towards the Jewish quarter, he marvelled at the cathedral, close to his home, and the Great Mosque along the banks of the Guadalquivir. There were hundreds of mosques in Cordoba but also many synagogues. The streets were well-lit and paved. Muslims, Jews, and Christians were able to follow their respective religion with almost complete freedom. How different from other parts of Europe! Everyone, irrespective of religion or status, had access to the libraries, to the hospital facilities, to the public baths, and to thousands of shops. Close to the Great Mosque was a magnificent citrus plantation which enhanced the mosque's religious architecture and provided a pleasure garden for the people to enjoy. Maimon marvelled at the opulence and bustling activity and was struck by how well dressed the citizens appeared. It was difficult to distinguish the appearance of a Jew from that of a Christian or a Muslim.

Although Arabic was the common language, Hebrew was frequently used by the Jews, and of course it remained the language of prayer. Cordoba was prosperous and dynamic with an ever-expanding population of now almost two hundred thousand, with Jews representing some 5 per cent of the total.

In the countryside, the introduction of new crops and new techniques, including irrigation, had made agricuslture a prosperous undertaking. Farmers brought their donkeys laden with fruit and vegetables to the marketplaces. Jewish craftsmen were renowned for their excellent leatherwork, and hundreds of Jewish weavers created wool and cotton fabrics that were sold throughout Europe. Al-Andalus (Muslim Spain) was booming, and Maimon was proud that Jews were key in contributing to the political, economic, and cultural life of Cordoba. Moreover, the caliph had a Jew as his foreign minister.

Despite all this, Rabbi Maimon was troubled by the Umayyad Caliphate dictat that labelled Jews and Christians, who shared Abrahamic monotheism, as *dhimmis*, the Arabic word for the protected People of the Book or, as cynically translated by Maimon, "second-class citizens". Yes, he enjoyed the freedom to practise his religion, but he could only do so by submitting to Muslim law and authority. Undoubtedly there were distinctions of privilege amongst the different religions, but he conceded that life was still very comfortable for most of the Jewish population, even though he was concerned about the inevitable intermarriages which occurred between the different cultures and that Jews were becoming increasingly Arabised.

Full protection by the Muslim rulers did not come for free. All *dhimmis* had to pay a specific tax, the *jizya*, to receive these benefits. *Dhimmis* who did not pay the tax had to either convert to Islam or face the death penalty. The tax burden was always increasing and became a major source of income for the kingdom. Maimon was frequently involved in assisting members of the Jewish community who were unable to afford the tax. He had set up several charities and was often an advocate for congregants who had fallen on bad times. At present he was particularly concerned about Meir and his family. Meir had recently developed a cough which had worsened and now left him incapacitated and unable to work. His wife took in washing. This was their only source of income. The family had barely enough to feed themselves and often had to rely on the synagogue hardship fund to survive. They were unable to pay *jizya*. The local council had warned that if payment was not honoured, Meir and family must convert to Islam. Meir was not particularly religious and had decided that this was the only option. He was too proud to accept additional charity from the Jewish community. Rabbi Maimon had tried to change his mind, but Meir was insistent.

Maimon was deep in thought as he strolled towards the Jewish quarter. The midday heat had become increasingly overpowering. He recalled that it was almost nine years since Sarah had died and six years since he had remarried. He respected his new wife as a caring, supportive partner who adored Moses, but she had initially lacked the warmth and charisma of Sarah.

The community had understood the difficulty Rabbi Maimon had in coming to terms with Sarah's death. It might have been thought that his deep religious fervour would have been dented by the tragic loss, but the reality was quite the opposite. He had immersed himself in prayer and study, possibly as a method to divert his bereavement sadness. His overall workload expanded, he was appointed as Rosh Beth Din, head of the religious court, in addition to his responsibilities within the synagogue.

As he strolled through the busy streets, frequently accosted by beggars and merchants, he remembered his first contact with Shoshanah.

"Rabbi, I want you to meet my sister's daughter. She is from a good religious family and loves children," demanded Rivka, the wife of Rabbi Shmuel ben Yitzach, who was well known for her forthright direct approach.

He and Rabbi Shmuel had been acquainted for several years but could hardly be regarded as close friends. Shoshanah was twenty-nine when they first met. She was tall and remarkably thin with dark curly hair and a rather elongated face with exaggerated cheekbones. Because of her height, she tended to walk with her head bent forward and portrayed a rather timid appearance. She could not be described as physically beautiful, but no one doubted her kind and considerate personality or her intense religious faith. She was at an age that her parents and friends despaired that she would ever marry. She taught in the girls' school attached to her father's synagogue and was hugely popular with both parents and children. However, the absence of children of her own was a constant source of stress to her.

A meeting was arranged with Shoshanah under the supervision of a family friend. Rabbi Maimon remembered that their conversation covered many topics of common interest, but it was not long before the subject of Moses's upbringing was broached.

"My life revolves around children. I would regard it as a pleasure and privilege to look after your son," she had remarked demurely.

"You must come and meet with him," he offered.

"I would be delighted to," Shoshanah replied. She paused a

moment and then added with obvious embarrassment, "I meant only that I would be happy to look after his needs should I be required to do so. I am often asked to care for my young nieces by my sister."

"I do understand." He had smiled reassuringly and knowingly.

This initial meeting convinced him that Shoshanah would be a sympathetic stepmother for his son. Rabbi Shmuel was delighted to give his blessing to the betrothal. Within six weeks wedding plans were put in place, and two months after the couple were first introduced, they were married.

As expected, Shoshanah was an ideal mother for Moses. Her experience in looking after young children was invaluable and much appreciated. She worked hard at being a good wife. However, she remained timid and introspective.

On their first wedding anniversary, Shoshanah announced that she was pregnant. She was ecstatic. Rabbi Maimon noticed that her whole demeanour changed. She became more confident. She seemed to blossom.

The pregnancy progressed uneventfully, as indeed did the labour. She delivered a healthy boy. Rabbi Maimon remembered how joyful Hannah was when she brought the happy news to him. He blessed and thanked his wife. She had survived childbirth.

The birth of his second son, named David following his circumcision eight days later, changed Rabbi Maimon's relationship with his wife. They were both more relaxed. Shoshanah enjoyed the challenge of looking after the two children. Her greatest desire, to have a child of her own, had been met. She made sure that Moshe received as much of her attention as David did. Moshe loved his brother and was fiercely protective of him. He showed no jealousy or resentment against his younger brother and was seen frequently playing with him.

Shoshanah deserved great credit for bringing up the rabbi's sons in an environment of love and joy. He was devoted to her and no longer compared her to Sarah.

Maimon arrived home exhausted from the heat. His tunic was drenched with sweat, and he needed a full ewer of water to refresh himself. He rested for a while.

When fully refreshed, he called for Moses. Even though his rabbinic lifestyle was onerous with a heavy workload, he personally undertook the Jewish education of Moses at home. This was traditional in his family. He fondly recalled how his own father had introduced him to Judaism when he was the same age as Moshe. However, teaching Moshe was a challenging task. It was obvious that the boy was gifted and possessed a prodigious memory, but Rabbi Maimon was increasingly exasperated by his lack of concentration and dedication to learning.

Moshe joined his father and sat on the floor by his side. He carried a book but seemed vague and disinterested. "Moshe, please concentrate. You seem so reluctant to learn. How can a son of mine prefer to daydream or to play rather than to learn Torah? Remember your background, your grandparents. You must put your mind to study."

Moshe was fluent in Hebrew and had learnt to write in Arabic using Hebrew letters, Judaeo-Arabic. Learning and study, however, had to be forced on him. He showed little interest or commitment. He was eminently capable of learning but lacked the enthusiasm to do so and failed to appreciate the significance of acquiring knowledge. Maimon was tired from his recent exertion and became increasingly irritated with his son, who appeared disinterested and soon lost all semblance of concentration. Maimon angrily dismissed him and went in search of Shoshanah.

"What am I to do, Shoshanah? He will only study when I coerce him to. After ten minutes he loses concentration and shows no interest. And the exasperating thing is that he has a brilliant mind but will not use it for learning." He confided regularly in Shoshanah with increasing frustration and apprehension.

The situation was distressing for Maimon because he recognised in his son not only a remarkable mental agility, essential for Torah and Talmudic study, but also the possession of a remarkable memory. He was certain that the Almighty had blessed him with a son whose future influence on the Jewish people could be significant. It was therefore his responsibility to lead Moshe along the path that God had identified for him. If Maimon failed to achieve this, then he would be failing the Almighty. The thought tormented him. He must not allow this to happen under any circumstances.

"Dear husband, with the greatest of respect, might I be permitted to question whether Moshe would do better with a teacher who is not his father?" suggested Shoshanah rather reticently. She was always careful to avoid any proposal that might seem to contradict her husband's views.

"I have also considered this, but the only person I could trust would be my good friend and colleague Rabbi Yosef ibn Migash in Lucena. This would mean Moshe leaving home for a few years."

Rabbi Migash was a prominent Talmudic scholar, a disciple of the great rabbi Yitzchak Alfasi. He had taught Rabbi Maimon as a youth, and they had enjoyed a good relationship ever since. Rabbi Migash's yeshiva was the most prestigious Torah academy in Spain.

Shoshanah thought for a few moments. "If you feel it is best for his education and future development, even though he will be greatly missed in our home, should we not provide him with the very best opportunity for learning?"

"You are right, of course, but at his age will he be happy so far away from his family? You know how he adores David, and he has many friends here in Cordoba. I am convinced he has potential to be a great scholar and that this must not be lost, but I feel reluctant to send him away."

"Dear husband, if studying with Rabbi Migash would provide an opportunity for Moshe to become a great *talmid chacham*, then surely the sacrifice is justified in God's name."

Maimon sat quietly for a few moments. He remembered his own experiences under the influence of Rabbi Migash. He knew that the learning programme would be arduous for Moshe, but on the other hand he was certain that his son had the mental capacity to cope. Shoshanah was correct: every opportunity should be made available to Moshe, and the change in environment in a yeshiva with Rabbi Migash may be the stimulus necessary for him to concentrate wholeheartedly on his studies.

Maimon was grateful for his wife's encouragement. The decision was taken. Provided Rabbi Migash was able to accommodate him, Moshe would be sent to Lucena to continue his Jewish education under the tutelage of one of the greatest Talmudic scholars of the time. They sat quietly, each reflecting on the implications of the decision.

The couple's quietude was interrupted by loud repetitive knocking on the door.

"Who can that possibly be this late at night?" queried an anxious Rabbi Maimon. His immediate thought was that a congregant had died or was terminally ill and a relative was requesting prayers to be said. Dina, their servant, appeared from the kitchen. "I will see who it is," she offered, and made her way to the door.

A visibly worried man in his early fifties, poorly dressed, breathless, and coughing, greeted Dina. "Can I help?" Dina looked concerned. "Would you like a glass of water?" she offered. She ushered him into the house, and he followed her to the room where Maimon and Shoshanah were seated.

"Meir, what is the problem?" Rabbi Maimon had recognised the visitor immediately. Meir had been on his mind recently; he had been worried about him.

"Rabbi." Meir spluttered and appeared unable to take deep breaths. "My eldest son, Shmuel ..." The coughing continued. He turned his head away.

"Shmuel has been arrested. He was caught stealing money

17

and goods from a trader in the market," he managed to blurt out with difficulty.

"Come, sit down, Meir." Rabbi Maimon guided him to a chair whilst Shoshanah collected a pitcher of water, poured a cup, and handed it to Meir, who thanked her. Meir drank the water, coughed some more, and sat quietly with his head bent, his eyes staring at the floor.

"It is serious, Rabbi. I am sorry to bother you, but there is no one else to turn to. I should have taken the charity you offered. It is all my fault. Shmuel tried to feed the family by stealing. He is a good boy. He only did this for the family."

Rabbi Maimon and Shoshanah looked at each other. Maimon immediately grasped the implications. Shmuel, if found guilty, would be punished according to sharia law.

In sharia law, theft was regarded as a *hudud* crime, in the same category of offences as drinking alcohol, unlawful sexual intercourse, and apostasy. The penalty was for a hand to be cut off from the wrist if the theft was taken by stealth or seized by force in front of other people and if the stolen property was above three Islamic dirhams or a quarter of an Islamic dinar in value. The theft itself had to be proven, either by the testimony of two qualified witnesses or by the confession of the thief twice.

"I beg you to represent Shmuel at the sharia court. You are our only hope." He coughed and spluttered.

"Obviously I will help and do my best. I will pray for Shmuel, and you should do the same."

The trial was conducted by a judge with a body of twelve members drawn from the neighbourhood who were sworn to tell the truth and who were bound to give a unanimous verdict. Shmuel had been caught in the act of stealing valuable goods and money by both the owner and two other witnesses, and the value of the goods was above the amount stipulated by law.

In court, Rabbi Maimon pleaded mitigation.

"Revered judges, Shmuel is only fifteen years old. He wanted the money and goods for his family, who are poor and desperate for food. This is his only offence. He is filled with remorse. It will not happen again. I beg you for mercy. The boy will repent, and I guarantee to repay the money in full."

There was silence as the judge read out the decision of the court: "Theft is forbidden according to the Koran, Sunnah, and Ijmā. Allah, the Most Exalted, has condemned this action and decreed an appropriate punishment for it. The legal punishment prescribed by Islamic law for a thief is to cut off the thief's hand. Allah Almighty says in the Noble Koran: 'Amputate their hands in recompense for what they committed as a deterrent from Allah. And Allah is Exalted in Might and Wise.'"

Shmuel stood rigid, his face contorted with fear and grief. His mother cried uncontrollably. Meir could only watch with a glazed stare. Rabbi Maimon tried to console the family, but they were impervious to comforting words. Shmuel was led away.

The punishment took place the following day in a public market. Maimon attended. There were several dozen spectators present to witness the punishment. Shmuel struggled as he was restrained by leather straps in a chair. Both hands were fixed firmly to a wooden board. His parents turned away; they could not bear to watch the proceedings. Rabbi Maimon tried to comfort them. The punishment was conducted quickly and efficiently. A corpulent guard with a black hood covering his face, so that only his eyes were visible, appeared wielding a large sword. An assistant applied a tourniquet over the upper right arm to reduce blood loss. The sentence was read out for the benefit of the enlarging audience, and a prayer was recited. The sword was raised and brought down accurately to amputate the hand just above the wrist. Shmuel screamed, and there was a collective sigh from the spectators. Tar was applied to the raw surface of the forearm and a firm bandage applied to reduce the bleeding. Shmuel lost consciousness and was released from the constraining straps. He was lifted and carried to a nearby divan, where he was laid down and covered with a blanket. His parents knelt by his side and wept. Shmuel awoke after twenty minutes and was taken home.

Rabbi Maimon visited the family later that day. A doctor provided appropriate balms. He checked the wounds regularly and was pleased that the raw surface appeared clean. Shmuel was provided with a sling and was able to mobilise, albeit with pain, after a few days.

Rabbi Maimon was visibly shaken and remained depressed for several days. He should have been more forceful in insisting that Meir take the money that had been offered him from the fund to pay the *jizya*. It was ironic that Meir, following the horrific events, now felt it necessary to receive the charity.

Shmuel himself never fully recovered from either the physical or mental effects of the punishment. He later left the family home and spent the rest of his life as a beggar on the streets of Cordoba.

3

Moses was both confused and nervous at the thought of leaving his family, but his father explained the reason why it was necessary and its temporary nature.

"You will return a happier and more learned Jew. God has given you special abilities, and they must be used for the well-being of all," his father explained.

"But I have been happy learning with you, Father. I promise to concentrate more if you allow me to stay," the boy pleaded.

"You must learn in Rabbi Migash's yeshiva. He will make you a brilliant scholar. You will return home as soon as he feels you are ready. Always remember that you are our treasured son and we will miss you. We look forward to your return."

Moses had mixed feelings. It would be an adventure, but would he be lonely and homesick? Could he cope on his own? He had only known the comfort of a close-knit family atmosphere. However, his father was wise, he told himself, and knew what was best for him. Perhaps it was important for him to concentrate more on learning. He was determined to benefit from the move and make his family proud.

His father arranged transport to Lucena through a congregant, known to Moses, a merchant in olive oil who was travelling to Aguilar, only about five legua (approximately ten miles) west of Lucena. Moses carried his possessions in a soft leather bag which contained food for the journey. Shoshanah had included his favourite home-made cakes and a specially baked bread. He climbed on the wagon and waved to his parents and David. He thought he saw tears in his father's eyes but could not be sure.

The wagon left the walled city through one of the southern gates and trundled along at a moderate pace through the countryside. There were numerous vine groves and olive trees and peasants tending their patches of land. Moses marvelled at the numerous citrus and avocado trees. He was aware that he had only once been outside the city of Cordova and was intrigued by the novel surroundings.

The merchant reached Aguilar as darkness fell. He left Moses at an inn recognised for providing comfortable accommodation. The following morning a friend of his father's met him, and they travelled in a horse-drawn carriage to Lucena. Moses estimated it was a journey of about three hours, but it seemed much longer. The closer they got to Lucena, the greater was the level of anxiety he felt. But he was determined not to show his nervousness when they reached their destination. They entered the walled city through the northern gate and headed directly to the famous yeshiva academy of Rabbi Yosef ibn Migash.

On Moses's arrival at the yeshiva, a surly elderly man dressed in a long black tunic opened the door. He had a most unwelcoming expression, although he did force a brief smile which revealed stained yellow teeth.

"You must be Moshe ben Maimon. I remember your father. He studied here years ago. Come in," he growled without introducing himself.

"Yes, sir. I am Moses." He was surprised by the brusque welcome and entered the yeshiva with trepidation. His father had warned him about a morose unkempt man called Lev who had worked in the yeshiva all his life and who rarely, if ever, smiled. *This must be him,* thought Moses as they passed down a narrow corridor barely lit by an occasional lamp in a niche in the wall. They stopped, and Lev knocked on a door.

"Enter," came an almost immediate reply.

Inside was a room with two small windows and a high ceiling. It was lit by a large candelabra with six oil lamps. Sitting at a table with an ancient scroll in front of him was Rabbi Yosef ibn Migash. He smiled as he recognised Moses.

"I am pleased to meet you, Moshe. Your appearance reminds me of your father. Your father is a great man. I am honoured that he chose this yeshiva to continue with his son's studies."

"Thank you, revered sir. My father wished me to pass on his most sincere regards to you."

Moses was unable to determine whether Rabbi Migash was pleased to see him or not. He seemed to be concentrating more on the scroll in front of him than on providing a welcome. Moses was aware that the rabbi had a reputation for extreme piety and as a man of few words, which could explain the lack of warmth in his welcome. Rabbi Migash was austere in countenance and seemed remarkably pale and gaunt. He spoke in a quiet gruff voice, frequently needing to stop to catch his breath.

"It is important that you be a credit to your father, and for this you must study diligently whilst you are here. Lev will escort you to your room. I am sure you must be hungry after the journey." He turned towards Lev. "Please ensure Moshe is provided with food and water. Maariv prayers will commence in one hour."

Rabbi Yosef then returned to studying the scroll.

Moses followed Lev. They walked up several flights of stairs until they reached a room on the top floor.

"Your father occupied this very same room when he was here," remarked Lev.

Moses carefully clutched his small bag of belongings and

entered the room. Six boys of varying ages turned towards him and began to laugh and snigger. They were busy tucking into food, which was laid out on a separate table.

"This is the new boy, Moshe. Which bed has a spare space?" asked Lev.

A tall boy pointed in the direction of a palliasse in the corner of the room.

"That is your place," said Lev. Then he left the room without further comment.

The sleeping arrangement was such that two boys slept on each palliasse, head to toe. Moses was pleased that one of the boys came to greet him.

"My name is Yaacov. Come and join us for supper. I apologise for laughing when you came in, but do not worry. It was only because you are so young. Rabbi Yosef does not usually accept children of your age to study here."

Moses had very little sleep during his first night in the yeshiva. Sleeping two to a bed was strange to him, and he was unhappy about being away from his familiar surroundings. He already missed his parents and David. At dawn he was awakened by a loud ringing bell. He dressed quickly and followed his roommates to morning prayers.

After the morning prayers, *shacharit*, he went to breakfast with Yaacov. The food was plentiful and tasty, bread with tomatoes, figs, onions, and grapes.

"How long have you been in the yeshiva, Yaacov?" he asked, trying to sound friendly.

"Just over a year. I am from Marrakesh in Morocco," Yaacov replied. Moses had noticed how dark-skinned Yaacov was, and this was the explanation.

"My parents want me to stay for at least another year. I find the study here very demanding. It is hard work. That is why I was surprised to see you. You are so young. You will find it very difficult."

Moses was pleased when it was announced that Yaacov would be his study partner. He liked Yaacov even though he was fourteen, five years older than he, but they seemed to get along amiably. Moses was determined not to be overawed by the level of learning. He would demonstrate to Yaacov, as well as to the other boys and his teachers, that he had the ability to keep up with the rigid discipline.

During the first study session, the topic of discussion was a tract of Mishna relating to ritual slaughter (*shechitah*) of animals and the significance of a blemish in the lungs and whether this would disqualify the animal from consumption. Moses was able to recite the Mishna verbatim after one reading and discuss its implications. He was aware of his innate ability to digest large quantities of complicated information, carry out an in-depth analysis, quote appropriate sources, and provide an opinion, all in a relatively short period of time.

Rabbi Migash then proceeded to lecture in depth on the topic and provide all the relevant source material. Without hesitation Moses was able to compose an erudite response to the issues raised.

"You are special, Moshe," complimented Yaacov. "I now understand why you have been accepted into the academy at such a young age."

After the first week, Moses settled into a routine, basically adopting Yaacov as an older brother. He was pleased and relieved that Yaacov seemed to enjoy his company and was always available to provide comfort when his homesickness became obvious. Time passed quickly, but he still missed being home.

One day whilst in the garden, two boys who had been bullying Moses approached. They were cruel and abusive, often deliberately pushing and tripping him as he walked past. The boys later admitted that they were jealous of his undoubted mental ability and thought he was receiving preferential treatment from the teachers. On one occasion they even poured water over him whilst he was lying on his palliasse. At least he thought it was water, until he realised it smelt more like urine.

Moses knew he'd have to deal with the two boys at some point, despite Yaacov's willingness to protect him. As they passed him, the boys shoved him to the ground.

"Why do you behave like this?" he shouted. "I mean you no harm."

They laughed.

Yaacov witnessed what had occurred from a distance and ran towards the confrontation.

"You are disreputable bullies, and you are upsetting my friend. Leave him be, or you will answer to me." Yaacov was incensed, and his aggressive manner had the desired effect. The two boys looked anxiously at each other and started to run in the opposite direction. When they were at what they thought was a safe distance, they turned and shouted towards Yaacov.

"Yaacov, why do you protect him? Is he your boyfriend? We can see you enjoy his company. Do you not remember what the Torah says about lying with a boy?" They sneered, but Yaacov was not amused.

"You are disgusting." He was enraged. "Apologise, or else you will regret those foul words." They laughed sardonically.

Yaacov's appearance changed dramatically. His face became taut and his lips whitened. A fine tremor was noticeable. He struggled to contain his anger but failed. With no warning he sprinted towards them. They ran, but Yaacov was much faster and soon caught up with them. He punched one of the boys in the face and the other in the abdomen. A teacher arrived to find one boy clutching his abdomen and the other with blood flowing from his nose.

Yaacov received a serious reprimand for his violence, but the investigating rabbi was sympathetic to the mitigating factors of the assault. Yaacov's punishment was lenient. He was instructed to learn by heart a major chapter of Mishna by the following week, which he achieved. The two boys were warned about bullying and threatened with expulsion from the yeshiva should it occur again. No further complaints were received about them. They had learnt a painful lesson.

Yaacov was studious, clever, and normally cheery and extroverted. He was tall for his age and handsome and had the beginnings of a substantial beard. Moses was extremely grateful to Yaacov but was concerned that at times he seemed depressed and withdrawn. And for no obvious reason he would become angry and aggressive even when not provoked by bullies.

"Do not be concerned. Moses," Simeon, one of the other students, in the dormitory remarked when Yaacov seemed withdrawn and would not communicate for several days. "His parents sent him to the yeshiva in the hope that his behaviour would improve under Rabbi Migash's influence. He is better than he was, but every so often his mind seems to alter and he becomes a different person. When he is angry or depressed, do not confront him until he settles down."

This worried Moses, who had noticed that when Yaacov became depressed, he refused to speak or socialise with his fellow students. On other occasions he became overly aggressive and shouted randomly whilst waving his arms aggressively.

"Surely Yaacov is unwell and requires help," Moses replied with concern. "This behaviour is not normal."

Moses observed that Rabbi Migash was becoming visibly frailer. His skin, originally pale, had now become a deep yellow. His cough was more pronounced, and he was rarely seen. Moses noticed that a man who he assumed to be a doctor had visited the yeshiva on several occasions. Rumour was rife, and prayers were recited for the rabbi's health by all the staff.

One Monday evening whilst learning a particularly difficult

passage from the following Sabbath's Torah reading, Moses's concentration was interrupted by a gentle knock on the dormitory door. One of the students answered and was surprised to see Dovid, Rabbi Migash's assistant.

"Rabbi Migash requests that Moshe accompany me," he murmured apologetically.

Moses stood up immediately and followed Dovid to Rabbi Migash's chamber. They entered. Rabbi Migash was surrounded by his closest family, and the doctor was present. His breathing was laboured and rattled noisily, but he was able to summon Moses to his bedside. He placed his thin, shaking hand on Moses's head and barely audibly muttered a blessing. He turned to kiss Moses's head and whispered, "You will become one of the greatest of the Jewish scholars." He then lay back on his pillow. Moses was bewildered. What did he mean? He looked around. Everyone seemed to be staring at him with gentle, knowing smiles. Moses returned to his dormitory with a feeling of despair and understandably high emotion.

On Tuesday morning, almost six months after Moses had arrived, it was announced that the great Talmudic scholar Rabbi Yosef ibn Migash had passed away. In accordance with Jewish law, his funeral took place within twenty-four hours of death. He was buried in the Jewish cemetery close to the main synagogue. Hundreds of worshippers attended, and many erudite *rabbonim* gave flowing eulogies about him. Moses's father came from Cordova for the shiva (seven days of mourning), but Shoshanah remained behind to look after David. At the end of the shiva period, Rabbi Maimon met with his son.

"Dear father, I now understand the importance of learning. I will be a good student with you. Rabbi Migash taught me many things, but his love of learning has inspired me. I miss being with my family. Can I come home and study all the Hebrew texts with you?"

Rabbi Maimon was wholly sympathetic. He himself had

come under the influence of Rabbi Migash and understood the change in Moses's attitude towards study.

"Moshe, my son, your mother and I have been saddened by your absence. Even David misses you. You will come back with me, and we will learn together. And the legacy and influence of Rabbi Migash will live on."

A wave of relief flooded over Moses. He'd wanted to go home right from the start, and he'd been worried that his father might yet insist that he remain at the school. Moses collected his belongings, said farewell to his fellow students, especially Yaacov, and to his teachers, and joined his father for the carriage journey back to Cordoba. The carriage pulled out of town, and soon Moses found himself back in the vast countryside. He felt oddly detached. He didn't speak to his father as he stared at the ever-changing scenery slowly passing by. He recalled his last conversation with Yaacov.

"Moses, you will be a great scholar, and people will respect you," Yaacov had said. "You have a loving family who want you to return to them. I, on the other hand, am worthless and disliked by everyone. My parents have abandoned me. They make no contact. They told me my mind is diseased and that my fits of anger are impossible to control and are a punishment from God. Only by studying hard will I be cured." Yaacov seemed resigned to his situation. "Thank you for your friendship, Moses. Please do not think too badly of me. I will not see you again. I will miss you."

What did Yaacov mean, "I will not see you again"? Should Moses discuss his concerns with his father or just ignore them? *Probably better not to mention anything to Father. He will not appreciate my anxiety and will think me foolish.*

They arrived back in Cordoba after dark, hungry and tired. Shoshanah was delighted to greet them and relieved that they had arrived safely. David clung to his brother.

On the following Sabbath, Maimon and Shoshanah prepared a special meal for the community in the synagogue to celebrate Moses's safe return. Maimon had asked his son to prepare a brief talk on the week's Torah reading. He was delighted to do so. He now felt energised by studying. His previous reluctance to learn had dissipated under the influence of Rabbi Migash's yeshiva. Moses confidently delivered an in-depth, erudite speech without notes. He was nervous at first but soon relaxed as he noticed that the audience seemed mesmerised by his rendition.

"How can a ten-year-old child have such a deep understanding of Torah?" commented a senior member of the community. Rabbi Maimon could barely hide his pride upon hearing the brilliant discourse.

A programme of daily study, interspersed with prayer, was organised for Moses. Each day under his father's tutelage, he studied the Talmud and Torah. He was introduced to books on philosophy, science, mathematics, astrology, and medicine. He seemed capable, almost effortlessly, of grasping detailed, complicated knowledge and committing the information precisely to his prodigious memory.

Moses remained true to his word to his father. He studied hard. By age eleven, he'd mastered much already. As his studies broadened, his capacity to concentrate in depth increased exponentially. And with directed learning proposed by his father, his knowledge of classical rabbinic works expanded. The Mishna corpus and the appendix to the Mishna—the Tosefta, the commentaries, Sifra, and Sifre—were all absorbed. He was able to translate the Babylonian Talmud as well as legal and nonlegal Midrashic literature. No amount of detailed information seemed to be beyond his intellectual grasp.

By the age of twelve Moses was able to read not only Hebrew and Arabic but also Aramaic, as well as understand Greek. He expanded his understanding of Judaeo-Arabic—Arabic using

Hebrew letters. This combination of languages enabled him to access everything of a rabbinic nature since the great majority of texts were written in Hebrew or Aramaic.

He was also attracted to philosophical texts. He read the works of the Muslim philosophers al-Kindi and al-Ghazali, both of whom followed the Kalam cosmological argument of the existence of the universe, its being the beginning of time and the cause of its existence being God. He became engrossed in the Aristotelian philosophical works on rationality. He explored in depth the Aristotelian conceptions of God, the universe, and humankind, concepts which were indelibly implanted in his mind at this very early age. He formulated a hypothesis that God is a wholly incorporeal being and that his essence is unknowable.

Maimon's long-standing interest in science, mathematics, logic, and astronomy enabled him to introduce these subjects to Moses. He was able to direct the boy to the libraries in Cordoba which were generously stocked with all the relevant standard texts. The caliphal library alone had some four hundred thousand books. It was one of seventy libraries in Cordoba.

Moses could not resist the lure of reading medical books. He learnt the rudiments of Galen's humoral theory of disease and studied Hippocrates's work, as well as the writings of all the great Arabic physicians such as al-Razi, Alfarabi, Avicenna, and Ibn Zuhr. Whenever he met a physician, he would question him relentlessly. He soon began to grasp the principles of diagnosis and treatment as well as medical ethics.

Despite his intensive education, Moses did not ignore his family, especially not David. He was deeply attached to his younger brother and played with him whenever he could. When Moses turned twelve, his studies consumed him more than ever. But he always took time to be with the family. He could see how much this pleased Shoshanah, who had always been a good, sympathetic mother to him.

"Moshe, your father and I wish to speak with you. Please

leave your book and join us." He was intrigued. He followed Shoshanah into the large room where his father was already seated on a low brocaded settee. On the table there was a large glazed bowl filled with fruit and smaller ones with nuts and olives.

"Moshe, I am going to have another baby." He smiled and threw his arms around Shoshanah and then hugged his father.

4

The first indication that Rabbi Maimon had of a possible Almohad invasion had been a few weeks earlier. He was aware of a commotion in the synagogue as he was teaching two of his students.

"Rabbi Maimon, I apologise for interrupting, but a merchant has just informed me that the Almohads have invaded Gibraltar," Shemtov reported with staccato nervousness. He had suffered with speech difficulties for many years, but the stress of passing on this worrying message had exacerbated the problem. The information had been sent to the merchant by carrier pigeon from Cortes and was now confirmed by signals from watchtowers along the coast.

Jews had lived a contented life in Cordoba since arriving in Spain following the destruction of the first temple in Jerusalem some seventeen hundred years previously. The Maghreb, comprised of the coastlands and the Atlas Mountains of Morocco, Algeria, and Tunis, was under Muslim control. In 1086, Spain had come under the rule of the Almoravids, a faction of Muslims who were part of a distinct tribe of Saharan Berbers called the Umayyad, their capital being in Marrakesh. The Almoravids gradually advanced militarily, and eventually the whole of Muslim Spain fell under their rule.

The relationship between Muslim Spain (al-Andalus) and the Maghreb had strengthened with time to the mutual benefit and prosperity of both. The Jewish population also prospered and practised their religion and culture unhindered despite their *dhimmi* status. The Almoravids were liberal in many of their concepts and favoured peaceful coexistence with all religions within their areas of control. This enabled Christians and especially Jews to prosper and contribute greatly towards society in general. However, the status quo was soon to change. Almoravid power in Spain began to crumble in 1124 when Mohammad ibn Tumart, a Berber from Morocco, initiated the Almohad movement. Ibn Tumart was a student of theology and a charismatic preacher. He professed that his movement was driven by religious motives. *Almohad* translates as "believers in the oneness of God". The movement's objective was to uphold the absolute unity of God. For this to occur, Ibn Tumart developed a religious doctrine which insisted on a scrupulous observance of Islamic law. Almoravid chieftains who failed to conform were brutally slaughtered. The Almohads systematically conquered a wide swath of the Maghreb, leaving a trail of blood and destruction wherever they went. Jews and Christians were spared on the basis that even though their religion was different, it was monotheistic. Nevertheless, there was concern amongst the Spanish Jewish community that things could change, but provided Ibn Tumart remained in power, they felt reasonably safe and were allowed, as *dhimmis*, to follow Judaism.

In 1139 Ibn Tumart died. He was replaced by Abdullah al-Mu'min, who took the title of caliph. His approach was quite different from that of Ibn Tumart. He was a ruthless religious zealot who believed that Islam was the only true religion and that nonbelievers should be slaughtered, although they could preserve their lives if they converted to Islam. He despised the soft luxury living which was prevalent among his fellow Muslims, and what is more, he was appalled by the wealth, status, and position of the Jews. They were *dhimmis* and should be treated as such. This comfortable existence had to end, and as caliph he would impose the change.

Al-Mu'min ruthlessly invaded all parts of the Maghreb. In Oran he put the Almoravid garrison to death. He killed the Almoravid governor, gibbeted his body, and placed his decapitated head on a stake outside the wall as a warning to any inhabitant who failed to support his doctrine. It was reported that in Fez he slaughtered 100,000 inhabitants and in Marrakesh some 150,000. His army killed the entire population of Tilimsen, apart from those Jews who converted to Islam.

The Jewish leaders of Morocco were gathered together by al-Mu'min and were told, "You are waiting for the Messiah, but we know that he was supposed to have come five hundred years after the death of Muhammad. Since he has not done so, you now have the choice of conversion or death." However, with persuasion al-Mu'min also allowed, as an alternative, emigration from Muslim lands.

There was a legend which the Jews of Morocco firmly believed in. They considered that the Almohads were the descendants of the Philistines. During the reign of King David, the Philistines were subjected to the wrath of David's military and escaped to North Africa. According to the legend, the Almohads never forgot their hatred of the Jews and enjoyed their revenge.

The messages coming from the north suggested that the Almohads had now set their sights on Muslim Spain. This could not be disregarded. It was obvious to Rabbi Maimon that al-Mu'min intended to absorb Spain's cities into a unified empire.

This thought had been foremost in his mind as he mingled with his guests at Moshe's bar mitzvah. The ceremony was over. Moshe had read from the Torah scrolls using the traditional Sephardic chant. Because he was born on the eve of Passover, he chanted the portion of the Torah from the book of Exodus, chapter 33, which is always read on the Sabbath which occurs during the eight days of Passover (called "Shabbos chol hamoed"). He was word-perfect and followed this by singing a section from the book of Ezekiel. He was then blessed by his father, who beamed with pride.

What an incredible few weeks it's been, mused Maimon. *It is only six weeks since Shoshanah delivered a healthy girl, Miriam, and now Moshe's bar mitzvah!* Both Shoshanah and Miriam had recovered well and were able to watch the ceremony from the women's balcony. Miriam was exceptionally good and slept throughout the entire proceedings, much to the relief of her mother.

After the service, Rabbi Maimon and Shoshanah hosted separate men's and women's ceremonial meals for the community. There was cold chicken and roast lamb with salads and vegetables. Wine was poured in abundance, and sweet apricots were served as a dessert, all prepared in accordance with the strict requirements for food during Passover. Maimon noted with pleasure the smell of jasmine which pervaded the room. Every so often the men stood and danced joyfully in a circle, whilst the women, in their separate section, peeped through the dividing curtain. It was a happy, relaxed occasion. Maimon listened, transfixed, as Moshe delivered a dvar Torah (a discourse on the portion of Torah he had read). He spoke brilliantly of the exodus from Egypt with assurance and maturity. The assembled company could only sit and admire his erudition and insight.

"Rabbi Maimon, you are surely blessed. Your son will be a great *talmid chacham*," whispered his good friend Aaron as he helped himself to yet another glass of the excellent wine.

"You are most generous with your praise, Aaron. Moshe is very special and has been an inspiration to me since his return from yeshiva. His capacity for acquiring knowledge is truly remarkable," responded Maimon.

The celebration was memorable. It was wonderful to have such a joyful occasion at a time when the Jews of Cordoba were becoming increasingly anxious about their safety and well-being. The community tried hard to ignore the worrying circulating reports about the Almohads; they just wanted to enjoy the moment. Maimon, especially, had anxieties, although he did his best to appear relaxed and reassuring.

Rabbi Maimon noticed a rather overweight, bearded young man, whom he did not recognise as a member of the community, standing alone in the corner of the hall. He went over to welcome him.

"My name is Judah," the man explained. I am a friend of Moshe. We were together and shared a room in the yeshiva in Lucena."

"You are most welcome. Come, Moshe will be delighted to see you again."

Rabbi Maimon ushered Judah through the crowd towards Moses.

"Moshe, look who is here. You remember Judah from Rabbi Migash's yeshiva? May his soul rest in peace." Rabbi Maimon then gave his apology as he wandered off to welcome other newly arrived guests.

"Judah, how nice to see you again. I am so pleased you are here." Moses beamed with delight to see a friend from yeshiva.

"I was travelling to Tudela and had heard your bar mitzvah was today, so I have spent Shabbos with friends here in Cordoba. I am honoured to join you on this special occasion. Rabbi Migash, may his soul rest in peace, would have been so proud of you."

"How are all my friends in the yeshiva, Judah?"

"I left soon after the tragedy, so I have not seen them recently," Judah uttered in an undertone. He was clearly distraught. "Everyone in the yeshiva is still in a state of shock."

"What do you mean? What tragedy?" Surely Judah was not

referring to the death of Rabbi Migash. Moses was anxious but reluctant to enquire what the tragedy was.

"Did you not hear? Yaacov, may his soul rest in peace, killed himself. He hanged himself from the dormitory rafters." Moses could only stare vacuously at Judah, unable to speak at first. He felt the blood drain from his face.

"Moses, are you all right? I am so sorry to bring the news to you. I thought you would have known."

Moses could not respond. He tried, but the words were stuck in his mouth. Eventually he murmured his thanks once more to Judah for coming to his bar mitzvah and for telling him about Yaacov. He needed to be alone. He excused himself and walked from the synagogue hall to a bench outside. He cried as he berated himself. With his eyes closed and his head held in his hands, he spoke directly to Yaacov:

"I knew you were ill, but I did nothing to help. You were a good friend to me. You took care of me, rescued me from the bullying. Oh, Yaacov, Yaacov. Why? Why? Now I know what you meant when I left the yeshiva and we said goodbye. *Thank you for your friendship, Moses. Please do not think too badly of me. I will not see you again. I will miss you.* You had planned to kill yourself when we last met and whilst your mind was diseased. I will never forget you, Yaacov, and I will never forgive myself for doing nothing when I was so sure you were ill. You had a disease of the mind. I should never have ignored you. I must learn in future to recognise when a person's mind is diseased."

It was late; the festivities were over. Afternoon and evening prayers were recited, and the guests slowly drifted home. Although the Maimon family were exhilarated by the occasion, Moses could not summon any feelings of joy as he repeatedly recalled his last contact with Yaacov.

Shoshanah, modestly covered, was feeding Miriam. She recognised that Moshe was in deep thought and unhappy. David was playing quietly with a mounted toy soldier that had been given to him by a guest at the bar mitzvah.

"Do you want to tell me what worries you?" she asked him.

He thought for a moment and then told her about his friend Yaacov. She was sympathetic.

"Do not feel guilty. He was ill and suffered from a disease which he could not deal with. He wanted you to remember him only during the good times. That is why he asked you not to think badly of him. He was so grateful for your friendship at a time when he was depressed and lonely."

"I will remember your sensible words, Mother, but I feel responsible. I hope the good Lord will forgive him and have mercy on his soul, even though he sinned by ending the life given to him by God to look after and to cherish."

5

Moses and his father were walking towards the yeshiva when they became aware of a commotion in the street ahead. The sun had not fully risen, but it was already hot and sultry outside.

"We must be careful, Moshe. There is much unrest in the city. Everyone is worried about a possible invasion. Whatever happens, it will not be good for the Jews."

The Jews of Cordoba had first-hand information of the consequences of an Almohad invasion. Many Jews from Morocco, who had decided to flee rather than convert to Islam, flooded into Cordoba, and their tales of persecution were harrowing. Their synagogues and yeshivot that had stood for centuries had been destroyed.

A group of scholars who had sought shelter with Rabbi Maimon reported that the Almohads had conquered Malaga, Granada, and Lucena. Even Rabbi Migash's yeshiva had been reduced to rubble. It was only a matter of time before similar events would happen in Cordoba.

The normally congenial relationship between the different religious groups in Cordoba visibly deteriorated as an invasion seemed closer and inevitable. The Muslim population were concerned that they would be held to account for allowing and indeed encouraging close contact with the Jews when they should have treated them merely as unworthy *dhimmis*. Would they themselves be punished?

Moses's attention was directed to a large gathering of Muslims in a square adorned with fragrant flowers. A tall speaker standing on a cart was gesticulating wildly and shouting raucously to the noisy audience.

"Too long have we suffered the *dhimmis*—the Jews and the Christians. The Koran commands us to treat them as inferiors. So why are the Jews so prominent, so wealthy, so honoured? Why don't we, the true believers, the Muslims, have the best jobs, the nicest houses? Fellow Muslims let us cast the *dhimmis* down!"

His face was visibly changing to a deep red colour, his arms were waving, and his voice was ever more strident. The audience were cheering in agreement.

"We must leave. We will bypass the crowd. It could get hostile," Maimon said as he turned sharply down an alleyway leading to a road in Juderia which he knew would be safe. Moses had rarely seen his father look so anxious.

Why is this happening? Jews, Muslims, and Christians have lived contentedly in Cordoba for generations. The city is one of the most advanced in Spain, an ornament to the world. How could such a change in attitude occur so quickly? Moses pondered. *Who could have imagined that such prejudice and anger against Jews could develop so rapidly? Why are things spinning out of control? I suppose the Muslims are becoming as concerned about the invasion as the Jews. If they do not demonstrate allegiance to the Almohad cause, then they too will be in danger.*

Word was spreading around Cordoba. The gatherings of Muslims were increasing in size and becoming more frequent. Active demonstrations were taking place throughout Cordoba, even in Juderia. A clear message was being sent to the Jews by their hitherto friendly neighbours: *unless you convert to Islam, you will not be welcome here.*

"I am worried, Moshe. The atmosphere in Cordoba is threatening. We must prepare for the worst." Moses's father was agitated.

They arrived home in haste, obviously anxious.

Rabbi Maimon sat on his upright chair in the library and addressed the family. "I fear Cordoba will soon be overrun by the Almohads," he explained with a look of resignation and despair. His voice was unusually quiet, and he was visibly anguished. His whole body appeared to shrink into the cushions and shudder. He tried to give an impression of confidence but was failing.

"I have considered our options. I refuse to consider conversion to Islam. We must therefore plan to leave our home." He paused. There was silence. Shoshanah looked at Miriam in her arms and hugged her even closer. She nodded in agreement.

"We must be ready to leave at short notice. We will pack our carriage with essential goods. I will also take as many books as reasonable so that our learning can continue." Moshe noticed that his father was looking directly at him.

Moses considered other options, including the possibility of converting to Islam. Conversion would allow the family to remain in comfort in the home they loved, but what would conversion entail? New converts were required to accept monotheism; this would not be a problem since the very basis of Judaism was monotheism. New converts were required to declare a belief in the Prophet Muhammad; this could be declared but would not be truthful. The family could build up an elaborate subterfuge about their belief in Muhammad and recite their own prayers. New converts were required to attend services in the mosque but only occasionally; they could do this, but instead of reciting from the Koran, they would quietly read from the Torah. The charade could easily take place in public whilst there was no system in place to check what converts did privately in their own homes. They could continue to practise Judaism, albeit with some risk, and not in a synagogue.

Moses didn't consider converting for a moment, and he knew that his father didn't either. Yes, the decision to flee rather than convert would lead to hardship, possibly even death, but Moses decided that the risks were worth taking. He knew he was of like mind with his father, and that at least gave him a little solace. He stood up and faced his father, who looked like he had aged suddenly to more than one hundred years old, and said, "Father, I think we're doing the right thing."

"Thank you, Moshe. Trying to bring up children in this environment will eventually have catastrophic consequences, however strong our belief in Judaism. It is far better to leave and seek a new life elsewhere. Admittedly this will lead to short-term physical and emotional hardship, but it will allow an honest continuation of our commitment to the Almighty."

His father was correct: exile was the only sensible option.

"We will travel to cities in Spain which are still under the rule of the Almoravids," Maimon declared. "Christian lands are unacceptable. Christians are reluctant to accept Jews, and their language and culture are quite alien to us," he explained. "I prefer the option, however dangerous, of remaining in Spain, certainly to begin with, although Morocco remains a possibility since I have many colleagues and ex-students in Marrakesh and Fez who might be able to assist us in finding accommodation and work."

The family listened quietly. Moses saw the sense in his father's analysis and agreed with the proposition that remaining in Spain was the least destabilising option. Moses loved Cordoba and would forever regard it as his home. He would miss his comfortable life, his books, and the synagogue that he had prayed in all his life. Nonetheless, Jews were no longer welcome in Cordoba, and they must plan to leave with some urgency.

"I have contacts in Almeria. We should go there first."

Two weeks later the Almohads invaded Cordoba and the surrounding area.

Soldiers on horseback, followed by hundreds of foot soldiers, entered the city through four gates. The other gates were closed and guarded by well-armed militia. The cavalry, in short tunics and mail with turbans wrapped around their helmets, wielded swords and brandished small round shields. They looked ferocious. The foot soldiers in surcoats were well-armed with long lances, Frankish bows, and shields. There was no resistance. The Muslim population cheered their invaders in the hope that they would be spared any retribution.

Within the Jewish quarter Moses witnessed the panic and mayhem. People were frantic, not knowing what to do, running to their homes and bolting their doors. He saw the Almohad horsemen heading for the synagogues and yeshivot. Each was entered, its contents destroyed. Torah scrolls were removed from their beautifully engraved and embossed metal cases where they stood upright, placed in a pile in the streets, and set alight. Libraries were vandalised, and books burnt.

Foot soldiers were deployed to enter homes and deliver a prepared ultimatum to all the Jewish residents: "You have a grace period of three days either to convert to Islam, be killed, or leave. We will return."

Moses was pleased that his family were well prepared thanks to his father's foresight. Their decision had already been taken. They would leave. A large cart had already been filled with essential requirements for a prolonged journey. Shoshanah had stocked up with fruit, vegetables, bread, and rice, and milk for Miriam. They took several flagons of water.

Maimon, in consultation with Moshe, had packed a few books to maintain their programme of learning. In addition, they had rescued key volumes of Mishna and a Torah scroll from the synagogue just prior to the invasion.

The loud banging on their door was frightening. Miriam was woken and began to cry.

"Open up immediately before we break down the door." The voice sounded uncompromising. Moses joined his father at the entrance to their house. He reluctantly unlocked the door to find three heavily armed soldiers with swords directed at him.

"You Jews have been given your conditions. Now listen carefully. I have requisitioned this house as billets for my men. I want you out of here by six o'clock tomorrow morning, understood?"

"I hear you, Sergeant. We have already decided to leave, but we need more time to prepare for our journey," explained Moses's father.

"Ah, so you have decided not to become a Muslim. You have taken a soft option. If I had my way, I would cut off the head of all nonbelievers. There is only one true God, and Muhammad is his Prophet. Now listen to me: be out of here by tomorrow morning, or you and your family will be gutted by this very sword, even the baby. Do I make myself clear?" At which point he turned without waiting for an answer, summoned his soldiers, and left.

"It is fortunate that we prepared ahead of time," remarked Maimon with a sense of inevitability. "Moshe, let us hurry to the synagogue before it is completely destroyed. We might be able to save some more texts. Shoshanah, finish the packing and prepare the children. We will be back shortly."

They rushed from the house and down the paved road to the synagogue. There was chaos all around as Jews huddled together in groups and discussed their options. Some were wearing the yellow turban as required by the Almohads. They were understandably distressed. As Moses and his father passed by one group, a dishevelled elderly gentleman with a long grey beard recognised Rabbi Maimon and shouted out to attract his attention. "Rabbi, what is your advice? I am too old to move from my home, and I will not betray my religion. I would rather die than become a Muslim."

"As Jews we cannot continue to live in Cordoba. My family and I will be leaving tomorrow morning and will travel north towards Almeria," explained Maimon. "You must also consider leaving."

Moses saw that Rabbi Ovadiah was in the centre of the gathering. He was a well-known religious zealot who followed a strict interpretation of all religious texts. He looked directly at the old man with a fervent glare and then pontificated to the audience, which had now swelled in size.

"Any acceptance of Islam is complete heresy." He turned to look at the old man as though trying to emphasise a point. "It is preferable to die for the sanctification of the name of God than submit. If you are too frail to leave, then your duty as a religious Jew is clear."

There was silence. Moses had been listening to the arguments and was dismayed. He nudged his way forward into the centre of the group.

"Forgive me, learned rabbi, for talking in your esteemed presence. I am just an ignorant youth and not as learned as you. But is it not true that in the days of the evil Nebuchadnezzar, all the Jews in Bavel except Hananiah, Mishael, and Azariah bowed to the idol? But no one ever called the people evildoers or non-Jews or said they were unfit to give testimony. God did not consider them to have served idols, since they were forced. If this gentleman submits to religious persecution to save his life because he is incapable of leaving, then he has not sinned willingly. God will not despise him. When Rabbi

Meir was captured and given ham to eat or be killed, he said, 'I willingly eat it. God will not regard me as an evildoer.' Please chastise me if my comments are incorrect, but perhaps the gentleman should be helped to save his life. He can still follow his Judaism but in secret."

Rabbi Ovadiah was not convinced and said so. However, the crowd dispersed. They had heard enough of the rigid uncompromising views and preferred the opinion of the young scholar.

Rabbi Maimon put his arm around Moses and led him away, towards the synagogue. The old man smiled and thanked him. "For such a young man, you are very wise."

When they arrived, the windows of the synagogue were smashed. The seats had been dismantled and the holy books put to the torch. Nothing remained. How fortunate they had removed at least some of the books before the invasion. It was a depressing scene; however, no one had so far been injured, which was a blessing.

They quickly walked home. Moses was apprehensive about the future, and he sensed that his father was too, although both were comfortable with the decision that they had taken.

Dina, their maidservant for many years, had decided not to join them but to return to her parents' home in the outskirts of the city. Maimon thanked her sincerely for her unstinting loyalty and handed her some money, which she accepted with gratitude. She had been with the family for over fifteen years and cried as she left.

Although they were entering the unknown, Moses was pleased that at least they were together as a family, even though they were changing their comfortable lifestyle in a city they loved to a life in exile with its inevitable disruption and uncertainty.

The legendary poet of Cordoba, Rabbi Abraham ibn Ezra,

wrote of the Jews' fate as they lamented, being forced to leave their beloved Cordoba:

> Great evil descended on Spain from heaven.
> And deep mourning on North Africa.
>
> Our hands are weakened and our eyes are filled with tears.
>
> I weep when I gaze on the city.
>
> Although it was not guilty the exile took root there.
>
> It was a city that was a thousand and seventy years old.
>
> And now this day arrived;
>
> The people left, and the city was widowed,
>
> Without Torah, without Tanach: the Mishnah was hidden
>
> And the Talmud abandoned for all its glory left it.
>
> Some people were killed, and others sought refuge.
>
> The synagogues were turned into Mosques—
>
> And a strange, cruel nation has called itself the true religion!

How abandoned is Cordoba, like a stormy sea.

The Jews have been injured and dealt a terrible blow.

I will cry out, I will speak bitterly, I will sigh and groan,

I will wail in deepest sadness.

PART II

EXILE

1148–1160

6

"It is so fortunate we have a large carriage for all our food and essential items, as well as four healthy and trustworthy donkeys," said Moses as they passed through the southern gate to leave the city of Cordoba for the last time. Moses knew it was especially hard for his father, who had spent his entire life in Cordoba and felt the pain of leaving more acutely than the others. But what else could they do? They had no choice; they were right to leave and seek a Jewish life elsewhere.

Moses had enormous confidence in his father's arrangements. He had accumulated adequate funds to ensure comfort in the short term. The money was hidden amongst their possessions, some sewn into the linings of their clothes. With his many contacts in the region, Maimon was confident that they would be able to live a reasonable existence in terms of food and shelter. Moses's stepmother, Shoshanah, was a most capable wife and companion, and her culinary skills were outstanding. David was capable and mature for his age and would be able to assist with all manner of duties. Miriam was a delightful toddler and seemed content with hardly a murmur during the inevitable disruption.

But Moses was aware that his father was worried that his desire for study and learning would be impeded by a scarcity of books and limited access to library facilities. He intended to teach him as much as possible from memory and from the books they had taken with them, but this would not be enough. They would need to find libraries and yeshivot along the way, should any still exist!

They journeyed towards Almeria, a Christian-held port city approximately sixty leguas southeast of Cordoba. Maimon estimated the journey would take six days. They probably had enough food to cover them for this period but would need to supplement with fresh provisions at each of the places they stopped for overnight rest.

Moses could see that they were not alone on their travels. Thousands of Jews filled the roads leaving Cordoba. Their destinations varied. Some were travelling north towards the Pyrenees heading towards Provence, others towards Christian Spain, and some even as far as Egypt. The wealthy had carriages full of precious possessions; others struggled on foot with ragged clothes and pitifully asked for food. His father often paused to hand out rations to the more obviously needy but was conscious of the requirements of his own family, particularly his wife and little daughter.

Along the way they met many Jews in similar circumstances to theirs and exchanged information. The stories they heard were filled with sadness and misery. Tales of death and destruction of synagogues and burning of books were commonplace. Almohad soldiers were frequently encountered on the roads and would hurl abuse. It was generally accepted that the best course of action when harassed was to ignore the insults and travel on regardless. There were very few reports of physical violence, so avoiding confrontation was deemed sensible.

The family usually rested in local hostels or inns overnight. The accommodation was invariably miserable and basic. Occasionally they were required to sleep in stables. On two occasions they stayed in the homes of acquaintances of Rabbi

Maimon. This was greatly welcomed and provided an opportunity for study.

Shoshanah's true character showed through despite the adversity. She was able to maintain a family atmosphere. Food was always thoughtfully prepared, and she even managed to prepare a Friday night Sabbath meal in a rather unprepossessing room rented out at an extortionate price from a Muslim innkeeper. Shoshanah's appearance was always impeccable. She dressed modestly but smartly and seemed relaxed with never a word of complaint. She ensured that David's education was continued, whilst Moses learned intensively with his father whenever possible. Miriam seemed unconcerned. She rarely cried and was a delightful toddler who gurgled, smiled, and played with anyone who paid her attention, whether family or others.

As each day passed they became more comfortable with the decision to leave Cordoba, although Maimon did express one troubling matter which needed sensitive and diplomatic discussion. On several occasions whilst on the road he had become aware of leering glances and lewd comments directed towards Shoshanah by passing Almohad soldiers. This was a source of great concern. Rumours were rife about rape and violence towards women. Maimon delicately raised the matter with Shoshanah, who seemed unconcerned but agreed to keep out of sight whenever soldiers were nearby and ensured she was always covered up and portrayed the appearance of an old woman.

They initially headed towards Montefrío before turning south along the Almeria river. The roads were dusty and dry. They passed numerous waterwheels and collected fresh water, an essential requirement in the summer heat. They passed many farmers working their crops and were able to purchase fresh fruit and vegetables.

On the sixth day, which happened to be a Friday, they stopped for the night three leguas north of Almeria at an inn owned by Benjamin, a cousin of Shoshanah's father. They would not travel on the Sabbath. Benjamin was delighted to welcome them and was honoured that a distinguished rabbi was staying in his home over the Sabbath.

"Please regard my humble abode as your own, dear rabbi," declared Benjamin very generously. "Shoshanah, your wonderful father was very kind to me a few years ago when I experienced money problems, and he generously arranged for supplies of food to be sent to me. I am so delighted to be able to repay the debt in some small measure."

"You are very kind, Benjamin." Rabbi Maimon was deeply appreciative. "Our intention is to stay only for a few days before leaving for Almeria. My only request is to be directed to the nearest synagogue or yeshiva so that my son Moses and I can study. We have been bereft of learning opportunities since leaving Cordoba."

"If only I could, dear rabbi," answered a clearly upset Benjamin. "The last synagogue in the area was destroyed a week ago and the Torah scrolls set to fire. The yeshiva has been converted into a hostel for Almohad soldiers and their harlots, although I did manage to rescue a few books. It has been devastating for us here. However, I understand things are much quieter in Almeria. The community there are not being too badly treated, although, of course, things could change."

Benjamin's wife entered the room carrying drinks and fruit. She also proudly displayed a recently baked cake.

"I am sure you must be hungry. I hope your children like cake." Moses, David, and even Miriam nodded vigorously and smiled appreciatively. Benjamin helped to serve. He had a rotund appearance. Indeed, everything about him seemed circular, including his pear-shaped torso and a rounded, bearded face. His smile was infectious but revealed teeth with a prominent gap at the front.

His wife, Rivka, was much younger than her husband and seemed overwhelmed by the occasion and embarrassed by her unkempt appearance. Her clothes were threadbare and dishevelled. She fussed around the children, especially Miriam, and handed out large portions of the fruit cake.

"Thank you so much. The cake is delicious." Moses beamed.

"My wife has a reputation in these parts for her excellent cooking. I am sure most people stay here just to sample her food. Thank God for that; otherwise, I would be out of business." He laughed loudly, but Moses thought that his observation was probably accurate.

"Please come with me, Rabbi, and I will show you the learned books that I managed to take from the yeshiva before it was burnt down. If they are of use, you can have them with my blessing. I am afraid I am not a very knowledgeable or observant Jew."

Moses and his father were pleased with what they found. Two volumes of the Mishna from Tractate Eruvim and Tractate Berachos would provide an extremely valuable learning resource.

"Thank you so much. We will commence our study of them. You are to be praised for saving these holy books." Maimon was visibly delighted, and Benjamin beamed with pride. Moses thought that was the first joy they had experienced since leaving Cordoba, and his smile reflected this.

As night fell, prayers were said by the men whilst the women lit the Sabbath candles.

Moses watched as Shoshanah and Benjamin's wife prepared a traditional Friday night meal. A chicken, slaughtered in accordance with Jewish law, was plucked by one of Benjamin's daughters. Vegetables, recently purchased from the local market, were prepared.

The meal was eaten joyfully, and songs were sung. *Despite the adversity, Jewish tradition continues,* thought Moses. *We will survive provided we remain true to our beliefs. Please, God, give me the strength to continue learning so that, in some small measure, I may pass on the vast body of knowledge in a form that can be understood by all Jews. I feel a responsibility has been placed on my shoulders to assist in this aim. The yeshivot have been destroyed, so I must act as a repository and use my memory and the intellect given to me by the Almighty to achieve this.* These views, which had been developing in his mind for several months, could be regarded by some as arrogant, but determination rather than arrogance would be required if he was to realise his ambition. He was still a teenager and yet felt inspired by some unknown force, which he considered to be God, to take on the challenge and be a leader of the Jewish people. Sitting around the Sabbath table with family and friends and witnessing the joy that can occur in adversity convinced him to take on the challenge.

"Moshe, you are quiet this evening. It is Shabbos. Sing and be happy," suggested Shoshanah as she lifted a gurgling Miriam in the air. Moses's father, David, and Benjamin were in full voice as they sang traditional joyful songs.

"You are right, Mother, but do not fret. I feel inspired." He joined in the chorus.

They sang the traditional Friday night songs heartily and with enthusiasm. The evening was a great success. It was a truly inspirational event for the entire Maimon family. Moses experienced tangible evidence of the importance of maintaining a Jewish identity despite all the hardship. As a family they were encouraged to carry on their journey with even greater motivation.

They left the inn well fed and content. Benjamin and family were delighted to have hosted them and said they were welcome back at any time. They continued their journey towards Almeria. Moses listened to his father's reminiscences of a visit to Almeria several years previous when he had been invited to sit on a Beth Din (court of Jewish law) tribunal in which a wife was pleading to receive a "get", a certificate to say that she was divorced, from her ex-husband so that, should she wish to remarry in the future, she would be allowed to do so. The husband had steadfastly refused to give her the get, but pressure from the Beth Din, with them explaining that he would be ostracised by the community and lose certain rights and privileges, had made him reconsider and reluctantly agree. It was a satisfactory outcome.

Moses looked in wonder at the hustle and bustle of the port city Almeria as his father guided the cart through the crowded streets. He knew that he'd embarked upon a new adventure. He saw ships that had arrived from around the world carrying a variety of goods including skins, rubies and other precious gems mainly from India, and paper and silks from China.

They arrived at a merchant's house near the docks, where his father had been told rooms were for rent. Their accommodation consisted of two rooms above the merchant's storehouse. It was a busy area with frequent noisy movement of carts and carriages. Miriam made friends with two of the merchant's children of a similar age. The merchant, a devout Muslim called Nadim, was friendly and always willing to help the family, undeterred by the prohibitions towards Jews. He told Moses that he had always enjoyed the company of Jews and that many of his business acquaintances were Jewish. Nadim's wife befriended Shoshanah, and the two women would often meet whilst their children played happily together.

Moses spent most of each day engrossed in learning with his father. He enjoyed this enormously. They studied from all the books they had managed to acquire and carry with them. Moses was able to memorise vast sections, and his overall knowledge expanded. Both Moses and his father offered their services as teachers to the Jewish community and enjoyed clandestine teaching to both children and adults. This filled an important void in Jewish education in Almeria since, prior to their arrival, there had been little or no Jewish learning. In this way they acquired small sums of money or food as a way of thanks and didn't rely solely on savings or on charity.

Moses was pleased that David had developed an obvious interest in the commercial aspect of the port. Even at his young age, David enjoyed the frenetic atmosphere around the docks and often wandered around, talking to the merchants. It was not long before he gained an understanding and recognition of gems and learnt how prices were calculated. He became so proficient that he was taken on as an apprentice by a jewellery and gem company owned by a Jewish merchant. For this he received a small salary.

When not learning with his father, Moses frequently studied alone. He would sit on a bench in a park or by the docks and commit to memory sections of the Talmud. He found this both relaxing and satisfying and began to conceptualise detailed philosophical ideas. Often these would be devoted to theological issues, but his scientific and embryonic medical knowledge enabled him to appreciate the importance of integrating religion and science into practical matters. He became fascinated with philosophy, especially pragmatic Aristotelian concepts.

Despite the paucity of Jewish scholarship and learning, Moses managed to acquire books hidden away in family vaults or secret places. Maimon was astounded by his son's immense appetite for knowledge, his remarkable memory, his understanding of complex issues, and his mature demeanour.

Almeria had remained reasonably safe and was comfortable for the Jewish community. The Almohad regime was present, but the captain of the guard was liberal and lax in his jurisdiction and allowed certain freedoms for the Jewish population provided they were not too overt. Moses was determined to avoid confrontation. Life was initially peaceful. Synagogues and yeshivot were officially banned; therefore, religious services took place secretly and quietly in private houses. Both Moses and his father were often required to conduct the services.

Jewish men were permitted to socialise and to trade as required, so they mixed freely with the Muslim population.

Although these freedoms were enjoyed by men, women had to endure many prohibitions. They were forbidden, for example, from venturing outside their homes whilst unaccompanied. This ruling was strictly observed. Accordingly, Shoshanah remained at home with Miriam, now a very active three-year-old, for most of the day. She became adept at improvised cooking and provided nutritious meals for the family on rather meagre provisions. Each week she went with her husband to the local market for vegetables and eggs. Occasionally a chicken was obtained for the Sabbath meal. When outside with her husband, her dress was modest in appearance and her head covered. It was considered improper for a woman to speak in public unless questioned.

Moses was convinced that despite, or perhaps because of, the adversity, the family had become even closer and more loving. In Almeria they were enjoying a settled and fulfilling life. Moses considered that the decision to leave Cordoba two years previously had been vindicated, even though rumours of radical Almohad influence getting closer to Almeria were rife. The family maintained a Jewish lifestyle and seemed content. And what is more, he was able to continue with his studies. Moses was not complacent but reasoned that they were in the optimum place at present, but should the situation change, they were prepared to leave at short notice.

It was inevitable that this harmonious lifestyle would not last.

The day of 15 July 1151 was hot and humid. Moses's father was attending a meeting of prominent Jewish leaders to discuss arrangements for the forthcoming Jewish New Year. Moses himself was studying a portion of the Talmud in a large olive grove which provided shade from the sun. He had discovered this area a few weeks previously and found that the environment and cooling breeze in the grove was conducive to learning.

When he first discovered the grove, he was joined by a young Muslim man who also appeared to be studying.

"Good morning." The man introduced himself. "My name is Abu-Walid ibn Rushd. I see you are also immersed in study." They soon realised that they had a common interest in theology and philosophy. Ibn Rushd was also a keen admirer and follower of Aristotelian philosophy. It was not long before the two of them were immersed in a discussion on how closely religion and science are connected.

"There is a widely held view that natural phenomena occur only because God wills them to happen. This cannot be right," Ibn Rushd insisted. "Phenomena follow natural laws that God created."

"I agree with you totally. That has always been my view. How refreshing to discuss a difficult topic with a like-minded individual." Moses was exhilarated by the chance meeting.

Today Moses was alone and was quietly contemplating the future. How would Jewish culture survive in Spain? Would it ever be restored? What about the continuation of Jewish learning? He was convinced that in the present environment with the current lack of facilities and loss of learning, a simplified compendium of Jewish laws for the benefit of the average Jew unable to acquire or understand the sources would surely be worthwhile. Could he possibly write such a text?

These thoughts, part of a recurring theme, were interrupted by Joshua, a neighbour and friend.

"Ah, there you are, Moses. You must come quickly." Joshua was distressed and had obviously sprinted from the house to the grove.

"What is the matter?" Moses was on his feet immediately and collected his books in a satchel.

"No time to explain. We must run. Your father is waiting."

Moses arrived at the house breathless and anxious. He was met by his father and David. Both were in tears, devastated, and incoherent. Moses looked on the scene which greeted him with horror and disbelief. A bloodstained sheet covered a body.

"What has happened?" he shouted.

"A terrible accident, a terrible accident, Moshe." His father could not control his emotions.

7

As far as Abdul was concerned, it had started out as a normal day. His elderly donkey required feeding with the fresh straw he had acquired from his farmer friend, although in payment he had agreed to take the farmer's elderly mother to market on the following Thursday. He meticulously hitched the donkey to his cart. Blinkers were applied. He later vehemently claimed to have carefully checked that the bridle straps were appropriately positioned. He then joined his wife and their five children for breakfast. He had three journeys to make during the day. The first was down to the docks to haul a cartload of spices which had recently arrived from India down to a merchant in the centre of Almeria. He estimated a round journey of three hours, including the loading. He guided the donkey at a gentle pace towards the docks. It was a hot humid day, and he reminded himself to make sure the donkey was well-watered.

Shoshanah had prepared breakfast for Moses and David, who were at a friend's house for morning prayers. They returned to be welcomed by the appealing aroma of fresh fruits, bread, and oats boiled in milk. After breakfast Moses decided to study a portion of Torah alone in the olive grove, which he visited regularly because it was both quiet and cool. His father would spend the day teaching young boys in preparation for their bar mitzvahs. As usual Shoshanah would remain at home with Miriam. She adored her daughter and gained great pleasure in observing her development. Miriam was demonstrably intelligent with an ever-increasing vocabulary. However, she was occasionally overactive and needed to be watched constantly; otherwise, she was in danger of running off or even harming herself.

Abdul needed to give his donkey very little encouragement. They proceeded at a steady pace. The roads were partially paved and busy. He wondered how much he would be paid for each delivery. Usually the merchants were generous, provided he was on time and the goods had not been damaged in transit. He was able to earn a reasonable income, but this depended on his trusty donkey, who was now getting old and approaching the end of his working life. Abdul also suspected that the donkey's eyesight was defective, but provided he was able to steer the beast in the right direction, he should be workable for another year or so. The donkey kept shaking his head. *I wonder if the bridle is irritating him,* Abdul pondered. *I will check it when we stop to unload.* He was heading for the central market and was close to Calle Camelia. The road was uneven, and the donkey was having difficulty, at one point having stumbled but managing to maintain his footing.

Miriam was playing quietly, so Shoshanah left her alone to continue with her cleaning in the other room. There was a commotion outside. Miriam toddled to the open window. Two men were arguing, and a crowd was gathering. Miriam recognised a friend who was passing by with her parents.

"Hello, Alia!" she shouted. "Can we play? I want to play with you." She ran towards the stairs, descending on all fours to the bottom, and then ran into the street.

Shoshanah went to check on her daughter and screamed as she realised she was missing. She looked through the window in horror. Miriam was wandering aimlessly in the road below. She shouted to her to come back, but there was no response. She dashed downstairs and into the road, her eyes scanning for Miriam. She saw her.

"Miriam," she screamed hysterically, "come here!"

She hadn't noticed the donkey behind her. It all happened so quickly. The disturbance and the noisy crowd upset Abdul's donkey just as Shoshanah was passing. The donkey raised up on his hind legs and turned. The poorly fitted bridle failed to control him. As his front legs came down, they crashed into Shoshanah, who was busy trying to attract Miriam's attention. Shoshanah had no chance to move away. The hooves hit the back of her head, and she collapsed to the ground. As she lay prone and unconscious on the ground, she was stamped on by the donkey and run over by the cart. She lay unconscious and bleeding from her scalp. She remained motionless. She was carried into the house by passers-by but failed to regain consciousness. A doctor was summoned, but all he could do was to officially pronounce her dead. The multiple broken ribs and serious head injury were incompatible with survival.

Moses wanted to see his mother's face. He gently lifted the sheet to display the terrible injuries. The hooves of the donkey and the wheels of the cart had trampled her head and chest. The injuries were horrendous. Her skull oozed jelly-like material which Moses assumed to be brain tissue. *How could this have happened to such a kind, good person? Why do the righteous need to suffer so much?* Moses was distraught.

Psalms were recited. Shoshanah's body remained in the house overnight, and the funeral took place on the following morning.

For the second time, Maimon buried a wife whom he had loved dearly. The funeral was followed by seven days of mourning. Throughout, Moses and David were inconsolable and had difficulty in coming to terms with the tragedy. Miriam was confused. "Where is Mummy?" she asked repeatedly.

Friends and colleagues rallied around Rabbi Maimon and his family, providing much-needed support. Maimon explained the situation as sympathetically as possible to Miriam. But how would she cope without a mother? Soon a decision would have to be taken on how best to cater for the needs of a small girl. Miriam would require a stable female carer, and her father was very conscious of this. Maimon and his sons felt incapable of taking on the responsibility. Miriam herself proved to be remarkably resilient. She seemed to appreciate the situation, and she soon realised that she would never see her mummy again.

Maimon tried his best to return to a normal life, but he found it difficult to do so. He had become so devoted to Shoshanah and only now realised how dependent he had been on her calmness and competence. As the weeks and months passed, another worrying situation was developing which he was becoming increasingly concerned about.

The liberal Almohad influence in Almeria was diminishing, and a much more radical approach was being adopted. This was because the commander in charge of Almeria, who'd allowed limited freedoms for the Jewish community, was replaced by a hard-line extremist. This radical Almohad doctrine was not limited to Almeria but was spreading diffusely and rapidly across the whole of Spain. Maimon anticipated the worst and realised a solution for Miriam was now urgently required. If they had to return to a life of travel from city to city, Miriam would not be able to cope. A solution would have to be found—and quickly.

Maimon had built up a close friendship with Nadim, who continued to have respect for Jews in general and especially for the Maimon family. He knew that Nadim regarded Jews as his cousins and had no animosity towards them. Nadim deplored the Almohad regime. He was aware that Shoshanah had developed a close relationship with his wife, and their children were always pleased to play with Miriam.

Maimon discussed his concern for Miriam's future with Nadim and his wife. Without hesitation they offered, with total sincerity, to take care of Miriam should the Maimons need to be exiled yet again.

"We would regard it as our pleasure. With Allah's blessing we will look after your daughter as our own," were Nadim's reassuring words.

"You are generous and thoughtful. I thank you sincerely. May you be blessed." Maimon reluctantly accepted the offer in the expectation that one day he would return and retrieve his daughter.

It was fortunate that arrangements for Miriam had been made well in advance. The invasion by the radical Almohad forces came rapidly and viciously. With no warning, Almohad soldiers charged into Almeria. Their horsemen galloped through the streets destroying any semblance of Jewish activity. Many innocent bystanders were put to the sword. There was no resistance. An edict went out to the Jewish population ordering them out of their homes.

Miriam was left with Nadim's family.

"We love you very much, Miriam, but you will now be living with Nadim and his family. We will come and see you again soon." Maimon tried to be as reassuring as he could.

"I want to come with you." She cried inconsolably as she struggled in the arms of Nadim's wife. Maimon was overcome with both emotion and guilt as he saw that his daughter was unhappy and confused.

"Please don't cry," he pleaded. "You have many friends here, and your dear mother would have wanted you to stay."

What else could he say? He prayed to God to keep her safe and to protect her.

The invasion was swift and brutal. Maimon, Moses, and David were rounded up by a group of marauding soldiers and, joined by several hundred other Jews, were marched into the main central square. A tall, fiercely aggressive army commander addressed them.

"You Jews have no place in Muslim Spain. We are now properly in control of Almeria. The privileges that were afforded to you by the previous weak commander have ended. We will put to the sword any Jew who does not convert to Islam. However, I am a generous man." He sneered. "I give you another choice. You can leave and travel wherever your feet take you. But remember, we will catch up with you as we advance, and then we will give you the same choice again." He laughed. "Now be gone, you wretched people."

Because spurious conversions to Islam were common, severe restrictions were now placed on converts. They could not engage in large-scale trading, hitherto a Jewish specialty, and they could not possess slaves or act as guardians. In addition, men were now required to wear degrading costumes: a long blue tunic with absurdly large wide sleeves, and a blue skullcap in the shape of a donkey's saddle that fell below the ears. Jewish converts were also made to wear a piece of yellow cloth sewn onto their outer garment.

Maimon and his sons packed their cart once again and joined the throngs of exiles leaving Almeria for an uncertain future, the difference from last time being that they had arrived in Almeria with Shoshanah and Miriam but sadly were now leaving without them.

Initially they travelled north towards Christian Spain. Their journey was tortuous. They passed through Grenada and Lucena, cities where they could rest and spend time with fellow Jews who were also fleeing. Moses continued to study with his father whenever possible from books they carried with them and some which they were able to acquire. Once they left the larger cities, there was no sign of Jewish life, but they persisted with their trek regardless. They stopped at sparsely inhabited villages and usually found places to rest or alternatively camped outside at night, worryingly conscious of wolves, which roamed freely.

The land covered with brush was inhospitable and provided little shade or sustenance. They headed relentlessly towards the Sierra Morena mountain range and eventually arrived at a mountain pass, which they crossed, and descended into a valley. Here they found woodland with clumps of conifers and oaks, along with comfortable places for shelter. Throughout the journey they set aside time each day for learning, much of which Moses committed to memory.

The pattern of movement from town to town, from village to village, continued year after year. On one occasion they entered Christian Spain but found the atmosphere intimidating; the Christians who themselves were persecuted by the Almohads took pleasure in similarly persecuting the Jews. The family constantly sought areas not yet under Almohad rule, but this option became increasingly elusive as the Almohad influence expanded.

Moses would enhance his knowledge of science, logic, mathematics, and medicine by finding secular libraries in the larger towns and cities. He would study voraciously and commit as much to memory as he could. Patterns of thought and novel concepts continued to develop in his mind. His father taught him basic rabbinics, adequate—when combined with his theological background—for him to become a rabbi in due course, which had been the tradition for generations of Maimons.

However, as the years passed, it was clear that Jewish culture and learning in Spain was disappearing. Jewish life was a wasteland, and the realisation of this depressing fact acted as a catalyst for the Maimons to maintain their Torah learning and to spread its influence whenever a possibility arose.

On occasions they were able to settle in one place for several months. In Tudela, for example, the Almohad regime had temporarily waned and the few resident Jewish families were able to live in relative safety. The family took advantage of this and stayed in a small, sparsely furnished cottage for over a year. The cottage had two rooms. One acted as a bedroom with rugs and pillows; the other, a small dining room and kitchen. There was a stove with a wood heater for warmth and cooking and a wooden table with three chairs—spartan accommodation but ample for their needs. It was a particularly productive period for Moses, who was able to focus his thoughts and begin to write. He was seventeen at the time.

Moses could see that his father was anxious to maintain David's Jewish education also, but it was evident that David had interests other than in Jewish studies. These were commercial in nature and were related to gems and precious stones. David relished every opportunity to enhance his expertise in this field. Whenever possible he would seek out merchants in the larger cities, ask questions, obtain information, and generally expand his knowledge. Occasionally he would find a trader willing to take him on as an apprentice, which pleased him enormously. David's long-term ambition was to become a trader in precious gems.

The atmosphere in the cottage was stuffy, especially in the summer, and not conducive to learning, so Moses often sat outside to read. One day whilst outside and seeped in study, he was approached by a young man. The youth who lived nearby had observed Moses studying intensively each morning but was initially embarrassed to approach him. He was the son of a local fruit merchant who worked in the city, and whose family were known to have maintained their Jewish identity.

"Good morning. My name is Daniel. I live down the road." He pointed in the direction of a row of small houses. "I have met your father, who teaches in our local school. He suggested I contact you."

"I am delighted to make your acquaintance," replied Moses. He recognised Daniel as a neighbour. His father had mentioned that Daniel wished to become a friend.

"Your father told me of your deep knowledge of Gemara as well as astronomy and mathematics."

Moses seemed rather embarrassed. "That is rather an exaggeration."

"Your father also suggested I ask you a question about a matter that has confused me," Daniel remarked hesitantly.

"You flatter me, but I will try to answer your query," Moses replied.

"I often sit out at night and look at the stars and the moon. I am puzzled by the timings of the new moon. I have studied the explanations in the Gemara but cannot understand them. Can you explain it to me? I have so little understanding of astronomy."

Moses considered for a moment.

"There is much knowledge in the Torah and Talmud," he replied. "But it is important to be familiar with science, logic, and mathematics in order to fully understand the messages contained within." The youth was tall and thin with an obvious purple birthmark occupying the skin of much of his right cheek. He nodded.

"I was not aware of that, but perhaps that is the reason for my ignorance."

This chance meeting was the incentive for Moses to consider writing responses to questions addressed to him. The timing of this query was particularly apposite since he had recently studied astronomy in detail in the well-stocked central library in Tudela. He was convinced that mathematical knowledge was crucial to understanding the link between the astronomical laws of the new moon and the Gemara explanations.

"I will try to explain the movement of the moon, but perhaps you would find it most helpful if I were to write the explanation as a booklet for you to study," offered Moses. The youth smiled gratefully.

Soon Moses set about the task with vigour. He reread the passages in the Talmud and the Gemara to refresh his memory and correlated the key points to accepted astronomical principles. He introduced mathematical formulae into his descriptions. The writing took several weeks, but at the end he was satisfied with the result. The booklet explained the movements of spheres in the sky, the way in which the seasons are divided, and most importantly how to calculate the timing of the new moon and the distribution of the leap years. He entitled the booklet *Maamar Ha'ibbur* ("An essay on intercalation"). The booklet was written in a lucid fashion that could be understood by a young man who might not possess a knowledge of astronomy or indeed mathematics.

Daniel was delighted and appreciative to receive the booklet. He found the explanations presented both rational and logical. Moses was pleased. This was the first occasion that he realised he possessed an important skill, a unique ability to explain and classify information in such a way that it was understandable to a man of average intelligence. This greatly encouraged him. He promised himself that he would continue with this approach whenever he was faced with a dilemma or difficult question.

Daniel's father asked if he could read the booklet because he, too, was intrigued by the movements of the moon and the recognition of the new month. He studied the booklet avidly and was hugely impressed.

"How I wish I had your understanding of science and logic, Moses. I am sure you are right: it would allow a better understanding of the wonders hidden in the Talmud," commented Daniel.

"Logic and science are as important to understanding the

Torah as grammar is to language," explained Moses. "Much of what I have written in the booklet is based on the observations of Aristotle, a philosopher whose work I have read extensively."

Moses was intrigued by the discipline of logic and the application of logical thought to everyday matters. Even before meeting with Daniel he had intended to write a treatise on logic to assist in the understanding of problems which arise in the Torah and Talmud. The serendipitous meeting was the stimulus he required to illustrate the basis of logic and its contribution to scientific thought for anyone of average intelligence who wished to grasp the finer points of the Talmud.

He set about his task of writing another treatise, this time on the principles of logic. He studied and incorporated numerous texts and works from Arabic philosophers such as Yaqub Abu Ishaq ibn Yusuf and Sina al-Mantik, in addition to Aristotle. He analysed their work and documented his thoughts and concepts in a treatise written in Arabic using Hebrew characters, Judaeo-Arabic. He entitled the short book *Biur Milos Hahegayon: A Treatise on the Explanation of Logical Terms*. He was gratified with the response and plaudits the work received wherever it was read.

Life in Tudela, although initially comfortable whilst the local population were willing to accommodate the few Jewish families who remained, became less pleasant when an Almohad militia approached the city. The local Muslim population, as in Almeria, were worried in case they be accused of collaboration with the Jews. This allegation was a serious matter. Tales of hangings and beheadings of Muslims in other places who had shown support for and given comfort to Jews were well publicised. Jews were no longer popular or welcome.

"We have an opportunity here," explained Omar to his motley crew of disorderly teenagers known to be troublemakers. They regularly roamed the streets frightening passers-by with their crude comments and implied threats. He described his plan.

The central mosque in Tudela had acquired ancient silver goblets which were known to be very valuable. They would fetch a good price, and Omar knew of an unscrupulous dealer willing to purchase them.

"The mosque has no security and can be entered very easily. The goblets are on display. The Jews will be blamed, especially now that the Almohads are on their way. No one will suspect a Muslim. We will be rich." His friends, although initially reluctant, were seduced by Omar's enthusiasm and were concerned that they would lose out on the proceeds if they refused to participate. They all agreed to join the scheme.

Entrance to the mosque at night was not difficult. There were no guards, and the windows were an easy target. They entered quietly and swiftly. The goblets were extracted from a cabinet and placed in a bag. They left the same way as they'd entered. The entrance, theft, and exit took less than fifteen minutes.

The theft was discovered the following morning, and word spread rapidly across the neighbourhood. The staff of the mosque were terrified lest they be held responsible. To avert the finger of blame, they spread the rumour that it was Jews who had robbed the mosque. The townspeople believed them, mainly because it was inconceivable that a fellow Muslim would have desecrated and robbed a mosque of holy relics. Omar and his friends reinforced the false accusation by claiming to have seen the perpetrators of the theft running from the mosque whilst they were enjoying a social evening in the vicinity. They identified one of the thieves as a Jew called Abraham del Capa. Omar claimed to have given chase, but the thieves escaped down a labyrinth of narrow streets before Omar and his friends were able to apprehend them and return the stolen goods to their rightful place in the mosque.

The local population were incensed. It was not long before groups rampaged through the streets, looking for Jews and storming houses. Many innocent Jews were arrested, including Del Capo himself. Abraham del Capo was a pious observant Jew who spent much of his day in prayer. Moses and his father knew him well and had great respect for his learning. They regarded the allegation against him as preposterous and intended to fully support him.

Del Capo had never been inside a mosque and would never enter one for religious reasons. Therefore, he could not have even known of the presence of valuable silver goblets. Moreover, he was too infirm to climb through a window; he had a stiff hip which resulted in him walking with a limp. How could he possibly have run away from Omar and his friends, who were young and fit? Rabbi Maimon also knew of Omar, a disreputable troublemaker and petty thief. Surely his account would not be preferred to that of Abraham del Capo.

Rabbi Maimon and his sons lay on their rugs discussing their plans for the day and how they would support and defend Abraham, when their conversation was shattered by a large rock hurled through a window. The glass shards narrowly missed Moses. A crowd had gathered outside and were shouting abusively.

"You Jews are thieves, and you have desecrated our holy mosque," one of them shouted. Moses went outside to confront the angry crowd. Further abuse was hurled, but Moses was undeterred.

"Please, friends, listen to me. We have great respect for your holy sites. You believe in one God, as do we. I am familiar with the writings in the Koran. We would do nothing to insult your Prophet. No Jew would desecrate a holy mosque, which we respect as your God's house on earth. Abraham del Capo is a respectful, pious gentleman who would never offend your religion." Moses's appeal was drowned out by continuous bellowing from the crowd. Maimon stepped outside, realising that the crowd were angry and impervious to reasoning and that he needed to calm the situation lest Moshe's safety be compromised.

"We do not wish for trouble. And as it is your will, we shall leave Tudela. We thank you for your hospitality. But you must know, Jews would never desecrate and steal from a mosque," shouted Maimon. The crowd seemed placated and slowly dispersed, but an elderly member stayed behind.

"I am sorry about this, but the Almohads will be arriving tomorrow in force. Your presence here is a threat to us. We will be punished if we are shown to harbour Jews. I hope you understand. You must leave before they arrive," he remarked apologetically.

"We have enjoyed our stay in Tudela," said Rabbi Maimon. "We understand your dilemma and will not make things bad for you. We will leave. I am sure other Jewish families will do likewise."

Moses later joined his father to visit Abraham, who was under house arrest. "Abraham, I am so sorry that you have been falsely accused of the theft. Is there anything I can do to support you? Should I speak to the general?"

"You are kind and considerate, but no assistance is necessary or required. I am content to leave the matter in the hands of the Almighty. He will defend me. I have no concerns. Please do not fret. Leave Tudela whilst you are still able."

Moses later heard that Abraham del Capo had been taken before a sharia court, accused of desecration of a mosque and the theft of holy relics. After hearing all the evidence, the judge found him not guilty. There was no evidence to support the allegations, and the witnesses to the incident were considered unreliable. Abraham was released and left Tudela. An investigation into the theft was carried out. The goblets were found in Omar's possession because the trader who he thought would purchase them refused to do so and reported Omar and his friends to the authorities. Even an unscrupulous dealer in stolen goods had refused to handle items taken from a mosque, however profitable they might be. Omar was arrested for theft, for desecration of a holy mosque, and for providing false testimony. He and his friends confessed to the crime when forcibly interrogated. Omar was publically hanged, and his friends were flogged.

The Maimon family left Tudela and drifted again into an uncertain future, resigned to a continuing life of exile.

8

Rabbi Maimon was comforted by the regular letters he received from Nadim about Miriam, although he was still worried about whether he had made the right decision to leave her. Miriam was adapting to a predominantly Muslim lifestyle. She admitted to occasional bouts of depression accompanied by tears as she remembered her family, especially her mother. Nadim and both his wives were sympathetic and able to comfort her. Nadim reassured Maimon that he repeatedly reminded Miriam of her Jewish background and said that he had found books to assist in this.

Nadim had recently married his second wife, who was twenty years younger than his first. She had provided Nadim with another child, a boy. Miriam was delighted and warmed to the opportunity of looking after the new arrival whenever possible.

"At least she is safe and well looked after," Maimon commented to his sons as he sought to reassure himself, even though he was dejected by the situation.

"She could not have coped with life on the road with its constant dangers. What would have happened to Miriam, for example, when we were attacked by those robbers in that village near Villafeliche?" Moses said, anxious to reassure his father. The incident he referred to was etched on his memory. He vividly recalled the horrific event.

A band of robbers burst into a wayside inn where the Maimon family were staying to extract money from the guests. A Christian family with a teenage boy and a ten-year-old girl were similarly seeking shelter. The gang of masked robbers demanded money and threatened to kill the girl if none was forthcoming. The family begged for compassion. They were poor and pitifully clothed and had no money to give.

Moses intervened and asked for mercy, quoting relevant passages that he had learnt from the Koran. He also offered the robbers his own money, wrapped in a cotton pouch, that he had saved. The money was snatched. The robbers laughed heartlessly and then ruthlessly snatched the screaming girl.

"Please be merciful. I beg you, let her go," pleaded the father. "Take me instead. I would be more valuable to you."

"I have in mind a wealthy sheikh who will pay more for a girl than for you," he sneered.

The father leapt forward but was unceremoniously knocked to the ground, unconscious. The mother screamed.

Maimon tended to the father. Moses stood before the brigands and again begged for mercy, but none was forthcoming. He was punched in the stomach for his efforts. The brigands left.

The family were devastated. The girl was never seen again. Such events were not uncommon, and rumours were rife regarding a slave trade in young girls shipped to faraway places.

"At least Miriam is safe from such atrocity," Rabbi Maimon commented, trying to reassure himself.

The Maimon family travelled extensively, stopping at villages and cities but always fearful of the Almohad presence. The persecution was relentless. Moses became increasingly anxious and very angry. How would it all end? When would they be free to lead a normal settled life? Would they ever be able to practise their religion in freedom? *Perhaps God is testing our resolve,* he thought. *We must remain strong, and whatever the provocation, we must remain true to our religion.*

Food was mainly fruit, rice, and vegetables purchased from local farmers or at a central market. Occasionally a chicken was slaughtered in accordance with Jewish law for the Sabbath and Jewish holidays. Throughout, the Maimon family meticulously observed the Sabbath and all festivals. Moses studied with his father each day, whilst David would listen and try to comprehend, although his main interest remained in commerce and particularly gems and precious stones.

On their travels they encountered Jewish families in a similar situation. They would exchange news and offer advice and sympathy if required. Warnings of impending Almohad movements were exchanged and places to avoid usefully noted.

In Calatayud they met a young man and his pregnant wife struggling on foot and offered them transport on their overladen carriage, an offer which was gratefully accepted.

"You are most generous. We have come from a nearby village. The Almohads destroyed it and burnt down our synagogue. We managed to escape, but many didn't, including my wife's brother. We are now desperate to find shelter. My wife is six months with child." The man was obviously indebted for the assistance but distressed.

"I am so sorry. I wish we could help further. We are travelling to Seville, but it is a long journey, and I do not think your wife will be comfortable." Maimon was sympathetic but felt he could do little more to help them.

"I understand. We would be most grateful if you could take us as far as Ateca, which is only two leguas away. We know people there who might provide shelter." Maimon agreed and headed in that direction. They arrived some two hours later.

"You must stay for a meal. My uncle Naphtali is a religious

Jew who would be pleased to have your company." The offer was enthusiastically accepted. They dismounted and entered the house. Rabbi Maimon introduced himself and his sons.

"Shalom Aleichem, Rabbi. You are most welcome in my home." Naphtali beamed.

"Shalom," replied Rabbi Maimon. "It is considerate of you to welcome us so generously."

"Rabbi, you were kind enough to bring my dear nephew and his wife. It is the least I can do to offer you and your sons a meal and accommodation for the night."

The house was modest, remarkably tidy, and well decorated considering that Naphtali had lived in it alone since his wife died three years previously. The room had a table on trestles covered with a colourful tablecloth. There was a bench in one corner of the room and a cupboard. Rabbi Maimon, David, and Moses were invited to sit on stools whilst Naphtali's nephew and wife occupied the bench. Naphtali laid out a modest but welcome nutritious meal of rice and stew with fresh vegetables.

"This is delicious," complimented David. The other guests nodded in agreement. Naphtali's nephew, a rather unkempt gangling man, had long black sidelocks showing from his turban and a flowing beard. Both he and his wife were devoutly religious. The conversation during the meal quickly turned to Torah studies.

"Moshe, I have just remembered where I have heard your name." Saul, the nephew, appeared pleased with himself. "Your reputation follows you. You are the young man who has written on science and logic. Am I not right that you have written booklets explaining these things? Let me think where I heard this." He stared at the ceiling, deep in thought.

"Ah yes, now I remember. A farmer from Tudela whose son, Daniel I think his name was, asked you some questions, and you produced a detailed response."

Moses was embarrassed and looked towards his father. Then he answered diffidently.

"I have read the works of the great masters on these topics and brought their ideas together to try to make them understandable to people without knowledge of science. In yeshiva we learn much Torah and Talmud, but an understanding of science makes the lessons more real," Moses explained.

"Jewish learning is disappearing," Naphtali bemoaned. "We have no yeshivot left, and most synagogues have been destroyed. Many Jews have converted to Islam to save themselves and their families. We have difficulty in obtaining kosher food. We are a dying religion," continued Naphtali in a resigned monotone. "How can we be true Jews and learn without the tools, without books? We must do something."

"My uncle is right." Saul appeared forlorn and looked towards his pregnant wife, who was in obvious discomfort with her arms wrapped around her bulging abdomen.

"Without our holy books, much is being forgotten. What is needed is a commentary, a summary on the Mishna, for example, which can be used to remind Jews of the importance of the oral teachings but which does not require all the sources. Moshe, what do you think? With your knowledge and ability to explain things clearly, have you ever considered writing a commentary on the Mishna with all its arguments for Jews with only limited knowledge and appreciation?" Saul said this whilst looking directly at Moses. Maimon grinned with pride.

"That is quite a challenge thrown at you, Moshe," his father remarked. "There is indeed a need in these dark times for a clear, concise exposition of the Mishna without complex Talmudic discussion which can be understood by the common man at a time when material for learning is no longer widely available. You have shown that you are able to write with clarity, and with your remarkable memory and the few books we have available in our possession—and with God's blessing—you could make it possible."

Moses could feel the glares of all present fixated on him whilst awaiting an answer. He remained silent as he collected his thoughts. It was an enormous challenge. He had written a treatise on the Jewish calendar that required a knowledge of astronomy and mathematics, and a treatise on logic and metaphysics, topics that intrigued his analytical mind and taxed his scientific knowledge. However, a commentary on the Mishna was a much greater task. He was just twenty-three, and the work would take many years to complete. The style would be crucial. It would need to be directed specifically at Jews without a deep background in Jewish learning and articulated in such a way that was both understandable and practical. Despite the enormity of the task, he reasoned that such a review of the Mishna in these dark days of exile was much needed.

Jews lived by complex laws, Halacha, based on interpretations by generations of erudite rabbis who provided commentaries and decisions on a multitude of issues. The deliberations had been passed down orally by individuals or in religious academies, and discrepancies were bound to have occurred. In 200 CE Judah ha-Nasi, a deeply respected patriarch of the Jewish community in Palestine and a forebear of Rabbi Maimon, compiled the huge corpus of oral tradition into a single text, the Mishna (which means "learning by repetition"). He divided the laws into six sections containing over sixty-three tractates, each of which were further divided into chapters. Much discussion and argument of judicial Halacha by generations of rabbinic scholars over several hundred years was then compiled into a text called the Gemara, a conglomerate of law, legend, philosophy, history, and science.

Moses was being asked to produce a compendium of only the most essential Talmudic precepts to enable an understanding of the Mishna for less-learned readers or for those who, in the difficult times they were facing, did not have the time, source material, or inclination to wade through difficult and complicated texts. Any commentary would need to be written in concise language and provide understandable explanations in such a way that the reader would not be left confused. People were not prepared to spend time trying to understand difficult concepts when actual survival was at risk and far more important. Discussions in the Gemara were often expanded to four or five pages on a single law, with arguments going backwards and forwards. Only well-trained experts in the discipline were able to clarify the convoluted disputes.

"I feel humbled and unworthy to be considered for such a task. The work would take many years to complete. It would require more texts, and I would need to live a more stable existence with scholars with whom I could exchange ideas," he explained. "Nevertheless, I will give it more thought and discuss the matter with my revered father and brother."

The following morning, the Maimon family thanked their hosts and bade goodbye to Saul and his wife. They mounted their cart and continued their travel towards Seville. Moses had much to think about.

The summer of 1158 was cooler than in previous years. This was a relief to the entire population. Whilst in Seville, David, even though barely twenty years old, set up a small business and commenced buying and selling gems for jewellery. He established good connections with expert designers and made return journeys to Tudela on occasion. He acquired expertise during his wanderings and gained a deserved reputation for being honest, fair, and ethical in his business dealings as dictated by his upbringing. His enterprise became profitable and enabled the family to lead a comfortable, but by no means luxurious, lifestyle. This was of assistance to Moses, who, after considerable thought and with much encouragement from his father and brother, had decided to attempt a commentary on the Mishna. To do this he required access to source material as well as a place of solitude to write and study. The fact that David was able to support him financially was a great help and allowed him to concentrate on the task at hand without undue money worries.

Moses called his work *A Commentary on the Mishna or Perush Ha'mishnayos*. Much of the source material was extracted from memory. He had a few books retrieved from Cordoba and other places, and his father's extensive knowledge of the Gemara was invaluable. Each of the laws and related discussions and arguments required careful appraisal and much concentration. For example, the Torah prohibits the slaughter of a cow or a sheep and its young on the same day. The oral law further distinguishes between animals dedicated for sacrifice in the temple and those that are unsuitable for sacrifice. Slaughtering either type in a location unauthorised for it, for example slaughtering a nondedicated animal within the temple premises or a dedicated animal outside of those premises, constitutes a sin. According to the oral law, meat from a nondedicated animal slaughtered within the temple premises and the parts of a dedicated animal that was slaughtered outside can be neither consumed nor placed on the altar. The Mishna makes numerous presuppositions. There are sixteen permutations individually dealt with and argued about within, each involving detailed explanations. Moses's objective was to summarise and simplify and to provide clarity by allowing the reader to dispense with unnecessary obscurities and yet understand the key points of the law, for example on the sacrifice of animals.

However, the instability of the family's circumstances made the task time-consuming and onerous. Moses struggled on to the best of his ability for two years, making slow progress. More books were needed, and discussion with scholars was required. The Almohad threat remained a constant worry. They were continuously required to hide their religion and be ready to move at short notice, making their situation intolerable.

The situation did not ease. Persecution of the Jews, if anything, was getting worse. One incident in the autumn of 1160 was the final affront as far as Maimon was concerned. He was returning from a friend's home where clandestine prayers were recited. A group of youths blocked his path, and one pushed him and spat into his face.

"You Jews are no longer welcome. Get out of Seville," the teenager instructed.

"Why do you hate us so? We are no threat to you. Why can we not all live in peace?" he shouted at the sniggering youth. Maimon was exasperated. He decided that he could no longer endure the perpetual stress of living in Spain, his homeland. Life was uncertain and dangerous. The miracle he had hoped and prayed for would not happen. Jews would not be able to return to the existence they had enjoyed in his beloved Cordoba. To add to the despair, he felt he was in danger of becoming spiritually bereft, God forbid, and he knew Moshe was struggling with his writing.

With regret and in a soft, hesitant voice, Rabbi Maimon addressed his sons quietly but with passion. "We have suffered long enough in Spain. It is now time to leave. May the Merciful One lead us to a land where we may rest, each man under the shade of his vine."

PART III

MOROCCO

1160–1165

9

Whilst in yeshiva in Cordoba as a young man, Maimon befriended Yehuda ibn Shushan. They'd studied together, shared the same room, and remained in contact at the end of their rabbinical training. Both were ordained as rabbis. Rabbi Shushan, like Maimon, heralded from a long rabbinical dynasty. He was the same age as Maimon but physically quite different. He was small in stature and was politely referred to by most people as being stout. In truth he was grossly obese. He had a voracious appetite and proudly consumed enormous amounts, especially on the Sabbath, when he claimed it was a spiritual necessity to overeat. He had a jovial nature and was popular amongst his teachers and peers. On completing his studies, he'd left Spain to stay with his uncle, also a rabbi, in Fez, Morocco. Soon after arriving there he was appointed as rabbi of a synagogue within the mellah, the Jewish quarter. He established a deserved reputation as a Talmudic scholar, and this resulted in his appointment to the judiciary as a dayan.

In deciding to leave Spain, the question of where to go was uppermost in Maimon's thoughts. Fez in Morocco appeared a possible destination. He was confident that he would be welcomed by Rabbi Shushan, his friend and colleague from yeshiva. Although predominantly Muslim, Fez was also known as a Jewish city and at one time had many yeshivot and synagogues. Jews had originally arrived in Fez on Phoenician ships during the reign of King Solomon. The city had frequently changed regimes and had been under the control of both Romans and Byzantines. Traditionally, as in Spain, Arabs and Jews lived together in harmony and flourished until the Almohad conquest in 1145, when Jews were given the customary choice of convert, die, or leave. Although some Jews chose to die and many emigrated, the majority remained on the pretence of accepting Islam whilst secretly and in fear practising Judaism.

Despite the threat of persecution from which he and his sons were trying to escape, Maimon reasoned that there was an advantage in travelling to Fez. Many forms of scholarship still existed there, such as secular schools teaching natural sciences, philosophy, and mathematics, topics which Moshe wished to pursue in greater depth. Moshe had also expressed a desire to study medicine as his broad knowledge and appreciation of natural sciences increased. In Fez, one of the most respected institutes of higher education in the world was to be found, the Karaouine (Quaraouiyine) school, which also provided an opportunity to study medicine.

Rabbi Maimon also reasoned that a period of stability without the need for constant travel from place to place would enable Moses to settle down to his project on the commentary. In addition, David was keen to pursue his business interests and would have the opportunity to do so since Fez had a thriving commercial industry, especially in gems and precious metals. On a personal level, Maimon much preferred living in Muslim countries. He had a strong aversion to Christians, whom he regarded as more unwelcoming even than Muslims, and what is more they had an alien culture and language. At least he had contacts in Fez and could expect a warm, friendly welcome with the strong possibility of some form of employment.

Maimon contacted Rabbi Shushan to enquire about the Almohad situation in Fez.

"My dear friend," Rabbi Shushan wrote in response, "you would be most welcome in Fez. I know of your travails in Spain and the difficulties you and your family have endured. I have also heard through a contact in Almeria that your son Moshe is a gifted scholar who already, at his tender age, has made important contributions to Jewish scholarship and education. The situation here in Fez has improved. We were initially subjected to severe persecution, but in recent months it has been peaceful. The local Almohad commander has shown signs of laxity in his dealings with Jews, and we are feeling less threatened. We keep to ourselves, and many communities have reverted to regular religious services, but in secret. The situation may change, of course, but at present we are enjoying a period of quietude, Baruch Hashem."

This positive, reassuring reply from Rabbi Shushan reinforced Maimon's decision. In consultation with his sons, and with their agreement, he decided to move to Fez. Once more they packed their possessions and made their way to Tarifa, the most southern port in Spain, where on a clear day it was even possible to see the coast of Morocco.

They were not alone at the port of Tarifa. Many Arabs and a few Jews were also seeking travel to Tangier. Maimon had been warned to be vigilant because of the prevalence of thieves, but more importantly because unscrupulous sea captains overcharged and overfilled their dhows.

They entered the walled city of Tarifa through the largest of the three gates. Having managed to sell their faithful donkeys to a local trader, they settled for the night in an inn close to Guzman castle. The innkeeper was friendly but obviously troubled as he sat with Rabbi Maimon on a table overflowing with food.

"I am ashamed, Rabbi, because I am Jewish and yet I have renounced my Jewish heritage. I converted to Islam so that I could keep my business and support my family. I feel wretched and guilty." He was almost reduced to tears. This admission of shame and guilt by Jews who had converted had been brought to Rabbi Maimon's attention by many people on their travels.

"I have given this matter much thought over the last few years," Maimon replied, "ever since my son Moshe was faced with a similar expression of guilt from a distressed gentleman in Cordoba." He hesitated a moment. "It is my intention to address this dilemma in the form of a community letter, but I have not yet found time to do so. When we have settled in Fez, I will do this and distribute its content to the Jews of Spain and Morocco."

He stared directly at the innkeeper. "Do not fret, my friend. A person who is forced to convert but says his Hebrew prayers quietly to himself and continues to perform good deeds remains a Jew. The preservation of one's life is a most important Torah edict."

"I bless you for those few words of comfort. I have been consumed with guilt for many years." The innkeeper looked relieved. He smiled and hesitated as he appeared to be collecting his thoughts. "I can repay your kindness. My cousin has a seaworthy dhow and is sailing to Tangier early tomorrow morning with the tide. I will contact him and make sure you and your sons are comfortable and safe. The dhow will be crowded, but make sure you sit on the prow of the boat, the part of the bow above the waterline. It is the safest and most comfortable area for the journey."

At dawn on the following morning, the Maimon family made their way to the port and found the dhow.

"Shalom Aleichem," whispered the captain, a swarthy, bearded Yemenite Jew in his early sixties. He looked around to make sure no one was listening. "I was expecting you. My cousin contacted me." He assisted Rabbi Maimon onto the boat. Moses and David followed, carrying their possessions.

He introduced himself, "My name is Gershon. I am honoured to have you on my humble dhow, Rabbi. Please remain seated whilst the other passengers board. And remain silent lest we have some unpleasant Arabs looking for a fight. It has happened before, believe me."

The dhow had five sailors. As soon as twenty passengers had boarded, they were huddled together in cramped conditions and set sail. The mainsail looked rather ragged but was effective. Throughout the journey there was a fair wind. The passage was uneventful. The Maimons had taken a small amount of dried food with them, adequate for the journey.

Moses spent the journey working on his book but had difficulty in concentrating. He was concerned lest they had made the wrong decision to move and feared they would experience a similar degree of persecution in Fez as in Spain. But he agreed with his father that life in Spain had become intolerable. He rationalised that he would be content if they could only enjoy a period of stability to allow him to work on his commentary.

He was preoccupied with these thoughts as he looked around at his fellow passengers. He could not help but notice with derision how many of the passengers, particularly the Jewish ones, wore amulets and other magical devices on their wrists or around their necks. There were tradesmen selling amulets on the dockside before they'd boarded, and even some had stayed on board to sell magic trinkets and other talismans to the passengers. This was a source of agitation to Moses. He could see no useful purpose in them and considered their use to be an insult to the Almighty. The practice was unnecessary and ridiculous. He made a mental note to argue at every opportunity against all forms of superstition as a substitute for faith and belief in Judaism. Faith in God was all that was required.

Superstitions were nevertheless understandable and indicated how frightened people were when travelling by sea, not only because of adverse weather conditions but also because of pirates. When pirates took over a ship, the passengers had little chance of survival. Those who were not killed were sold as slaves and would rarely be heard of again.

By late afternoon they arrived in Tangier. Rabbi Shushan had given Maimon the address of a reliable Jewish friend who he knew would be able to accommodate them. The family made their way to the house, having been directed there by passers-by.

They arrived at the home, tired and dishevelled from the journey. They were warmly greeted by Adam and his rather ebullient and overpowering wife. A table with large amounts of vegetables, couscous, and chicken stew occupied the centre of a large room. The food was particularly welcome considering they'd had little to eat on the journey from Tarifa. They sat on the floor on large padded cushions, an unusual seating arrangement for the Maimons. A servant brought a pitcher and bowl and poured water over the men's hands. The appropriate blessing was recited.

"You have come to Morocco at a good time," explained Adam. "The Almohads conquered us almost fifteen years ago, and we suffered greatly. They were ruthless to the Jews in the beginning, and who can blame many for professing to convert to Islam, although secretly remaining Jews?" He smirked with a degree of satisfaction.

"We have clung to our Jewish way of life and faith in secret, whilst in public we pretend to be Muslims. Many Jews, not surprisingly, are now beginning to question their faith. They wonder whether Muhammad's truth is greater than the truth of Moses himself. However, Baruch Hashem, in recent months we have noticed a change. Al-Mu'min, as you know, has left Morocco for Spain, and the local commander of the Almohads in Morocco is much more tolerant. People are beginning to hold services in makeshift synagogues, and I even hear that a yeshiva has been set up in Fez."

"This is a sign of God's continuing love of the Jewish people," remarked Maimon. "My son Moshe has much work to do with his writing, David will develop his business interests, and I hope to teach. However, you have made sacrifices which should be recognised, and Jews must not feel guilty about their actions. I have promised to address the issue of forced conversion in a letter which I will finalise when we have settled in Fez and ensure it is distributed to the Jewish population within Morocco and Spain."

Early the following morning, Maimon and his sons made their way to the local market to purchase camels for the journey from Tangier to Fez. The scene facing them was one of organised chaos. Hundreds of merchants were showing their wares— clothes, fabrics, metals, foods, and sweets—all in abundance. The noise of bargaining and arguing was deafening.

They had no knowledge of the quality, cost, or types of camels available but had been given rudimentary advice by Adam, who'd provided them with the name of an honest and reliable camel trader. Eventually they found his compound, which contained about a dozen dromedaries, one-humped camels. The dealer explained the important aspects of looking after camels, principally to feed them on foliage and desert vegetation. Camels survive for long periods without water. Indeed, they can lose more than 30 per cent of their total water content and still thrive.

Three male camels were selected on the recommendation of the dealer and a price agreed. The Maimons were shown how to mount and were provided with a *hawia*, a baggage saddle. Content with their purchases, they returned to thank Adam and his family for their generosity and loaded up their possessions for the journey.

Adam had explained that it was not safe to travel to Fez unaccompanied; robbery and even murder were not uncommon. They therefore joined a properly organised land caravan for the journey which was led by a group of Berbers. The Maimons kept their Judaism hidden, and since they were fluent in Arabic and dressed in appropriate clothes, they avoided any trouble.

The journey to Fez took four long, tedious days. The heat

during the day was stifling and humid, but thankfully it was pleasantly cool at night. The caravan stopped twice a day to refill with water and allow for some rest. The camels seemed to relish the experience and required minimal food and water. On one occasion the caravan was stopped by a group of Almohad soldiers who demanded food. They questioned the Berber leader and accused him of smuggling goods. Seemingly this was a relatively common occurrence. A payment to the soldiers was necessary for them to drop the fabricated allegations and to allow the caravan to continue unhindered.

Maimon was aware of the commercial reputation of Fez but was not prepared for the sights that greeted them as they approached the city wall with its great gates. Fes el-Bali (Fez) was founded in the ninth century by the Idrisid dynasty. The entire medina, the central walled city, was heavily fortified with crenelated walls containing watchtowers and eight elaborate gates. Along the walls were many forts constructed as a defensive perimeter.

The caravan dismounted outside the wall, and the travellers entered the medina through Bab el-Seba gate. Maimon sold the camels to a local dealer for a reduced price compared to how much they originally cost, but he was happy to see them taken into reputable hands for resale.

The initial impression of Fez from within the wall was far less favourable than from outside the wall. Once their eyes had accommodated to the darkness in the medina, compared to the glaring sun outside the wall, the Maimons were astonished by the general dismal gloom. The narrow, winding streets were littered with filth. The houses had high walls and seemed generally in a state of disrepair. How different from Cordoba, where the streets were always clean and the centre had numerous parks and fountains. *Not so in Fez,* mused Maimon as he struggled to find his bearings amongst the warren of streets. Most houses were greyish in colour with doors painted in blue for good luck.

Unquestionably there are advantages for us in this structure, he thought. *With such a large population in a confined area, Jews could mingle anonymously, and it should be an easy matter to hold religious services and study groups without being noticed.* He reasoned that these advantages could well overcome their initial disappointment.

Their first task was to locate Rabbi Shushan's residence. This would not be easy. Burdened with their packs, they followed the narrow streets towards the mellah, the Jewish quarter. Rabbi Shushan would be expecting them but obviously did not know the exact day of their arrival. Maimon was confident of a warm welcome and knew that accommodation had been obtained for them.

Moses noticed an elderly gentleman with a long grey beard and a black fading tunic sitting on a low wall at the side of a narrow alley reading a book. Moses came closer and recognised it as a volume of Talmud.

"Excuse me, sir. I am so sorry to disturb your studies, but I could not help noticing that you are reading a portion of Talmud. My revered father, my brother, and I are also Jewish and require some directions. Perhaps you would be kind enough to direct us to the residence of Rabbi Shushan."

The elderly gentleman nodded. "You must be careful, young man. Never reveal that you are Jewish when you are outside. Me, I do not care. I am old and no longer worry for myself." He smiled. "I am sure you are a sincere, honest Jew and not a spy." He laughed to himself. "Everyone knows Rabbi Shushan. He is a great tsaddik and *talmid chacham,* a kind and learned gentleman. Please follow me. I will direct you to his home."

"Sir, you are most kind," responded Moses.

Progress was slow as the elderly gentleman shuffled rigidly, rather than walked, but it was obvious that he was familiar with the area. He also gave a commentary as they passed different points of interest.

"I am sure you have noticed the smell. Over there is the tannery." He pointed to a large building behind a wall. The tops of several vats could be seen. They walked towards the tannery and looked through a hole in the wall. The smell was all-pervasive. There was a large courtyard with many vats. Sweating workers were dipping hides into the vats, some filled with saffron for yellow, others with indigo for blue or poppy for red. The offensive smell was from the dyes being mixed with cow urine for preservation. The hides were then hung up to dry over walls or on rooftops.

The elderly gentleman was evidently well known and was often stopped by both Jews and Muslims, who enquired about his health.

"I have many friends in Fez," he said proudly to Rabbi Maimon. "I have lived in Fez all my life, and I am now approaching seventy. Jews have lived in Fez for centuries. For over a hundred and fifty years we had a golden age, but not now. My father, may his soul rest in peace, was a famous rabbi. He was a Rosh Beth Din, head of the rabbinical court. We used to have dozens of yeshivot and synagogues in Fez. Now look at us; we have been crushed, and learning is disappearing. You are lucky to be visiting Rabbi Shushan. He is a great scholar and works hard to maintain a Jewish life in these terrible days."

He led them along several narrow zigzag passages populated my merchants showing their wares of silks and fabrics and others with stalls displaying fruits and sweets. Maimon became totally disorientated and lost all sense of direction. It would take a long time to confidently find his way around Fez, he decided.

Eventually they reached an attractive alley which led to a large courtyard with a mosaic floor. The elderly gentleman pointed to a whitewashed door. "That is Rabbi Shushan's house."

"We are most grateful to you, sir. I hope we will have an opportunity to meet again," said Maimon.

The elderly gentleman smiled and shuffled away.

Rabbi Shushan had been expecting them, and his greeting was genuinely warm. He wore a long white blouse with a brown robe. His head was covered with a red fez. Rabbi Maimon and Rabbi Shushan embraced, although Rabbi Shushan's rather large waist, even larger than Rabbi Maimon had remembered, made this somewhat awkward.

"How good to meet again after all these years." Rabbi Shushan was clearly delighted to re-engage with his old yeshiva partner. After the introductions, he ushered them into his house, where his wife and their seven children were waiting. After a delicious meal in which the two rabbis reminisced about the "old days" in yeshiva and caught up with all the news, it was time to make their way to the house which Rabbi Shushan had identified as being ideally suited for their needs. They were taken there by his eldest son, Joshua. Before they left, however, Rabbi Shushan warned them again of the dangers.

"The Almohads are more liberal and tolerant than in previous years, but you must be careful. Do not pray in public or show any signs of your Jewishness lest you be arrested or worse. We have organised secret religious services, and your teaching will be greatly appreciated."

The house was not far away in the very heart of the mellah. Joshua opened the door and handed the keys to Rabbi Maimon, who thanked him for his assistance. The house had previously been owned by a Muslim family. The door was painted blue and opened onto a narrow passage. Mezuzahs, the parchment of Hebrew script placed in a container and attached to the doorpost of a Jewish house, were no longer used since they were a clear sign of a Jewish presence within. The furniture was adequate and the two bedrooms well appointed. Each had a large chest to store clothes. The floors had woollen carpets on which were two large divans. There was also a room devoid of all furniture which appeared to be a study. The accommodation was comfortable—sparse but adequate.

Maimon was relieved. They had arrived safely in Fez after a long and tortuous journey. It was time for evening prayers, maariv. He recited the HaGomel blessing, mentioned in the Talmud and traditionally said after a dangerous journey, especially by sea: "Blessed are you, Lord our God, King of the Universe, who bestows good on the unworthy, who has bestowed on me much good."

The family faced an uncertain future but did so with renewed optimism and no little ambition.

10

Moses always felt elation as he walked past the Karaouine university building in the centre of Fez. Founded in 859, it was the oldest degree-awarding educational institution in the world. Attached to it was a madrasa and mosque with a remarkable ribbed dome standing on an octagonal base. The Karaouine library contained a vast collection of Islamic literature as well as tomes on philosophy, science, mathematics, natural science, and medicine. How Moses wished he could gain access to the mass of scholarship contained within. However, entrance to the library and to the university was limited strictly to Muslim scholars.

Soon after arriving in Fez, Moses concentrated on his commentary. He had already made a good but rather staccato start during his travels in Spain, but now he found the work easier because of the more settled environment. He structured his days so that in the mornings, after prayers had been said with a minyan (a group of ten men) in Rabbi Shushan's clandestine synagogue, he concentrated on analysing and structuring his thoughts on each book of the Mishna in turn. He classified and codified sections before committing them to paper. He was fortunate to have access to Rabbi Shushan's personal library and was able to discuss difficult sections both with him and his father.

"I am humbled to be in the presence of such learned scholars," he remarked with sincerity. "You make my task easier and enjoyable." He often thanked them for their contribution. The work was difficult and tiring, but he continued with enthusiasm and fortitude.

In the late afternoon and evening he concentrated on expanding his knowledge of philosophy, mathematics, and science, even though the books he had access to on these subjects were limited in scope. He knew he could benefit enormously from access to the Karaouine institute and library, but he recognised that this would only be achieved by conversion to Islam. The thought troubled him. Would a fake conversion for this reason be religiously immoral? Would it diminish him before God? Would the end justify the means? Would his father allow it? As the days and weeks passed, he became increasingly fixated on the concept. He would need to speak to his father. Without his blessing it would be impossible.

As time passed, Maimon took great satisfaction in playing a major part in the Jewish community. He assisted Rabbi Shushan at the clandestine Beth Din and was a popular and inspiring teacher. Although life in Fez was easier than it had been previously, nevertheless the Jews of Fez had suffered from Almohad rule for fifteen years, and sadly there was a state of malaise and spiritual torpor within the Jewish population. Many Jews had converted outwardly to Islam whilst inwardly clinging to their Jewish beliefs and were now beginning to question their faith, but in doing so they were racked with guilt.

Maimon decided it was now time to compose the letter he had promised to circulate to Jews in Spain and Morocco. He called the letter "Igeres Hanechamah, the Epistle of Consolation". It was a long and detailed account based on Torah precepts to explain the suffering of the Jews and the measures that they were justifiably required to implement to survive. It was written sympathetically and with an understanding of their plight.

"Dear brothers, Jews in suffering, may God have mercy on us soon. We need to know that the sufferings that God inflicts on his people are the ultimate good."

After the opening, the letter then explained the need for maintaining faith and keeping all the commandments that had been laid down: "The evils that we suffer today are merely passing circumstance. From troubles will spring salvation, and from groaning will come tranquillity."

He also addressed the worries that Jews had in falsely converting to Islam in public: "God would condone this way of life, and you are still considered to be Jews. Even if you cannot pray during a set time in the synagogue, it does not matter. A silent prayer from the heart will always be welcomed by a merciful God."

He emphasised the Torah commandment to preserve life, paramount in Jewish law, which justified forced conversion to Islam.

Many copies of the letter were written by scribes and messengers were appointed to distribute them surreptitiously to Jews in Morocco and Spain, with great effect. The letter provided much-wanted reassurance that their efforts to observe the Torah, despite all the dangers they faced, were meaningful and would bring them reward. For many it strengthened their belief that God still loved them. Maimon was delighted with the positive feedback he received from all sections of the community, and Moses was deeply moved and proud of his father's efforts. The letter also presented an appropriate opportunity for him to approach his father about access to the Karaouine library.

"Father, I have a yearning to study medicine and become a physician. I do not wish only to study religious texts. I want to make a practical contribution." This ambition had been secretly nurtured for many years, ever since he had watched doctors in Cordoba and later read about the basic precepts of diseases and their treatment.

"I am greatly troubled. I have studied many Talmudic sources, and like you, revered father, I do not believe it to be a sin to disguise oneself at a time of religious persecution to save one's life. For me the disguise would not be to preserve my life but to be able to study medicine at the Karaouine institute. For this I would need to convert to Islam." He hesitated at this point and looked directly into his father's eyes to gauge any response.

"The type of apostasy would not require transgression of God's laws. Only lip service is required, only a verbal formula. I believe I can justify the action since it would provide me with the ability in the future to help people. In this way, it would be done for the greater good."

His father remained quiet for what seemed like an age to Moses. Moses watched his father stroke his beard. His brow furrowed, he walked solemnly towards the window. He gazed outside with his hands firmly held behind his back. He then turned to face Moses.

"Moshe, you present me with a difficult quandary. I need to give the matter detailed consideration and will consult Torah and Talmudic Halacha to identify any prohibitions against apostasy which does not involve a matter of life or death. I must also obtain the view of Rabbi Shushan. Please be patient. I will give you my decision shortly."

"I appreciate your consideration and will, of course, abide by your eventual decision since it will be based on Halacha and adherence to Jewish ethical behaviour." Moses was sincere in his response. His love and respect for his father knew no bounds. He was sorry that he had presented his father with such a predicament, especially since he himself was aware of the ethical and moral dilemma with all its implications. But at least he knew that whatever decision his father took would be the correct one, based on consideration of all the major sources.

It was a week later that Maimon spoke about the matter to Moses and gave him his considered response.

"Moshe, we are living in difficult times. We are asked to recite an empty formula which the Muslims know we utter insincerely. Muslims worship the same God as we do. They pray to a single all-embracing being. They call Muhammad a prophet, not a deity. The Almighty has presented you with unique gifts of intellect. You must be allowed to fulfil the potential that you have been given. You possess the ability to become a great physician as well as a great Jewish thinker. I have given the matter deep consideration and reviewed all the key sources." Moses waited with nervous anticipation for his father's decision. Maimon looked directly at Moshe and placed his hands on his son's shoulders.

"You have my blessing to pursue your medical ambitions in any way you wish."

With that Moses kissed his father's hand. The initial sense of elation that Moses felt was in later days mixed with a feeling of guilt. Was he really justified? Was he being ethically dishonest despite having received his father's blessing?

The process of conversion to Islam was not difficult. He approached an imam who led the services in a mosque close to where they lived. He was a kindly elderly man dressed entirely in white. Even his long beard was totally white.

"You must be sure about your decision to convert to the holy Islam," he explained. "You must also know that false conversion and return to your previous faith, thereby renouncing Islam, is totally unacceptable. The penalty for falsely converting and then reverting back to Judaism, when proof is obtained or the event witnessed, is death by stoning or decapitation. There are no mitigating factors and no discretion. The sentence is irrevocable. Do you understand?"

"I do," replied a subdued Moses.

"In that case, please repeat after me the Testimony of Faith, the Shahada: 'There is one true God, Allah, and Muhammad is the messenger of God.'"

"There is one true God, Allah, and Muhammad is the messenger of God." Moses had done it. He had converted to Islam. Unbeknownst to the imam, he'd also recited the Shema prayer in his mind at the same time.

Following the "conversion", Moses was able to enter the Karaouine institute and acquire full access to the vast library. He was also accepted into the school of medicine after a detailed appraisal of his ability by the senior teachers. He provided his Arab name on entrance: Abu Amran Musa ibn Maimon.

He now spent all his time concentrating on his commentary and on his medical studies. He did so without the worry of financial matters. David had been employed by an established and respected Muslim gold and gem merchant in the central medina district who immediately recognised his expertise. And because he trusted David absolutely, he gave him increasing responsibility.

"I recognise you as a Jew," the merchant had told David. "Do not deny it. I have worked with Jews and have many Jewish customers. I know Jews to be honest and trustworthy. I dislike the Almohads intensely; they are bullies and rogues. I would trust a Jew before any Almohad. But do not repeat what I have said. I am going to appoint you as my manager."

David's salary supported all the family's needs. Moses was eternally grateful. He and his brother had enormous mutual love and respect which persisted throughout their lives.

With this rapid progression in his chosen career, David decided it was an appropriate time to consider marriage. This was made known to the clandestine Jewish community, and within a few weeks he was introduced to a young woman, the niece of a local leather merchant who was her guardian. Her name was Rachel. Her parents had been killed some years previously at the hands of a vicious Almohad soldier who had stormed into her house and put both her parents to the sword in front of a screaming Rachel. It was the soldier's intention to rape Rachel, but she was saved only by good fortune. As she was grabbed, her brother, who had not been in the house at the time, appeared and pinned the soldier to the floor before plunging a knife into his eye and through to his brain. The soldier died soon after in agony. Rachel was only twelve at the time but still suffered from stress and recurrent nightmares.

A formal meeting in the presence of a chaperone was arranged. Conversation between David and Rachel flowed easily. David explained his business ambitions and Rachel showed great interest and insight.

"You should know that my father and dear brother are erudite Jewish schloars and as a family we rigidly adhere to all the Jewish customs and beliefs," David explained.

"I too have a love of our faith and with encouragement could become even more devoted. Do not fear. As a Jewish wife I would obey and respect all that my husband requires of me," she blushed with embarrassment. David smiled knowingly.

With her guardian's and his father's blessing, David and Rachel were married in Rabbi Shushan's house. It was a joyful occasion but of necessity rather low-key so as not to attract the attention of any Almohad sympathisers. Rachel was radiant at the wedding. In keeping with Moroccan tradition, she had her face painted red and white, and her hands and feet were stained yellow with henna. She was only seventeen, but after years as an orphan and dealing with adversity, she seemed older and had acquired maturity beyond her age. Her joy at the celebration was tainted by the memory of her parents. She was certain that they would have approved of the marriage. She reflected on how they would have loved to be at the wedding. The memory of their murder still haunted her and would do so for many years to come.

David's managerial experience and expertise provided him with the confidence to launch his own import and export business shortly after the wedding. This soon attracted influential clients, especially in India, where jewellery was particularly fashionable. His commercial success continued, and he was able to continue supporting Moses's medical studies at the Karaouine.

Moses was officially and formally ordained as a rabbi following an induction by Rabbi Shushan and adopted the name Moses Maimonides (the Greek *ides*, meaning "son of"—in this case, "son of Maimon"). He worked intensively on the commentary, which was becoming far more structured. By detailed analysis of specific sections of the Mishna, he was able to compose and itemise the thirteen principles of faith which make up the fundamental pillars of traditional belief. He took for granted that God is an incorporeal being, that God's essence is unknowable, and that God does not possess physical attributes. He was able to clarify the meaning of the Mishnaic and Talmudic passages and make them rational and understandable for the average Jew.

Moses approached his medical studies with a similar degree of resolute determination. Each day he attended classes and seminars, listening intently to his teachers, many of whom were famous Arab physicians. The Karaouine school was the foremost medical institution in the world. Arabic medicine was many years ahead of anything that was available in the Christian world, where the priest was often the only source of medical advice and comfort. Christianity rigidly held to the view that illness was a God-given punishment for sin and that failure to heal was evidence that a person had sinned. Priests were committed to a literal translation of Exodus 15:26: "I am the Lord that healeth thee." This approach was an anathema to Moses.

Moses studied Hippocrates and Galen as well as the philosophical concepts of Aristotle. Contemporary medical teaching involved the writings of the great Arabic physicians al-Razi, al-Farabi, Avicenna, and Avenzoar. He was already familiar with much of their writings, having read their works whilst a young student in Cordoba, but now he was able to study them in depth. His spiritual and philosophical knowledge complemented his medical studies as he began to appreciate and conceptualise the importance of an ethical approach to the healing of disease and the importance of a healthy soul as well as a healthy body. He found that his medical studies assisted his work on the commentary. He formulated these concepts in *Eight Chapters—Shemonah Perakim*, which became an introduction to *Pirke Avos*, translating as "The ethics of the fathers". The eight chapters included discussions and debates on ethics and how to lead a good life, on how to keep one's soul healthy, on the importance of good and bad character traits, and on serving God by showing moderation in all activities (the "golden mean").

The unchallenged hypothesis for the cause of disease, laid down by Galen and Hippocrates in 600 CE, was that disease developed when there was disequilibrium in the amount and quality of the four humours (or biles) which were found in the body. These were red bile (blood), white bile (phlegm), black bile (melancholy), and yellow bile. The humours were characterised as cold or warm and moist or dry. Illnesses developed when one humour was in excess; for example, excess black bile resulted in cancer, confusion, and fever, whereas an excess of red bile was responsible for chest and heart disease. Avoidance and treatment of excessive humours could be achieved by regular exercise, proper diet, rest, and good bowel movements. Venesection (bloodletting) was used when red or black bile was thought to be in excess.

Moses learnt important practical skills such as being able to examine a patient, to perform a venesection, to feel the pulse, to drain an abscess, and to examine urine by comparing its colour to a standard colour chart and by tasting it to assess sweetness.

He progressed well and was frequently complimented by his

teachers not only for his diligence but also for his remarkable memory and rapid acquisition of knowledge. Throughout his time in the Karaouine he managed to keep his Judaism secret. When it was time to enter the mosque for prayers, he followed the rituals but whispered to himself the Shema prayer (Hear, O Israel, the Lord our God, the Lord is one).

Moses deliberately tried to avoid social contact with his fellow students lest his false conversion be recognised. However, friendships did develop.

"I cannot help but notice how diligently you are studying each time I come to the library." Moses looked up from his book to see a young student whom he recognised from his class.

"My name is Abul Arab ibn Moisha. May I share the table with you?"

"Certainly," Moses replied. He introduced himself.

"I see you are reading a philosophical text," Abul commented. "I too am interested in the Aristotelian approach to philosophy."

"My interest in philosophy is because I find it helps my understanding of scientific and ethical dilemmas in medicine," Moses replied.

Their friendship established, they would discuss difficult concepts for many hours, often well into the evening. Moses found this liaison hugely helpful and gratifying. They also discussed religious matters, and Moses realised how much Islam had in common with the Jewish attitude towards life. Moses, of course, concealed the fact that he practised Judaism despite his conversion, although he suspected that Abul was aware of the subterfuge but deliberately avoided any comment that might compromise his position.

Surprisingly, Moses also encountered an acquaintance from the past. He was in the entrance to the Karaouine when a handsome, smartly dressed student approached.

"Excuse me, sir, but with respect, are you not Moses ben

Maimon, my friend from Almeria?" The young man appeared familiar. Soon Moses recollected.

"Of course, Abu-Walid. How wonderful to see you again. It is many years since we last met. It was indeed in Almeria. Are you also a student here?"

"I am studying medicine," said Abu-Walid.

"As am I," responded Moses. "It was fortuitous that we met in Almeria and equally fortuitous that we meet again in Fez."

They were delighted to re-form their acquaintance after many years, recalling the meeting in an olive grove in Almeria where they had discussed philosophical concepts and formed a friendship based on their intellectual prowess. They began similar discussions on mutual interests in philosophy and medicine, and Abul often joined in. Abu-Walid (soon to be known throughout the Arab world as Averroes) had been a student at Karaouine for three years and lived with his uncle in the centre of Fez. He acknowledged Moses's conversion to Islam and did not question his motives.

"You must be careful, Moses. I know of your conversion. There are people who would try to expose you." He seemed genuinely concerned. Moses nodded in agreement but said nothing further. Throughout their time in Fez, they took every opportunity to discuss matters of mutual interest.

Jews continued to enjoy a settled existence in Fez despite the Almohad presence, which, although obvious, was tolerant and in general noninterventionist in the way they policed the population. At home Moses wrote his *Commentary* with ever-increasing fortitude. He took every available opportunity to discuss issues with his father and especially with Rabbi Shushan. The Maimon family, after many years of uncertainty, seemed at last to be enjoying a period of serenity. It was much appreciated.

Unexpectedly and to the surprise of the community, a controversy developed which would have wide ramifications.

It had been a year since Moses's father had written the letter of consolation regarding forced conversion, and few concerns remained other than those amongst certain ultraorthodox sections of the Jewish community. One of these individuals wrote to a famous rabbi who lived outside Fez, where the Islamic decrees were not in force, suggesting that Maimon was wrong and that it was preferable to die rather than convert to Islam, even if secretly following Judaism. The distinguished rabbi provided the following considered opinion:

"A person must deny that Muhammad is a prophet and must allow himself to be killed. Whoever declares that Muhammad was a prophet is like a denier of God of Israel. Whether or not he keeps all the mitzvahs of the Torah, he is considered a non-Jew. Even if he was forced to make that statement, he is wicked and is to be counted among those who are unfit to give testimony."

The Jews were once again thrown into doubt and confusion. Many even considered going to the Muslim authorities to admit to remaining a Jew despite their conversion, thereby forfeiting their lives and even the lives of their children.

Moses was appalled.

"Father, they are ignoring your letter. With your permission I will respond on your behalf. We cannot allow such an intolerant and uninformed response to go unchallenged." He was outraged by the response.

"Moshe, I am too upset to provide a considered reply. I am grateful for your offer. Your deep knowledge of the sources makes you an ideal person to counter this ridiculous assertion."

The situation and controversy escalated. Serious doubts were raised, and anguish inevitably followed. Maimon became the object of abuse and derision. "How dare he make such heretical assertions?" was often heard.

Judah, a strict Orthodox Jew, decided to accost and challenge Maimon to redact his letter.

"You have misled us in the sight of God. You have encouraged us to blaspheme. We should never have listened to you. I will now confess to the authorities in the hope that the Almighty will forgive me." He was tearful.

"Please, Judah, wait. My son is composing a response which will counter the claim. Do nothing until you have read it."

"How can your son's view be compared to that of a senior rabbi of distinction?"

"I beg you to be patient. Life is too precious, and we live in difficult times. My son's reply will be sent shortly."

Moses realised the urgency. He wasted no time in composing his Epistle on Apostasy (also known as the Epistle on Conversion, Igeres Hashmad).

His response was detailed. He used rigorous Halachic reasoning from well-referenced Torah and Talmudic sources to support his argument. He gave numerous examples to show that the famous rabbi who had sent his opinion had provided a misinterpretation of Judaism. Using examples from the Talmud, Moses showed that it was not a sin to disguise oneself in times of religious persecution to save one's life. He illustrated this with examples from Roman times of great rabbinical leaders who had taken this approach to save their own lives and the lives of fellow Jews. No Jew would claim that these great rabbis had ceased to be Jews. He also referred to Achav, who denied God and worshipped idols. And yet when he fasted for two and a half hours, the heavenly decree against him was nullified. He reminded them that the Talmud declared only three capital offences that would justify martyrdom: idolatry, incest, and murder. He stated that there is not a single mention in the entire Torah of God punishing a person who acts under duress.

"A person under duress is not considered liable by God." Moses used his medical knowledge. He claimed that the writer of the ludicrous letter could not be of sound mind or body, stating that he must be ill and that there was no need to listen to him.

He ended by asserting, "This is my opinion. And God knows the truth for sure."

The letter was distributed not only in Fez but also throughout Morocco. It was read widely and understood. Moses's style of writing and communication revealed an extensive breadth of knowledge and yet was simple and easy to understand.

The epistle was accepted. It saved the Jewish community of Morocco from further despair and disintegration. It was clear: during persecution instead of choosing to martyr, opt for a double life to survive until better conditions prevailed.

The letter established Moses as a man of intellect and eminence even though he was relatively young and inexperienced. Criticism of a senior rabbi was unheard of, especially when it was suggested that he may be insane or ill. Moses wrote the letter out of love for a suffering people rather than as a show of arrogance.

11

The newly appointed Almohad commander decided he needed to assert his authority over the so-called Jewish converts who seemed to be leading a far too comfortable existence.

"All these Jews who claim to have converted, are we sure it is not a charade?" he barked at his subaltern. "We must be stricter and more vigilant. They are making fools of us. I will not stand for it. I will offer a reward to anyone who provides proof of a false conversion. Put the word out."

"Yes, sir. Immediately." The subaltern could only agree but was concerned. Life had been peaceful in recent years. The Jews were law-abiding citizens. They were hard-working and caused no trouble, making the soldiers' lives easy. *If we start looking for false converts, and especially if rewards are offered, our workload will escalate and things could get unpleasant. Why look for trouble?* But he had his orders.

It was never established with certainty who'd reported Rabbi Shushan to the authorities. One theory was that a disgruntled Arab labourer who worked as a caretaker at a school predominantly for Jewish children and in which Rabbi Shushan surreptitiously

117

taught Torah to boys up to bar mitzvah age was the culprit. However, the caretaker vehemently denied responsibility.

The commander was delighted to receive the allegation.

"See, I told you so," he addressed his subaltern. "We have proof, a witness who saw this rogue. What is his name?" He extracted a crumpled piece of paper from his tunic. "Shushan. Do you know him? He is a fraudulent convert who still practises Judaism. The time has arrived to set an example," he exclaimed joyfully. "Bring the charlatan to me."

His subaltern was defensive. "Sir, Yehudah ibn Shushan is an elderly man who commands great respect."

"Are you questioning my orders? You will bring him to me immediately. We will soon find out how much of a Muslim he really is."

The subaltern reluctantly assembled his men and explained their mission. They were to arrest an alleged elderly false convert. They had been instructed to wear full armour and brandish both swords and lances. They were to terrorise and frighten any onlookers and use the whole episode as an example of what happens if false converts are found. He felt embarrassed. All this heavy armour to arrest an old man! How ridiculous. But what could he do? Orders were orders.

The subaltern led his company as they charged into the courtyard of Rabbi Shushan's home. They burst through the door to find the elderly rabbi sitting with a group of young boys. They were reading from the Talmud.

"You are under arrest!" shouted the subaltern. "You profess to have converted to Islam, and yet you still study the Jewish filth." Rabbi Shushan was hauled out of the house by two of the soldiers and led away to the fort, where he was imprisoned.

The following day he was taken to the commander.

"My subaltern informs me that the allegation against you is true. You remain a Jew, and you were caught reading Jewish books. You falsely converted to stay in Fez. What do you have to say?"

Rabbi Shushan looked unconcerned. He knew his fate was sealed. He did not care. All his life had been devoted to his love of Judaism. He had served God to the best of his ability, and he was prepared to die and was ready to meet with his Maker.

"I was born a Jew and I will die a Jew," responded Rabbi Shushan with a look of disdain and defiance. "Your threats will have no influence on an old man."

"I give you a final chance since I am a generous man," barked the commander. "You will accept Islam and abandon your Judaism, or you will die a painful death."

"Your threats mean nothing and have no influence on me. Jews have died painfully for their religion for generations. We are accustomed to it."

With that he was led away and thrown into a dark, damp cell without food for three days, during which time he prayed incessantly. He recited the liturgy by heart. He felt no hunger. He enjoyed the experience as he felt closer to God. He was pleased to await his fate with equanimity.

As he was dragged through the streets to the central marketplace, he recited psalms quietly to himself. He was then forced to kneel. A hooded soldier stood behind him wielding a large-bladed sword. With a double-handed single swish, Rabbi Shushan's head was decapitated. Blood poured onto the surrounding sawdust as the head fell into a wicker basket. Rabbi Shushan was reported to be muttering prayers as he knelt, and his face, as it lay in the basket, appeared relaxed and at ease.

The effect on the Jewish community was profound. There was general gloom as well as anxiety. Even greater care was now required by the thousands of pseudo-converts to avoid any suggestion of practising Judaism in secret.

Moses and his family attended the funeral. Rabbi Maimon officiated and openly wept as he gave the eulogy to his long-time friend and colleague. Moses was equally affected and cried as he watched the coffin being gently lowered into the ground. On leaving the cemetery, his mind turned towards the future. Did he really wish to remain in Fez for the rest of his life? When they returned home from the cemetery, Moses broached the subject with his father.

"Dear father, do you think it would be sensible to plan in case we need to leave Fez?" He could see how upset his father was following the funeral, and at first there was no response. Moses regretted raising the topic.

"You are correct, dear Moshe. I have also feared we may need to leave. But where should we go? Elsewhere in Morocco would not be sensible since the same situation would arise as here in Fez. Similarly, a return to Spain would not be appropriate." He was morose and deep in thought.

"We will discuss again at a later date when the memory of dear Yehudah is less vivid." With that he left the room, his head bowed. Moses thought he heard his father weeping. This confirmed to Moses that he could no longer contemplate a long-term future in Fez. He must finish his medical studies and then, once more, approach his father with his concerns.

Moses was able to retrieve many of Rabbi Shushan's books before the remainder were placed in a large pile by the Almohad soldiers and set on fire in the street for all to see.

The crackdown on the Jews continued with even greater ferocity. Regular invasion of properties occurred with no warning as whistle-blowers chasing rewards increased in number. Moses could only risk working on his *Commentary* in the early morning hours, fearing that the manuscript might be discovered. Any Jewish activity during the day was too dangerous. This forced him to pursue his medical studies with even greater determination.

Interestingly, as his medical knowledge increased, he began to question many of the established concepts of disease, which brought him into conflict with his teachers. But he was heartened by the approval he received from his friend Abu-Walid, who held similar views.

Moses's acquisition of medical knowledge filled him with a desire to explore all aspects of the human condition. He was particularly fortunate to be taught by Ibn Zuhr, one of the most prominent physicians of the time. Moses was convinced that disease should be treated only on a scientific basis and not by guesswork, superstition, or rule of thumb. This view remained with him throughout his years as a clinician. It was a concept proposed and strongly advocated by Ibn Zuhr, who'd acquired it from his father, the great physician Abu Marwan. Also, he considered that a diagnosis should be essential before surgery is contemplated. When a teacher disagreed with this view during a seminar, he supported his opinion with a quote from the Arab physician Albucasis: "One should never undertake surgery until there is proof that the usual treatments are not effective. If the physician has not diagnosed the nature of the illness and has been unable to determine its cause, it is a crime to attempt an operation, which may endanger the life of his fellowman."

He followed this with, "I believe this to be a most important principle, respected teacher, which I intend to follow in my own practise of medicine."

Moses's attitude towards the practise of medicine was also influenced by his deep religious background, which made the preservation of health and life a divine commandment. He found much in common between religion and medicine and pursued this theme rigorously. For example, within his *Commentary* he wrote: "The art of medicine although it treats only the body plays a very large role in acquiring both the ethical virtues and knowledge of God, and hence in attaining a contented state of being happy and healthy. Learning and studying medicine is an important form of divine worship. For through medicine we calibrate our bodily actions so that they become genuinely human actions, actions that render the body a tool for the acquisition of the virtues and scientific truths."

He also argued against the view of some religious scholars, both Jewish and Christian, who deprecated reliance on the medical art because they claimed it implied a lack of trust in God. He discussed this concept in his *Commentary*, convinced that it was an unnecessary, dangerous, and illogical concern.

"If this nonsensical and foolish reasoning were carried to its logical conclusion, anyone who feels hungry and eats is equally blameworthy for failing to trust God to assuage his hunger without food. The truth is," he argued, "that we eat when we are hungry and thank God for providing us with the means to do so. A healthy body is accordingly desirable not only for itself but also as a platform upon which the soul can strive towards its proper perfection. A soul is desirable because it will serve the intellect. Perfection of the intellect is what God and nature intend as the goal of human life. Man must direct his heart and every one of his actions solely towards knowing God."

This view was not accepted by all, but Moses was convinced he was correct. Both his father and David could see sense in the argument and were happy to lend encouragement.

Rachel, blissfully happy in marriage, was worried and could not avoid feelings of guilt. She had been married for more than two years and still had not been blessed with a pregnancy. She was worried that the trauma she'd suffered as a child was responsible for her barren state. *Watching my parents being brutally murdered must have effected my body,* she argued. David tried his best to reassure her. She was only nineteen, still very young, but the desire to have a child was overwhelming. The frustration she felt often spilt over into anger. She was argumentative at times and then depressed and withdrawn. David was sympathetic but realised that her concern over fertility was adversely affecting their marriage.

"If you wish to leave me because of my barrenness, I will understand. You deserve to have children, and you would be more fulfilled with a different woman."

She had considered this for many months and was sincere in her offer, although tearful.

"My dear Rachel, I love and respect you dearly. You must not be so stressed. If it is God's will, we will have children. I would never leave you or even consider having another woman." He gently caressed her and wiped away the tears. He reminded her of the biblical Rachel, one of the matriarchs.

"When Jacob married Rachel, she too was unable to conceive for many years, but eventually she was blessed with a son, Joseph, who would become Jacob's favourite son. Joseph was special and shows that pregnancy is an act of God. Do not fret. I would not accept a Bilbah, Rachel's maidservant, to be a substitute mother." He smiled and hoped the biblical reference would amuse and relax her.

They embraced. Rachel was comforted.

The message from Nadim was received by Rabbi Maimon some three weeks after it was sent. Nadim, who was caring for Miriam in Almeria, explained in detail the problems he was facing. His first wife had recently died following a fever, and his second wife was having difficulty in coping with his five children. To make matters worse, he recently sustained an injury to his back and was unable to maintain his business to the standards he wished. He hinted that financially he had serious problems. Maimon read the letter with increasing foreboding. Poor Nadim, he was a good man and deserved better fortune. How would this affect Miriam? He continued to read: "Miriam is now twelve years old, and reluctantly I can no longer continue as her guardian. I hope you understand my dilemma."

Maimon had harboured feelings of guilt and regret ever since taking the decision to leave Miriam with Nadim and his family, albeit for her own safety. She'd been too young at the time to cope with the discomfort and dangers involved in travelling from place to place in Spain. The message from Nadim was timely. Maimon had been considering for many months whether it was now time to reunite Miriam with her family since she was of a more suitable age. He would be forever grateful to Nadim for his generosity and goodwill.

"My dear Nadim," he wrote in reply. "As a family we were distressed to hear of your unfortunate circumstances. We are so grateful to you for caring for our dear Miriam and agree that the time has come for her to return. May God bless you and your family."

David collected Miriam from Almeria and brought her to his father's house in triumph. A party was held in her honour when she arrived.

Miriam seemed embarrassed at first but soon relaxed. She was embraced by her father and Moses, and psalms were recited in thanksgiving. She was petite and pretty. Rabbi Maimon could clearly recognise the similarity in her appearance to that of Shoshanah. Her eyes and lips were so reminiscent. She wore a floor-length tunic held in place with a cord and with long sleeves. Her hair was long and wavy, so much like Shoshanah's.

David suggested that she live with Rachel and him. She would be good company for Rachel and could possibly help to alleviate her frustration at not having a child. He considered, rather selfishly, that the unfortunate circumstances faced by Nadim could be a blessing for their marriage, even though in recent weeks Rachel appeared less agitated now that she had openly expressed her concerns to David and had learnt he had no intention of abandoning her.

Miriam embraced the Jewish lifestyle effortlessly even though she had spent so long a time in a Muslim environment. Rachel took on much of the responsibility for her well-being and was instrumental in teaching her the Jewish way of life, especially regarding the role of women, much of which Miriam vaguely remembered from Cordoba. Rachel's whole persona changed for the better with the return of Miriam. She became more relaxed and at ease. David was delighted, and their marriage, which had become tense, began to return to normal.

Miriam understood the difficulty her family had in hiding their Jewish identity, but she herself had no real problem. She had been brought up in a Muslim household and had never really been taxed by the subterfuge. The accommodation provided in David's home was luxurious compared to what she was accustomed to in Almeria, where she'd shared a tiny room with three other children. Rachel was overly friendly and hospitable and enjoyed Miriam's company.

"We must consider our future." Moses decided it was time to raise this matter again with his father and David.

"The matter has occupied my mind since you raised the issue after Rabbi Shushan's funeral," Maimon replied thoughtfully. "I now believe we should leave Fez. It is becoming more dangerous for Jews, and I fear we could be exposed at any time."

"I agree, Father, but where is safe?" David asked. "Elsewhere in Morocco would not be sensible. Similarly, a return to Spain is impossible."

"I agree. But we must get away from Almohad rule." Moses had been considering the options for some time and felt this was the appropriate time to propose his idea.

"Even though Palestine has been under Christian rule since the Crusade in 1099, it is still Eretz Israel, the land where God had made a covenant with the Jewish people. I believe that is where we should go."

Initially there was silence as the proposal was considered. Moses waited anxiously for a response.

Maimon was excited by the thought of travel to the Holy Land. He would walk on its sacred soil, would pray at the Wailing

Wall in Jerusalem, and would be in the land of his forefathers. David was also enthusiastic and gave the idea his full support but wondered how Rachel and indeed Miriam would manage with the arduous journey to a new country.

"We must make plans for a rapid escape should it become necessary," said Rabbi Maimon as soon as the idea was accepted. David would collect and hide his most precious gems and store them so that if they were required to leave precipitously, they would have adequate finance. Moses and Rabbi Maimon would collect key books and conceal them in a safe place.

Moses was pleased that his suggestion had been accepted so enthusiastically, but he had much to do before a move could be undertaken. His medical education was almost complete after three years of intensive study. He had memorised much of the teaching, and he was beginning to feel confident in his ability to practise as a physician. But his heightened intellect often threw him into conflict with both his teachers and fellow students.

He continued to clash with his teachers when he voiced a nonorthodox concept. He remained convinced of the importance of the scientific method, of the need for independent observation, and of the requirement to be rational in delivering treatment. His teachers were not impressed. During one session, unsubstantiated therapeutic superstitions relating to a patient with a skin infestation were claimed to be of benefit. Moses disagreed.

"Men should believe nothing which is not attested by rational proof as in mathematical science, by evidence of the senses, or by the authority of prophets and saints," he stated forcefully, contradicting one of his teachers.

His teacher was annoyed at being challenged in this way but could not fail to be impressed by Moses's argument and conviction.

"Your view has been noted, Abu Amran, but not fully accepted. There is much in medicine that is unknown, and unusual treatments must be tried, even without proof of efficacy, lest a patient be prevented from receiving benefit."

Moses disagreed and was particularly argumentative on that day.

"Revered teacher, you are correct provided the treatment does not result in weakening the body."

"You have forthright views, Abu Amran, which is commendable. But please remember that not all treatments have been proven to be effective but should still be used in certain circumstances."

Moses was aware of this and was able to agree with his teacher.

"I would prescribe remedies known to be futile if withholding them would cause distress resulting in mental deterioration. I believe it is crucial for a patient's psyche to be at ease when they are ill. This can help them to overcome their disease and recover."

"I am so pleased that we can agree on at least one important concept of medicine," replied his teacher rather sardonically.

Yet Moses's forthright views and his undoubted intellect annoyed some of his fellow students, especially Muhammad ibn Malik, who became obsessionally jealous and regarded Moses as serious competition in the student hierarchy. He disliked Moses intensely and harboured suspicions that he was a pseudo-convert who secretly followed Judaism, to the extent that he began to observe Moses's activities closely. He secretly followed him and carefully observed him during prayers in the mosque. However, he was unable to be certain. Moses, for his part, had suspicions about ibn Malik and realised he would have to be very careful. The family would shortly be leaving Fez, and to be found out now, with the end of his studies in sight, would be devastating.

And then unexpectedly ibn Malik was presented with the evidence that he had sought so assiduously and which he knew if presented to the authorities would result in serious consequences, even execution, for Moses.

12

It was Ibn Zuhr, the great physician and Moses's teacher, who passed on the news to Moses in person.

"Abu Amran, it is my pleasure and privilege to inform you that your progress and the assessments by your teachers have been of the highest standard. We confer upon you the right to undertake the duties of a physician. On a personal level, I have no doubt you will be highly successful and a credit to the profession."

Moses beamed with delight. He had achieved his ambition. He was also pleased that his close friends Abul and Abu-Walid were similarly successful. He was required to recite the Hippocratic oath, which committed him to lifelong devotion to the well-being of his patients and required him always to practise medicine in an ethical fashion for the good of humankind. He was proud to declare this in front of his teachers and fellow students. He was now a doctor.

The Maimon family were ecstatic. With close friends they spent an evening of dancing, with good food and wine. Moses's father beamed with obvious pride throughout the evening. Moses thought about his mother, Sarah, whom he never knew, and his stepmother, Shoshanah. They would have been so proud of him.

"May their souls continue to rest in peace with the angels in heaven," he whispered to himself.

A rather forgetful elderly Jew had inadvertently left a copy of Moses's letter the "Igeres Hashmad" in the pocket of an old tunic which he subsequently gave away to a beggar as a charitable act. The beggar decided that the tunic might be worth a few dinars and sold it to a second-hand clothes merchant who had a stall in the central market. The tunic was then sold at a significant profit to a student only able to afford second-hand clothes. When the student returned to his meagre accommodation and changed into the tunic, he discovered the letter, the content of which made little sense to him. Nevertheless, he was concerned that it might be encouragement by a Jew to fellow Jews to pseudo-convert to Islam. This was a serious offence, and he was aware of the potential danger to himself if it were discovered that he had deliberately hidden the information from the authorities. He would be regarded as equally guilty as the writer of the letter, and the punishment would be severe.

He showed it to his friend, who suggested that because the writing was so clear and erudite, it was probably written by a student or teacher at the Karaouine institute. He asked several of his fellow students for their opinion on the content of the letter. Eventually the letter came to the attention of a medical student, Muhammad ibn Malik. Muhammad could not believe his good fortune. The letter was signed by none other than Abu Amran Musa ibn Maimon, who'd also added his Hebrew name, Moses ben Maimon. He had been correct all along. At last he had definitive proof that Abu Amran was an apostate.

Before reporting Moses to the authorities, Muhammad showed the letter to a fellow student, Abul, for confirmation that it provided absolute proof of apostasy. Abul Arab ibn Moisha examined the letter in silence. This was definitive evidence: his good friend Abu Amran was a false convert. He was not unduly surprised; he had suspected this to be the case all along. But now he was looking at a letter which amounted to a death sentence for his close friend.

"I agree this looks very suspicious," Abul remarked, trying to look as indifferent as he could. "However, it could be a forgery designed to falsely implicate him. Before going to the authorities, if you wish I could obtain a copy of Abu Amran's handwriting to compare with this writing and provide confirmation that the letter was written by his hand. It would only take me a day or two at the most."

Muhammad considered the offer. Perhaps he should accept it. A few days would not make much difference, and at least the evidence would be unequivocal. He would be rewarded for his diligence in confirming the provenance of the letter and in reporting the pseudo-convert.

"Thank you for the suggestion, Abul, which I agree is worthwhile. Perhaps we can meet in two days' time when you have obtained the proof."

Abul was worried. What should he do? Abu Amran was his closest friend at the Karaouine, and he respected him greatly not only for his kind and considerate nature but also for his exceptional intellect. In all honesty, he had suspected that Abu Amran was a pseudo-convert but had deliberately ignored his suspicion. Abu Amran had completed his studies and was now accepted as a doctor, so he was no longer required to remain in Fez. Abul had managed by subterfuge to allow two days of warning, enough time for Abu Amran to leave Fez. However, if the authorities ever found out that Abul had assisted in the escape of an apostate, he would be severely punished.

He made his decision: despite the danger to himself, he would warn his friend. He could not allow him to be executed.

Moses was sitting in the courtyard of the institute. The sky was cloudy and drops of rain were beginning to fall on the whitewashed cobblestones. He often sat on a bench in this open space to contemplate. On this occasion the logistics of a move from Fez to Palestine was occupying his thoughts. He decided to take shelter from the rain when he saw his good friend Abul heading towards him in haste.

"Abu Amran, my friend, you have been discovered to be the writer of a letter encouraging apostasy." Abu was breathless but felt he needed to impart the information rapidly. "You must leave Fez immediately before the offence is reported. You and your family have at the most two days to escape before the authorities are informed."

Moses was stunned and thought about the implications of the discovery for a few moments.

"I will not deny the accusation. I know that you have put your own life in danger by giving me this warning. I will always remember you in my prayers. I am a Jew at heart and cannot change." He realised how much he owed his good friend for providing a warning, which could also have serious ramifications for Abul himself.

"Do not tarry, good friend. I fear for your safety."

With that they embraced. Then Moses left to inform his family and prepare for a rapid departure.

The preparations they had already made for travel saved much time. All the valuable items were collected together. David, Rachel, and Miriam joined Rabbi Maimon and Moses as they prepared themselves for departure. David carefully collected his gems, and Moses ensured that his unfinished manuscript of the *Commentary* was carefully and safely stored.

To leave during the day would be dangerous in case they were seen. They therefore decided to leave under cover of darkness and to head for the port city of Ceuta, approximately one hundred Arabic miles due north of Fez. Ceuta was the centre for commerce in northern Morocco and was home to a Jewish population. From there it was their intention to book passage on a ship to Acre in Palestine.

They had a day-and-a-half start, assuming Muhammad would wait until Abul informed him that the letter was indeed genuine and was undoubtedly written by Abu Amran. However, Moses was concerned that Muhammad would not wait. He decided that they must leave this very evening.

Moses's fears were well founded. Muhammad indeed decided not to wait. He did not trust Abul, whom he knew to be friendly with Abu Amran. He informed the authorities that evening.

The commander, dressed in traditional red fez and white blouse, carefully read the letter. "This letter clearly shows that this Abu Amran is an apostate. He has fooled the authorities. He has encouraged others to falsely convert. Look, he has signed the letter." He was convinced. Muhammad was pleased.

A company of soldiers were dispatched to Moses's house. They were too late, but only just. The family had left one hour previously at dusk. The house was ransacked, but there was no sign of the occupants. A witness explained that the family had just left, but he did not know where they were headed to. The subaltern sounded the alarm. The entire garrison were deployed to go in search of the family. Muhammad was later reprimanded for his delay in informing the Almohad authority. By the grace of God, Moses and his family had escaped just in time.

The family arrived in Cueta after seven days of arduous travel. They stayed in an inn whilst awaiting a ship to Acre in northern Palestine. Eventually one with suitable accommodation docked, and passage was booked. The ship was large, 150 feet long, but overloaded. The journey was anything but uneventful.

Below deck were numerous barrels of merchandise, including dates, cinnamon, and sugar. Initially the wind was brisk and the huge triangular sails ensured steady progress. The ship anchored at night, and the fish that the sailors caught during the day were cooked over a clay barrel.

Moses used his medical knowledge to treat the seasickness that both his family and many of the other passengers experienced despite the journey being reasonably smooth. The treatment he advised was sniffing cut lemons and stuffing both ears and nose with papyrus, which proved remarkably effective.

Moses was exhilarated by the thought of walking in the Promised Land but was conscious of yet further disruption to their lives. Another move. Would they ever be really settled? Would he ever complete his *Commentary*? These thoughts were foremost in his mind when suddenly dark clouds boiled on the horizon. Fear ran through Moses. He'd never been so far out to sea before, nor had he seen such ominous swells. The waves were massive, mounds of water that looked like mercury. He noticed the worry on the captain's face as he stood at the wheel. Thunder rumbled in the distance.

Water smashed over the deck. Gusts of wind churned up the ocean until it became a mass of huge waves. The sailors struggled to keep control. The mast swayed dangerously, and the bow creaked under the pressure. For a whole day the ship pitched from side to side and the rain poured continuously. Rabbi Maimon and his family huddled together and prayed. And then as suddenly as the storm had started, it faded away. The rain stopped and the sea became calm. The relieved passengers thanked God for their deliverance. Moses made a written vow:

"On the evening of the first day of the week, the fourth of the month of Iyar [which correspond to the month of May], I went to sea, and on the Sabbath of the tenth of Iyar, 4925 [corresponding to 1165], we had a dreadful storm; the sea was in fury and we were in danger of perishing. Then I vowed to keep these two days as complete fast days for myself and my household, and all those connected to me, and to command my children to do the same throughout all their generations. I will speak to nobody and only pray and to study as on that day I saw no one on the sea, except the Holy One, praised be his name, so will I see no one and stay with no one on that day in the years to come."

They sailed along the coastline of Algeria and Tunisia past Libya and Egypt, occasionally stopping at ports to take on fresh supplies of water and fruit. Moses felt increasing excitement the closer they came to Palestine. He was aware of the Christian nature of the country since the First Crusade, but nevertheless it had historical significance as the home of the Jewish people.

The whole journey lasted a month, but eventually they reached Acre, the major port of Eretz Israel, the land of Israel. It was the third of Sivan 4925 (1165).

PART IV

PALESTINE

MAY 1165 (SIVAN 4925)

13

The sails were lowered and rowing vessels towed the ship to the dock, where it was made fast. Moses and his family carefully disembarked from the ship along a rickety gangplank, having ensured they had collected all their precious luggage. They merged with the bustling crowd.

Moses had done his homework on the port. He knew that Acre was the chief port of the crusaders and provided them with a foothold in the region with access to trade, especially the Asiatic spice trade. It had a population of some twenty-five thousand—only Jerusalem had a larger population—and contained the largest Jewish population in Palestine, some two hundred families. It was a busy cosmopolitan city since the port served as the disembarkation point for pilgrims, predominantly Christians, and immigrants. There was no persecution of Jews. Indeed, Jews were permitted full civic freedoms and were encouraged to settle there, although relatively few did.

Only about one thousand Jewish families lived in the whole of Palestine. Since the first Crusade in 1099, Amalric, who referred to himself as King of Jerusalem, ruled Jerusalem, the Galil, and the coast from Ashkelon in the south to Acre. He recently tried to invade Egypt but was not successful. He taxed everybody harshly to pay for his exploits. Muslims and Christians had been at war for over a hundred years.

The port itself was crowded with hundreds of ships from all over the world trading in weapons, spices, silk clothes, and Eastern luxuries, especially jewellery, which Moses knew to be of especial interest to David, who intended to set up a trading partnership with a reputable merchant.

The wall surrounding the city was so massive and wide that a chariot could ride along its top with no difficulty. Moses stared in wonderment as he watched the teeming life, the peddlers, merchants, and knights all busily going about their business.

Moses and his father knew by reputation Rabbi Yaffes ben Eliyahu, a dayan, and it was their intention to seek him out for advice and possible assistance. Moses approached a tall well-dressed man wearing a *tarbush* (oblong turban) and a loose-fitting blue tunic supported by a belt. He recognised him as Jewish, although probably of Ashkenazi rather that Sephardi origin.

"Sir," he spoke in Hebrew, "would you be so kind as to direct me and my family to the home of Rabbi Yaffes?"

"It is my pleasure. Everyone knows Rabbi Yaffes. He is a great Torah and Talmud scholar and a most benevolent man," he replied, clearly pleased to assist. "It is not far. He will probably be in the synagogue. I will take you there myself."

With that he offered to carry some of their luggage, and they happily followed him in single file through narrow streets festooned with stalls. Moses realised that this was the first time in many years that he was not required to hide his Jewish identity. He felt invigorated. In Palestine the Christians did not persecute the Jews. As they walked through the streets, he was fascinated by the large number of churches and pleasant stone houses fitted with glass windows and roof gardens. He noticed larger grandiose buildings, which their guide explained were for the orders of the Knights Templar and the Knights Hospitaller.

The kind gentleman showed Moses and his family to the

nearby synagogue, where Rabbi Yaffes was leading a service. The decorations inside were ornate. There were wooden pews in rows and a large ark containing Torah scrolls at the far end. Ten men wearing tefillin and prayer shawls were engrossed in prayer. Moses took the opportunity whilst in the synagogue to thank God for delivering them safely to Palestine. When the rabbi was done, he greeted the family warmly, saying that he'd heard of Moses and his father and had read the letter on conversion. He offered to show them a house he knew had recently become vacant and was for rent. Moses was delighted as they made their way to the house. When they got there, they could barely believe their good luck. The small brick house was perfect.

Having unpacked and walked around the nearby streets to familiarise themselves with their bearings, the Maimons returned to Rabbi Yaffes's house for a welcome meal. The house itself was small, crammed with books, and rather sparsely furnished but comfortable. They were warmly welcomed by Rabbi Yaffes's wife, Devorah, who sat with Rachel and Miriam in another room, whilst the men sat on a large divan and embarked upon a deep rabbinical discourse.

The meal provided by Devorah was delicious, especially since it was the first that the Maimons had really enjoyed since their month at sea.

"It is our intention to visit Jerusalem and the burial places of our forefathers in Hebron," said Moses.

"When you decide to go, I will accompany you. You will need a guide. It has been many years since I visited Jerusalem and the Temple site. It will be a good opportunity for me," the rabbi offered. "However, whilst you are in Acre, you are welcome to enjoy all the facilities in our community and synagogue. And this house is at your disposal."

Rabbi Yaffes is such a kind and hospitable man, thought

Moses. *How comforting to relax knowing we are free, at last, to openly practise our Judaism.*

Moses settled into the new surroundings, as did the whole family. His father was employed as a part-time teacher and helped in the synagogue. Moses himself spent most of his time on the *Commentary*, which was now approaching completion. He showed parts of the draft to Rabbi Yaffes, who was critical of some interpretations but generally very impressed. Rabbi Yaffes's overall knowledge of Talmud was immense, and he was able to provide incisive and thoughtful suggestions for improvement, which Moses appreciated and was happy to include within the text.

David was able to make useful commercial contacts and to continue with his business interest in gems, which was proving highly profitable. The fact that he was happy and content pleased Moses, who still relied on his generosity.

After five months in Acre, during which they experienced the sights and sounds of living in the Promised Land and during which they enhanced their relationship with Rabbi Yaffes and his family, Moses, his father, and David decided to journey to Jerusalem and Hebron. As promised, Rabbi Yaffes was pleased to accompany them, although the journey was regarded as unsafe for Rachel and Miriam. Miriam told Moses that she was very pleased to stay in Acre. Initially she found being in a religious Jewish household strange, but Rachel and Devorah were sympathetic, and she now felt fully integrated and able to assist in the school. Moses was pleased that his sister had settled and developed many friendships. She was obviously content with her new life.

The journey to Jerusalem was predicted to take three days. Rabbi Yaffes made all the necessary arrangements. They required sturdy donkeys and adequate provisions. Rabbi Yaffes mapped out the route and described the hazards they were likely to encounter, particularly from thieves. It was not uncommon for travellers to be robbed on the road by crusader soldiers or mercenaries.

Moses was so pleased to be travelling in Israel, even though his donkey was not the most comfortable he had ridden on. But the surrounding countryside acted as a pleasant distraction. It was still hot even though autumn. There was little greenery, and shade was sparse although olive trees were plentiful. They passed small villages with primitive houses and tents and saw many children playing with family members and animals. There were frequent wells for water and traders from whom to purchase fresh fruit and vegetables. Moses relished the opportunity to take stock of his situation and reflect on his time in Acre.

He had found little opportunity for socialising and had worked incessantly on the *Commentary*, often into the early hours of the morning. He incorporated difficult philosophical ideas, which he was worried that the ordinary reader, not familiar with Mishnaic background, might have difficulty in comprehending. He would need to include appended comments to explain them. He had identified important ancient Talmudic texts in Rabbi Yaffes's library which he had not previously encountered and reflected that Palestine, especially Acre, was ideally conducive to his writing.

As the hours passed and he became bored by his surroundings, which were now very familiar, Moses focussed on two philosophical conundrums which had been troubling him: the purpose of the world's existence and the reason for the existence of the human species. He argued in the *Commentary* that everything in the lower world inhabited by humankind is directed towards a single goal, to achieve excellence in knowledge and in practice. Surely human existence is to seek an understanding of God. He wrote, "The goal of the human species is the conceiving of intelligible thoughts, and that goal is attained by persons who are students of science and philosophy.

An understanding of science and philosophy becomes essential for an understanding of the Torah."

He argued that we should aim to achieve moral perfection, which requires "balance in natural matters, taking only what contributes to the maintenance of the body and the improvement of one's qualities". In other words, avoidance of physical indulgence is necessary when aiming towards moral perfection. The concept was occupying his mind, and he was determined to obtain corroborative evidence from relevant sources as soon as he returned to Acre.

They met many travellers on their journey. It was a popular pilgrimage both for Christians and Jews. They stopped at wayside inns at regular intervals. Moses was certain that David and his father were also pleased, as indeed was he, to be in the Holy Land and on the road to Jerusalem.

They were close to Nablus. Moses was uncomfortable on the donkey and noticed his father appeared weary.

"I think we should stop for the night. I see there is a hostel over there." He pointed to a building in the distance.

His father seemed relieved.

They arrived at the inn, where they dismounted, hitched their donkeys, and entered the hostel.

"Kind sir, we wish accommodation for the night, and our donkeys require food and water," his father addressed the owner, who was helpful and provided them with reasonable accommodation at a fair price. They had two rooms. Maimon and Rabbi Yaffes shared one and Moses and David the other.

The owner prepared a meal in accordance with their strict dietary requirements. The inn was quiet, and Moses was pleased to listen to the amusing conversation between his father and Rabbi Yaffes. Both appeared relaxed as they exchanged humorous anecdotes about their respective congregations.

A noisy group of Christian soldiers stormed into the inn. They were festooned with crosses affixed to their garments, indicating their crusader status. They spoke in Arabic, presumably Christian Arabs from a Middle Eastern country working as mercenaries.

"Your finest wine, innkeeper. We are thirsty, so don't keep us waiting," bellowed the leader.

Moses noticed that one of their number was limping and that a rather foul smell emanated from him. Moses was concerned. The soldiers became increasingly abusive as they consumed large quantities of wine. Rabbi Yaffes had warned the Maimons about marauding soldiers with an appalling reputation. The leader suddenly and without provocation grabbed the innkeeper by the throat and pulled him towards him so that their faces were frighteningly close.

"What sort of grog do you call this? It tastes like camel's piss. I am not paying for this rubbish." He laughed raucously and took another swig from the jug.

"I see we have some Jews with us!" he shouted, looking directly at Moses, who tried to appear calm and unperturbed.

"We are crusaders, and we have saved this land for you Jews. I think we deserve some reward." The other soldiers nodded in agreement.

"How much do we deserve? I would think at least the cost of this filthy wine."

Moses stepped forward and confronted their leader, who seemed content to carry on drinking.

"We are pilgrims on our way to Jerusalem. We are from Spain, where we also suffered from Muslim cruelty, but we are now in the Holy Land, and we thank you for helping to return it to its rightful owners. You are noble men, and as you can see, we are unable to defend ourselves. We are able to pay for your drink if you wish, but I beg you not to harm the innkeeper."

The soldier released his grip on the innkeeper and looked at Moses with incredulity.

"I see you are a sensible man. Like me you do not seek trouble." He and his friends guffawed in unison.

"I accept your offer. Innkeeper, you heard what this sensible Jew said. Fill our jugs. Our friends here will be paying." Turning to Moses, he asked almost politely, "Tell me, what is your trade?"

Moses thought for a few moments then replied, "I am a physician. We are on our way to Jerusalem to pray and to see the holy sites."

"How fortunate. We have met a doctor." He pointed to one of his fellow soldiers. "He was wounded in the leg by a lance two weeks ago, and it is now stinking."

The soldier limped forward and revealed his calf. The odour coming from the leg was offensive. The soldier was sweating profusely. Moses examined the exposed calf. It was swollen and inflamed. He recognised the problem. There was an abscess where the lance had penetrated the skin. He remembered the treatment that he was taught in Fez for dealing with this problem.

"He has an abscess in the calf. Surgery is required," Moses said, trying to sound as authoritative and professional as possible.

"Do you hear that? You are going to get another knife in your calf." The leader laughed.

The soldier was held down by his comrades, and wine was poured into his mouth. Moses nervously incised the abscess using a heated blade provided by one of the soldiers. Pus poured from the wound. Moses then added vinegar to the raw area and bandaged the calf.

"The malign fluid is removed. The wound will require bandaging each day," he explained. "Olibanum, pulverised beans, butter vetches, and white lilies should be placed in the wound to keep it clean and help the healing." The soldier was thankful that the pain had subsided.

"We are grateful to you, kind sir," said the leader. "Innkeeper, we will pay for our own wine." Turning back to Moses, he said, "We are also on our way to Jerusalem and will accompany you to make sure your journey is safe. We don't want you being troubled by ruffians on the way." He smiled at his joke and shook Moses's hand.

The following morning, they set out on their journey to Jerusalem accompanied by the guard of soldiers, although their injured colleague was left behind for appropriate medication and bandages provided by the innkeeper.

They met many groups of crusader soldiers and mercenaries on the way but were treated respectfully thanks to their bodyguards. The soldiers accompanied them to the outskirts of Jerusalem and bade them farewell.

"We wish you well," said the lead soldier, "and thank you for your care. Be warned, Jerusalem can be dangerous for pilgrims. There are many thieves and beggars." With that they remounted their horses and departed.

14

Moses with his father, his brother, and Rabbi Yaffes approached Jerusalem on 14 October 1165, a time when many pilgrims came to Jerusalem to pray. They stood on the Mount of Olives and saw the land that had once been the site of the holy Temple. Moses ritually tore his outer garments as he looked on the area and uttered the lines from the book of Isaiah on the wasting of the Temple. The area known to Muslims as Haram al-Sharif, the noble sanctuary, was also venerated by Christians. Moses noted, as though to emphasise this, numerous churches.

The road to Jerusalem first descended into the valley of Jehoshaphat and crossed the ridge which extended between Scopas and the Mount of Olives. Moses gazed on the domes and minarets. The sun glittered on a square tower and the broad yellow walls of some buildings. Beneath he could see immense uniform rocky grey stones. He and his group walked until the rocks diminished, and suddenly they faced the walls of Jerusalem.

They entered the city through the eastern Jehoshaphat gate, which consisted of two towers with battlements, the stone foundations of King Herod's ancient enclosure. It was obvious to Moses that Rabbi Yaffes was familiar with the area. With no hesitation their guide was able to direct them towards Temple Mount.

Jews were forbidden by the Christian authorities to reside within the walls of the city, but they were permitted to enter the city for prayer. The only Jews they encountered were beggars outside the walls trying to exploit the Torah for credulous visitors. Moses reminded his father and brother of the words of Judah Halevi: "For their sins, Jews have been punished by the transformation of the city of David and Solomon into the lair of owls and jackals."

Street life was centred on the Roman cardo, leading from St Stephen's Gate, passing the Holy Sepulchre and Patriarch's Quarter, to enter the three parallel covered market streets joined by crisscrossing alleyways. Moses was charmed by the smell of the many and varied spices with cooked food on open stoves. There was a street where only herbs and spices were sold, a separate street for the sale of fish only, and another where cheese, chickens, and eggs were available. Close to the street of herbs was a *malquisinat* (bad cooking) street, where food was cooked for pilgrims. Near the central market was a row of shops housing Syrian gold workers which were of interest to David. Taverns full of boisterous knights could be seen everywhere. Harlots displayed their wares throughout the city, having been shipped in from Europe to service and satisfy the soldiers.

The Maimons followed Rabbi Yaffes and arrived at the western wall, the Wailing Wall, the nearest site to the holy of holies in the destroyed Temple. Moses was overcome with emotion. He prayed incessantly for hour after hour until nightfall, at which time they were required to leave the city. He experienced a deep spiritual force as he touched the wall wearing his prayer shawl and tefillin. He recalled in his prayers the history of the first Temple with its destruction and then the building of the second Temple, the history of the Romans and the Greeks, the story of the Hasmoneans and the many battles and loss of life around this very site.

They slept overnight under the stars at Rabbi Yaffes's suggestion since accommodation outside the walls was difficult, if not impossible, to find. Moses was wary of thieves and beggars and offered to stay awake to keep guard, but this was refused. Instead they organised a two-hour rota to keep guard.

Moses was disturbed to see the extreme poverty of the Jews, who numbered no more than two hundred in total. The only way Jews could survive in Jerusalem was by begging and charity.

Each day they walked around the city and the Tower of David, surrounded by ruins wrought by the Crusade, but they always returned to pray by the wall. Moses was inspired by his proximity to the site of the Temple but was disappointed by the lack of a Jewish identity within the walls of Jerusalem.

"Rabbi Yaffes, how can there be so little Jewish learning or culture here, in our Holy Land?" he asked in bewilderment.

"I ask myself the same question each time I come here," commented Rabbi Yaffes in sympathy. "But there is no answer. As Jews we continue to suffer."

After three days of wandering through the narrow streets and visiting other religious sites, they decided it was time to leave Jerusalem and make their way to Hebron to visit the Cave of Machpelah, where the patriarchs Abraham, Isaac, and Jacob and the matriarchs Sarah, Rebecca, and Leah are buried. Rabbi Yaffes proved to be an expert guide as they made their way southward towards Hebron.

Each day Moses wrote a detailed account of their visit in a diary, which he had brought specifically for the purpose, so that every experience they encountered in the Holy Land was documented.

The countryside surrounding Hebron had villages spread out in all directions. There were numerous vineyards and orchards. Moses was intrigued as he watched farmers drying the fruit for sale. He saw mills worked by oxen and mules producing flour for bread, one of which had a small guest house where they stopped for a meal of bread and lentils with olive oil.

Moses was energised the closer they came to the Cave of Machpelah.

"There is a custodian of the tombs," explained Rabbi Yaffes. "As Jews we are required to pay him for entrance."

"Whatever the cost, it is of no consequence compared to the joy and spiritual uplift that we will feel," replied Moses. Both Maimon and David were as exhilarated as Moses when the iron gate leading to the cave of Machpelah was opened by a youth who was the son of the official custodian. They descended the steps, each holding a lighted candle.

Moses was awestruck. The history of his forefathers raced through his mind. The first two sections of the cave were empty. The third section had six stones, on each of which was a carved inscription: "This is the tomb of Avraham"; "This is the tomb of Yitzchak ben Avraham Avinu"; "This is the tomb of Yaacov ben Yitzchak ben Avraham Avinu"; "This is the tomb of Sarah"; "This is the tomb of Rivka"; and "This is the tomb of Leah." He bent down on his knees and kissed each of the stones, as did his father, his brother, and Rabbi Yaffes.

The four men recited the traditional hymn of praise to God in which they magnified and sanctified God's name. Then they rested and reflected. They revisited the cave on two additional days. Each time he entered and left the cave, Moses did so in a state of heightened spirituality, a level that he had never previously attained.

Moses struggled to express his emotions in his diary. He wrote: "On the ninth of the month of Marcheshvan [October], I left Jerusalem for Hebron, to kiss the graves of the patriarchs in the Cave of Machpelah. On that day I stood in the cave and prayed: 'Thanks be to the Father of all for everything!' The two days, the sixth and ninth of Marcheshvan, I designated by a vow as festivals devoted to solemn prayer and festivity. May God give me strength and assist me to fulfil my vows; and may I and all Israel soon be permitted to see the land in its glory, even as I prayed there in its state of desolation! Amen."

They also visited other holy sites nearby. At the end of three days, they decided it was now time to leave and make their way northward back towards Acre.

Moses was troubled. In truth Palestine had been a disappointment to him. He was exhilarated by the visit to the site of the Temple in Jerusalem and to the Cave of Machpelah in Hebron, but the small Jewish population and the lack of opportunity for study in Palestine was a worry. The few Jews whom he encountered seemed forlorn and impoverished. They were overwhelmed by the large Christian population, many of whom were lured to Palestine by religious zealotry or to become crusaders and mercenaries. Indeed, Moses and his travelling companions had met numerous brigands and unsavoury characters. Jerusalem had become a frontier town, a Christian melting pot, and a military headquarters. As a serious scholar, Moses was crestfallen. He considered the matter in depth and decided that he would obtain the views of his father and brother before expressing his own personal concerns.

During their travels Moses was not able to work on his *Commentary*. He did not have source material available, and the uncertain day-to-day activity and movement did not allow much time for thought and meditation. However, it did allow more time to talk and to discuss matters of importance with his father and David, which was useful. Consequently, he was soon able to raise the important issue of their future intentions. Were they going to stay in Palestine?

"Father, you once told me that it is the nature of man to orient himself in his character and actions according to his friends and companions and the practices of his compatriots."

"That has always been my view, Moshe," replied Maimon.

"A man must associate with the righteous and always dwell with the wise to learn from their ways of life. He must stay aloof from the wicked, who walk in the darkness, so that he will not learn from their actions."

"I agree," responded Moses. "Therefore, dear father, we must consider the future. The environment in Palestine is, regrettably in my view, not conducive to a contented religious life. I agree that if a man lives in a place whose customs are repugnant and whose inhabitants do not walk in the right path, he must migrate to a place whose inhabitants are pious and have good morals."

Rabbi Maimon listened thoughtfully.

"Those are indeed my views," he answered with obvious sadness and resignation. "I have also been troubled by the disappointment of living in our holy land. I think you are implying that we should consider a move."

Moses nodded. David remained silent.

"I am in agreement," replied Maimon. "Regretfully it appears that we must contemplate a future outside Palestine."

David was quiet during the discussion but did not dissent from the argument. Moses was deep in thought. They had spent many years wandering through Spain and Morocco under constant fear of persecution. In Palestine, admittedly they had freedom to follow their Judaism, but not in the kind of environment they were hoping for. He had concerns for David, though, who had, in difficult circumstances, developed a business which was now thriving. He had contacts in Spain, Morocco, and Palestine and was active in exporting gems to the Far East. He was even hoping to export to India. Moses was so proud of and grateful to David, but might yet another move be detrimental to his commercial ambitions? Surely he had the ability to develop a successful business wherever he lived.

"Dear David, you are quiet. What is your view?" asked Moses. "Can your business be moved elsewhere?"

"I have built up contacts in many places, and God willing,

the business will survive," replied David. "I understand your concerns. We must live in a place where we are able to practise our religion in comfort. And you Moshe must be able to spread your influence for the greater good of our people."

Maimon looked at both his sons as they embraced with genuine love and affection. *Sarah and Shoshanah, you can rest in peace knowing how blessed we are.* Maimon thought of his wives whenever an emotional event involving his family occurred, and this was one such occasion.

Rabbi Yaffes was present at many of the discussions. He fully understood their concerns.

"On occasions in the past I too have harboured similar thoughts," he said. "I also would have liked to live in a larger, more dedicated community, but because I have developed a reputation and am an essential part of the Acre community, I could not contemplate leaving."

"You are to be praised by the Almighty for your wonderful work in Acre," said Maimon in total sincerity.

Moses had another concern. He was approaching thirty years of age and was unmarried. This was not because of a lack of desire to find a wife but rather because no suitable opportunity had presented itself. He had been unsettled for most of his adult life and had not encountered a sufficiently religious woman with whom he felt he could be comfortable. He was fully aware that most Jewish communities would consider it unseemly for a man of his age not to be married. Remaining a bachelor was unacceptable. He had a duty to marry and father children. He argued that it was therefore necessary to move to a place with a large Jewish community so that there would be the opportunity to find a wife. Also, he needed to live in a community where he could freely practise his Judaism and continue with his theological work. Neither of these objectives was likely to be met in Palestine.

They started on the long return journey to Acre. They stopped for rest at the inn near Nablus where they had encountered the soldiers on the way to Jerusalem. The innkeeper recognised them immediately and was delighted to provide accommodation. He told Moses that the soldier he treated had improved greatly and left the inn after two days.

Once on their way again, they passed through the towns of Jenin and Afula, both populated by Arab farmers. The fields were rocky with little vegetation, but they were able to purchase water and vegetables from wandering Bedouins. It was overbearingly hot. Maimon especially seemed distressed by the heat. He needed to make frequent stops and complained of dizziness and headaches. Moses was concerned and assumed that the heat was the cause of his problem. However, his father seemed less energetic despite drinking water at regular intervals.

They made a slight detour. Both Moses and his father expressed a desire to visit Tiberias on the Sea of Galilee. They particularly wished to visit the tomb of Rabbi Yohanan ben Zakkai, an important Jewish sage in the era of the second Temple who was buried in Tiberias. Ben Zakkai was a primary contributor to the core text of the Mishna and one of Moses's great heroes. They found the tomb in a secluded area and recited prayers. Moses looked out onto the Sea of Galilee and pondered on how wonderful it would be to have this spot as one's final resting place. They then travelled to Salam and Majd al-Krum before eventually arriving back in Acre.

During the journey they continued with the discussion regarding their future travel plans and eventually came to a decision. They would go to Egypt, where there was a large Jewish community with religious freedom and stability. The Jewish community was based mainly around Alexandria and in the old city of Cairo, an area called Fustat. Both cities had achieved a degree of prosperity, with most Jews proudly following Torah law.

15

"Why do you look so sad, Rachel? Don't worry," reassured Devorah. "My husband knows the area well and will take good care of them. I am sure they will be back very soon."

Rachel and Devorah had become good friends and were often seen in each other's company. As they walked through the gardens, Rachel looked wistfully at small children playing, with their mothers looking on.

"That is not the only worry I have." She seemed restrained.

"Please tell me what ails you. Perhaps I can help." Devorah was concerned. She had noticed how sullen Rachel had appeared for several weeks. Rachel was desperate to confide in Devorah about her barrenness and how it was making her depressed. Devorah was so sensible and knowledgeable.

"I feel only half a woman. I am barren," she revealed with obvious reluctance and with tears running down her cheeks.

"David has been so reassuring and understands, but I know he feels let down that I have not conceived. I worry that he will ask for a divorce because I am a barren woman, although he says he never would. David is a loving and devoted husband, but I know how desperate he is for children."

This was the first occasion that Rachel had expressed her anxieties to anyone other than her husband.

"If the Almighty wishes it, you will have children. I will pray for you," Devorah remarked with sincerity.

"I thank you for your prayers. I am also worried that David now has little desire for me, and that is the reason I am barren. I become angry and tense and am unable to relax. We try every Friday night just after the start of the Sabbath, but to no avail."

Devorah was able to sympathise. She realised how much joy she had from her three married daughters and twelve grandchildren.

"I have heard from many reliable sources that eating large quantities of artichoke hearts mixed with cabbage can help to conceive. Why not at least try it?"

Miriam had developed into a mature, attractive young woman. She had many friends and was totally re-engaged with her Judaism. Life in Acre suited her well; she could think of no better place to live. She was a great help to Rachel, and Devorah regarded her as one of the family. She had experienced so much disruption in her life, and now that she was settled and not fearful of Almohad persecution, she made a conscious decision to spend the remainder of her life in Acre. She had a forceful character, and even though as a young woman her views were regarded as of little or no relevance, she wished to take control over her life. She knew this was unusual for a young woman, who was expected to be obedient and subservient to her parents, especially to her father, who would determine the pattern of her life without any dissent. Traditionally the desires of a daughter were irrelevant and never taken into consideration, but Miriam was different. She was strong-minded and resolute, and as soon as her father and brothers returned, she would explain this to them.

Rachel's demeanour improved. This was clear for all to see.

She seemed livelier, had a permanent smile, and was evidently more relaxed. She was heard singing quietly to herself. Miriam was the first to notice and mentioned it to Devorah, who agreed.

"At last she is enjoying being in Acre and appreciates the land of Palestine," was her response. However, the real reason was more personal. Rachel was now sure she was pregnant. She must have successfully conceived just before David left for Jerusalem. She remembered the occasion and blushed. David had become far more attentive towards her, and she was able to relax during their lovemaking. It was after their Sabbath meal, during which they had consumed a great deal of wine. Her only regret was that she was unable to tell David immediately. God willing, she would be advanced with child when he returned.

"I am not barren," she repeated to herself. She was certain that Devorah's prayers were important. She waited another week and then told Miriam, who beamed with joy.

"Baruch Hashem. I am so pleased for you. David will be so happy." Miriam embraced her.

Rachel tried her best to remain calm, but she was desperate to inform David of her pregnancy, which was progressing well. She was pampered especially by Devorah, who provided the healthiest of fine foods and would not allow her to do any form of housework or cooking.

Moses was delighted and overcome with emotion when they arrived back in Acre. They were tired and hungry, having run out of food a day earlier, so the meal which Devorah prepared was much appreciated. They had a great deal to relate. Over a sumptuous meal, Moses recounted their adventures, with contributions from David and Rabbi Yaffes. He noticed, however, that his father was less vociferous and seemed unusually reserved. Moses recounted the escapade at the inn near Nablus and told of being in Jerusalem, praying at the Temple site, visiting the Cave of Machpelah, visiting Tiberias, and undertaking the journey back to Acre.

He then brought up the decision they had taken to leave Acre and to travel to Egypt. Rachel seemed in favour, but Miriam looked glum.

"What is troubling you, Miriam? You do not seem happy with the idea," commented Maimon, who now looked pale and appeared to be struggling with his speech. Moses also observed a slight tremor of his hands.

"Father, I have been so happy in Acre. For the first time that I can remember, I feel settled in a city and a country that I love. I enjoy being with Rabbi Yaffes's family, and his children and grandchildren, and I am now caring for children in the school. I would prefer to stay here in Acre."

"You will always be welcome in Acre, Miriam. You could live with us. You are part of our family," said Devorah with complete sincerity.

Moses was astounded by Miriam's dissent. It was not usual for a daughter to argue with a father's decision, but he understood the situation. Miriam was a young, intelligent woman who wished to develop a life for herself without being continually displaced. It was different for men, who had many opportunities as well as the strength to travel and build new lives and homes whilst not necessarily taking the wishes of the women into account. Miriam, however, had experienced independence following her time in Almeria and now wished to direct her own life. She had a determined, steadfast character, and although her decision would appear to be in conflict, Moses hoped his father would accede to her request.

Moses watched as everyone looked towards his father. Maimon was hesitant before he replied and seemed to be struggling to find the words.

"My dear Miriam." Maimon spluttered. "You have my blessing to stay with Rabbi Yaffes and his family in Acre should you wish. I appreciate your reasons and would not try to change your mind. You must live your life in the manner which provides you with the greatest happiness. You have had a troubled childhood, and now you are a woman."

Miriam was noticeably relieved. "I thank you so much, revered father," she replied.

"We will look after Miriam as though she was a daughter of our own." Devorah beamed.

Moses noticed that Rachel and David had left the room earlier, and now they returned, both with beaming smiles.

"We wish to inform you that Rachel is with child." David could not hold back his joy. Rachel could only smile and timidly, blush with embarrassment.

Detailed plans were made for travel to Egypt. It was their intention to travel to Alexandria, an exodus in reverse.

Moses spent the final weeks in Acre working with determination on the *Commentary*, which was reaching completion. He adhered to all the precepts in the Mishna but included his own observations on free will and miracles. He added criticisms of superstition embraced by certain rabbis which he considered to have no substance in Jewish law. These included belief in astrology, divination, amulets, and the "evil eye", views which had matured ever since he observed the sale of amulets to passengers on their sea journey from Tarifa to Morocco.

He was distracted, however, by concerns for his father, as were David and Miriam. Since returning from Jerusalem, Maimon had become noticeably more tired and weaker. He was unable to talk for more than a few minutes, and his speech seemed slurred. His condition was deteriorating day by day. A doctor was summoned.

"I think he has mild apoplexy," was the view of the distinguished-looking physician.

"It is an illness of the black bile. I recommend keeping the bowels loose and bleeding the blackish blood."

Moses looked puzzled. He could see no rational reason to bleed his father, who was already weak and increasingly disorientated. He was fearful of the dangers of bleeding, even in younger patients. He also noted that his father had short rapid breaths and a cough with sputum. He remembered one of his teachers mentioning the role of myrrh and hyssop given with sweet wine to improve breathing and aid speech. The doctor considered this and reluctantly agreed that it be tried initially.

"But I consider that bleeding will eventually be necessary," he responded.

Within hours of being seen by the doctor, Rabbi Maimon's condition markedly worsened. The right side of his body lost all movement, as did his face. His breathing became laboured and rattled, and he lost consciousness. Moses was distressed. He knew his father had progressive apoplexy and was dying. Nothing could be done. He sat by his bed with David and Miriam. His father looked so old and frail, very different from how he remembered him in his beloved Cordoba. They recited the traditional psalms said for a person who is dying. Moses observed his father's breathing to be increasingly shallow, and then it stopped. Moses put his ear to his father's mouth. There was no breath. He kissed his father, as did David and Miriam. Maimon had peacefully passed away with his family gathered around him.

Rabbi Maimon's funeral was attended by almost the entire Jewish community of Acre. After ritual purification of the body, it was wrapped in a shroud and then transported to the grave on a bier covered by drapery. He was buried in the cemetery adjacent to Rabbi Yaffes's synagogue, and Rabbi Yaffes himself conducted the proceedings. Moses and David walked with their heads bowed, their hands hidden under their robes. The coffin was lowered into the ground and covered with earth. Rabbi Yaffes spoke passionately and respectfully about the great rabbi and dayan and discussed how his wise words and empathy had helped so many Jews in Spain and in Fez. Prayers were recited, and seven days of mourning commenced. Numerous letters of condolence and tributes were received, which provided a great source of comfort to the family and especially to Moses, who was so proud to have confirmed what he already knew, that his father had been a great and respected rabbi.

And so, Rabbi Maimon, the father of Moses ben Maimon, was peacefully laid to rest in the land of his forefathers, the land of Israel.

PART V

EGYPT

1166–1193

16

fter the tearful farewell to the Yaffes family and Miriam at the dockside, Moses stowed his gear in the cabin and told David and Rachel that he wanted to be alone. He strode to the bow, turned his back on the open sea, and gazed at the land fading fast astern as the ship surged through the water, the strong wind filling the sails. Palestine had been a disappointment to him. It had taken his father, and it had instilled in him the ardent desire to be with his own people which had led to this latest journey. He passed the three days it took to get to Alexandria in a similar routine, keeping to himself while welcoming the sombre reflections.

The accommodation in the bow of the ship was comfortable. It was the end of the summer, and a stiff wind blew during the entire journey. They had made the decision to travel to Alexandria by sea rather than by land caravan because passage through the Negev and Sinai deserts was fraught with danger from marauders and bandits, irrespective of how well armed the caravans. Nonetheless, travel by sea also had its dangers. There was the inevitable threat of storms and assault by the crew, as well as attacks by pirates, who frequently overcame merchant and passenger ships, robbing and holding passengers for ransom.

Alexandria by sea was approximately two hundred Arabic miles due west from Acre.

Thankfully the passage was smooth, and they arrived at the sea wall of Alexandria three days later. Rachel felt nauseated during the entire journey and was sick on a few occasions, but despite this she did not complain and otherwise tolerated the journey well. David provided constant comfort to her and was astounded by her strong constitution.

Alexandria was a most impressive city. It was built in style by Alexander the Great in 332 BCE and had become a thriving metropolis characterised by wide straight streets. Benjamin of Tuleda, a rabbi and merchant who documented his visit to Alexandria, said of the streets that they were so straight and long that "a man could see from one city gate to the other", an unobstructed view of approximately three Arabic miles. *How very different from the claustrophobic and narrow streets in Fez,* thought Moses, as he looked at his surroundings in wonderment. The more prosperous citizens lived in large houses which lined the avenues and were surrounded by tall decorated walls. A long pier which Benjamin described as a "King's highway" stretched into the sea and ended with a large, impressive lighthouse. There were twenty institutes of higher education in the city, including the famous Academy of Aristotle. Alexandria was a beacon of scholarship.

Merchant ships arrived at the port from Europe, North Africa, the Arabian Peninsula, and India. Not surprisingly Alexandria was generally regarded as the trading city for all nations. On the dock were numerous sailors, fishermen, and merchants, all scrambling around trying to find a source of income.

Alexandria was predominantly Muslim but had been home to a large Jewish population for generations, indeed since the time of the second Temple. There were some three thousand Jewish families, a significant proportion of the city's population of fifty thousand. Jews lived in almost complete religious freedom and had autonomy over their own internal affairs. Many Jews were prominent in politics and became involved in the life of the ruling court of Egypt as well as in the government in Alexandria. The Jewish schools, religious institutions, communal functions, and system of justice were under the administrative responsibility of the government-appointed nagid, or leader. The nagid was able to formally appoint rabbis, judges, and other officials and was in effect the Jewish representative at the caliph's court, an extremely important position held only by the most respected individuals. These political and religious rights for Jews in Egypt were found in no other country.

Moses was now the patriarch of his family. He would take his responsibilities seriously as his dear father would have wanted and expected. His initial task was to seek out the Jewish quarter, where he knew they would be welcome. His father had contacted rabbis in Alexandria several weeks before his death. They had responded enthusiastically, were looking forward to the family's arrival, and promised to assist them. David identified a donkey trader close to the port and purchased three robust animals with saddles.

Following directions from passing Jews and Jewish traders, they made their way to the main Jewish quarter. The aroma of strong Turkish coffee wafted around amidst the sweet scent of tea and herbs. Groups of swarthy men with thick beards sat in circles puffing at bubbling water pipes.

They eventually arrived at the Great Synagogue of Alexandria with its tall colonnades and its yeshiva with a large sign on the outside reading, "Beis Mishna". They introduced themselves in the synagogue and were warmly welcomed by the religious leader, Rabbi Simeon, who Moses thought looked rather young to hold such a senior position.

"You are most welcome. Your reputation precedes you, Rabbi Moses, and of course we all know of your father. Please accept my most sincere condolences on his death. I wish you a long life."

The synagogue was astonishing. Moses and David had never seen a synagogue that could compare with it in size or opulence.

"I see you are impressed," Rabbi Simeon said. "The synagogue is so large that we need to employ a system of flags to ensure the proper responses from worshippers, many of whom sit so far away from the reader that they are unable to hear him when he is reading from the Torah or reciting prayers." He smiled as he looked at their expressions.

"You must be tired from the journey. Please join me for refreshments. I will arrange for Gideon, my assistant, to guide you to the accommodation I have identified for you. I do hope you find it suitable."

Moses, David, and Rachel followed Gideon. The streets were cobbled and lined by stalls with merchants selling fruit, fish, and vegetables. They passed numerous mosques and several synagogues. Eventually they reached the accommodation which Rabbi Simeon had recommended. It was located above a bakery. There were three rooms and space for cooking. Moses was favourably impressed and thanked Gideon for his assistance.

Moses had several pressing matters to deal with, but undoubtedly his main priority was completing the *Commentary*. He had been working on it for almost nine years, and it was approaching completion. *What a relief, but how sad,* he thought, when he considered that he would not be able to show the completed version to his father, who had encouraged him and supported his efforts throughout. In the introduction he reviewed the fundamental principles of Judaism and chose Tractate Sanhedrin, Chapter 10 of the Talmud, called Pereq Helek, to illustrate this. He included explanations of monotheism, prophecy, revelation, providence, and reward and punishment in a way that, he hoped, would be understandable to all Jews. He showed Rabbi Simeon a draft of the manuscript and asked for comments. Rabbi Simeon told Moses that the writing overwhelmed him with its erudition.

"My synagogue attracts a large congregation, and there is

need for another rabbi to assist. I and several of the most senior and respected members are so impressed by your knowledge and piety that we wish to invite you to take up the salaried post. I do hope you will accept." Rabbi Simeon was certain of an affirmative response.

"Your offer is both generous and humbling. I feel honoured to have been asked," replied Moses. "However, I must decline. I will of course be pleased to assist in rabbinical duties and teach should I be considered worthy of doing so, but I cannot take a paid post as a rabbi. I cannot use the Torah as a spade. I believe it is important for rabbis to work in other positions to earn a living and support themselves. The great Hillel was a woodcutter, and Shammai was a carpenter. Rabbis have been potters, weavers, sandal makers, and the like. Rabbi Karna was a water carrier who asked his community to replace his wages if he had to leave work to judge matters of law. I will not accept money for doing the work of God."

Rabbi Simeon was taken aback. He looked embarrassed and bewildered.

"I respect your decision and will inform the synagogue members accordingly."

David and Rachel settled into their new life with little difficulty. Rachel took pride in acting as a capable wife and sister-in-law. She excelled in cooking and created a comfortable homely atmosphere. David was proud of his wife, who blossomed as her pregnancy advanced. The initial morning sickness subsided, and she delighted in planning for the birth and afterwards. David took on responsibility for financial matters. Each day he met with local traders in gems and was able to expand his business contacts. He gained a reputation for honesty and integrity and became highly respected in the profession.

Moses, however, even though content with the present situation, had a major concern. He was still unmarried. He was eager for marriage but realised that his background and social isolation as a young man whilst wedded to his studies and occupied with escaping persecution had not been conducive to finding a wife. His years of deprivation seemed to have supressed his sensual nature and desires, and he adopted a puritanical approach to life. One of the reasons he had wanted to move to a large religious Jewish community was to find a suitable wife. He hoped that Alexandria would provide the opportunity, but he was disappointed. There was little observance and a dearth of learning amongst the Alexandrian Jews. Despite being a large and prosperous community, in general they favoured a lax lifestyle and had taken undue advantage of the many nonreligious opportunities available to them. As far as Moses was concerned, they had become far more secular than he would have liked or expected. For example, he noticed that many unmarried women were careless in their dress and modesty, which was unbecoming. He saw women in the streets unaccompanied by their husbands. This was unacceptable. Furthermore, he had been reliably informed that most married women were neglecting the rabbinic rules for purification after their menstrual periods. This was repugnant to him. To exacerbate the situation, rabbis in Alexandria were less learned in Torah and Talmud than he would have expected, and the religious academies were not of an adequate standard.

Because of his acknowledged erudition and wisdom, Moses was often asked to provide opinions on difficult religious matters. A prominent lay member of the Great Synagogue approached him with such a request.

"We would appreciate your opinion on a problem we are facing with the Karaitis," he said. "How should we treat them? Are they to be regarded as Orthodox Jews or not?"

Moses was happy to oblige but knew that there would be controversy with whatever judgement he delivered regarding Karaitism.

Karaitism is a movement that rejects anything but the Hebrew Bible as a source of all divine law. It was established in the eighth century in Persia and is analogous to Shiism in the Muslim religion. In repudiating rabbinic Judaism, Karaitism was considered as heretical by Orthodox Jewish congregations. A natural sympathy, however, existed between the Karaitis and the Shiite Fatimids, to their great advantage, and as a result many Karaitis had become influential and wealthy throughout Egypt. Conflict between the Orthodox and Karaiti factions was inevitable. They would not eat in each other's homes nor bury each other's dead. Moses was now being drawn into the dispute.

After considerable thought and a thorough review of Talmudic and Torah sources, Moses replied to the request in the form of a responsum, a written reply. A responsum carried great weight when written by an acknowledged rabbinical scholar.

His reply reflected his revulsion of Karaiti practice and raised the hope that the Karaitis could be brought back into the Orthodox fold. But in the interim they should be afforded tolerance and respect. For example, social relationships should be encouraged and strengthened. He advocated that rituals such as circumcision and burial rites previously denied them should be offered. However, the Karaitis should be considered a corruptive influence, having violated the intentions of God. They were not, he insisted, authentic Jews and should not be allowed to make up a quorum of ten men required for religious services. Nor should they be included among the three men needed to pray after a meal.

This suggestion of exclusion from communal Jewish rituals upset the Karaiti community, and even some members of the Orthodox community who considered that Moses's views were too harsh. Moses was not surprised but annoyed that his judgement was ignored by the Orthodox community as well as the Karaiti. What is more, he was considered by the established wealthy Karaitis to be a young provocative upstart who should be encouraged to leave Alexandria. He was also socially ostracised by many in the Orthodox community who feared his extreme views. Life was made very difficult for him.

Having fled from Spain and from Morocco, and now troubled in Alexandria, Moses still could not find peace and harmony. Supported by David, he had no choice but to consider yet another move. However, the time was not right. David's business amongst the wealthy Jews who delighted in purchasing jewels was expanding, and his dealings in India, where he had established excellent contacts, required time to mature. Rachel was approaching childbirth and did not feel capable of more travel. Nevertheless, Fustat in old Cairo, where the Jewish community were comfortably settled and far more observant than in Alexandria, would be a possibility. After all, it was the seat of the nagid.

Moses was now fully concentrated on the final part of the *Commentary*; the end was in sight. He was happy with the content. His aim, as he constantly reminded himself, was to provide a text which could be used to guide the life of an Arabic-speaking Jew of average intelligence and educational background. Wherever possible he simplified the text. If he did not agree with the teachings of the Gemara and the later rabbinic commentators, he either ignored them or provided his preferred explanation, avoiding the tortuous pathways they had negotiated. He also included a historical description of how the oral law developed from Mount Sinai to the completion of the Mishna by Judah ha-Nasi.

An important point which he repeatedly emphasised was the need to follow the "golden mean", not an ascetic lifestyle or one of excessive behaviour, for example, but a lifestyle which was in between. But he needed to obtain considered opinion on his hypotheses. When his father was alive, this was not a problem. His father would always be available and willing to offer advice and suggest modifications. But now he needed to rely on David. He found David to be an ideal sounding board to gauge how acceptable and pertinent his interpretations were to an "average" Jew. David was usually conducive to this approach and rarely resented his brother's requests. The only problem arose when he offered an opinion. It was invariably rejected by Moses with a relevant quote from the Torah or Talmud. Nevertheless, he felt flattered at being regarded as an "average" Jew capable of following the discourse.

"David, I apologise for intruding, but I would appreciate your opinion on whether you consider that adopting a middle course in one's life would result in a happy and satisfying existence." He was careful to approach David only when the latter seemed relaxed.

"An argument I propose in the *Commentary* is that man is blessed with a free will which should be directed towards acquiring wisdom and knowledge of God. To follow a path of hedonism or to pursue a life of asceticism is a choice. Surely happiness can only be attained by following the middle course, the golden mean?"

David had heard this argument previously and found it persuasive. But all Moses's concepts, based on the Torah, seemed sensible, and David never considered that he had the intellectual ability to dissent. He nodded in agreement.

Moses was also anxious to clarify the meaning of Olam Ha'ba, the next world. He wrote about this in detail in the *Commentary* since it was a matter of deep philosophical interest to him and a concept which he considered to be often misunderstood. He was annoyed at the fanciful perceptions surrounding the afterlife and what it would be like. Since he appeared to have held David's attention with his first interruption, he now took the opportunity to expound his hypothesis about Olam Ha'ba.

"David, I condemn the fanciful notion of what the afterlife would be like. Olam Ha'ba is traditionally believed to be a place of sensual pleasures, of infinite satisfaction, and of reunion with family and friends, and for those who have been wicked, a place of unhappiness and pain."

David showed renewed interest. This was certainly a topic that he, like most people, had considered at some time or another on a personal level.

"The Mishna states, all Jews have a share in the Olam Ha'ba," continued Moses. "The problem is that many Jews have misunderstood what this means. It should not be taken literally. Foolish people fail to grasp the allegorical nature of what the sages were trying to explain about Olam Ha'ba. The sages attempted to provide rewards to the common man for following the law, like promising sweets to a child for studying or behaving well. Olam Ha'ba is not a place of physical rewards, but of divine glory. The goal any thinking man wants to achieve is the enlightened state in which God's existence is understood." Moses was becoming quite animated.

"The afterlife is a form of intellectual enlightenment, achieved through a heightened state of spiritual communion with God." David was not sure he understood, but he remained quiet as Moses continued.

"This is the form of afterlife that man, who thinks of pleasure as deriving from the senses, cannot comprehend as long as he is alive. Just as a blind person cannot understand colour or a deaf person cannot imagine sound, the body cannot understand spiritual pleasure. As for punishment of the wicked, it will consist of the destruction of their souls so that they may not achieve what is granted to the righteous. Rather than punishment by some form of torture, their destiny is nonexistence."

Moses had not yet finished testing his concepts on David.

"A person must always have one purpose in mind, which is to come close to knowledge of God. He must do this when he eats, when he drinks, and when he rests. The purpose of keeping the body healthy is that this is for the sake of the soul. Only when the body is healthy can the soul be healthy. In this way the soul will have a healthy complete vessel with which to acquire wisdom and good character traits. David, a healthy soul is as important as a healthy body and should be equally looked after."

David realised that he was listening to a great teacher of Torah, a physician of the soul as well as of the body, whose wisdom would survive and be referred to for generations to come.

"Moshe, your knowledge and erudition are truly outstanding. You must continue with your writing, which must be made widely available to Jews everywhere. Be assured that I will do everything I can to help you in your holy endeavours."

"David, without your support I would be unable to fulfil my ambitions," responded Moses. "You are worthy of a prominent place in Olam Ha'ba." With this they laughed and embraced.

The *Commentary* was finished at last. The final words were written with great relief. Moses was certain that nothing pertinent, either legal or ritual from the Torah or from the obligations instituted by the rabbis, was omitted. He expected criticism for his views, so in the introduction, he expressed a humble request for understanding. He also became self-congratulatory.

"The reader should read the book over and over again and reflect on it carefully. If the reader felt he understood the book after one reading, or even ten readings, he is misled by his own foolishness. This book was written after long research and reflection."

By studying all the key texts, Moses was, in addition, able to compile a *Book of Commandments, Sefar Ha'Mitzvot*, a list of the 613 commandments given to the prophet Moses: 365 negative ones paralleling the days of the year, and the 248 positive ones paralleling the number of bones of the human skeleton.

The commandments were originally elucidated by the Gaon Shimon Kairo in the eighth century. But exactly what were these commandments? There was disagreement, and the sages had remained silent. Moses undertook a clarification. He wrote a detailed overview of the commandments with principles and teachings for Jews who did not understand their significance.

Copies of the completed *Commentary* were written by scribes and sent to Palestine, Morocco, Spain, Yemen, and Iraq, as well as to the Jews of Cairo and Fustat.

Rachel adored her daughter and devoted herself to ensuring the child's comfort and well-being. She had been remarkably stoical throughout the pregnancy and undertook labour in a similar fashion. The midwife claimed that she had never known such a smooth and speedy delivery. Rachel seemed to enjoy the experience, probably because she had been looking forward to having a baby all her adult life. The little girl was named Shoshanah in memory of her grandmother. Both Rachel and David doted over her, and even Moses was emotional towards his niece.

Shoshanah was a placid child who rarely cried. She was invariably dressed in pretty clothes, and Rachel ensured she was well fed. Breastfeeding proved no difficulty. Rachel's diet included honey, fresh goat's milk, olives, dates, and moist bread, designed to provide good quantities of nutritious milk. She seemed so content and relaxed, doubtless because David was equally happy as his business interests expanded. Nevertheless, there were tensions in living in Alexandria which could not be ignored. Moses was anxious to move. He was unpopular in Alexandria because of his views on Karaitism, and he was troubled, as well as irritated, by the lack of learning and commitment amongst the Jewish community. David was successful in Alexandria, but he was certain that opportunities for expansion existed in Fustat. He anticipated little difficulty in moving his business. The family agreed to revisit their earlier decision to move to Fustat now that Rachel was no longer pregnant and Shoshanah was old enough to travel.

"I am comfortable with the move," David explained to Moses. "Cairo is only one hundred and thirty Arabic miles from the ports on the Red Sea. I have heard that many traders sail from there to India. Also, in Cairo, there is a thriving trade in imported gems because of the many palace officials and their harems."

He seemed visibly excited by the prospect of a move to Fustat, but Rachel looked worried. David had mentioned on several occasions his business contacts with traders in India. He had also mentioned travel to India, which filled her with dread. The journey was treacherous with a terrible reputation. Moses was equally concerned whenever travel to India was raised.

"You must promise never to take unnecessary risks for the sake of your business. The journey to India is long and dangerous. The sacrifice is too great." Moses was adamant on this matter and left David in no doubt about his concern.

David seemed unperturbed and reassured his family that he would only ever pursue a sensible business strategy.

In 1168, the year that the *Commentary* was completed, Moses, David, and his family moved to Fustat. The move was not regretted by the Alexandrian community, who had found Moses arrogant and far too learned for their comfort. Rabbi Simeon was especially relieved. He regarded Moses as a serious threat to his authority. He accepted that Moses's knowledge and expertise on theological matters was far superior to his own but was annoyed that this detracted from his credibility as the rabbi of the main synagogue in Alexandria. In addition, the views that Moses had expressed regarding the Karaiti community had been an embarrassment to him. As a rabbinical colleague he felt unable to publically contradict Moses's edicts, and as a result several senior members of his community expressed annoyance with him and held him partly responsible for the situation. Once Moses had left, he had reasoned, the matter would soon be forgotten and he could return to the previous mutually agreeable understanding with the Karaiti community. Things would return to normal.

17

They joined a land caravan. Moses and David travelled on donkeys, with Rachel and Shoshanah in a separate carriage. They passed many villages with cultivated fields and palm trees and watched Arab farmers beat the branches of olive trees with large rods, knocking down the ripe olives and catching them in a net. When they reached a Nile delta they were enthralled by thousands of beautiful white and pink flamingos on tall sticklike legs hunting for fish.

"When one gazes at God's wondrous creatures, one immediately loves, praises, and glorifies his name and desires to know God," stated Moses as he said a short prayer in wonderment and humility for the flamingos.

Fustat was approximately 170 Arabic miles southwest of Alexandria. They reached Cairo in four days. The walls of Cairo had large fortified gates, one of which, Bab Alfutuh, was over twenty metres high. It was the entrance to the royal city and had a massive turret on each side. They travelled the length of the city wall as they headed south towards Fustat, two Arabic miles from Cairo.

Fustat had been the capital of Egypt until Cairo superseded it when the Fatimids seized control in 969 CE and began their dynasty. It was a prosperous centre of commerce with the main industries being in ceramics and glassware. The Jewish community had done well in Fustat and lived on friendly terms with their Muslim neighbours. Being the traditional home of the nagid, the religious Jewish leader, Fustat was regarded by the Jewish community throughout Egypt as their religious and administrative centre.

Whilst in Alexandria, Moses contacted the Fustat Jewish community and sent a copy of his completed *Commentary* to them, so when the family arrived in the Jewish quarter, they were warmly welcomed. A house had been identified close to Knesset Ilshmiyin, the synagogue, and was ideally suited for their requirements.

Moses settled into the new surroundings remarkably quickly, and it was not long before he was involved in religious activity. Resulting from the widespread distribution of the *Commentary*, which was held in high esteem, his opinion was frequently sought on Halachic issues based on his proven knowledge of both the Torah and Talmud. This gave him immense satisfaction. He gratefully accepted the challenges presented to him. He had a feeling of worthiness and was pleased to be able to contribute in a meaningful way. It seemed to him that his lifetime work and intellectual gifts were at last being used as they should be, to spread the Word of God and to provide Jews with an understandable view of their religion.

As his reputation spread, Moses became accepted as the leading rabbi of Fustat. He was a popular teacher of Torah in addition to the person to approach for challenging Halachic decisions. David similarly prospered. Whilst Moses was heavily involved in Jewish affairs, David expanded his flourishing business interests and was pleased to support his family in a comfortable, albeit not luxurious, style, allowing Moses to continue unhindered without financial worries.

Soon after they arrived in Fustat, the whole of Egypt become worryingly volatile. The reasons for the political unrest were complicated, unsettling, and difficult to understand. In 1167, Amalric, king of Jerusalem and the crusaders in Palestine, marched against Cairo but was defeated by Shirkuh, a Syrian leader based in Damascus. Later that year another attempt was made by Amalric, but this time Shirkuh was accompanied by his general, An-nasir Salah ad-Din Yusuf ibn Ayyub, otherwise better known as Salah ad-Din or Saladin. Once again Amalric failed after a bitter, bloody battle.

Constant battles followed between Amalric, the Syrians under Sultan Nureddin, and the Fatimid Egyptians themselves. The situation was even more complicated by the division, which had been present for hundreds of years, between the orthodox Sunni Muslims (the Almohads were in this group) who ruled Syria and the Shiite Muslims who controlled Egypt. Shiites rejected the oral tradition of Islam, accepting only the written Koran, whilst the Sunni, considered the more orthodox, accepted both the oral and written law. The Christians, Sunnis, and Shiites battled each other, often forming temporary alliances, betraying one to the other, and engaging in frequent assassinations.

The caliph at the time was al-Adid, a rather weak and ineffectual leader, the last of the Fatimid dynasty. In reality, Egypt was ruled by the vizier Sharwar, who recognised the lacklustre leadership of the caliph and worked hard to rectify the disasters which he had imposed on the population. Al-Adid, whilst recognising Sharwar's virtues, disliked him intensely and was suspicious of his motives and ambitions. Nevertheless, he relied totally upon his loyalty and support.

Following an embarrassing battleground defeat by the powerful Seljuks, al-Adid agreed to pay a regular tribute to Amalric, to act as his protector. But in September 1168, al-Adid decided to stop paying the tribute without any discussion with Sharwar. In response, Amalric invaded Egypt. He marched northward against very little resistance, and his army looted everything in sight, pillaging cities and cold-bloodedly murdering unarmed civilians. A major atrocity was committed in the town of Bilbay, where thousands of innocents were slaughtered. Cairo, being a heavily fortified city, was able to defend itself, but Fustat was an open city with no realistic means of defence. Losing Fustat to Amalric with the concomitant loss of life would have been an unmitigated disaster, especially since the city occupied a key strategic position in Upper Egypt.

Sharwar decided that the only way to prevent Amalric from taking Fustat was to immediately evacuate the citizens and burn key parts of the city to the ground so that Fustat could not be used as a strategic centre to attack the remainder of the country. The implications of losing Fustat to the Christians were far too great for the vizier to contemplate.

The sudden, unexpected order for the population to evacuate and take refuge in Cairo was met by panic and pandemonium. The people were given no choice. They were warned about the impending invasion and were threatened with certain death if they were to stay behind. Moses and David were shocked but remained calm and level-headed in the face of this latest adversity. They were accustomed to leaving their home with little warning and did not panic. Rachel took responsibility for domestic possessions and made sure Shoshanah was well cared for. Moses rapidly amassed his manuscripts and books whilst David ensured that his valuable stock of jewels and gems were well hidden.

The carriage which they had brought from Alexandria was packed to absolute capacity and their trusty donkeys bridled up. They were fortunate in possessing transport. Many people were not so lucky and were desperate to buy or even steal animals for their escape. Many families had members separated from one another; others left with nothing but the clothes they were wearing. The scene in Fustat was one of sheer terror. In the panic to escape, people were running aimlessly. Some were trampled on, and some were seriously hurt or even killed. The fleeing crowd took refuge wherever they could, in mosques, in bathhouses, anywhere. They were fearful of a similar Christian massacre as had occurred in Bilbay.

When Fustat was totally deserted, slaves were dispatched with inflammable liquids, which were spread over a wide area, and fires were lit. A huge bonfire greeted Amalric as he approached the city. It could not be extinguished. Fires raged for six weeks. Amalric was frustrated but would not be denied. He camped outside Cairo and laid siege whilst waiting for the opportunity to attack.

The delay gave Sharwar time to contact Nureddin, the sultan of Syria. He begged Nureddin for assistance to help his Muslim brothers against the Christian invader. The emissary who delivered the message to Damascus also carried with him hair from al-Adid's wives as a warning of what would happen to the Muslim women should they be taken by the Christians troops.

Nureddin was persuaded and sent his finest troops under the command of his most experienced commander, Shirkuh, accompanied by his nephew Saladin. The approach of advancing troops was ample message for Amalric to retreat in haste. He knew full well that he would be defeated by a far superior fighting force.

Shirkuh assumed control of Fustat and, with Saladin, set about governing and rebuilding it with the full support of al-Adid. They were very effective. New buildings were rapidly erected. The speed of the restoration greatly impressed the refugees, who began to return in large numbers. The vizier Sharwar, however, resented losing control of Fustat to Shirkuh and Saladin and began to plot against them. Saladin was sensible enough to realise the danger to his plans and had planted spies everywhere. He soon learnt of a plot by Sharwar and his henchmen to regain power and reported this to al-Adid. The news was of great delight to al-Adid, who disliked and feared his aggressive vizier. This was the excuse he had been seeking for years. The plot was an insult to him personally. He had Sharwar arrested, and the vizier was subsequently tried, found guilty of treason, and beheaded. Shirkuh was appointed as the new vizier and as commander-in-chief of the army. Saladin was appointed as his second-in-command.

In March 1169, Shirkuh died suddenly after grossly overeating at a banquet arranged in his honour. Al-Adid immediately appointed Saladin as his new vizier. As Saladin's power increased, he justifiably restored the Sunni dominance in government, since they were the majority population, and in so doing reversed the Shiite emphasis of the Fatimids. Saladin, a Sunni, was guaranteed to have the allegiance of the suppressed Sunni majority. Al-Adid did not object, probably because he had developed a progressive mental illness, which soon led to his death. Saladin, still only thirty years old, was able to claim the caliph's crown without opposition.

However, he had little time to enjoy his spectacular rise to power as he faced serious trouble from the Christians. Amalric joined forces with Byzantium, formally an ally of Egypt, and launched a major attack on the port of Damitta on the Mediterranean coast east of Alexandria. A fierce battle took place with hundreds of casualties on both sides, but by superior strategic knowledge and expertise, Saladin and his forces fought off the assault. This was a spectacular victory. Any doubts about Saladin's leadership abilities were now effectively dismissed. Saladin's triumph confirmed his position as caliph. Under his leadership, Egypt continued to follow a progressive and illustrious course with the complete rebuilding of Fustat.

The entire community of Fustat returned from their refuge in Cairo to find a regenerated city with attractive buildings. As a result of the economic boom following the restoration, the city flourished, and prosperity returned. There were numerous gardens with ox-drawn waterwheels for irrigation and shaded streets with a profusion of markets. High-rise buildings appeared, some seven stories tall, often with roof gardens, which could accommodate hundreds of people.

It was fortunate for the Jewish community that the main synagogue survived the fire almost intact, as indeed did much of the Jewish area, which was built predominantly of stone. Moses and David were pleased to return and set about making their own contributions to the new city and foundations in their inimitable fashion.

Although Moses was justifiably proud of the acclamation the *Commentary* received, nevertheless he considered it insufficient and felt that more needed to be done. It was necessary, in his opinion, for an even more daunting undertaking: to compile a compendium of the entire body of Jewish law. It was his intention to codify and clarify all the complex regulations and diverse facts, making them more comprehensible to Jews everywhere. It would be a code of Jewish law. He would call it the *Mishneh Torah*, "Repetition of the law".

Moses served the community as a local judge, and as the most knowledgeable rabbinic legist in Egypt, he was regularly presented with questions related to Halachic issues, not only from Fustat but also from Jewish organisations in countries that had received copies of the *Commentary* and needed advice. As his reputation spread, students came to learn under his tutelage. One of his students was Rabbi Shlomo Hakohen from Yemen.

Rabbi Shlomo was pleased that Moses agreed to his visit. He was older than Moses but was intrigued by his reputation for erudition and wanted to see for himself how justified it was. Shlomo was always anxious to learn. He sat at the back of the room whilst Moses conducted a seminar for a group of young rabbinic students.

At the completion of the session, Shlomo approached Moses.

"I have listened and learnt from many great rabbis," he remarked to Moses, "but your deep knowledge and understanding of humanity and the Torah is truly amazing, a gift from the Almighty."

"You honour me with your kind words, which are not deserved," Moses replied humbly.

"You are most modest. In Yemen we have many problems with interpretation of Torah precepts. There are differing views between the ultraorthodox and the more liberal. I try to calm what can be stormy waters but often fail. Your knowledge and reputation could be of great assistance to me and thereby the Yemeni Jews. Might I be permitted to contact you if I am faced with intractable dilemmas?"

"But of course, dear Shlomo. I desire that any knowledge or insight that the Almighty has bestowed upon me should be used for the greater good."

Shlomo thanked him. He realised how similar they were in their approaches to Judaism. He returned to Yemen wiser and contented. He felt confident in having an ally to consult for the problems that he anticipated lay ahead in Yemen.

"Moshe, perhaps you will permit me to raise an issue of a personal nature, which I hope will not embarrass you," Rabbi Mishael said rather diffidently.

Moses was delighted when Mishael, one of the elders and one of the most learned men in Fustat, was complimentary about his *Commentary*. They became good friends and colleagues and often sat together after synagogue services or Torah teaching classes to discuss meaningful topics of Talmudic interest, which Moses invariably found both relaxing and stimulating.

"Dear Mishael, good friend, please feel free to do so. You are not known for causing offence, and I respect your views as much as any person I have known," replied an intrigued Moses.

"You will be aware of the wise words of King Solomon: 'He who has found a wife has found goodness.' I can assure you from personal experience over the last forty years that these words are true as well as wise."

Moses smiled and slowly stroked his beard. "Who could disagree with the wisdom of Shlomo Hamelech?" He nodded, anticipating the hidden reason for the comments.

"In addition," Rabbi Mishael continued, "our sages teach us that 'he who is without a wife is without completeness and without joy.'" He paused for a moment before continuing. Moses now had no doubt where this was leading.

"I would be honoured if you would consider meeting with my daughter, Jamilah. Would you have any objection?"

"I have seen your daughter leaving the synagogue and would regard it as a pleasure to make her acquaintance," Moses replied.

Moses had indeed noticed Jamilah from afar and often wondered why she was unmarried. She was tall, always modestly but well dressed and had an elegant deportment which gave her a confident air. This could be misconstrued as arrogance, but he doubted that this was accurate.

Moses was formally introduced to Jamilah by Rabbi Mishael, accompanied by his wife.

18

The wedding took place six weeks after they'd first met in Rabbi Mishael's house. There was no need for a prolonged courtship; it was obvious to Moses that they were suited to each other. David strongly approved, and Rachel was overjoyed.

Miriam came from Acre for the wedding, accompanied by Rabbi Yaffes and his family. Miriam seemed so much older and more mature than Moses remembered. It was obvious that she was happy and settled in Acre. Although he thought it would be desirable, Moses was reluctant to encourage her to move to Fustat.

At last he was getting married. He was forty, but as he stood under the wedding canopy, he reflected that his father was thirty-two when he'd married. Moses was sure that the wait was right and that his father would have approved of Jamilah. He looked at Jamilah and experienced a surprising degree of affection towards her, even though her face was covered with a lace scarf throughout the proceedings.

At the ceremony, Rabbi Mishael delivered a dvar Torah in which he discussed the section of the Torah that was to be read on the following Sabbath. Rabbi Yaffes recited the ketubah, the marriage certificate, written in Aramaic, to the assembled congregation. Moses gave a discourse relating to Talmudic concepts on marriage and emphasised the need for mutual understanding and adherence to all the required religious stipulations to ensure a happy and productive union.

After the wedding, he and Jamilah were left together without a chaperone for the first time. They entered their house together. Moses was aware that he had no previous experience with the opposite sex, and neither had Jamilah. He was, of course, familiar with female anatomy and physiology following his medical training in Fez, but his scholarly work and medical training had consumed his sensuality and almost his very essence. He was aware of his responsibility to ensure that the marriage was consummated. It was a Torah precept. Jamilah gave the appearance of being totally relaxed and at ease, but nothing could be further from the truth. Deep down she was nervous and embarrassed. She undressed in private. When they drew close to each other, to his astonishment Moses experienced unexpected sensations which he recognised as being erotic in nature. He recited some blessings and felt a sense of inner self-contentment which he had never previously experienced. They gently consummated their betrothal. Jamilah expressed audible pleasure during their sexual encounter and visibly enjoyed the experience, which was a great relief to Moses. They fell asleep in each other's arms. Jamilah wondered whether Moses would regard her obvious pleasure with lovemaking to be improper. She felt ashamed and blushed as she lay in the darkness.

Moses returned to his busy schedule immediately after the seven days of traditional celebratory festive meals, the Sheva Brachot. His first task, delayed because of the wedding, was to provide responses to two difficult problems which had been directed to him in his role as dayan. A rabbi from Alexandria requested clarification on the Talmudic prohibition against a twice-widowed woman who had married for a third time, the Talmudic scruple being that following the death of two husbands, a third marriage is forbidden since it is deemed dangerous. The woman therefore had broken the stipulation by marrying for a third time. Moses was asked for an adjudication.

After prolonged consideration, Moses responded, "The matter can be sidestepped. There should be no prohibition since they have already married and cannot be divorced. The marriage should be blessed. This is the way I have decided and acted in Egypt since arriving here."

Some thought that Moses was being far too lenient, but they accepted the ruling.

He was less lenient in his reply to another matter and advocated strict punishment. He was asked to adjudicate in the case of a Cohen, a member of the priestly class who had married a divorcee, a forbidden act, under the auspices of a Gentile authority. His response to this misdemeanour was forceful.

"The sinful priest and his harlot should be excommunicated from the synagogues in Fustat and Cairo," he stated. "No Jew should be permitted to conduct business with them or, eat or drink with them, or sit down within four cubits with them, or participate in their celebrations or mourning. Should the two miscreants repent, they must return to the Gentile authorities and be divorced, appear in a Jewish court and be punished, and then undertake by solemn oath in the presence of the sacred Torah scroll of the law never to repeat the sin. However, if the man and woman remain recalcitrant, the ban should be publicised throughout the Jewish community of Egypt. For we cannot be remiss in the face of an evil act of this magnitude, the lifting up of a hand in rebellion and the open repudiation of Moses, our teacher, and his perfect Torah."

The response to this ruling was that it was excessively harsh, but Moses remained adamant. He was unforgiving because of the clear commandment that members of the priestly caste were identified by God as being pure and without blemish. The concept of marrying a previously married woman, who was therefore not a virgin, was strictly forbidden and in direct noncompliance to God's affirmed wish. Moses explained that individuals involved must receive harsh, uncompromising punishment.

Conversely, he developed a reputation as a most caring community leader in his approach to the problem of Jewish hostages. Many Jews were being held in captivity following various battles, mainly against Christian aggressors, although some had also been abducted by pirates on the high seas. They were held as hostages, and ransom demands were commonplace. Moses set about raising funds to buy the captive Jews back and return them to their families. The cost, however, was enormous, with a rate of one hundred gold pieces for every three Jews. He wrote numerous letters to all the community leaders throughout Egypt, set up action committees, and laid down guidelines for exchanges. His personal appeal and involvement proved successful beyond everyone's expectations.

He was far less effective, unfortunately, in his attempts to bring together the disparate Jewish religious factions. Because of his prestige and status, he was asked to adjudicate in an intransigent communal problem, the rift between the descendants of the Babylonian Jews and the Jews of Palestinian origin. Both groups were firmly established in Fustat.

"We have a problem." A senior representative of the Babylonian Jewish community approached Moses at the end of a morning service. "You know that we have different customs from the Palestinian Jews, and you have seen the difficulties this can cause." He was referring to a dispute that had arisen regarding the order of synagogue services.

"Surely it is far more sensible for the cycle of Torah readings to be one year instead of the three years required by the Palestinian Jews."

Moses remembered painfully his failure to reconcile the Orthodox and Karaiti Jews in Alexandria, so he approached this latest communal dispute warily. After significant consideration, he agreed that a one-year cycle was preferable to a three-year cycle and quoted Talmudic sources to support his opinion. He mobilised all his powers of persuasion, but the representatives of the Palestinian Jews would not be moved. The three-year cycle for the Palestinian Jews was to remain. Moses had learnt from his previous experience in Alexandria and provided his judgement in such a way that he avoided offence to either side.

"Moshe, Rachel confided in me about a worry she has with David." Moses could see that Jamilah was troubled. "She tells me that David intends to travel to India to sell jewels to his customers there. He says he must do this personally to get the best deal and because of the value of the gems. It is a hazardous journey. The seas are dangerous. She is filled with anguish and foreboding."

Moses was aware that Rachel was worried about David's impending trip to India. His business enterprise had expanded, and he had acquired a reputation for honesty and ethical behaviour as a trader in gems in Fez and Alexandria—and this was known in Fustat. He had told Moses of his extensive trading deals with merchants in India, his main customer base being amongst Muslims, where the precious stones were in demand. But many ships had been shipwrecked on the journey to India, and pirates were known to be active on the high seas.

"Dear Jamilah, my love for David is boundless. I also have concerns about the dangers of travel to India. I will speak to him. I will try to dissuade him from this dangerous travel." However, Moses was not sure he could deter him. David had already mentioned that he had established a major commercial deal with traders in India which he was reluctant to abandon. He would, nevertheless, speak to David again at the earliest opportunity, but currently his mind was occupied with a serious matter involving the Jews of Yemen.

19

Rabbi Shlomo Hakohen in Yemen was deeply distressed by the situation. He addressed his fellow rabbis at a rapidly convened special meeting in the large community centre.

"We must find a leader who can convince the community to resist the proselytisers and remain within the faith. We must destroy this ridiculous false messiah and his nonsense views," Rabbi Shlomo Hakohen argued vehemently to his council.

Many Yemenite Jews had converted to Islam out of terror and others because they had little religious background or interest in Judaism and were poorly educated. There was a prevalent feeling amongst the Yemenite Jews that Muhammad had brought a new religion which represented a suitable replacement for Judaism, which they considered had let them down. To make the situation even worse, many Jews volunteered to proselytise for Islam. One such individual was particularly vociferous and regarded himself as a forerunner of the Messiah. He claimed to have the power to perform miracles and actively encouraged conversion.

"We agree with you, Shlomo, but where are we going to find such a person?" replied Rabbi Judah.

Rabbi Shlomo recounted his conversation with Moses in Fustat when he'd attended a teaching session. He reminded the council of Moses's epistle to the Jews of Fez which was so beneficial in providing comfort and assistance. He argued that Rabbi Moses could also help in the desperate situation now unfolding in Yemen. Surely it was worth an approach to him. The proposal was discussed in detail by the council and resulted in unanimous approval. Rabbi Shlomo arranged to meet with Rabbi Yaacov ben Nesanel Alfayumi, the senior and most respected leader of the Yemenite Jews, to get his agreement for an approach to Moses.

"Rabbi Alfayumi, dear respected colleague, I have been impressed by the writings of Rabbi Moses ben Maimon in Fustat. You will be familiar with his *Commentary on the Mishna*. He also assisted the Jews in Fez when they were faced with a similar situation to ours regarding forced conversion. He wrote to the Fez community and provided a comforting response which was a great help to them. Do you think we should approach him to provide comfort and reassurance to our own distressed community? Would this be worthwhile?"

"My dear Shlomo, I am willing to try anything that might comfort our people," Rabbi Alfayumi responded. "I know of Rabbi Moshe's reputation and his undoubted erudition. I am familiar with his *Commentary*. I think your suggestion is excellent. And since I am uncertain what to do myself, I will make an immediate request to him."

As Moses sat at his desk and read the letter, his thoughts turned to the depressing military situation which had developed in the Yemen. The reign of the Sunni Muslims had been attained throughout the Arab world except in Yemen, where the Shiite Muslims still ruled. Unlike the Sunnis, the Shiites were far less tolerant of other faiths and considered Christians and Jews to be infidels and not deserving of life amongst the true believers. They were vicious towards the Jewish population and held them under oppression in a similar fashion to the Almohads in Spain. Moses was only too aware of the persecution in offering the Yemeni Jews conversion to Islam or death.

Moses read the letter with mounting sorrow.

"We are suffering so much. The people are losing faith. We must have some hope, some consolation. I believe God is testing us," Rabbi Alfayumi wrote. "The grief has shattered our hearts, and the apostasy is destroying our lives. What is more, a false messiah is leading our people astray. We seek your assistance and draw on your brilliance to restore our faith and hope."

Moses walked to the balcony and stared at the scene in front of him, people actively pursuing their business or leisure, free to do so, unlike the situation in Yemen. He would, of course, assist but was aware that in responding to the request, his reply inevitably would be critical of the persecution by the Shiites and hence result in potential danger to him and his family. However, he considered that it was a risk worth taking if his intervention could benefit the suffering Jews of Yemen.

As Moses reflected on what to do, Jamilah came onto the balcony to join him. He was pleased. He would confide in her as he had done previously. She was so sensible and always reassuring. As he explained the request he had received, he held her hands and then gave her a spontaneous loving embrace.

"My dear Moshe, only you can make the decision, but should you decide to write an appropriate response, it will have my total support since I believe it to be the correct decision even if there are dangers. The Almighty has given you the ability and power to help fellow Jews, so you must always accept the challenges whatever the consequences."

Moses found solace, once again, in his wife's wise countenance. How fortunate he was to have married Jamilah. How much he respected her. He would respond. He knew that the request had been instigated by Rabbi Shlomo, whom he regarded as a scholar of repute. This was an additional incentive for him to acquiesce to the request.

He carefully considered his written response and decided to address it not only to the Yemenite people but more generally to all who were living in torment under oppression. He entitled the response "Iggeret Teman", "Letter to Yemen", and "Petah Tikvah", "Gate of hope". He was anxious that his message would be understood by the entire community, men, women, and children. He therefore wrote in Arabic and in a style that was simple to follow, even by people not familiar with the sources of Torah and Talmud upon which it was based.

It was late Moses sighed, rubbed his eyes, and gazed out the window into the darkness of night. He yawned, got up from his desk, and went to bed, falling into a deep sleep. When he awoke the next morning, he ate a light breakfast, told his wife that the process was going well, and returned to work. He wrote:

> Our brothers, scholars, all the disciples of the communities in Yemen, be assured, my brethren, that our three opponents, namely, the system of coercion, that of sophistry, and that which seeks to impress a high origin to which it is not entitled, will vanish. They may continue to prosper for a certain time, but their glory will shortly disappear.

> Our brethren of the house of Israel, scattered to the remote regions of the globe, it is your duty to strengthen one another, the older the younger, the few the many. ... My brethren, it behoves us to keep ever present before our minds the great day of Sinai, for the Lord has forbidden us ever to forget it. Rear your offspring in a thorough understanding of that all-important event. Explain before large assemblies the principles it involves. Show that it is a lucid

mirror reflecting the truth, aye, the very
pivot on which our religion turns. ... Know,
moreover, you who are born in this covenant
and reared in the belief, that the stupendous
occurrence ... stands alone in the annals of
mankind. For a whole people heard the word
of God, and saw the glory of Divinity. From
this lasting memory we must draw our power
to strengthen our faith in times of persecution.

He stood up for a break and walked to the nearby park,
continuing to order his thoughts. He needed to emphasise that a
campaign of apostasy against the Jews should not decrease their
faith in God.

We were promised by God via Yeshayahu that
whoever tries to overcome our Torah, whether
by force or by argument, will be vanquished.
"Every weapon made against you will not
succeed, and whatever tongue rises against you
shall be condemned" (Yeshayahu 54:17).

There has never been a time that did not have
a new persecution and trouble; and afterwards,
God has always removed it.

He decided to document examples of persecutions which
were subsequently overcome, to provide reassuring evidence.

During the second Temple period, the
evil Greeks pronounced terrible decrees of
persecution against the Jews in order to wipe
out the knowledge of Torah. They forced Jews
to desecrate the Sabbath, not circumcise their

children and to write on their clothing and carve on the horns of their cows that they have no portion in the God of Israel. This continued for fifty-two years. And then God destroyed their Kingdom and laws altogether. God already promised Jacob that even though other nations may subjugate the Jews, the Jews will always remain. He promised that He will not reject us all, even if we rebel and transgress His mitzvos.

He included a harsh judgement on the Islamic nation with its rigid legislation.

Never has a people arisen against Israel more hurtful than it, nor one which went so far to debase and humiliate us and to instil hatred toward us as they have.

He argued the fallacy and inadequacy of the false messiah who had tried to convince the Jews that Islam had replaced Judaism as the true religion.

The man is more madman than fraud. He should be put away. In that manner the people will be saved from persecution and peace and harmony will be restored to the community.

Moses requested at the end of the letter that it be copied and distributed widely to all the scattered communities in Yemen. That is why it was not specifically addressed to Rabbi Alfayumi, but to "our brothers, scholars and communities of the Yemen". He was anxious for it to have the maximum impact, "in order to strengthen the people in their faith and put them on their feet".

He wanted the content to be read "in public gatherings and in private, and you will thus become a public benefactor".

He was also adamant that it should not be seen by non-Jews lest it result in severe retribution. The letter took several days to complete, during which time Moses separated himself from all distraction and worked into the early hours of each morning by the light of a brass lantern. He signed the letter and handed it to his trusted messenger, who hid it carefully and then travelled to the Red Sea by caravan and sailed southward to Yemen.

The letter reached Rabbi Alfayumi two weeks later. He read it carefully and was impressed. He would do as Rabbi Moses requested. It would be copied and distributed to communities throughout Yemen.

The effect was dramatic. Wherever Jews met, the only topic of discussion was the letter. It became apparent to Rabbi Alfayumi that the underlying objective was being met. The detailed references and quotations from biblical events added greatly to the positive response and provided relief and comfort to the suffering people of Yemen.

"Only a man of great knowledge and understanding could have constructed such an epistle," Rabbi Alfayumi told Rabbi Shlomo.

"I and the Jews of Yemen are grateful to you, Shlomo. It was at your suggestion that I wrote to Moshe."

The people overcame their fears and trepidation. It was no longer considered improper to undergo pseudo-conversion if it provided safety. The community was prepared to wait patiently, renewed in their faith that the ancient bond between Israel and God would be maintained and strengthened and that their oppressors would soon be vanquished. They ignored and ridiculed the rantings of the deranged false messiah, who was forced to leave Yemen.

One year later Saladin's brother, Turhan Shah, invaded Yemen and took control of the government. Because of his long-standing admiration of Jewish culture, his first act was to liberate the Jews from their difficulties and provide them with the same freedoms that existed in Egypt. Moses's letter had proved prophetic. He was revered throughout Yemen for his spiritual rescue of a despairing people. A special prayer in which his name is mentioned was inserted into the Yemeni daily religious service.

20

Rachel and her maid prepared a most delicious Sabbath meal for the entire family. Candles were lit by Rachel, whilst David held Shoshanah, and separate ones were lit by Jamilah. They were all dressed in their finest clothes, as was traditional on the Sabbath. Moses felt a warm glow as he always did whenever the traditional Sabbath songs were sung. The main course was chicken with rice and vegetables, followed by a variety of succulent fruits.

"Your reputation has spread far and wide. The epistle to the Jews of Yemen and your *Commentary* have established you as a true leader as well as a *talmid chacham*." Moses looked self-conscious, but David was delighted to praise his brother.

"My dear brother, without your support, which allows me to pursue these activities, nothing would have been possible. It is you who deserve the praise as much as I," he responded with appreciation and gratitude.

"Did you hear what happened to the false messiah in Yemen?" David asked rhetorically. "He was apprehended by the Arab authorities and asked to prove that he was a messiah. The man said that his head should be cut off and claimed that it would immediately be reinstated on his neck and he would survive. His wishes were followed, and that is the end of the story."

Moses was uncomfortable. "I am sorry this occurred. The poor man was obviously mentally deranged and needed help. It is sad that he died in this fashion." He remembered the fate of his friend Yaacov in Rabbi Migash's yeshiva in Lucena. Yaacov had suffered from mental problems and had killed himself. Moses was convinced that recognition of such afflictions and providing support was required, rather than ignoring or condemning the unfortunate person. "It is an illness. His mind was diseased. Sympathy for his mental plight was more appropriate." The family were silenced. Moses was correct.

The silence was broken by David, who decided that this was a good opportunity to raise his proposed business plans with the family.

"Up to the present I have conducted my business from Fustat, with occasional journeys to North Africa and to places in Egypt. This has been successful as far as it goes, but now a very special opportunity has arisen which I cannot ignore." Moses listened quietly but was worried.

"I need to travel to Bombay in India for an important business venture." There was silence again.

"I am in possession of some very valuable gems which will provide significant profit not only for us but also for several local merchants who have entrusted them to me and invested in the venture," he continued. "I need to complete the deal with the buyers in India personally. I have no choice."

David had previously informed Moses, in confidence, that he had invested his entire capital in the venture, so there was a major financial incentive for him to personally deliver the gems. He did not mention this to Rachel to limit the concern, which was already considerable by the thought of the sea journey alone.

"My dear brother, we love you dearly, and your safety is more precious to us than all the gems in the world." David could see that his brother was expressing all their emotions. "The Lord alone knows the anguish and heaviness in my heart when parting from you. I see you are determined to go, and all the arguments I can make will not change your mind. May the Lord guard you from harm and reunite us in Egypt, if the Lord so wills."

David embraced his brother, and they kissed cheeks with affection. He recognised that his brother loved him dearly and could not disguise his anxiety. There was no more to say. Rachel accepted the decision whilst hugging Shoshanah even more tightly than normal.

The thought of David travelling to India by sea distracted Moses from his work on the *Mishneh Torah*. His concentration lapsed whenever he thought about David's proposed journey, which had an inevitable degree of risk. He knew that David could not be persuaded to abandon the venture because of the huge investment involved. Moses could only pray to the Almighty and hope for a smooth passage.

Moses decided that the *Mishneh Torah* should be written primarily as a legalistic work but should also contain philosophical theology, ethical concepts, and even medical concepts. He planned to group the laws under rubrics such as the laws of Sabbath, the laws of the tabernacle, the laws of civil damages, the laws of the murderer, and so on. He was confident, because of his knowledge and understanding of the sources, that he could combine all the relevant literature into a comprehensive format, but he was under no illusion. It would take many years to complete.

Another matter which was occupying his thoughts was the news that Jamilah was pregnant. He was, of course, pleased, but he realised how unprepared he was to have a child. He would need to rely upon Jamilah for the child's upbringing but had no worries in that regard. Marriage to Jamilah had exceeded all his expectations. She was an ideal wife. She displayed thoughtful independence and would argue with and contradict her husband when she felt it appropriate, but she absolutely understood all his requirements. She was modest and intelligent and engendered universal admiration and respect. Jamilah devoted her life to ensuring her husband was comfortable and satisfied. She supported his long hours of work and made herself available whenever required. He knew how delighted she was at the prospect of being a mother. She had prepared herself accordingly.

Moses's reputation and responsibility as a community leader in Fustat was widely acknowledged and appreciated. As a result, and with acclamation, he was appointed Ra'is al-Yahud, the leader of the Jews. He was also appointed chief rabbi of the Jews of Fustat and Cairo, with the honorary title of *ha-Rav ha-gadol*, or Great Rabbi. He was often referred to as Rabbi Moses Maimonides.

David had listened carefully and understood the warnings given by his family and business colleagues regarding travel in the Indian Ocean. But he was troubled. The deal that he had negotiated was tortuous and involved risk, but the financial rewards would be considerable, more than adequate to secure a long-term future for all his family. He had committed his entire wealth and funds invested by others to purchase a large quantity of rubies, sapphires, and emeralds of the highest quality and purity at a generous price from a dealer who had fallen on bad times. David felt a degree of guilt lest it be considered that he had taken unfair advantage of the dealer's misfortune, but he was reassured by the dealer, who was happy with the agreed price, and thanked him sincerely. David did not try to bargain for a lower price and as usual acted responsibly and ethically.

He had a buyer for the gems in Bombay, an exceptionally wealthy Indian prince called Yuvraj Mishra. They had agreed on a price which would result in a handsome profit. However, in view of the significant value of the gems, David could not trust a courier to deliver them; he had to deliver them himself. He had no option; his entire assets were invested in the project.

It was now time to leave. He bade farewell to his wife and daughter. Rachel tried desperately to avoid shedding a tear, but she failed.

"Do not fret, my dear Rachel. The good Lord will protect me. My love and devotion to you and Shoshanah will be my strength during the journey." He then hesitated and seemed deep in thought before continuing.

"Please do not think badly of me. Keep Shoshanah safe ..." He could not continue.

Moses gave him a letter on parting. It read:

"May God be your trust and keep your foot from slipping. Peace, peace to the far and near. The exalted God knows the pain and sorrow in my heart because of the departure of my dear and most beloved brother. May God save me by allowing no harm to come to you, and may we again be together in Fustat, with God's help."

David had carefully hidden the gems in various locations on his clothes, sewn into inside pockets on his tunic and hidden in a belt.

He made his way by caravan to the city of Kus on the Nile, passing strips of green irrigated land where papyrus grew in thick profusion. From there it took seven days to reach the Sudanese port of Aydhab. The journey through the desert was arduous. The travellers were constantly vigilant and apprehensive. Bandits were known to roam in the area. In Aydhab David took the opportunity to send a letter to Moses. It read as follows:

"Do not worry. I have arrived in Aydhab. I have endured much in the desert yet have been saved. It appeared to me that it would be a comparatively easy matter to set sail. I will be sailing on the Malabar Sea. Who saved me from the desert will save me while I am on the sea. Please calm the heart of my wife. Do not frighten them, and do not let them despair, for crying to God over what has passed is a vain prayer. I am sure this letter will reach you at a time when I, with God's help, will have already sailed most of the way. But the counsel of God shall stand.

"Written on the twenty-second of Iyar, whilst on the point of leaving."

The journey to the west coast of India across the Indian Ocean took eleven days. The winds were favourable and the journey smooth with no major incident. The ship was large and held over a thousand passengers and crew. David was impressed by the efficient way the crew ran the ship. He decided not to fraternise with other passengers and kept his own counsel. The gems never left his person. On the eleventh day he was relieved to see mountains and landscape as they approached their destination.

Bombay, however, was not a city to his liking. The Silhara dynasty of Konkan ruled Bombay, and the predominant religion was Hinduism. David was astounded that idols were to be found everywhere. There was an elephant god and a monkey god, as well as many others. *How different from Judaism,* he thought. Bombay was oppressively hot and noisy with narrow streets full of impoverished and destitute men, women, and children. Beggars with horrific physical malformations were to be found everywhere. Cows roamed the streets and shared accommodation with the people.

In the centre of Bombay was the impressive Walkeshwar Temple, which had been built in the tenth century from marble and was massive. Yuvraj Mishra arranged to meet David at his warehouse near the temple. When David arrived, he was greeted warmly. Yuvraj was tall and handsome with a neatly cut beard. His dress was impressively flamboyant with golden brocade covering his achkan (a long coat to the knees) and traditional churidars (tight-fitting trousers). The two men exchanged pleasantries through an Arab-speaking interpreter and ate a simple meal of rice and figs. David handed over the gems, which were closely inspected by an expert gemmologist, who was able to confirm their authenticity. Both David and Yuvraj seemed happy with the purchase, and the agreed amount of Egyptian gold dinars of recognised quality and minting were handed over to David. The two shook hands.

"You must be careful in handling such a large amount of money in Bombay." Yuvraj was concerned. "I will arrange for one of my men to act as a bodyguard, and I have organised accommodation for you until your ship sails."

"You are most kind. It has been a pleasure to conduct business with you in such a gentlemanly fashion," responded a relieved David, who indeed had anxiety about his security.

He had booked passage on a ship due to leave two days later and would not venture from his accommodation until the ship sailed. The gold dinars were hidden in two wallets attached to a belt around his waist beneath loose-fitting clothes.

He boarded the ship carefully and made his way to the confined accommodation. They set sail at the appointed time, and the weather was fair with a pleasant breeze. The first four days at sea continued to be calm, and David was at last able to relax. The deal had been completed satisfactorily, and he was on his way home. He had missed his family and looked forward to being with Rachel again and playing with Shoshanah. He realised that he had been tense and anxious for many months before the journey as he contemplated the enormity of the task ahead of him and the recognised dangers of travel in the Indian Ocean. Moses would be especially pleased to see him. He was so proud of the achievements of his brother and loved him dearly.

The first suspicion David had that things were not quite right was whilst he was lying on his hammock reading psalms that Moses suggested he recite on the journey home. The hammock began to swing from side to side, and he heard a cacophony of noise from the deck above. He rushed to the deck and was immediately aware of concern amongst the crew.

"There is a gale approaching!" shouted one of the sailors. The captain was bellowing orders as the wind gained rapidly in intensity and the huge sails became unmanageable. It began to rain. Passengers were rushing around in chaotic fashion. David was fearful as he recognised that the crew were unable to control the sails. The ship heaved from side to side as the wind and waves battered the timbers.

Before long the situation became untenable. The rain had intensified, and thunder and lightning were heard and seen. Waves smashed over the deck. There was no remission. The storm persisted. The rain lashed down. Although no seaman, David feared the worst as he witnessed a nearby passenger become engulfed in a wave and be unceremoniously swept overboard.

"Jettison the cargo!" screamed the captain. The sailors attempted to follow his order, but it was too late. The ship lurched from side to side. Huge waves pounded the deck relentlessly. The main mast creaked and, after a short time, cracked and collapsed. The ship began to list to the port side. David uttered prayers and accepted his fate. His family had been right. The risk had been too great.

"I am so sorry. I am so sorry," he whispered to himself repeatedly as images of Rachel, Shoshanah, and Moses flashed through his mind.

He prayed: "Hear, O Israel, the Lord our God, the Lord is one."

The worst fears of his family were about to be realised. Within thirty minutes the ship overturned and slowly sank beneath the colossal waves. David managed to grab a plank of wood and held on to it for several minutes but to no avail. The suction effect of the sinking ship dragged him away from the wood, and he descended into the darkness below. He never surfaced. He was never seen again. There were no survivors.

The message with news of the tragedy was relayed to the family by a merchant who had heard of the shipwreck from a colleague in Aydhab. The family also received a letter of condolence from Yuvraj Mishra.

The period of mourning became a community affair. People flooded into the house, offering heartfelt condolences. The entire community took a day off work to attend the funeral. Rachel was overcome with grief and sought comfort by holding and playing constantly with Shoshanah, who, although still a toddler, seemed to understand the solemnity of the situation.

Moses lay in bed. He was still deep in depression and inconsolable. He hardly ever left the house. It had been almost five months since the tragedy and still he was unable to come to terms with the shipwreck. He could not work. However hard he tried, he found it impossible to write or deal with any of his community work. In addition, he developed recurrent fevers and a rash which covered his whole body. Jamilah was dismayed and fearful for her husband. She cooked nutritious food, provided unstinting support, and was always available whenever he wished to talk or ask for comfort. The strain, however, was enormous, especially since her pregnancy was limiting her activity and ability to cope.

As she approached the end of the pregnancy, she noticed a distinct change: she was perturbed. The baby had previously been active, but now Jamilah was unable to feel any movements. She discussed her worries with Rachel, who tried to hide her concern. The midwife was called. The baby was due in two weeks, but the midwife could not disguise her foreboding. She was sure that the child was no longer alive. It had died in the womb; that was the only plausible explanation for the lack of movement. Alas, this proved to be correct. The baby girl was stillborn. She had died in utero due to significant congenital deformities of the head and limbs. Jamilah cried, but not in front of Moses. The tragedy was yet another source of grief for Moses. However, it was also the catalyst for him to overcome his grieving for David. He decided that he must comfort Jamilah. He must return to his normal self. He was being selfish. His brother would not have wished for his health to suffer like this. David was always so proud of his achievements and supported him. For David's sake he must now return to normality and fulfil his ambitions.

"My dear Jamilah, I have thrown off my depression. I thank you for your support. Do not worry. We will have children," he reassured her.

Moses was worried lest his infirmity and David's death had contributed to the stillbirth, but he reasoned that this was not so. The dreadful congenital malformations must have occurred much earlier, before David had left on his travels.

"Moshe, our daughter could not have survived even if she had been born alive. We must not blame ourselves. If it had been God's will, we would have had a healthy child. We must return to our normal life." Jamilah smiled, and Moses felt a huge weight had been lifted from him. Jamilah was so rational and wise.

Moses began to show visible improvement. He regained some of the weight he had lost, the skin rash resolved, his sunken eyes filled out, and his mental state improved.

A priority for Moses was to deal with a pressing practical matter that had been disregarded since his brother's death but now needed to be resolved. The family were financially bereft. All their assets, apart from a few small gems that Rachel had kept, were lost when the ship went down in the Indian Ocean. The community had assisted in the interim in a most generous fashion, but now a long-term solution had to be found. Moses was responsible for both Rachel and Shoshanah and a servant whom David had employed to assist Rachel, as well as Jamilah. He was incapable of restoring David's business since his knowledge of gems was minimal. He refused to be paid for being a rabbi or for teaching Torah. He had made this abundantly clear previously. The very concept was an anathema to him. He obstinately refused to use the Torah as a spade.

There was one obvious solution. He had studied medicine and was a doctor, having completed his studies at the Karaouine institute in Fez. He had continued to read medical literature whenever he had the opportunity to do so and knew he was up to date. He would set up a medical practice and become an active physician. Provided he attracted a large enough patient base, he should be able to earn a good living and support his extended family. This activity would also deflect his thoughts from his beloved David and lost child. But he was also aware of the pressing need to work on the *Mishneh Torah*, which he felt must not be ignored.

Moses felt a psychological necessity to document his feelings about David before he could achieve closure of the tragic event and fully return to a normal life. After much deliberation, he decided to write to his friend and colleague Rabbi Yaffes in Acre. He wrote as follows:

> In Egypt the most terrible blow befell me, a blow which caused me more grief than anything I have experienced in my life: the death of the most perfect and righteous man who died whilst travelling in the Indian Ocean, and with him was lost considerable money belonging to me, himself, and others. He left me his widow and a little daughter to take care of.
>
> For many months after I received the sad news, I lay on my bed struggling with fever and despair. I still mourn him for there is no consolation. What can console me? He grew up on my knee; he was my brother, my pupil. He was engaged in business and earned money that I might stay at home and continue my studies. He was learned in the Talmud and in the Bible and was an accomplished grammarian. My one joy was to see him. Now my joy has been

changed into darkness. He has gone to his eternal home and left me prostrated in a strange land. Whenever I come across his handwriting or one of his books, my heart grows faint within me and my grief reawakens. Were not the study of the Torah my delight and did not the study of philosophy divert me from grief, I should have succumbed in my affliction.

21

Moses had seen several patients during the day and had been to the palace to hear the decision against Zuta. He was walking back to the synagogue for an appointment, deep in thought. Could he cope with another influential and prestigious responsibility? Would the additional work be too much of a strain? What would Jamilah think? So many matters to consider.

Undoubtedly it was the political situation in Egypt that had indirectly led to el-Fadil's appointment as vizier and therefore Moses's own change of circumstances. He pondered on the remarkable series of events that had occurred.

Saladin was caliph but was still subservient to the rule of Nureddin in Syria. Saladin wanted independence, but Nureddin had no intention of allowing this; he planned to take charge of Egypt himself. However, unexpectedly but to Saladin's great delight, Nureddin died suddenly from a mysterious illness. King Amalric of Jerusalem had seen this as a wonderful chance to annex Syria to Jerusalem and then move on to attack Egypt.

Whilst this was being planned, another remarkable event took place. King Amalric also died suddenly, also from an unexplained and mysterious illness. Civil war was about to break out in Syria, and Saladin saw his opportunity. With his superior forces, he successfully attacked Syria and declared himself king of both Egypt and Syria. Saladin had become, in a remarkably short period, the dominant force in the area and ruled a vast kingdom unopposed. He moved his capital to Cairo and appointed Al-Qadi el-Fadil as his vizier in Fustat.

This had important consequences regarding the position of nagid, the Jewish leader in Egypt. An unscrupulous man named Yahua Zuta held the position of nagid but used his power to bribe, to corrupt, and to obtain great personal wealth. He was not trusted and was unpopular amongst the Jewish community. Moses as chief rabbi opposed Zuta and joined a delegation of senior colleagues to petition el-Fadil for his removal as nagid. El-Fadil was pleased; unlike his predecessor, he disliked Zuta intensely. El-Fadil was aware that Zuta was nagid only because his predecessor had willingly accepted bribes, which enabled Zuta to keep the position. El-Fadil could not be corrupted in this way. He prided himself on honesty and integrity.

Moses had presented the case against Zuta in el-Fadil's reception chamber in the inner court of the eastern palace, which was close to the communal entrance. The palace contained over one thousand rooms. There was an outer court surrounded by colonnaded porticoes, paved with marble of various colours, and set off with gold. In the centre of the courtyard, a fountain poured water into canals and pools.

El-Fadil listened carefully to the arguments presented and agreed to consider the matter. Three days later Moses was summoned back to receive the decision. Zuta was brought before el-Fadil. Moses sat with other senior rabbis at the back of the chamber and listened intently to the deliberation.

"The chief rabbi of Fustat claims that you are corrupt and that the Jewish community no longer desire you to continue as nagid." El-Fadil seemed pleased to be giving his ruling. "I have considered the matter in great depth. I accept the allegations. You are therefore summarily dismissed from the post."

Zuta looked askance. "Your Excellency, this is most unfair. Have you taken into consideration the contribution that I make each year to the royal coffers?" Zuta was referring to the bribes that he paid annually to keep the post of nagid, money that was illegally removed from the hardship fund designed for distribution to the impoverished Jews in Fustat.

El-Fadil looked incensed. "It is no surprise to me that the Jews no longer wish you to serve as nagid," he replied with obvious anger. "You are dangerous, unscrupulous, and untrustworthy. I have given my ruling; I will repeat it: you are formally stripped of the title of nagid. You are dismissed."

Zuta was crestfallen. He left the chamber looking menacingly at Moses. He was furious. Moses made a conscious decision to be wary of Zuta in the future.

As a consequence of Moses's community work resulting in the release of Jewish hostages and his reputation as a scholar and chief rabbi, the community unanimously recommended to el-Fadil that he, Moses ben Maimon, be appointed as the new nagid. El-Fadil had no hesitation in agreeing and in offering him the title.

Moses was close to the synagogue. He stopped. He sat in a nearby garden. He needed time to think. He needed to be certain that he could cope with three parallel strands to his life: his work as a physician to earn a living for his family, his work in writing the *Mishneh Torah*, and his work as chief rabbi and now nagid to the Jewish community. Individually each could be regarded as a full-time obligation, but all three at the same time ... Moses was undeterred. He reasoned that the harder he worked, the less likely he was to think about David and his deceased child. Work was important to him. It acted as a defence against depression. If Jamilah agreed, he would accept the post of nagid. He got up from the bench, left the garden, and returned home to speak to Jamilah. He wanted her opinion as soon as possible. His appointment in the synagogue could wait.

They sat together. Moses held Jamilah's hand as he described the offer that el-Fadil had made on the recommendation of the community. Did she approve?

"My dear husband, there is no one better suited to the post than you. I can see that you are excited. You look healthier and invigorated. I support you wholeheartedly. The good Lord has put his faith in your ability. You must accept." Jamilah appeared sincere and overjoyed.

"Jamilah, your encouragement is so important to me. It will provide the strength that I will surely require." Moses had anticipated that the support would be forthcoming but was pleased nonetheless. How fortunate he was to be married to Jamilah; he now realised how much he relied upon her.

He would accept the post of nagid.

As a physician, Moses was required to change aspects of his lifestyle if he was to become successful and earn a reasonable living, at least one adequate to support his extended family. Doctors wore a white cloak and white turban, and Moses dressed accordingly. He had obtained the necessary medical equipment, such as surgical tools, lancets for venepuncture, and a urinometer. In keeping with the health needs of the population, he was available for consultation day and night. His fees were adjusted to what he considered the patient could afford. He followed strict principles in his management of patients and disease based on his knowledge and experience, on evidence rather than anecdote, and on his adherence to Torah teaching.

Moses lingered outside the synagogue, his mind lost in all manner of thought. Like a butterfly, his thinking now flitted from a discussion he had just had with a distraught congregant concerned about his son's upcoming marriage, to a recent conversation he'd had with Joshua, a medical colleague and friend. They had been involved in an intense debate on the importance of achieving a diagnosis before treating a patient.

"I consider it important to treat disease according to the causes that bring it about," Moses had explained. "And a physician should treat not only the disease but also the patient who is suffering from it."

"I agree," Joshua had replied, "but the problem is that we do not know the cause of many diseases and so must treat only the symptoms."

"Unquestionably you make a good point, but a physician must be watchful and try to identify causes. For instance, I did not see any case of diabetes in the west, nor did any of the teachers under whom I had studied mention that they had seen any. However, here in Egypt I have seen many cases. This leads me to the conclusion that this illness is associated with a hot climate and the waters of the Nile because their sweetness may play a part."

Moses was keen to stress his belief that physicians should carefully observe and try to understand how and why diseases develop. In this way effective treatments can be administered in a logical fashion.

"Yes, but a patient is only interested in relief of symptoms whatever the cause. We must not be detracted by looking for causes. Just treat what worries the patient," Joshua responded.

"I beg to disagree. Medicine is a science, and we must be scientists to deal with disease. A cause should be sought and dealt with if possible. Then the symptoms will be relieved," Moses responded.

Moses practised medicine always conscious of the divine influence. He considered that everyone should strive to maintain their body in a healthy state since life is a gift from God and must be looked after. He expressed these views on illness in Hilchot De'ot ("Laws of humankind"). In a chapter in the *Mishneh Torah*, he wrote:

"Since when the body is healthy and sound, one directs oneself towards the ways of the Lord—it being impossible to know anything of the knowledge of the Creator when one is sick—it is obligatory on man to avoid things which are detrimental to the body and seek out things which fortify it."

His mind now clearer, Moses felt able to enter the synagogue to inform the council that he had accepted the post of nagid. He was confident that with Jamilah's support he could fulfil all his differing responsibilities. He was energised.

A worried mother dressed in pauper's clothes attended for a consultation with a scrawny child of about five years old who was crying pitifully and obviously in pain.

"Please help me. My child has been crying all night and has pain in his belly. He will not eat," she explained anxiously.

Moses examined the boy as his mother held him in her arms.

"The tummy is swollen due to colic," he explained. "You should feed him with barley gruel and barley soup. Also boil water and add fresh fennel and cinnamon. This will soothe and relax the bowels. He will recover, God willing, very soon."

The mother was relieved.

"Thank you so much." She took a few coins from the pocket of her torn robe and handed them to Moses.

"I hope this is enough. We have very little, and I have three other children to feed."

The few coins were of very little value. Moses thanked her. "It is sufficient."

"I would like to see him again in two days to check that he is better. No further payment will be necessary."

His next patient was a middle-aged Muslim woman who was a secretary to one of el-Fadil's wives. She was elegantly dressed and soft-spoken. Moses knew that her religion would not allow him to carry out an examination of her. He would need to take a detailed history of her complaint to make the diagnosis and be sure he was prescribing the correct treatment.

"I have problems with my excretion," she whispered with embarrassment.

Moses was gentle with his questioning and eventually understood the problem. She was constipated.

"You must soften the excretion by taking a mixture of rhubarb and tamarind," he advised. "You must have regular meals which include saffron seeds, sugar, and beets. You must eat vegetables mixed with sauce made from barley and good oil. Following each meal, suck on a quince, pear, or pomegranate."

When she returned to see him two weeks later, she was happy and grateful.

"I am much better. I thank you sincerely for your attention."

The following day Moses received an invitation from el-Fadil himself to visit the palace. He assumed the request was related to his work as the recently appointed nagid. When he arrived, he was immediately ushered into the inner court of the eastern palace, el-Fadil's residence.

"Please be seated, Rabbi." El-Fadil was alone and addressed him directly. "You recently treated the secretary to one of my wives, very successfully I understand."

Moses remained silent. He remembered the patient he was referring to but respected the importance of patient confidentiality.

"I have the same problem as she with my excretions." El-Fadil seemed in discomfort and was holding his abdomen.

"I have received advice from my court physicians, but their concoctions are of no benefit."

El-Fadil described his symptoms. They were not life-threatening but did cause him much discomfort and occasionally restricted his activity. Moses diagnosed constipation and prescribed the same treatment that he had given to his female patient. The outcome was equally successful. El-Fadil was delighted and grateful. He liked Moses and was impressed by his calm approach. He also knew him to be respected amongst the Jewish community and a man of integrity. It was el-Fadil who had appointed him as nagid, and now, in addition, he invited him to join his court physicians. Moses was delighted to accept. It would enhance his medical reputation, but more importantly the post attracted a generous annual salary.

El-Fadil was often underestimated because of his small stature and rather benign countenance. Despite this appearance, he was a highly intelligent, insightful, and powerful leader. He prided himself on being able to assess a person's character and on recognising falsehoods. He admired Moses, had agreed to his appointment as nagid, and now welcomed him into his court of personal physicians.

The relationship between el-Fadil and Moses was one of genuine mutual respect. El-Fadil, although a fiercely orthodox Sunni Muslim, had an enlightened understanding of other religions, especially Judaism, and this was the basis of the strong bond with Moses, whom he recognised as a brilliant scholar and a respected leader of the Jews.

El-Fadil had been an advisor to several Fatimid rulers before working for Saladin. However, his relationship with Saladin was by far the strongest, and Saladin trusted him absolutely. Saladin was rarely to be seen in Cairo since he was predominantly involved in campaigns in other countries or in opposing the crusader invasions. These successful exploits brought growth and prosperity to Egypt and especially to Cairo but meant that el-Fadil was left in charge of Cairo and Fustat for long periods and had complete authority for the administration of the government.

Both el-Fadil and Saladin were committed to education and built many libraries and madrasas, which provided free education, lectures, and courses of study. El-Fadil even founded one of these at his own expense. This was contrary to the activity of Saladin's eldest son, al-Afdal ibn Salah ad-Din, popularly known as al-Afdal, who had a post in government but was far more interested in his own personal comfort than in the welfare of the people.

Moses was privileged to be held in such high esteem by el-Fadil, which resulted in obvious benefits when representing the Jewish community.

22

Moses, sitting at his desk in the synagogue, was deeply immersed in a particularly difficult chapter in the *Mishneh*. The loud knock on the door was initially ignored. It took several seconds before he responded, so deep was his level of concentration.

"Enter!" he shouted with annoyance.

The messenger was flustered. "Revered sir, you must come straightaway. The midwife insists. Your wife is in labour."

It was a heart-warming surprise and relief that Jamilah's latest pregnancy, after almost ten years of marriage, seemed to be progressing well. She felt different this time and was convinced it would result in a successful birth. Prior to this she had experienced a disastrous obstetric history, including not only a stillbirth but also three miscarriages.

Both Moses, who was now fifty, and Jamilah had prayed fervently each day for a healthy baby and a smooth, safe delivery. Moses had insisted that Jamilah rest, and he refused to allow her to undertake any strenuous chores. A maidservant was available to provide constant assistance. Moses prescribed regular doses of fenugreek and garlic, which were known to be beneficial in reducing excess humours within the unborn child which were the cause of premature birth. The couple had worried throughout the pregnancy about the possibility of another stillbirth, but happily progress had been uneventful. Most importantly, Jamilah noted no diminution in strong movements towards the end.

"I believe God has listened to our prayers, Moses. This pregnancy feels right," she had told him. Jamilah was positive about the outcome.

"Yes, but you must continue to rest and eat healthy food as well as fenugreek. I too feel that God has blessed us." Moses looked pleased but knew that problems could still occur.

Moses, with the maidservant, ran to his house, arriving in time but breathless. The midwife and a local doctor were present. Moses waited patiently and anxiously outside the birthing room. He heard screams from Jamilah, and then silence. He feared the worst. And then he heard a baby crying. He was overcome with emotion. At the midwife's request he entered the delivery room and saw a smiling Jamilah holding their son. Jamilah had delivered a healthy boy. The midwife was relieved. Delivery of the afterbirth was accompanied by a flow of blood, which initially caused concern, but the haemorrhage ceased spontaneously.

"Baruch Hashem, Moses. My dear husband, we have been blessed." Jamilah smiled as she held the boy to her breast and he began to feed.

Moses prayed to the Almighty to express his thanks.

After the ritual circumcision, the baby was named Abraham ben Moshe. The ceremony was followed by celebratory drinks for the numerous guests. Moses delivered a passionate discourse on the covenant between God and the Jewish people.

Moses was determined to complete his *Mishneh Torah* despite his many conflicting responsibilities, but he struggled to find the time. He was aware of a gradual reduction in the energy and dynamism that he'd enjoyed before David's death. He suffered, even now, from bouts of lethargy and was depressed whenever he thought about his brother. Each day was filled with activity. He awoke at five o'clock each morning. After prayers, he began work on the *Mishneh Torah* and on replying to legal dilemmas sent to him from around the Jewish world. He answered each letter personally, refusing to have a secretary to assist. He feared that having a secretary might make him appear arrogant. He then began his medical work, seeing patients in his home, visiting the sick, and attending the *bimaristan* to treat urgent problems. He was also required to attend the sultan's palace each day as a court physician. He returned home for a brief supper in the late evening before continuing to write his *Mishneh Torah* until after midnight. In between, he found time to pray three times a day in the synagogue and to deal with congregants' questions.

The scope of the *Mishneh Torah* was so great that even Moses was plagued with doubt that he would ever complete it. He planned for the fourteen volumes to consist of eighty-six monographs divided into one thousand chapters. He wrote the text in Hebrew so that it could be read and understood by Jews everywhere. He included all that is found in the Talmud, the Sifra, the Sifre, and the Tosefta—interpretations, additions, and commentaries, as well as insertions from later leading rabbis. He organised the text in such a way that a reader would be able to go directly to any aspect of the oral law without having to negotiate the tortuous, disorganised commentaries which led to abstruse and often contradictory discourses. Fundamentally he wanted the *Mishneh Torah* to function as a complete legal system.

His work as nagid was also onerous, but he gained great satisfaction in serving the community as both the political and religious leader. He took these responsibilities seriously and was often approached to adjudicate on difficult matters. Even Jamilah brought to his attention a topic which she was concerned about: the issue of serious discrimination against women. This was a matter that he had never really considered. Women could not enjoy the same rights as men and were expected to conform to strict guidelines.

"My dear Jamilah, I will consider the matter and decide whether changes are possible. But any change in women's rights must conform to the requirements of Jewish law. I will especially review any examples of ill-treatment of women."

He was aware of gross injustices when unscrupulous men married women, took their property, and then deserted them. Many Jews from foreign countries married women in Egypt, removed their property, and returned to their first wives in their country of origin. Moses was appalled by this unacceptable behaviour and was determined to strictly regulate marriage. As nagid he had the opportunity and power to do this. He decreed that marriages and divorces could only be performed by an appointed judge. Also, a foreign Jew could only marry in Egypt if he swore on the Torah to the judge that he had not been married previously. Once married, if the foreign Jew had to leave the country, he was required to fill out a bill of divorcement, which became valid after an agreed deadline. These regulations had a big impact and prevented many women from facing a life of ruin.

Another innovative case ruling related to a disadvantaged woman but was considered so radical that it met with disapproval. The case involved an unmarried Jewish man who had bought a young Christian woman initially as a sexual slave and converted her to Judaism. Islamic law states that a Christian can only convert to Islam. A rather vindictive individual reported the matter to an Islamic court. In court, the young woman claimed that she was the daughter of a Jewish mother and was therefore Jewish herself, even though sold as a Christian. The Islamic court accepted that she was Jewish and referred the matter to Moses. He interviewed both the young woman and the young man.

"You will be aware that according to Jewish law you have lived illicitly together and therefore are forbidden to marry," Moses informed them.

"But we have lived together for several years and have a strong attachment and longing for each other. We wish now to marry according to Jewish law, revered sir," replied the dismayed young man.

Moses deliberated. Turning the young woman away would have serious emotional consequences and would be cruel and senseless. She had been a slave and had no family. What if she were pregnant? There would be a fatherless child. Moses decided that common sense and humanity were far more important in this situation than rigid adherence to the law. The young woman had not caused the situation; it was the man who was responsible—and he must learn to mend his ways. Moses called them back to deliver his judgement. He addressed his comments to the young man.

"You must learn to behave lawfully and to lead an orderly and correct Jewish life. I consider that this will be of greater benefit to you than a harsh punishment. You will immediately emancipate the young woman from slavery and marry her. You will follow the ways of the Lord and lead a respectful Jewish life. That is my judgement."

There was some disapproval of the verdict from rabbinical colleagues since it appeared contrary to Jewish law. The couple had lived illicitly together, which meant that they were, according to the strict letter of Halacha, forbidden to enter into holy marriage.

"I remind you of the words of the sages," Moses replied to anyone who expressed doubts about his carefully considered judgement. "Pay regard to God with both wisdom and humanity."

The community accepted the decision without further argument, illustrating the huge respect for the opinion of the nagid Moses. The judgement did not fade into history but served as a precedent for other women faced with a similar situation.

It was inevitable that Moses would face another confrontation with the Karaiti community. His responsum on Karaitism in

Alexandria had engendered resentment, and his controversial views were known in Fustat. He still refused to accept that Karaitis were authentic Jews. His edicts, however, were all designed to entice them into orthodox rabbinic Judaism rather than to punish or wage war against them. He was also determined to reduce the hardship that Karaiti women were expected to endure by their husbands. This matter was vividly illustrated to him one morning when a Karaiti woman attended his surgery for a consultation.

"How may I be permitted to help you?" Moses enquired.

"I am embarrassed. I am a Karaiti Jew, and my husband has forbidden me to seek advice from a doctor." She was reluctant to explain her problem, but Moses waited patiently.

"My husband says the Torah forbids it. In Exodus 15:26 it says, 'I am the Lord your God who healeth you.' Nobody but God can heal. But I need help. Please do not tell my husband I am seeing you."

"You need have no concern. I will tell no one. You have my promise."

She hesitated and then quietly related her symptoms with obvious embarrassment. She had recently delivered a child and, following the birth, developed pain in her left breast. The pain had become more intense, and the skin of the breast was now reddened.

Moses examined the breast and confirmed a tender red area around the nipple. An established treatment was cupping to remove the black humour which was responsible for the abnormal lactation. The great physician Albucasis, however, advocated a more radical approach involving cauterisation of the skin over the affected area. Moses considered these two therapeutic options.

"A physician should treat not only the disease but also the patient who is suffering from it." He remembered these words from one of his teachers in Fez. Cauterisation is painful and can be dangerous, and afterwards the woman would be incapable of breastfeeding for many weeks.

He muttered the words of Hippocrates to himself: "Primum non nocere. First do no harm." He would advise cupping.

"You have malodorous milk in your breast which must be removed," he explained. "It will be necessary to apply a cup to the area and to dress with honey and bean flour with added vinegar. Salt should be added to the dressing."

Moses applied a vacuum cup over the affected area on the breast for twenty minutes. The procedure was uncomfortable, but when the cup was released, there followed a flow of greenish-white milky fluid with an unpleasant pungent smell. The area was then dressed. The woman was relieved. The pain had diminished.

"I thank you, most respected doctor, for your attention."

This episode was one of many which convinced Moses that the Karaiti community must change their ways. He recognised that this could be most effectively achieved through the wives, who generally had less interest in the Karaiti religion than their husbands. He decided to introduce edicts which would be popular amongst the women irrespective of what their husbands believed.

With nine other scholars, Moses pronounced that women who followed the Karaiti rituals of purification after menstruation instead of the rabbinical ones were disobeying the rules set down by the sages of the Torah and should be divorced and lose the dowry they had brought to the marriage. This appealed to many women who much preferred changing the purification ritual rather than going through an unpleasant divorce and losing money. In addition, women began to realise how rabbinic law resulted in a much more comfortable lifestyle than Karaitism. Rabbinic Jews ate warm food on the Sabbath, were permitted to light a fire on the Sabbath to help a childbearing woman, were permitted to seek medical advice from a doctor, and were allowed to break the laws of the Sabbath whenever there was a danger to life. This had great appeal to the majority of Karaiti women, who began to persuade, even nag, their husbands to accept the rabbinical laws.

By using his powerful position as nagid, he was successful in encouraging many families to change to rabbinic Judaism. Moses, with the full support and encouragement of Jamilah, also lifted the rigid prohibitions on women who wished to work. Women with religious knowledge became teachers. Others were trained in crafts, especially embroidery. Indeed, Jamilah was an accomplished needlewoman and enjoyed making fancy clothes for Abraham.

Jamilah and Rachel were fortunate to enjoy a comfortable lifestyle, but this was not universal amongst many contemporary women, not so much because of their inequality to men but because they were treated as a separate group and not allowed social activity outside the confines of their homes. There was little communication between men and women. A man was only allowed to converse with female relatives.

Moses became one of the first letter writers to break the taboo of greeting a woman directly. When writing letters, he openly sent his regards and blessings to the woman of the house, a practise that was traditionally frowned upon. He insisted that women should be treated with honour and respect. They were not slaves, and their husbands did not own them. They had a right to property and divorce.

It was usually on Sabbath afternoons after the synagogue service that Moses and Jamilah found time to discuss family matters and happily play with Abraham.

"Moses, my elder brother, Uziel, wishes to marry and has asked whether we are aware of any suitable unmarried young women," remarked Jamilah.

"Your enquiry comes at a most propitious time," replied Moses as he stroked his beard thoughtfully. The question was posed at a time when Moses had been thinking about his sister,

Miriam, who was still living in Acre. To Moses's great surprise, she had recently contacted him with a request to visit. Miriam was still unmarried.

"Miriam will be visiting soon. I think she would be an ideal wife for your brother. But she has a passionately independent nature." He smiled as he remembered her determination to remain in Acre and how she was able to convince their father to allow her to stay. He wondered how she had managed whilst being alone in Acre. Miriam visited some weeks later. Moses was impressed to see how capable and mature his sister had become. However, she still maintained her fiercely independent personality.

Jamilah's brother, Uziel ben Halevi, was a delightful young man with a pleasant temperament who came from a respected rabbinic family. He had followed in the family tradition and had become a rabbi himself. He was reputedly highly knowledgeable. When Uziel and Miriam met, accompanied by Moses and Jamilah, they appeared at ease.

"I must thank you for introducing me to Uziel, dear brother. I thought I would resent it, but I do not. Your brother is most personable, Jamilah." Both Moses and Jamilah were relieved. Miriam's esteemed brother and Uziel's father approved of the marriage.

Miriam would need to leave Acre, but this would no longer be a disappointment to her. In recent months she had found life in Acre to be less appealing, especially as there was continuing friction between the Muslim and Christian communities which was impacting on the Jews.

Uziel was a rabbi but had also learnt a trade. He was a merchant dealing in flax. Flax had become the most important industrial crop of Egyptian agriculture and a leading export commodity. Uziel had worked as an apprentice to a flax dealer in Fustat and learnt all aspects of the production, distribution, and export of the material. Bales were exported mainly to

Tunisia, Sicily, and Spain. Uziel was in a profitable industry and would have no difficulty in providing for Miriam without needing to resort to his rabbinical background to earn a living. Moses was pleased.

23

As with his own father and his grandfather before him, Moses took personal responsibility for Abraham's Jewish education. As soon as the boy was four years old, and despite his enormous workload, Moses spent at least one hour each day teaching his son Torah and Talmud. It reminded him, rather embarrassingly, of his own teaching in Cordoba when his father grew increasingly frustrated with his lack of interest in learning and sent him to Rabbi Migash's yeshiva in Lucena. Abraham was different. He enjoyed learning and being with his father. In fact, during learning was the only time they were together. Abraham had a sharp mind and quickly grasped key principles.

Of all his medical work, the one aspect that Moses had most difficulty with was his work as a court physician. Each day he was required to carry out consultations within the palace and deal with problems that had arisen overnight. He was expected to see not only courtiers and palace workers but also senior staff, including wives and concubines. Occasionally there were also important visitors to the palace, such as Saladin himself and his retinue, and Saladin's oldest son, al-Afdal Nur al-Din Ali, a notorious playboy, much to the embarrassment of his father.

Moses's consultations with staff members were conducted in a room in the eastern palace; senior staff and the vizier's family were examined in the inner court close to el-Fadil's personal quarters.

It was still early morning when Moses arrived home from morning prayers. He was surprised to see a large carriage outside his house. A courtier dismounted from the carriage and appeared anxious and stressed.

"Aisha, the vizier's second wife, is ill. You must come immediately."

The palace had never previously requested medical attention in this dramatic fashion, which was an indication to Moses that the situation must be serious.

Moses knew Aisha. He had treated her previously for a minor ailment of no significance. She was highly intelligent and very beautiful. El-Fadil had married her six months previously in the hope that she would produce many children for him. She was junior to Palmira, who was now el-Fadil's senior wife because his favourite wife, Saniya, had died one year earlier from an unknown cause whilst pregnant. El-Fadil had been distraught by the tragedy. He had lost not only his favourite wife but also his unborn child. Palmira, on the other hand, was now past childbearing age, was overweight, was rather unattractive in appearance, and was not particularly desirable. El-Fadil had lost interest in her, which caused Palmira much anguish, and so he had acquired a much younger, attractive wife to compensate, Aisha.

Moses was taken in haste directly to Aisha's chamber to find her lying on a large, highly decorated four-poster bed surrounded by two court physicians and a retinue of agitated servants.

"These idiots do not know the cause of her malady." El-Fadil pointed to the physicians and was clearly displeased. "I have confidence in your ability, Maimonides. Please examine her." He looked directly at Moses, who towered above him. "I am relying upon your skills. Don't let me down." His words were accompanied by a harsh and uncompromising stare, which was totally out of character but indicated how worried he was.

"I will practise to the best of my ability," replied Moses. El-Fadil grunted and walked out with the two court physicians. One female servant remained as a chaperone.

Moses was worried by Aisha's overall appearance. She was pale, lethargic, and incapable of answering the questions Moses addressed to her.

"How long have you been unwell?"

"Do you have pain?"

No satisfactory response, and yet Moses knew she had previously been a healthy young woman.

He addressed the questions to the servant, Seema.

"She awoke this morning feeling unwell and tired. She did not want to eat. She was sick—pain in her head," stuttered the overwhelmed servant. "She was getting worse but would not let me get help," she added defensively. "I insisted and requested the doctor. I did my best."

Moses looked at Aisha carefully before examining her. She hardly stirred. Her eyes appeared vacant. She was unresponsive. The pulse was rapid. He tested the urine, which was of normal colour, and by tongue he tasted that it was neither sweet nor bitter.

"What did she eat last night? Could she have eaten food which upset her?" asked a bewildered Moses.

"She had her normal meal prepared by her cook," the servant answered, obviously stressed by the situation, wondering if she would be blamed for Aisha's illness.

Moses could think of no possible diagnosis. The situation was serious. Even as he was looking at Aisha, she was deteriorating. Perhaps he should bleed her. It might help, although his previous experience had suggested that when patients look pale and have a rapid pulse, removal of one or two bowls of blood seemed to make the situation worse. But he had to do something. El-Fadil was very fond of Aisha, and to let her fade away without doing anything active would not be accepted.

And then suddenly Moses noticed it. How could he have missed the indicative sign earlier? He remembered the lecture from Ibn Zuhr, his tutor in the Karaouine school in Fez.

He looked carefully at Aisha's eyes again. The eyelids were shut, but this time he raised the upper eyelids. Yes, he had been correct: her pupils were dilated. He lit a candle and placed the light in front of her. She tried to close the lids; the light obviously upset her. Another indicative sign, light sensitivity. The cause of her illness was now obvious to him. Aisha had been poisoned with belladonna, deadly nightshade. Speed was of the essence if she was to survive.

"Quick," he shouted earnestly, "get me a jug of hot water and dill leaves, also some oil. Hurry. This is an emergency!"

Moses nervously awaited Seema's return. *Hurry. Hurry.*

Seema rushed back into the room with the cook, who helped transport the boiled water. Moses allowed the water to cool before he mixed in the oil, crushed dill leaves, and divided stalks.

"She must drink this mixture. It will make her vomit." The concoction was a recognised emetic, particularly favoured for belladonna poisoning. The servant and Moses sat Aisha upright, and the solution was poured into her mouth. She swallowed most of it but spluttered.

They waited.

A bowl was placed beneath her chin by the servant. Within minutes she vomited and vomited and vomited.

She was given fresh milk and butter with honey. Again, she vomited—and vomited some more.

Moses waited until the vomiting ceased. Aisha was looking ashen grey, but her eyes opened. It was now time to administer the appropriate antidote. But which one? He carried three in his medical bag: the electuary of Mithridates, the asafoetida theriac of Razi, and the theriac of Ibn Zuhr. After some consideration he decided on the third option. The theriac consisting of fennel seeds, mugwort and mallow was mixed with water and administered to Aisha. She tolerated it. Moses knew the theriac would take time to be effective, so he patiently sat beside the bed and waited in silence. He thanked Seema for her assistance. Aisha seemed peaceful.

El-Fadil, followed by two courtiers, returned to the chamber. He looked at Aisha with obvious concern.

"Have you decided what is wrong?" he asked Moses in a polite manner.

"I have provided her with appropriate medication and am waiting to see whether it has been effective," replied Moses.

"But what ails her?" El-Fadil was respectful but still agitated.

"I believe she was suffering from poisoning with deadly nightshade. I have administered an antidote, and we await the response."

"What?! Poisoned?! Are you sure?" El-Fadil was shocked, his expression one of disbelief.

El-Fadil had always employed the services of a taster for himself but had never considered the need for tasters for his wives. His present taster had worked for him for over five years, with no ill effects, which was an indication of his popularity. The tasters were expected to sample all meals and drinks before el-Fadil consumed them.

"Who could possibly want to poison Aisha? She is so young and innocent," commented an incredulous el-Fadil.

Aisha stirred. She opened her eyes and smiled. Moses inspected her eyes. The pupils were no longer dilated. The theriac had worked. The antidote had cleared the belladonna from her body. She no longer looked ashen grey. She would survive. Moses was delighted with the outcome. It was the first case of poisoning he had been required to deal with, and he thanked God that his treatment had been effective. He made a mental note to write to

Ibn Zuhr, who would be pleased to hear that his theriac had been an effective antidote.

El-Fadil could see the improvement and thanked Moses with relief and sincerity. Moses, having provided Seema with further instructions for Aisha's care, left the palace feeling pleased with himself and returned home.

As soon as Moses left, el-Fadil's thoughts immediately turned to identifying the culprit. Somebody in the palace had tried to kill Aisha by administering the poison. But who? The perpetrator must be found and face the consequences. The responsibility for finding the individual was placed in the hands of el-Fadil's senior general, Saif ad-Din Ghazi. Saif was known to be ruthless, and his very presence was threatening. He would set about his task of finding the poisoner with characteristic enthusiasm. He was tall and muscular. He had a jagged scar down his left cheek which even his beard could not hide, a reminder of the many battles he had fought on behalf of Saladin before being appointed as a general in Fustat. If anybody could find the villain, it was Saif. He was given a free hand but was expected to have identified the individual within a month.

El-Fadil had other pressing matters to deal with. Saladin was on his way back to Fustat after a prolonged series of battles which had successfully resulted in Aleppo, Damascus, and Mosul being brought together to form the Ayyubid dynasty. Saladin was now able to formally proclaim a return of Sunni Islam to the whole of Egypt. But the financial cost had been great, and he required additional funds to be raised in Fustat to support his continuing ambitions and to defeat the crusaders.

El-Fadil had much work to do to ensure that Saladin's returning forces were appropriately honoured. There were ceremonies and lavish banquets to be arranged. He would be expected to organise fundraising as well as extract additional taxes. The latter would not be easy. He would need to leave the poisoning matter entirely in Saif's hands until Saladin had left Fustat.

Saladin and his army were welcomed with much pomp and ceremony. Flags were displayed, and the official trumpeters heralded a triumphant return through the city gates. Saladin was hugely popular. Thousands lined the streets to cheer his return. He arrived at the palace with his entourage. He enjoyed his visits to Fustat and had complete confidence in el-Fadil, whom he knew to be a good and reliable vizier in his absence.

At a banquet in his honour, Saladin complimented el-Fadil on his collection and management of taxes and explained to him his future strategy.

"How are your wives?" Saladin was conscious of the need to discuss family matters as well as business with el-Fadil.

"Palmira is my first wife following Saniya's death. Aisha is now well, but she nearly died following a poisoning. Fortunately, I have an excellent physician who spotted the problem and was able to administer an antidote which saved her life."

Saladin expressed great interest. "Have you found the culprit yet?"

"No, but I will. I have left Saif to investigate, and you know how thorough he can be," responded el-Fadil.

"I should meet this physician," suggested Saladin. "I am conscious of the large number of poisonous animal bites my soldiers are receiving in the field, and they are dying before an antidote can be found. I need advice on how to deal with the problem and which antidotes to take with us into battle. Do you think your physician could help by producing a field manual to tell what a bitten soldier should do in this situation?"

"I will insist that he does so. He is not only a physician but also a distinguished rabbi whom I appointed as nagid. His name is Moses Maimonides. You may have met him. He acts as physician to you and your son when you are in Fustat."

Moses was later approached by el-Fadil, who informed him

that the request for a written manual had come directly from Saladin himself. A refusal would not be tolerated. Moses had no choice and agreed to write the treatise despite all his other responsibilities. He began work on it immediately.

Saif's initial investigation involved the vizier's main kitchen, which supplied food to the inner court.

"Who is in charge here?" he bellowed to the cowering staff. Rumour had already reached the staff of a poisoning in the royal household, and they were expecting a visit and inspection. A nervous-looking Nubian man called Hamza stepped forward. He was even taller than Saif but much thinner. Hamza was bought as a slave from Nepata in Upper Nubia, but soon his culinary skills became recognised. He had worked his way up from a lowly cleaner in the kitchens to becoming the senior chef. His mother tongue was Nilo-Saharan, but he also spoke excellent Arabic.

"It is I, sir," he replied with a broad smile which was his normal countenance.

"Who is responsible for preparing the food for the vizier's wives?"

"I cook for the wives, but the concubines have separate arrangements."

"I am only interested in who prepares food for Aisha!" shouted an agitated Saif.

"I am proud to say that I am personally responsible for preparing all Aisha's food." Hamza showed no sign of concern.

"Do you have a helper?"

"Yes, sir. Raza is my apprentice," he replied, pointing to a young woman who appeared nervous. "She is an excellent cook and totally trustworthy."

Saif knew that often it was not the food that was poisoned but the wine, since the bitter taste is masked by the wine and the victim is unaware of a different flavour. Aisha was a strictly observant Muslim and would not take alcohol. However, grape juice could similarly mask the taste.

"Does Aisha drink grape juice with her meal?"

"Aisha enjoys grape juice with her evening meal, and I always take responsibility for pouring from the flagon."

"Who delivers the food to her?"

"Her personal servant, Seema, always takes the food from the kitchen directly to her."

"So, am I correct in saying that the only people who come in contact with the food and wine that Aisha consumes are you, Raza, and Seema?" Saif was pleased that he had reduced the possible suspects to three.

"It would seem so, but there are many cooks and workers who have access to the kitchens with deliveries and in waiting on other members of the royal household. Even Palmira herself often checks on the cooking," Hamza replied defensively.

"I would like to interview Raza and Seema individually. Make the arrangements for tomorrow morning." He left, followed by his officers.

Saif prided himself on judging a person's character and especially in recognising when lies were told. He doubted that the three were involved. They had no obvious motive and would have had little, if any, opportunity to administer the poison secretly, unless of course they were part of a conspiracy and all three were involved, but again he doubted this. Nonetheless, he would apply pressure to each of them individually in the morning after they'd had a night's sleep to reflect and to worry about what was in store for them.

The following morning Saif conducted an aggressive, threatening interview of each individually, in which he professed that he was certain of their guilt but promised them a reprieve if they confessed. However, all three protested their ignorance and seemed totally sincere. Saif believed them. But who else had access to Aisha's food other than these three? Ostensibly nobody.

Furthermore, the lack of any obvious motive worried him. They were lowly kitchen staff and would have no reason to try to poison a vizier's wife, unless they'd been paid by spies. But even so, what possible benefit could accrue for enemies of the state by the poisoning of Aisha?

Yet something was bothering Saif. He recollected the unexpected and unexplained death of Saniya, el-Fadil's senior wife, a year previously. The court physicians at the time were baffled and had assumed that the pregnancy had put too much of a strain on her heart and that she'd died because of this. Surely it was too much of a coincidence that Aisha also almost died from an unknown cause and survived only because Maimonides recognised the symptoms and signs of deadly nightshade poisoning.

Something else was troubling him. It was nagging at him—something that a member of the kitchen staff had mentioned, but he could not think what it was.

He made an appointment to meet el-Fadil to provide an update on the progress with his investigation thus far. He expected to be reprimanded but still had time to identify the culprit.

He met with el-Fadil in his private chamber. Palmira, his senior wife, was with him.

"What progress so far, Saif?" was el-Fadil's opening remark.

Saif was unable to verbalise. He stood rigid with a vacant stare and an open mouth. His tongue was dry, and he began to sweat. He had suddenly remembered what had been tormenting him about the poisoning.

24

It was the presence of Palmira in el-Fadil's private chamber that jogged Saif's memory about what had been troubling him. He suddenly remembered what Hamza had said: "There are many cooks and workers who have access to the kitchens with deliveries and in waiting on other members of the royal household. Even Palmira herself often checks on the cooking."

Moreover, during his aggressive interrogation, Raza, Hamza's helper, had burst into tears because of his shouting and bullying. "Was there anybody else who entered the kitchen that morning?" he had shouted at her.

"No, sir," she had replied whilst drying her tearful eyes. "The only person I saw all morning was Her Highness Palmira, who wanted to check that the kitchens were clean."

Palmira was known to have been jealous of Saniya, and since the latter's death, Aisha, not Palmira, had occupied el-Fadil's bedchamber. Palmira had been in the kitchen the morning that Aisha was poisoned. Was she also in the kitchen a year earlier on the day that Saniya had died?

When he had completed his audience with el-Fadil, Saif returned to speak to Raza, on this occasion using more conciliatory language.

"Raza do not be afraid. I do not suspect you, but I have a few more questions." He tried his best but had difficulty in appearing pleasant and friendly.

"When Palmira was in the kitchen the day that Aisha was poisoned, was she ever in the kitchen by herself?"

Raza thought for a moment.

"I am always in the kitchen. I never leave. Hamza insists." Once more she was defensive.

"You will not be blamed. Think carefully. Was Palmira ever alone in the kitchen?"

She was silent and then appeared to recollect something.

"She asked for oxymel, a drink of vinegar and honey, because she had a cough. I went to the storeroom to get it, but I was only away for a few moments."

"Thank you, Raza. You have been most helpful."

Saif visited Palmira. He was certain she was the culprit. She had the opportunity to poison Aisha, and most importantly she had a motive. She had been sidelined by a younger and more attractive wife in Aisha. But in addition, he suspected that she had also poisoned Saniya, and therefore had tragically poisoned her unborn child as well.

Initially Palmira denied the allegations and feigned indignation. She then attempted to bribe Saif not to inform her husband, but she did not foresee Saif's absolute loyalty to the vizier. The matter was reported to el-Fadil. He was uncontrollably angry. Palmira confessed under torture administered by Saif. A brief trial was held, and she was found guilty. Sharia law was applied. The penalty was death by stoning, but *qisas* law was applicable by which the murderer could be set free and pay financial retribution (blood money) if the victim's relative agreed. However, el-Fadil did not agree. Palmira was painfully stoned to death in the public marketplace on the following morning.

In keeping with his status as vizier, el-Fadil replaced Palmira by marrying two wives shortly after.

Moses structured his treatise on poisoning for Saladin into two main sections. The first section dealt with snakebites, dog bites, and the stings of scorpions.

"When someone is bitten, strive to immediately tie and bind a ligature above the site of the bite as tightly as possible so that the poison does not disseminate throughout the body. Another person should make incisions with a knife at the site of the bite and suck with the mouth as strongly as he is able. To avoid absorbing any of the poison, he should coat the mouth and palate with oil. He should spit out all that he sucks. Empty the victim's stomach with a mild emetic, then administer the great theriac. Then on the site of the bite, apply a medication which draws out the poison, either a simple or compounded medication."

Moses documented all the recognised efficacious preparations and remedies for drawing out the poisons when applied to the bite or sting. He also included a detailed description of the diet that should be taken by the person who was bitten. Dishes rich in salt, honey, and butter were recommended.

In the second section, he described vegetable and mineral poisons and their antidotes. He also provided precautionary advice. Poisons were a common method for assassinating prominent people; Moses advised that such people be aware of coloured foods, thick broths, and astringent liquids with strong odours. He advised careful examination of all sharp or bitter foods before their ingestion. When a poison has been imbibed, vomiting should be induced and then the specific antidote administered. He listed the universal antidotes with their composition: the great theriac, the electuary of Mithridates, the small theriac, the asafoetida theriac of Razi, and the onion theriac of Ibn Zuhr.

The treatise was well-received by el-Fadil, who proudly delivered it to a delighted Saladin. Copies were made and distributed to all his commanders in the field. Moses's treatise on poisoning became a standard text used by both military and civilian populations to good effect for decades.

25

Moses completed his *Mishneh Torah*. It had taken almost ten years of intense application and dedication, but at last he had achieved his long-standing ambition. He had produced a work which he hoped would serve all Jews by presenting a single, well-organised systematic source to which anyone could turn for rapid resolution of points of law. The judgements were based not only on the oral law but also on his knowledge and understanding of philosophy—particularly Aristotelian—science, and the medical literature. He intended the *Mishneh Torah* to be both a legal guide and a guide on how a Jew should live his life and worship his God. He highlighted the requirement to lead a moral and balanced life, one which followed his famed "middle path", the golden mean.

> One should be neither constantly laughing and a jester nor sad and depressed but happy. Similarly, one should not be greedy, rushing for wealth and possessions, nor lazy and an idler from work. Rather they should be of a goodly eye and limit their business endeavours so that they may occupy themselves with Torah

studies. They should be happy with the little that is their lot.

Liberality is the mean between sordidness and extravagance; courage, between recklessness and cowardice; dignity, between haughtiness and self-abasement; contentedness, between avarice and slothful indifference; munificence, between meanness and profusion; modesty, between impudence and shamefacedness. The really praiseworthy is the medium course of action to which everyone should strive to adhere, always weighing his conduct carefully, so that he may attain the proper mean.

In addition, the *Mishneh Torah* included instruction on how to achieve a healthy lifestyle, a matter of great importance to Moses. He aimed to provide evidence in support of all his assertions, especially scientific or medical ones, but often evidence did not exist and his concepts were then reliant on simple observation:

Only eat when you are hungry and drink when you are thirsty. Do not eat to the point that your belly is full, but leave a fourth unsatisfied. Do not eat until you have taken a walk or done some work in order to warm your body.

Foods such as melons should be eaten a little while before the meal, and not together with the meal. In the summer one should eat cold foods, and in the rainy season, one should eat hot foods and many spices.

Maintaining physical health is a vital part of serving God. It is impossible to understand and gaze at the teaching of wisdom when one is hungry or ill or if one's limbs ache.

He expressed his disgust at making excessive profit or preventing others from earning a living and had particularly harsh words for any fraudulent practice, such as using inaccurate scales when weighing goods for sale: "The punishment for incorrect measures is more severe than the punishment for immorality, for the latter is a sin against God only, the former against one's fellow man also."

Moses was adamant that the honour and dignity of an individual should be regarded as sacred and must not be violated under any circumstances, especially when charity is given. Charity must be a motivating force for every Jew, whether in the form of money, benevolent deeds, or just ordinary kindness. It should be dispensed in such a way that the recipient is not ashamed to accept it. It must be given with an open heart, without conditions, without benefit to the giver, and whenever possible anonymously.

"Whoever gives charity to the poor with bad grace and a downcast look," he wrote, "loses all the merit of his action even though he may bestow a thousand gold pieces."

Copies of the *Mishneh Torah* were written by scribes and sent to communities in Spain, Morocco, Palestine, and Yemen and throughout Egypt. Many distinguished rabbis replied with fulsome, ecstatic praise, which enhanced Moses's reputation as the most eminent Jewish intellectual and spiritual scholar in the world. One letter which made a strong impression on him was from Joseph ibn Aknin, a student from Cueta in Morocco, who requested that he be allowed to come to Fustat to study under Moses. Joseph wrote:

Before your work came to Spain, the learning of the Talmud was so hard that people had to rely only on what the rabbis said, for they did not know how to find clear Halacha from the complex discussions. But when they learned the composition of the Rambam, which was understandable to them in a simple language, and were amazed at its beautiful order, their eyes opened, and they recognised its great worth. They studied it deeply. Youth and elders gathered to learn it. Now there are increased people who know Torah and who can make Halachic decisions and study the Halachic decisions of the judges. And just as in Spain, so it is everywhere, even in the Eastern lands, where they spend more time learning the Talmud. The praise of the great teacher grew day by day, especially when it became gradually known that his private life is in keeping with the ideal of a scholar as he describes in his work.

Moses was flattered by the letter and delighted to hear that his *Mishneh Torah* had such a positive effect on encouraging Torah study. He was impressed with Joseph and willingly accepted him as a student. When Joseph arrived in Fustat, Moses soon confirmed that he possessed the necessary attributes to study under his tutelage.

"I am impressed by your knowledge of Torah, science, and logic," he told him. "I see you have an intense longing to learn the secular sciences as well as the sacred religious texts. Your desire for learning Torah is as great as your capability."

"I am humbled. To receive acclaim from the great rabbi Moses is indeed praiseworthy. May God give me the ability to learn under your brilliance," Joseph replied. He was elated when Moses suggested he stay in Fustat as his pupil.

Nevertheless, as with his *Commentary*, there were also critics of the *Mishneh Torah*. Moses was clear in his own mind what he intended to achieve, but some scholars misinterpreted his motivation. In his anxiety to complete the work, he failed to reference all his sources, and this omission was justifiably criticised. Other detractors accused him of arrogance in claiming that he saw no need for any other book since everything of relevance was contained in the *Mishneh Torah*. Moses flatly denied this accusation, which he regarded as crass stupidity, and denied having stated such a ridiculous notion. To answer the criticisms, he wrote to communities explaining his reasons for writing the *Mishneh Torah*:

"In our days, severe vicissitudes prevail, and all feel the pressure of hard times. The wisdom of our wise men has disappeared; the understanding of our wise men is hidden. Hence the commentaries of the Gaonim and their compilation of laws and responses, which they took care to make clear, have in our times become hard to understand, so that only a few individuals properly comprehend them. On these grounds, I, Moses son of Maimon the Spaniard, bestirred myself to compose a work from which the entire oral law might become systemically known to all."

There were other criticisms of the *Mishneh Torah* which required considered responses. An obvious one was that codifying the Jewish law in such a structured manner would inevitably stifle innovation. The oral law came into existence through constant reinterpretations of the Torah and early commentaries. The *Mishneh Torah*, on the other hand, represented the judgements of a single man with decisions appropriate for the present era. There was no mechanism for amendments. It risked ossifying the law and preventing discussion and debate. Judaism would be frozen in time! Moses had been aware of this potential criticism as he was writing the *Mishneh*, but in his own mind he was predicting the imminent coming of the Messiah and was therefore writing for a changeless society.

Other criticisms came from judges and were vituperative. Many judges felt threatened and were displeased with the wide availability of the *Mishneh Torah*, which could result in ordinary citizens being able to check decisions on Halachic matters. This would diminish their authority as judges, so they resisted the book.

A particularly harsh critic was the Gaon of Baghdad, Samuel ben Ali, who regarded Moses as a dangerous rival and mounted a strong campaign to diminish his status in the eyes of fellow Jews. Ben Ali lived in a luxurious palace in Baghdad surrounded by some sixty slaves. He had great learning but rejected any pretext of modesty as he pursued an extravagant lifestyle. He was jealous of Moses's fame and saw an opportunity to undermine his authority by emphasising aspects of the *Mishneh Torah* which he considered to be heretical. Moses tried to stay aloof when answering the criticisms. He wrote to Ben Ali and his followers in his usual temperate style to try to pacify the conflict of views:

"For ten straight years I worked day and night to put this work together," he said. "But who can be free of errors? One forgets, particularly when one grows older. For all these reasons, it is fitting to examine my words and to check after me. The scholars have done me a great favour. I will be grateful to whoever finds anything and lets me know about it, so that there will be no stumbling block, God forbid, for my only purpose in this work was to open the roads."

His responses, however, resulted in further malicious attacks. Ben Ali became increasingly desperate and persisted in the condemnation of Moses's integrity. On one occasion Ben Ali objected vehemently to a responsum that Moses sent in reply to a rabbi from Baghdad who asked whether it was permissible to sail on the great rivers—the Tigris, the Euphrates, and the Nile—on the Sabbath. Moses answered that it was permissible to sail, provided one did not board or exit the boat during the Sabbath. He supported his view with a detailed explanation and source material directly from the Torah, where it is never stated that travelling the rivers on the Sabbath is forbidden. Ben Ali was furious. The responsum trespassed on his authority in Baghdad. He considered the Tigris and Euphrates to be his own personal territory, and he had forbidden sailing on them on the Sabbath. Moses replied politely to Ben Ali and proved how wrong the latter was in his ruling, to the satisfaction of most of the people. Nevertheless, the jealous and vindictive Samuel ben Ali continued to forbid sailing on the Sabbath.

Despite all the vicious criticism, the reputation of Moses throughout the Jewish world was so assured that even as powerful a figure as the Gaon of Baghdad could not sully it. The status of the *Mishneh Torah* became the unquestioned source of authority on Jewish law after the Talmud itself. Hundreds of additional copyists were employed to supply the demand for the *Mishneh Torah*. As a result, Moses's name was recognised in every corner of the Jewish world, whereas Ben Ali's name descended into obscurity. But alas the unwarranted criticisms affected Moses's health. Bouts of depression recurred.

26

Moses was pleased that Joseph continued to study with him. He found inspiration in the young man's appetite for learning, which had the effect of improving his own mood and health. This was noted by Jamilah and was a great relief to her. Moses regarded Joseph as part of his family for the two years he lived with them. He assisted with the education of Abraham, who enjoyed Joseph's less rigid style of teaching.

Both Moses and Joseph had an interest in philosophy, astronomy, and logic and a mutual appreciation of how knowledge of these disciplines was integral to understanding the Torah. Whereas the Greeks and Muslims had produced the greatest philosophers, few Jews had made an impact. But with his belief that the Torah provided answers to the deepest questions of life, Moses was convinced that the Jewish religion had much philosophical wisdom and knowledge to offer.

The *Mishneh Torah* now completed, and with prompting and encouragement from Joseph in particular, Moses embarked upon his next great work, *Moreh Nevuchim, the Guide of the Perplexed*.

"Joseph, your presence and your questioning of Torah has stimulated me to think more deeply about philosophical issues which have perplexed many in the past and continue to do so."

Moses was discussing a particularly difficult concept with his student.

"Revered teacher, a detailed guide to explain difficult concepts for those with knowledge and understanding of Torah and Talmud would be influential. Confusion and perplexity do exist." Joseph was excited.

"The purpose of the guide will not be to make itself understandable to the unlearned or to those who are only beginners in philosophy, nor will it be meant for those who have engaged in no other study than the Torah. The work will be addressed to the religious man who believes completely in the validity of the Torah and whose belief is expressed throughout his being. Such a person must be complete in his religious obligations and character but may be confused and perplexed."

In the introduction to the *Guide*, Moses was careful to indicate explicitly for whom the *Guide* was written.

"The person should be pious, learned and of high character, engaged in learning philosophy. He has studied the sciences of the philosophers and understood their works. And now this has confused him, he has felt distressed by the externals of the Torah. He is in a state of perplexity and confusion as to whether to follow his intellect."

Moses found Joseph's presence invaluable. Without his student's infectious enthusiasm for the project, Moses might have abandoned it. Jamilah was available for support when necessary, but Joseph was the key, the inspiration. He was constantly at Moses's side, available for discussion or for help with interpretation of obtuse concepts. They worked well as a team, teacher and pupil. Joseph was the companion that Moses needed to remain focussed on the project, especially since the latter suffered from mood changes and at times was incapable of continuing.

Moses was experiencing an exceptionally dark phase when Joseph reluctantly gave him the news.

"Revered teacher, it is with the greatest sadness that I now find I must leave Fustat."

Moses was devastated. A wave of gloom and desperation consumed his body. Joseph noticed the change in his appearance. His forehead furrowed, his face blanched, and his hands shook uncontrollably.

"My family requires my presence in Aleppo. I am so sorry."

"But for what reason? Why are you required?"

"I cannot reveal the reason, revered sir. I will miss being here. Your teaching has been of inestimable value to me. I hope you will permit me to continue my learning with you by exchange of letters."

Moses was silent. His countenance was one of desolation. Eventually he spoke, but in a timorous voice, seemingly struggling to find the words.

"It will be my privilege to maintain our productive association, and we will exchange views on the *Guide*." Moses was genuinely despondent. Abraham cried bitterly when he was told.

Why would he not tell me the reason his family wanted him in Aleppo? Was this true? Perhaps it is I who drove him away. Perhaps I was expecting too much from him. Moses had difficulty in accepting the loss of his student on whom he had become so dependent. He took to his bed with exhaustion, with depression, with an overriding feeling of foreboding. How could he carry on? Were the critics of his writings correct? Was it he who had misunderstood the scriptures? The depression impacted on his self-esteem. He began to doubt his own ability.

Jamilah was worried. There was a distinct change in her husband's behaviour. He was easily angered, he looked constantly morose, his appetite was poor, and he began to lose weight. He spent increasing time in bed, and he lost his desire for work.

And then Moses received a letter from Joseph which explained the reason for his sudden departure. Joseph's father had suffered major debts as his business ran into difficulties and was no longer viable. What remained of the business was sold, and the family were required to move. Joseph, who was the only son, felt honour-bound to return home to assist in providing for his family. He was appointed as an assistant rabbi to the local community and received a regular salary.

Moses was relieved. Joseph's initial explanation for the move was true. It was not he, Moses, who was responsible for the departure. His disposition slowly improved. Jamilah saw the difference. He soon felt able to return to work and looked forward to his communications with Joseph.

Vicious allegations against Moses continued to be distributed, orchestrated by Rabbi Zerachiah ben Berakhel, who delivered scathing attacks on both the *Commentary* and the *Mishneh Torah*. Interestingly, Rabbi Zerachiah was married to Rabbi Samuel ben Ali's daughter!

In his anger at the unjustified criticisms which had even reached Aleppo, Joseph wrote to Moses telling him of the slander and how he was determined to defend Moses's honour. Moses appreciated the information but remained calm and undeterred. He realised how upset Joseph was becoming and replied to him in such a way that Joseph would relax and not become overly agitated.

> My son, my character traits are not like yours. I am already older and experienced. I forgive the attacks on my honour. But you are unable to hold yourself back and suffer these incitements.
>
> As God knows, I wrote the *Mishneh Torah* in the first instance only for myself, in order to dispense with investigation and searching the rabbinic sources for whatever I might need on any occasion, as well as for my old age when

I shall find it difficult to search through the classic sources. And for the sake of God as well, for I have been zealous for the sake of God. I saw a nation lacking a comprehensive composition in the true sense and lacking sound, authenticated opinions. I therefore did what I did solely for God. I knew even as I wrote it that it would fall into the hands of fools who would denigrate its virtues, who do not know how to learn, who confuse matters, who would be puzzled by passages in it because they don't know them well, or who would be unable to follow my conclusions.

I knew that it would fall into the hands of people who believe themselves to be pious and who would attack its description of the fundamentals of Jewish faith. But I knew it would also fall into the hands of men who would appreciate the work, men of justice, judgement, and healthy mind. You are the first of them. Even if I had no one but you, that would suffice for me.

And how much happier I am that I have received a letter from the sages of France, who claim to be overwhelmed at what I have composed and requesting that I send them a complete copy.

Indeed, the overwhelming support that Moses received from several Ashkenazi rabbis in France was of solace and encouragement. He benefited from the acclamation. It vindicated his decision to write the *Mishneh Torah*. But in addition, it gave him the incentive and encouragement to continue his work on the *Guide*.

Moses and Joseph corresponded frequently and debated the teachings of philosophy with the beliefs of Judaism. As he wrote the *Guide*, Moses continued to teach Joseph by sending him chapter after chapter. He took serious note of the responses he received.

The structure and organisation of the *Guide* was not as straightforward as his previous books, but this was deliberate. Moses considered the *Guide* to be dangerous to those who were not qualified to understand it, so he concealed many of his true thoughts. The book explores topics such as the incorporeality of God, the nature of creation, miracles, prophecy, the nature of evil, and the purpose of life. Moses not only raised questions that had been troubling man for generations but also provided answers based on his interpretations, many of which were in line with the views of the sages of the Talmud and Mishna, but others which were totally original.

Jamilah was concerned. Her husband was working with ever-increasing intensity, and the strain on his health was apparent. She did not feel at ease. She was pregnant again, but the pregnancy felt different from the one she had with Abraham. She did not want to tell Moses and add to his worries.

At fifteen weeks, her worst fears were confirmed. She suffered another miscarriage.

"Moses, once again a pregnancy has ended in failure." She was crying. She knew that Moses wanted more children, as indeed did she. "I am so sorry," she sobbed.

"Do not fret, dear Jamilah. If that is the will of the Almighty, we accept with gratitude for our beloved Abraham. You have developed an abundance of phlegm in the opening of the vessels of the womb," Moses explained. "This weakens the connection between the womb and the afterbirth."

Jamilah was resigned. They would have no more children.

The presence of Shoshanah in the house provided some comfort to Jamilah. She regarded her almost like a daughter. This pleased Rachel, who never remarried following David's death and was pleased to devote herself entirely to the well-being of her daughter, who was blessed with an intellectual capacity above her years, as well as a placid personality. *Her father would have been so proud of her,* pondered Moses on many occasions. Moses missed his beloved brother. He thought about him every day and continued to include him in his daily prayers.

Rachel, nonetheless, harboured concerns about Shoshanah's physical development. She was small for her age and suffered from recurrent episodes of coughing and wheezing. At times she had difficulty with breathing. On one particularly frightening occasion when the shutter to her room was open with a damp breeze coming directly from the Nile, she began to cough repeatedly. She was struggling to breathe. The episode lasted a few minutes and was witnessed by Moses. He immediately sprinkled the air with aromatic water to provide humidification. He diagnosed her as suffering from asthma. He had seen many young patients with similar symptoms, including one of the palace courtiers.

Treatments for asthma were designed to purge the body of noxious substances thought to be the cause of the symptoms. Moses advised a healthy diet of efficacious foods such as fennel, mint, and radish, with avoidance of poorly digestible and fattening foods, as well as wheat flour, black beans, peas, onions, nuts, and garlic. To suppress the cough, he recommended aromatic herbs combined with liquorice root and fresh poppy heads in a honey syrup. When the asthma was accompanied by a fever, he advocated maidenhair, fennel, and cucumber seeds.

His suggestions were often but not invariably effective.

"I am disturbed by the environment that we live in and the air that we breathe," he told Rachel whilst they were sitting in her home with Jamilah and Abraham. "The air in Fustat is not clean. I am convinced that clean, fresh air and clean water help breathing and prevent asthma. Environmental factors surely must contribute to the illness." He suggested to Rachel that on hot days the air be conditioned by spraying with aromatic water and encouraging a circulating draft. On cold, rainy days, he said the air should be fumigated with perfumes which warm the body.

"These measures will be helpful to Shoshanah. I am convinced."

On the insistence of Jamilah, Moses brought his views on improving the environment, and thereby achieving healthy living, to the attention of el-Fadil. It was unusual for Jamilah to express such strong opinions to her husband, but on this subject she was adamant.

El-Fadil was grateful to Moses for saving the life of Aisha and for his medical expertise, which was appreciated by the entire royal household. He was always pleased to meet with Moses and listened attentively when Moses presented his views on health and the environment.

"Your arguments are persuasive. I will arrange for you to meet with Saladin's eldest son, al-Afdal. He has the authority to commit to introducing changes to improve the environment. He also needs a focus to his life; improving the health of his people may be just the thing."

The meeting was attended by all the court physicians and some ministers. However, al-Afdal addressed his comments directly to Moses and appeared to ignore the presence of anyone else.

"You are late. You have kept me waiting," an obviously irritated al-Afdal uttered as opening words of welcome. Al-Afdal had a raucous threatening voice which he utilised whenever he was angry. His dress was flamboyant with much gold brocade. This was in contrast to Moses', whose dress was modest and lacked colour.

"I would like to hear your views on improving the health of the population. This is a very important matter." Al-Afdal lay on a settee, eating a large bunch of grapes whilst being fanned by two of his concubines. Everyone else stood.

"I am honoured and humbled to receive such a request. In my religion the maintenance of a healthy body is regarded as a divine requirement," Moses replied. He was indeed flattered but struggled to avoid showing his contempt for al-Afdal and the lewd and wasteful behaviour attributed to him.

"I am not surprised you feel honoured. I do not usually give an audience to a member of my staff. Now what have you got to say?"

"You are most thoughtful and generous. Nothing could afford me greater pleasure than to use my modest ability to provide advice on how serious health problems might be prevented," Moses added. But he was not so naive as to be fooled by al-Afdal's apparently altruistic request to improve the health of the population. He knew that the meeting was merely an excuse to obtain advice on al-Afdal's own medical problems, which were many and varied but predominantly related to his unhealthy, excessive lifestyle. Moses had been told this by el-Fadil, who could only get al-Afdal to agree to convene the meeting on the promise that Moses would give him a private consultation. Moses was convinced that al-Afdal, unlike el-Fadil, cared very little for the well-being of his subjects. Al-Afdal expected to be adulated. He was an arrogant, egocentric leader with no concerns other than for his own personal comfort.

"As a doctor, I see patients with illnesses which I am convinced are due to the environment, the air that we breathe, and the water that we drink." Moses decided to offer general advice. "Your Excellency, the city air is stagnant, turbid, and thick, the natural result of its big buildings, its narrow streets, the refuse of its inhabitants. One should at least choose to build residences in wide-open spaces. Living quarters are best located on an upper floor with ample sunshine. Toilets should be located as far as possible from living areas. The air should be kept dry at all times by sweet scents, fumigation, and drying agents. Clean air and clean water are foremost in preserving the health of the body and therefore the soul."

Moses also offered his views on the importance of preventative medicine, a topic he had included in the *Mishneh Torah*, although he avoided referring to this source.

"A person should be advised not to eat until he has walked prior to the meal so that his body begins to become warmed, or he should perform a physical task or tire himself by some other form of exertion." Moses noticed that al-Afdal was showing little interest and yawned ostentatiously.

"When a man leaves the bathhouse, he should be dressed and have his head covered so that he avoids the cold, even during the summer. He should drink no cold water on leaving the bathhouse and certainly not while having a bath." He could see from the body language of those present and from the guffaws and chuckles of the assembled court physicians that his views were being discounted.

"This is all pure speculation," commented Muhammed Assaf, a senior physician who had been a member of the court for over twenty years and who was regarded as al-Afdal's personal doctor.

"The air and water are gifts of Allah and are provided by his great power, through the mighty Nile. You insult his name by your insinuations about the environment." Turning to al-Afdal, he said, "Your Highness, you must ignore these baseless rantings from an ignorant Jew."

Al-Afdal was amused. "You see, your views are not popular, Rabbi. The people are not complaining. Why should I listen to you? We cannot follow your suggestions. How can we change the air? How can we rebuild the city? What people do in the bathhouse is their own concern. Your ideas are ridiculous. I agree with the view of my senior physician."

There was a spontaneous nodding in acquiescence from the entire group. No one would dare to dissent from the view of al-Afdal.

"Have you any *sensible* suggestions to make? I cannot waste any more time with your fantasies. I have work to do," said al-Afdal as he looked in a rather lascivious manner at his concubines who were continuing to fan him.

"I also advocate the need for moderation in all activities." Moses was annoyed that his suggestions were unreasonably dismissed by people who lacked a moral compass and were so obviously hypocritical. He was pleased that this latest suggestion seemed to upset al-Afdal.

"Explain yourself, and for your own sake I hope you are not publicly criticising *my* behaviour," replied an obviously outraged al-Afdal.

"Your Highness, I apologise if my comment has been misinterpreted. As your lowly servant, I would never publically discuss your maladies. I believe this is a matter for private consultation." Moses was very careful with his words. Al-Afdal was known to have a vicious temper and was incapable of accepting any criticism or dissent.

"I will assume you are not being deliberately impertinent," replied al-Afdal, "and so I will allow you to conduct a medical consultation with me in private since there are matters of a personal nature which are troubling me." He looked around and, with a wave of his hand, dismissed his concubines, ministers, and physicians.

It was clear to Moses that al-Afdal had little interest or concern for his subjects' welfare and merely used his position for self-aggrandisement, a concept abhorrent to all that Moses believed in.

"I am flattered that Your Highness does me the honour of allowing me to carry out an examination. I agree that for the sake of confidentiality this should be conducted in private."

Moses was confident that his sycophantic, patronising approach would please al-Afdal. He intended to provide him with general advice regarding his lifestyle, in the certain knowledge that it would be ignored. Al-Afdal led Moses into his personal chamber, where a full medical examination and consultation could be undertaken in complete privacy.

Al-Afdal reported two medical problems to Moses which not only were an embarrassment to him, but which also were infuriatingly resistant to all prescribed treatments: painful haemorrhoids and intermittent impotence.

"Excretion is painful, and I have protrusions," explained al-Afdal. "Nothing makes them better. In fact, I had bloodletting on two occasions, but that only made them worse. Assaf wants to extirpate them with cautery. I have refused. What is your opinion?" Moses was familiar with the use of cautery in this situation but was not impressed by the results of this excruciatingly painful approach.

"Your Highness is very wise. The procedure is dangerous. I am a great believer in the writings of Hippocrates, who stated, 'First do no harm.' Haemorrhoids are very common, and there are different types. Some people have a type of haemorrhoids which, when extirpated, result in others developing. This is because the causes which gave rise to the original ones remain, and therefore new ones develop."

"So what do you advise? The pain is insufferable, and I want a cure. Do you understand?"

Moses examined the rectum and was impressed by the size of the haemorrhoids.

"The way to treat haemorrhoids is to address the underlying

cause." Moses was clear what the treatment would consist of and would explain it to al-Afdal in detail. In addition to general advice, however, he would also need to prescribe treatment for the substantial prolapsing haemorrhoids.

"What do you mean?" Al-Afdal was becoming irritated and wanted immediate relief.

"Let me explain, Your Excellency. Haemorrhoids arise from poor digestion. One must be careful to eat food of good quality with much residue, refrain from overeating, and observe the correct order, taking, for example, light food before heavy food. Meals should be eaten only when genuinely hungry and after exercise so that the body's inner heat is aroused and facilitates the digestive process, and never before exercise and vigorous movement, since physical activity interferes with digestion."

"But what about the haemorrhoids? I have them at present. I am not concerned about why they develop. I want you to do something about them *now*!" shouted al-Afdal.

"Permit me to continue. Haemorrhoids result from an excess of black bile in the body." Moses realised that al-Afdal was losing patience and was only interested in immediate cure.

"Black bile causes the problem by thickening the blood. The limbs and organs reject such blood, being weighed down by black bile. The black bile gravitates to veins in the vicinity of the rectum and distends them, the result being haemorrhoids."

"Very interesting, but how does all this theory help me?"

"You must avoid foods that produce black bile and thicken the blood," answered Moses. "The foods to be avoided are beans, lentils, dates, goat meat, and unleavened bread."

"You will make a list of these and the beneficial foods and provide it to my chef."

Moses decided that this would be worthwhile and made a mental note to write a treatise, an information guide, on haemorrhoids not only for al-Afdal but also for distribution to all patients with similar problems.

"When the haemorrhoids develop, I do not recommend bloodletting or cupping. In my experience, those treatments do not benefit the condition."

"I am pleased to hear that, but I am still waiting to hear what you *do* recommend, not what you *don't* recommend."

"I recommend that you have twice daily warm sitz baths. I will make up for you a medicine consisting of dried snakeroot, wheat flour, and sesame oil which is kneaded and pulverised into a spiced honey drink. This should relieve the pain and reduce the size of the haemorrhoids. I will also give you an ointment to rub into the area. This will also ease the pain." Al-Afdal was listening carefully.

"I also advise fumigation."

"What is that? It sounds dangerous." Al-Afdal looked bemused.

"It is simple but effective. A hole is dug in the ground and a fire started in it. I will give you some special herbs to place on the fire. An earthenware pot with holes in it to allow the resultant fumes to pass through is placed upside down over the hole, and you then sit on the pot so that the fumes pass through the holes and into your anus. By this means the haemorrhoids will be dried and obliterated."

"I have not had this treatment previously, but I will try it. Your advice is appreciated. And now to my second problem." Al-Afdal seemed reluctant and discomfited. "I am having increasing difficulty in satisfying my wives … and concubines. You must help me to increase my sexual potential."

Moses listened intently as al-Afdal explained in graphic detail his level of impotence. It was also made very clear to Moses that he had no intention of entertaining any suggestion that he reduce his sexual activity. Quite the opposite, he wanted advice and treatment to enhance it.

"I understand your problem. The treatment resides in nutriments which are more effective than medications. All foods that cool the body, as well as those that dry the body, are detrimental," explained Moses. "The foods known to be of benefit since they heat the body include the meat of lambs and pigeons and all brains, especially the brains of chickens. Foods which should be avoided include all seeds and condiments, since they are known to cool the body. The aphrodisiac plants are the turnip, lettuce, fennel, sesame, and asparagus."

Al-Afdal listened carefully. Moses also suggested a balm of pulverised ox testis mixed with almonds, onions, and syrup to massage into the area. He described the preparation of a cake which had originally been proposed by Avicenna, the great Arab physician, and was known to strengthen sexual intercourse. It consisted of brains of doves and yolks of chicken eggs mixed with lamb's meat and carrot juice, eaten after a meal.

Moses provided much additional information with detailed nutritional and medication advice which al-Afdal had difficulty in absorbing. He again instructed Moses to provide written information for his various servants to follow.

At the completion of the consultation, Moses was exhausted and decided that he would approach al-Afdal on another day to try once more to persuade him of the importance of public health measures for population disease prevention. But he was not very hopeful of success.

27

Moses's reputation as nagid was enhanced because of his admirable understanding of human nature as well as his knowledge of Torah and Talmud. His adjudications were usually met with acclamation. But still he was subjected to criticism, not least the persistent disparagement from Samuel ibn Ali. He was becoming increasingly weary of the attacks, and although initially he'd responded to each criticism in detail, eventually he became disillusioned and ignored them. Moses was now fully committed to the *Guide* and still had much to do. Nonetheless, he accepted the criticism relating to the lack of source references in the *Mishneh Torah*, and it was his affirmed intention to include these once he had completed his *Guide*. He would ask Joseph to assist in this task.

He divided the *Guide* into three sections, and subdivided each, resulting in a total of some 175 chapters. The intense work adversely affected Moses's health. He was aware of this but refused to be distracted. The esoteric subjects he tackled were ones which required detailed consideration, but only by those individuals who were qualified by their learning and who appreciated that faith and reason can be shown to share common ground with similar perspectives.

He wrote to Joseph with his deep convictions on this issue.

"While the uninitiated see vast conflict," he declared, "careful study leads to the conclusion that this only seems to be the case. It disappears when the text is scrutinised with the more analytically learned eyes of the highly trained observer. When faith and reason clash, the Torah can often be seen to be speaking in allegory. There are statements in the Holy Book that can be refuted by proof and therefore must be interpreted in some other way. But its words must never be dismissed, for they were dictated by God to Moses and are therefore not only infallible but also divine."

Completion of the *Guide* became a priority and an obsession even though his medical practice was ever expanding and was obligatory for financial reasons. Moses was still the source of income not only for his immediate family but also for Rachel and Shoshanah. He was pleased therefore to have been handsomely rewarded for his private examination and treatment of al-Afdal, who had also appointed him as his principal physician. El-Fadil told him that Muhammed Assaf was enraged that he had been replaced and that he regarded it as an affront to his competence and seniority.

Miriam delivered a beautiful little girl, which delighted the family. Moses and Jamilah were very proud of their first niece and showered her with gifts. Uziel was ecstatic and relieved that the labour was rapid and without incident. His father, Rabbi Mishael, visited. He held the little girl and wept as he remembered his beloved wife, who would have been so happy to have a granddaughter but who had sadly passed away six months earlier. Rabbi Mishael took the opportunity whilst he was there to teach Abraham, his grandson, some Torah. He was gratified that both his children were happily married into the Maimon family.

"God has been good to us," he proclaimed to Moses. "The

next generation will hand on our legacies. I am grateful to the almighty that Jamilah and Uziel are so happy and fulfilled."

"We are indeed blessed, Mishael. Uziel is a hard-working and dedicated man. I understand his business in flax is successful, and he is also an assistant rabbi to the synagogue. You must be very proud of him." Moses was also pleased that Uziel was such an attentive husband to Miriam.

"I have heard that you are writing another theological book. You are a remarkable man, Moshe. The *Mishneh Torah* is brilliant and will be studied for generations to come. I am sure your new contribution will be equally important."

"You are too generous with your praise and confidence in my ability," replied Moses. "I am writing the *Guide of the Perplexed* in response to questions that have been raised by intelligent religious Jews who have difficulty in comprehending some aspects of our holy law which they find confusing."

"That is important. Many Jews, and I include myself, have often questioned tenets of Torah but have relied upon the great sages of the past to provide interpretations. It is appropriate that you, as the most prominent Jew of our time, should continue this trend." They were sitting in an anteroom to the synagogue. Mishael was pleased that Moses appeared relaxed and obviously anxious to talk about his project.

"The intention of the *Guide* is to enlighten a religious man who finds it difficult to accept as correct the teaching based on a literal interpretation of the law. Accordingly, he is lost in perplexity and anxiety." Moses could see that Mishael was giving wholehearted attention to his every word.

"If he be guided solely by reason and renounce his views which are based on faith, he would consider that he had rejected the fundamental principles of the law; and even if he retains the opinions which were derived from those expressions, instead of following his reason, it would still appear that his religious convictions had suffered loss and injury. For then he would be left with fear, anxiety, and great perplexity."

"You are indeed a extraordinary person. You express the feelings that I and many others have struggled with for years. Baruch Hashem. You must remain strong. You must continue with your work."

That was the problem for Moses. He knew that his health was deteriorating whilst his work was ever increasing. As a physician he seemed to be constantly in demand, especially from the palace, and as nagid he was required to deal with an increasing number of Halachic conundrums and questions. He hoped that the Almighty would indeed continue to provide him with the strength to continue until his work was completed.

He was also determined to convince the palace of the importance of improving environmental conditions and thereby the health of the population. His first attempt had been unsuccessful, but he would persist. Another opportunity to address this matter arose when he heard of the imminent visit of Saladin to Fustat.

Saladin had gained a deserved reputation as a virtuous but firm ruler who was modest and devoid of pretence. Militarily he was successful in turning the balance of power in his favour in his struggle with the crusaders. In 1187, as a direct result of his outstanding military expertise, he destroyed an army of crusaders at Hattin near Tiberias. Under cover of night, Saladin's troops surrounded the Christian army. They set fire to the dried thick brush. Great clouds of smoke were swept by winds into the Christian camp. The heat of the flames and the thick smoke suffocated them. The crusaders struggled to pull off their burning armour. Volleys of arrows were fired into the camp. Saladin's soldiers then engaged the Christian soldiers in bloody hand-to-hand combat, killing many and taking many prisoners. As dawn broke, the losses to the crusaders were seen. There was indescribable carnage with thousands of bloody corpses and disembowelled horses. Fifteen thousand Christians lay dead, and fifteen thousand were prisoners. The crusader losses were so great that Saladin was able to rapidly overrun the kingdom of Jerusalem. The city surrendered after eighty-eight years in Christian hands. The entire population of Jerusalem ransomed their lives with payment of ten dinars per man, five per woman, and one per child.

A triumphant Saladin returned to Cairo after an absence of two years. His intention now was to supervise the building of colleges and improve the well-being of the population. He was extraordinarily generous and donated vast amounts of money, much from his personal wealth, to achieve this. He attracted scholars and preachers and founded colleges and mosques for their use.

Saladin was aware that during the Christians' long occupation of the land, they did not allow Jews to dwell in the holy city of Jerusalem. This distressed him. He sent out the following order:

"Islam, which is a just and righteous faith, now allows Jews who had been persecuted by the Christians to return to their ancient home."

Jews began to return to the ancient capital of the kingdom of Israel and again rebuild the ruins of synagogues and study halls. Moses heard of this from el-Fadil. Jews returning to Jerusalem! It was truly a miracle. The Almighty had not forgotten his people. Moses was also informed by el-Fadil that following his triumphs, Saladin would soon be visiting Fustat. Could this present another opportunity for Moses to explain his views on the environment?

During a routine visit to the palace to provide medical advice, Moses brought to el-Fadil's attention his own failure to impress al-Afdal with his views on the environment and health improvement generally. Knowing that Saladin would be visiting Fustat, he politely enquired whether el-Fadil thought an approach to Saladin would be more successful.

"I am convinced that al-Afdal is far too self-centred to worry about his subjects," scoffed el-Fadil. "Your reputation is known to Saladin. I will request an audience for you to speak to him directly. I am sure you will be given a hearing. Saladin is anxious to improve the lot of the people, and his recent victories have heartened him. He is the only person who would be able to talk some sense into his son."

"I hope so. The living conditions of many of the residents of Fustat is poor. And they lead unhealthy lives."

Moses was particularly concerned about the squalor surrounding the Jewish quarter, which he was convinced contributed to much ill-health, including malnutrition, nausea, and vomiting, as well as breathing problems. He was also troubled by Jamilah's implication that environmental factors might have an influence on the unborn child in the womb. He looked forward to discussing the issue with Saladin as soon as it could be arranged. He reported back to the council of Jews, in his position as nagid, and received their full backing for his negotiations with Saladin.

Moses confided in Jamilah. "I will be meeting with senior courtiers at the palace tomorrow, and hopefully with Saladin himself. I will try to convince him of the need to improve the quality of the environment, especially the quality of the air. I am worried about the high incidence of chest infections. Even Abraham has a cough. And you know of the problem with Shoshanah."

Shoshanah continued to have bouts of breathing difficulty, although less often than previously, but still enough to worry Rachel.

"Al-Afdal has little interest, but I hope that Saladin will agree to action. We have a responsibility to help people who are afflicted and change conditions for the better whenever we can. The Torah states in Leviticus, 'Neither shalt you stand idly by the blood of thy neighbour,' which means that we must not ignore a person's difficulty when we can see how it can be improved."

28

Prior to the rise of Saladin, Egypt was the centre of the Shia Fatimid Caliphate. The Fatimids had long sought to completely supplant the Sunni Abbasid Caliphate based in Iraq. With Saladin's rise to power, which resulted in a return of Egypt to the Sunni fold and the Abbasid Caliphate, Saladin took the title of sultan. Supreme power in the caliphate rested with the sultan of Egypt, so Saladin deservedly became an extremely powerful leader. But despite his undoubted wealth and power, Saladin preferred and maintained a modest lifestyle. When Moses was brought to his chamber in the palace, he was expecting to encounter a room of opulence and extravagance. Instead, he found Saladin seated on a large cushion on the floor, dressed in an unpretentious brown robe with traditional wide sleeves. He wore a green turban. His beard was neatly trimmed, and his facial appearance was the epitome of leadership. His eyes were deep blue with a piercing stare when anyone spoke in his presence, which recipients often found off-putting. He was surrounded by several courtiers and had positioned el-Fadil by his side. Al-Afdal formally introduced Moses to his father.

"I believe you know of Rabbi Moses Maimonides. He was the person who wrote the manual on poisoning which is now used by all our soldiers in case of snakebites and other poisonings whilst in the field or in battle," explained al-Afdal. "He is also a court physician, and many of us have reason to be thankful for his knowledge and skill."

"I am pleased to make your acquaintance." Saladin seemed genuine. "I understand that you are also a nagid. You must be an exceptional man, praise be to Allah. Jews will always be welcome in Egypt. We are cousins; we have the same forefathers and believe in the one God. I was born in Tikrit in Iraq and had many Jewish friends. As a child and young man, I was far more interested in religion than in joining the military." Saladin spoke in a quiet, thoughtful way and looked directly at Moses, seemingly insistent on making eye contact.

"I understand that you wish to discuss ways to improve the lives of our people. I am interested in your ideas. You will know that my ambition for Cairo is to supervise the building of new homes, of colleges, and of madrasas. I am also concerned about the many diseases affecting our people."

Moses was certain of Saladin's sincerity. The positive body language and mutual respect between the two men was palpable.

"Father, these are my ambitions also," proudly boasted al-Afdal. "My priority has always been for the welfare of our people. That is why I persuaded Maimonides to speak to you before I implemented many of his ideas."

"When you are ready, Rabbi Maimonides, I would be grateful for your views. But first, please be seated and get comfortable."

"The sultan honours me by allowing my views on the environment and on improving hygiene and sanitation to be expressed in your distinguished presence. I am flattered by the support of your son." Moses looked towards al-Afdal, who nodded rather coyly. Moses was offered a large embroidered cushion to sit on but found the position uncomfortable.

"Bring the rabbi a chair. He is not used to our ways." Saladin smiled. Moses was grateful for a seat rather than a cushion.

"If you are comfortable, perhaps you can begin," said Saladin.

"Your Excellency is most kind." Moses was conscious that many of the views that he was about to express had previously been rejected by al-Afdal, although they were supported by el-Fadil. Accordingly, he was mindful to be wary lest he appear to undermine al-Afdal.

"In my medical practice I see many patients of all ages suffering with breathing difficulties, and others with ailments of the bowels. I am convinced that much of this illness is related to the air that we breathe and the quality of the food that we consume."

Moses had spent a substantial amount of time considering these issues from both a medical and religious standpoint. He had included personal hygiene and sanitation in Hilchot De'ot, a chapter within the *Mishneh Torah*. However, he again decided that it would be inappropriate to use quotations from his religious writings or from the Jewish sages of the past in his presentation to the sultan. He would restrict his opinions to medical and scientific argument only.

"I respectfully propose that the first topic to consider is the quality of the air that we breathe. Your Excellency will be aware of the large number of citizens of Cairo who suffer with breathing difficulties, including my own niece." Moses was still troubled by Shoshanah's continued wheezing and breathlessness and was certain that the air quality was a factor.

"The city air is stagnant and has a foul smell which is unpleasant and nauseating. The air is trapped between large cramped buildings and narrow streets. I believe there should be more open spaces. In Cordoba, where I was born, there were numerous parks and green fields which were pleasant for the population to enjoy. There was never such a high incidence of breathing problems in Cordoba as I now see in Fustat. I am convinced that clean air is important in preserving the health of the body."

Saladin was listening intently and asked Moses to continue.

"I notice that there are tanneries in the centre of the city. I humbly suggest that because tanneries emit a foul, pungent odour, they should be placed at a minimum of fifty cubits from the city. A tannery should be set up only on the east side, because the east wind is mild and reduces the unpleasantness of the odours produced by the tanning of hides."

"I find your proposals appealing. Despite some obvious difficulties, I will instruct my engineers and builders to consider them whenever construction is taking place. Now what about digestion problems?"

"All my medical teachers followed the great physicians, Hippocrates, Galen, Razi, Albucasis, and Alfarabi. They advised that food should always be prepared in clean surroundings. Hands should be cleaned before eating, and toilets should be located as far as possible from living rooms," Moses explained.

"These are sensible measures that I understand and that should be conveyed to all our people. Do you not agree, al-Afdal?"

"Of course. These are matters which I have always considered to be important."

"Do you have other advice, Rabbi Maimonides?"

"It is important that people understand which foods are detrimental to health and which are beneficial and when foods should and should not be consumed." Moses had studied and documented these matters within the *Mishneh Torah*. They were derived from teachings within the Torah and from writings of the sages, but again he deliberately omitted to mention the sources. The irony of describing Halacha to a Sunni Muslim leader was not lost on him.

"Some foods are extremely detrimental to health and it is proper never to eat them, such as old salted fish, old salted cheese, truffles, mushrooms, and a cooked dish which has been kept until it acquires a foul odour. Likewise, any food whose odour is bad or excessively bitter is like a fatal poison to the body."

Moses was in full flow and provided lists of foods which were less detrimental but under certain circumstances should be avoided. He explained the importance of proper cooking of meats and the avoidance of excessive fatty foods. He also emphasised the golden mean, not to overeat or to suffer malnutrition, both of which are unhealthy.

"Anyone who leads a sedentary life and does not exercise or who postpones his excretions, even if he eats good foods and takes care of himself according to proper medical principles, will suffer pain, and his strength will wane. Excessive eating is like a deadly poison to the body and is a principal cause of all illness."

Moses was pleased with the level of attention he was receiving.

"Finally, one should be careful with consuming unclean water. A person should not put his mouth to a flowing pipe of water and drink from it, or drink from a river or pond at night, in case he swallows a leech which he is unable to see. Also, a person must not drink water which has been left uncovered. These actions lead to disturbance of the intestines and illness." Saladin seemed impressed but remained silence as he deliberated.

"With the greatest respect, Your Excellency, I wish to bring to your attention another matter which I think is important." Moses had decided that this issue should also be regarded as having relevance to the quality of life.

"Please continue, Rabbi Maimonides. You have my complete attention," responded Saladin expectantly, although al-Afdal looked apprehensive.

"I am convinced that for a healthy mind it is important to have a healthy body. Also, the physical well-being of a person is dependent on mental well-being. A healthy person is cheerful and content, whilst a sick one is always depressed and dissatisfied. If a person is emotionally upset or mentally agitated, his physical well-being suffers and eventually he becomes physically ill. By improving the environment, health will improve. Pleasant surroundings, encouraging exercise, listening to music, and avoiding overindulgence in wine and women are all important to maintain a healthy mind and thereby a healthy body." He looked directly at al-Afdal at this point, but al-Afdal deliberately turned away.

"Your views are most interesting and persuasive," interjected Saladin. "It will be necessary for you to write a report including all the points you have raised which can be used and acted upon. El-Fadil, please be kind enough to assist Rabbi Maimonides in this task and ensure that the information is widely distributed." Al-Afdal looked aghast.

Consequently Moses was tasked with even more work. He would write a *Treatise on Hygiene and Sanitation.* He left the meeting confident that he had presented a strong case and convinced that his words would be heeded, but once more he was required to produce a detailed written document. He enjoyed meeting Saladin and had admiration for all his achievements, both on and off the battlefield. He had little respect, however, for his son al-Afdal, who seemed inadequate and a pale shadow of his father. He knew that further battles were likely with the crusaders and hoped that Saladin would remain safe.

As Moses rode back to his house on his faithful mule, other concerns were in his thoughts. He was fully committed to completing the *Guide* and was continuing to communicate with Joseph. He sent him regular chapters to review and was grateful for Joseph's input, but he was struggling with time constraints. Although Moses had hoped that the *Guide* would be completed in a year, this was totally unrealistic.

On reaching home, Moses was welcomed by Jamilah with refreshment and freshly baked bread of the type that she knew he enjoyed.

"Dear husband, you must rest. You are working too hard and are pressured by many different people who want your opinion and counsel, but the strain on your health is too great."

Moses sat down and was about to respond when there was

a loud knocking on the door. It was Dovid, the caretaker from the synagogue. He was flushed and flustered and had obviously been running.

"Esteemed nagid, the members of the Beth Din await your presence." Moses had forgotten about the important adjudication that he was required to make regarding a difficult and controversial case.

"Tell the Beth Din that they will have to wait. My husband requires rest before embarking on further work this afternoon," Jamilah interrupted before Moses could reply.

Moses had reflected on the case for several days, but he was still troubled. A religious student at the yeshiva called Yehoshua, the son of a rabbi, was accused of a practice which was regarded in Jewish law as an abomination. He was accused of "lying" with an eight-year-old boy. Initially Yehoshua denied the accusation, but the child's testimony was so credible that he was found guilty. Yehoshua broke down and wept openly under intense questioning. He claimed he was only trying to comfort the boy who, he said, was lonely and unhappy. He insisted that no sexual contact took place. The boy himself was unclear on this matter and did not seem to know what carnal relations were and whether they'd taken place or not. Yehoshua admitted his liking and desire for men and boys rather than women but denied any abuse of the boy. Moses had listened carefully to the evidence. The young boy's parents insisted on full retribution, which meant stoning to death. The student's father begged the Beth Din for leniency.

Although he was exhausted, Moses knew he had to attend the court. He rose slowly from his chair, apologised to Jamilah, and left with Dovid. When Moses and Dovid arrived at the court, everyone stood. Moses made his way to the front of the hall. He sat, and so did everyone else. The time had now arrived for the nagid to discuss the appropriate punishment with his council. Moses was the court president and would be required to write the main adjudication, with his colleagues adding concurring opinions.

In the *Mishneh Torah*, Moses quoted unambiguously the Torah prohibition against lying with a man, but he had sympathy for Yehoshua. He did not believe that sexual activity had taken place. He was aware that the entire assembly were awaiting his adjudication. He began his ruling with a statement of Jewish law.

"This is a most troubling matter. In the case of a man who lies with a man or causes a man to have connection with him, and if sexual contact has been initiated, the rule is as follows: If both are adults, they are punishable by stoning, as it is said in the Torah, Leviticus 18:22, 'Thou shalt not lie with a man.' This is irrespective of whether he is the active or the passive participant in the act. If he is a minor aged nine years and one day, or older, the adult who has connection with him or causes him to have connection with him, is punishable by stoning, whilst the minor is exempt. If the minor is nine years old or younger, both are exempt. It behoves the court, however, to have the adult flogged for disobedience, as he has lain with a male, even though one less than nine years of age." Moses hesitated and looked at Yehoshua, who was gazing with a vacant stare at the floor. The boy was with his parents and seemed bemused and unsure of his surroundings.

"The boy, aged eight, has therefore no case to answer and is dismissed with our sympathy. I expect that as parents you will ensure he is comforted and made to understand the situation. There is no evidence that a sexual act took place, and in Jewish law it is this that is an abomination. Therefore, I have decided to express leniency."

There was absolute silence in the room. Moses faced Yehoshua. "Yehoshua, as a religious man you knew that your action was unacceptable, and although you may have been merely trying to provide comfort to the boy, the fact that he was in your bed indicates to me that you are mentally ill and deserving of medical assistance. You will recompense the family financially with a sum that I will decide, and you will submit yourself to strengthening your mental and moral convictions through study of the moral exhortations of the prophets and philosophers until you are able to regulate your life accordingly. Peace of mind, even in adverse circumstances, is an essential requisite for the well-being of the soul. You will surely be able to purge the desire for men from your very soul."

Moses rose from his seat and slowly walked from the room. The nagid had made an adjudication which would be followed.

29

The two keepers of the nilometer on the island of Roda were pleased. Throughout the summer they recorded the flood level at 30 cubits, which was high. By autumn it had risen to 50 cubits. They spread the word by messengers to the central market so that the population and particularly the farmers could be informed. They would be happy.

The fields were flooded again, generously watered with the richness provided by the Nile. The waterwheels turned, filling the canals passing through the fields. It would be a good harvest. The Nile had fulfilled its responsibility, and the people were guaranteed ample food for another year. The mosques would fill up, and thanksgiving prayers would be recited. The situation had been quite different two years previously. Then the Nile was green with duckweed, and the meagre waters hardly covered the thickets along the border. Dead fish floated to the surface, the harvest failed, and the people faced a year of misery. This year would be quite different. Food would be plentiful, and life would be comfortable. It was all in the hands of the Almighty.

Saladin was pleased not only because of the news from Roda but also because he had met Moses. He had been addressed by a man of stature and integrity, one who had the interests of humanity at heart. The Jews were fortunate to have such a leader. Saladin hoped that his administration would work to implement the proposals, but he had misgivings. Al-Afdal was his eldest son and would follow him as grand sultan, but Saladin doubted his ability. Al-Afdal was shallow and self-seeking and could not be trusted. Saladin knew that al-Afdal sought credit from the meeting with Maimonides and undeservedly hoped to be showered with praise for considering the living and health conditions of the people, even though el-Fadil had told him he had tried to block the proposals when Maimonides initially discussed them.

Nevertheless, Saladin had no choice but to leave the implementation of the proposals to al-Afdal. He had other important matters to deal with. The crusaders were planning revenge attacks for their recent defeat and were determined to recapture Jerusalem. There would be many bloody battles, and he, Saladin, would be leading from the front as was his custom. He could be killed but was not frightened of his own mortality in the holy cause.

Saladin was proved correct in his prediction of crusader revenge. The fall of Jerusalem prompted the Third Crusade. Richard the Lionhearted, King of England, led a siege of Acre, conquered the city, and executed three thousand Muslim prisoners, including women and children. How pleased Moses was that Miriam had left Acre and was now living happily in Fustat. Multiple battles followed in which Saladin's armies suffered heavy losses and were forced to withdraw. Richard began to restore inland castles on the coastal plain beyond Jaffa in preparation for an assault on Jerusalem. After Richard reoccupied Jaffa, he and Saladin discussed terms and reached an agreement. Christians would be allowed to travel as unarmed pilgrims to Jerusalem, and Saladin's kingdom would be at peace with the crusader states for the following three years.

In September 1191, Richard once again mounted an army and attacked Saladin's forces, forcing him to retreat. Saladin had no strategic options. He destroyed the walls of Ashkelon and the town of Jaffa so that they could not be used by the Christians. This failed to stop their progress, and they moved closer towards Jerusalem. In a frantic attempt to halt them, Saladin destroyed towns, burned farms, and poisoned all the wells. The strategy worked. Richard realised that without the resources present in the countryside, a siege of Jerusalem would result in the loss of thousands of Christian lives.

Richard reluctantly agreed to a truce with Saladin which was acceptable to both parties but temporary in nature. Saladin had much to do to strengthen his forces and prepare for inevitable future crusader attacks. Sadly, however, his personal commitment was cut short. During a visit to Damascus, during which he tried to reinforce his army with local men and to strengthen his coffers, he developed a fever which gradually intensified. He became delirious, and within a few days he died. There was a period of extensive mourning, both from the civilian population and from his soldiers who had trusted him wholeheartedly and never hesitated to follow him into battle whatever the risk and however unfavourable the odds.

At the time of his death, his entire possessions consisted of one piece of gold and forty pieces of silver. He had given away all his wealth to improve the living conditions of his subjects. He was buried in a mausoleum in Damascus.

Al-Afdal, as Saladin's eldest son, had expected to be appointed as sultan and head of the dynasty, but his ambition was thwarted by his siblings who considered that he lacked the required leadership credentials and was deceitful. Egypt was claimed by his younger brother, al-Aziz.

Moses was saddened when he heard the news of Saladin's death. He had great respect for the illustrious leader who had devoted his life to the well-being of his people and who fought bravely for his deep religious beliefs. Moses was comforted when he heard that al-Aziz, supported by el-Fadil, gave an undertaking to work towards Saladin's recommendations on improving the environment, knowing that this is what his father had wanted. To this end Moses's treatise on hygiene was used as the basis for the implementation.

Moses's reputation and standing in the Jewish community as a religious leader and physician of repute reached stellar heights. He was constantly in demand and was expected to deal with copious medical and religious issues. Jamilah became progressively more concerned, but despite her protestations, Moses refused to relax. His main objective, despite all his other commitments, was to complete the *Guide*. He devoted every spare moment to the task.

One concession he made to Jamilah was to cut down on the number of visitors who requested an audience with him for whatever reason. Meetings of this type often consumed many hours of his precious time, and it was time that he could least afford.

Moses continued to send instalments of the *Guide* to Joseph for comment and so was able to maintain his interest in Joseph's education and development. He eagerly awaited Joseph's responses on the *Guide*, which were usually incisive and thoughtful, confirming to Moses that Joseph was developing into a talented scholar.

In the *Guide* Moses consolidated teachings of philosophical truths that he had identified in the *Mishneh Torah* in such a way that they did not hinder religious commitment. The *Guide* urged people to become fully human by living in accordance with reason. He argued that religion is not merely a mythic representation of rational truths but is what takes over when science reaches its limits. He hypothesised that human intelligence is limited, and the *Guide* instructs humankind to contemplate the beauty and harmony of the universe and to experience the divine presence everywhere, in a room, in the sky, in a storm at sea, so that one comes to a passionate love of God. He wrote of his belief in the order and harmony of the universe and a conviction that there is a supreme intellect manifesting itself in nature.

Philosophical discussions on the nature of God, including His incorporeality, as well as the problem of the anthropomorphic description of God in the Bible, the nature of creation, miracles, the question of evil or its absence, and prophecy, were difficult to comprehend even by the most gifted of individuals but were questions which had occupied the mind of thinking people for generations. Moses not only posed these questions but also provided answers, some of which, with their interpretations, were in line with the thoughts of the sages of the Talmud and Mishna, but others were entirely original—and some even contradicted the sages' opinions. There can be little doubt that the kind of philosophy Moses proposed was designed not merely to be intellectual but to lead one towards a life of wisdom and contemplation in the pursuit of happiness.

In 1190, after three intense years, Moses, at the age of fifty-five, successfully completed his masterly work the *Guide of the Perplexed*. The huge effort took its toll on his already failing health and well-being. Even at times when he was mentally exhausted and lethargic, he refused to allow his medical practice to suffer. The combination of the two activities brought him to the very edge of what is humanly possible without a complete breakdown. He suffered from bouts of depression and exhaustion akin to those which he had experienced on hearing of the death of his brother David. Jamilah's constant attention and the reassuring presence of his young son, Abraham, were mainly responsible for maintaining his sanity during these especially arduous times.

The *Guide* generated widespread interest very quickly. It was read not only by religious scholars but also by philosophers who were attracted to Moses's line of reasoning. The book was also read outside Muslim countries. In France, Jewish scholars requested a copy translated into Hebrew since they could not read Arabic. Moses was honoured but did not have the time or the energy to personally undertake a translation. They were sent copies of the book, and they arranged for a translation to be undertaken by Rabbi Samuel ibn Tibbon.

Moses was pleased with the choice. He did not know Samuel ibn Tibbon but was familiar with the writings of his father. He wrote to Samuel saying that he was honoured that such an eminent scholar with such an illustrious father had been chosen to translate his work. Moses was aware of the difficulties that might accrue with the translation and made suggestions to assist Samuel and to help him with difficult parts.

"Do not rigidly follow each word but be sure that the thought is clear and understandable, and transmit that thought, even if some of the words or phrases must be changed or even omitted," wrote Moses. "You should first try to grasp the sense of the passage thoroughly and then state my intention with clarity. This cannot be done without changing the order of words, putting many words for one, or vice versa, and adding or taking away words, so that the subject may be perfectly intelligible in Hebrew."

Samuel completed three sections and sent them to Moses so that he could check them for accuracy. Moses was delighted with the result. The translation was excellent and had exceeded his expectations. Ibn Tibbon went on to complete the task and asked whether he could have the honour of visiting Moses in Fustat. The request came at a particularly difficult time for Moses, when his health was deficient and his energy sapped. He was also cognizant of his promise to Jamilah to refuse all requests for visits. He declined but gave a detailed account of his reason:

> Now God knows that in order to write to you,
> I have escaped to a secluded spot, where people
> would not think to find me, sometimes leaning
> for support against a wall, sometimes lying

down on account of my excessive weakness, for I have grown old and feeble.

With regard to your wish to come here, I cannot but say how greatly your visit would delight me, for I truly long to commune with you and would anticipate our meeting with greater joy than you. Yet I must advise you not to expose yourself to the perils of the voyage, for beyond seeing me, and my doing all I could to honour you, you would not derive any advantage from your visit. Do not expect to be able to confer with me on any scientific subject, for even one hour by day or night, for the following is my daily occupation. I dwell in Fustat, and the sultan resides at his palace. These two places are two Sabbath days' journey [a mile and a half] distant from each other. My duties to the sultan are very heavy. I am obliged to visit him every day, early in the morning and when he or any of his wives or children, or any of the inmates of the harem, are indisposed. I dare not leave but must stay during the greater part of the day in the palace. It also frequently happens that one or two of the royal officers fall sick, and I must attend to their healing. Hence, as a rule, I do not return until the afternoon. Then I am almost dying with hunger. I find the antechamber filled with people, both Jews and Gentiles; nobles and common people; judges and bailiffs; friends and foes—a mixed multitude, who await the time of my return.

I dismount from my animal, wash my hands, go forth to my patients, and entreat them to bear with me whilst I partake of some light refreshment, the only meal I take in the twenty-four hours. Then I attend to my patients and write prescriptions for their various ailments. Patients go in and out until nightfall, and sometimes even, I solemnly assure you, until two hours and more into the night. I converse and prescribe for them whilst lying down from sheer fatigue, and when night falls, I am so exhausted that I can scarcely speak.

In consequence of this, no Jew can have any private interview except on the Sabbath. On this day the whole congregation, or at least the majority of its members, come to me after the morning service, when I instruct them as to their proceedings during the whole week; we study together a little till noon, when they depart. Some of them return and read with me after the afternoon service and until evening prayers. In this manner I spend that day. I have here related to you only a part of what you would see if you were to visit me. Now when you have completed for our brethren the translation you have commenced, I beg that you will come to me, but not with the hope of deriving any advantage from your visit as regards your studies; for my time is, as I have shown you, excessively occupied.

It pained Moses to respond in such a negative fashion, but he felt it important to give an honest realistic assessment to ibn

Tibbon of what he could expect if he were to visit. The letter was also useful in clarifying Moses's impossible work schedule. How perceptive Jamilah had been in her insistence that his health was now suffering. But time was against him, and he knew he had so much more to accomplish.

The *Guide* had an influence on both Arab and Christian philosophy. But it also generated much controversy. Whilst many fellow Jews regarded it as a magnificent attempt at unifying knowledge, others condemned it as heresy. Animosity was expressed, as had been expected, from Samuel ben Ali, but also surprisingly from rabbinical colleagues in Egypt who had difficulty in understanding several precepts.

"Rabbi Moses, can it be true that you believe that God is some kind of nonphysical Being, heaven forbid?" Rabbi Shaul ben Yosef, a senior member of the community who had lived in Fustat all his life and who, even at the age of seventy-five, attended prayer services in the synagogue three times every day, seemed agitated as he accosted Moses with his concerns. "Do we not learn in the Torah and in the words of our sages that God speaks, God raises his hand, God sees, God listens?"

Moses tried to remain calm and polite.

"My dear Shaul, the Torah is not always meant to be understood according to its superficial meaning. It speaks allegorically. Like a veil worn by a princess, so do the images used by the Torah cover the beauty of the hidden meaning of the words."

Moses had intended that the *Guide* be read only by the small coterie of intellectual Jews who wished for a deeper philosophical explanation of key religious concepts which cannot be found elsewhere. But the book had been distributed widely and was not fully understood and indeed was misinterpreted by many, either through ignorance or vindictiveness. Interestingly, Moses received supportive letters from Muslim theologians who had expressed similar views. He was particularly delighted to hear from his old friend Ibn Rushd (Averroes), whose writings he was familiar with. They had remained in intermittent contact since their days in Fez. Ibn Rushd was now a respected Muslim theologian and, like Moses, was a physician of some repute. Although his field of study was the Koran, he blended it in with the teachings of Aristotle. He claimed vehemently that the Koran must not be read literally but interpreted allegorically.

"My dear Ibn Rushd, how similar we are in our thoughts," Moses wrote to him, "and how grateful I am for your concern and good wishes."

But many of Moses's fellow Jews were far less impressed, and the criticisms continued unabated. He was distressed to receive a letter from Rabbi Nasanel ibn Alfayumi in Yemen, the father of Rabbi Yaacov, to whom Moses had addressed his famous letter of consolation (Igeres Teiman).

"My friends and I are confounded. It seems that everything is a symbol. No simple meaning of any doctrine remains. Do you really believe in the resurrection of the dead, or is this also like the descriptions of God, merely a symbol?"

Nasanel copied his letter to Samuel ben Ali in Baghdad, who was appalled that resurrection, a basic tenet of Jewish teaching, was being questioned. This was another opportunity for ben Ali to undermine Moses's authority and to assert his own position as Gaon. He wasted no time in responding and accusing Moses of heresy. He then wrote a detailed essay on the topic of the resurrection and sent copies to Damascus, Yemen, and Egypt.

Moses had already responded to Rabbi Nasanel, upholding his firm belief in the resurrection as a fundamental principle of Jewish belief. At no time had he ever disputed the concept, he said. He had been deliberately misrepresented.

Moses read ben Ali's essay with mounting distress. He was deeply upset. Despite his growing weariness, he felt compelled to respond, stating his position on resurrection. The letter, "Igeres Techias Hameisim", reflected his anger:

"I declare that the resurrection, which is well-known to our people, a generally accepted belief, which is agreed upon by all factions, which is so often mentioned in the prayers composed by the prophets and greatest sages, which is discussed in the Talmud and Midrash, is a concept universally accepted by all Jews. The concept has no 'interpretation' at all. And if one has heard that a religious man has said the opposite, one may not believe such a report."

Whilst writing he realised how incensed he was becoming, so much so that he flushed with anger and developed an unusual pain in his chest which moved up to his left arm. He rested on his divan for a short while before getting up and continuing with his writing.

"Someone has claimed that I have said that the resurrection mentioned in our holy books is allegorical. But this is a clear falsehood and totally different from what I have actually said. It appears to me from the statements of our sages that after people are resurrected, they will eat, drink, engage in marital relations, have children, and die after a very long life, as will be in the days of Mashiach. The life that has no death after it is the life of the world to come, which is a life without physicality."

However, the feud and attacks on Moses's integrity continued, fuelled in the main by Samuel ben Ali. Moses decided that he could do no more to persuade the sceptics, and in view of his failing health, he decided to ignore further criticisms. His approach was not unlike that which he used when the *Mishneh Torah* was subjected to similar abuse.

Moses's failing health was a worry to Jamilah. He was looking older and greyer. His sleeping pattern was disturbed, but most concerning of all were the bouts of depression during which he remained silent and withdrawn for several days. Jamilah was certain that he needed rest to recover. Eventually, as Moses himself became aware of a lack of energy and an increasing frequency of chest pains, he succumbed to her wishes. He took a three-month break from his medical practice with el-Fadil's and al-Aziz's blessing. He also stood down as nagid for the same period. He would rest and recover from the strain of his heavy workload and criticism. His only concession was that he would continue with his writing. He had decided that his medical treatises should be completed.

PART VI

Egypt

1193—1204

30

braham was proud of his father and knew how much he was respected for his work both as a doctor and as a Jewish theologian and philosopher, not that he understood what these latter were. But every time Moses entered a room, everyone stood; each time he spoke, everyone listened attentively. Abraham knew that his father was a very religious man, but religion to him appeared to be a way of life which determined how he conducted himself. Abraham understood, even though only seven, that his father wanted him to lead a similar lifestyle, and he was determined not to disappoint. He was going to follow in the footsteps of the Maimon and Mishael dynasties.

Abraham was conversant with portions of the Torah and Mishna which he could recite by heart, but most notably he enjoyed learning. He relished the teaching sessions with his father, and this established a close relationship, heightened during Moses's prolonged enforced period of rest. They spent many hours studying together in a bonding exercise during which his father related stories of his life in Cordoba, his travels throughout Spain and Morocco, the periods of hardship and persecution, his study of medicine in Fez, his journey to Palestine with visits to Jerusalem and Hebron, and the untimely death of his uncle, David. Abraham was enthralled.

"My son, your grandfather Rabbi Maimon, may his soul rest in peace, was a learned man who devoted his entire life to study of the Torah and to helping his fellow man. He died in Israel, where he is buried. In the same way that I am teaching you, so your grandfather taught me and his father taught him. Our family has fourteen generations of rabbonim. From generation to generation that is how Judaism has survived." Abraham always listened intently whenever his father recalled their family history.

"When we were forced to leave our home in Cordoba, your grandfather cried. It was always his desire to return one day, but he never did."

"What about your mother? Did she wish to return?"

"I never knew your grandmother. She died after giving birth to me. My father often talked about her and how happy they were during their year of marriage. My father remarried an *eshet chayil*, a wonderful woman of worth, Shoshanah, whom I always regarded as my mother. She looked after me as her own son, and I loved her very much. Sadly, she died in a dreadful accident when I was very young. My father was devastated and never really recovered from the bereavement. She had a son, my dear brother, your uncle David." Moses paused. Abraham could see the colour drain from his face. This happened every time he talked about his uncle. The boy sat quietly and waited for his father to recover his composure.

"Your uncle David developed a thriving business in gems which provided money to support the family whilst I continued to study and learn medicine. He was shipwrecked whilst returning from India, where he'd completed a successful business deal. I say a prayer for him each day during the morning service in the synagogue."

"Father tell me more about Cordoba. What was it like to live there?"

"Ah, Abraham, life in Cordoba, when I was your age, was idyllic. We lived in a comfortable house. I had many friends, not only Jewish but also Muslim and Christian. Do you know Cordoba was one of the most advanced cities in the world? It was a centre of education where learning was taken seriously. It was a Muslim city. Jews were called *dhimmis*, 'subservient ones', but we lived in peace and harmony with our neighbours. Christians and Jews participated in all aspects of the life of the city. We had many synagogues and yeshivot, where we were free to pray and study. When I was thirteen, everything changed. The tolerant Almoravid regime was taken over by the vile Almohads, who were vicious and would not accept that Jews should live so comfortably. They forced us to leave if we refused to convert to Islam."

Abraham could see that his father was becoming increasingly more distressed as the memories came flooding back to him.

"Your grandfather would not consider conversion, so we left with very few of our possessions and travelled throughout Spain, from city to city, from village to village, looking for refuge. It was hard, but we managed until we were driven from Spain and travelled to Fez in Morocco. But your grandfather's heart always remained in Cordoba. Even when we travelled to Palestine and visited Jerusalem and Hebron, he could not settle."

Moses was quiet for a while and stared into the distance. His eyes seemed to lose all vibrancy, and tears appeared.

"I want to be like you, Father, a rabbi and a doctor. I will not let you down."

"You will be better than me. When I was your age I could not study. I had little concentration. I understood ideas but would not learn. Your grandparents were worried, and I was sent away to a yeshiva in Lucena to study with the famous rabbi Migash. He taught me many things, but most notably he taught me the importance of achieving the potential which is given to each of us by God. We are all here to do his bidding. If we fail, then we have let him down and ultimately will regret it. You must go your own way in life. We all have free will, but you must follow the righteous pathway. You know your path, and you must follow it."

Abraham decided it was time to leave his father to rest. How he loved his father, and how much he enjoyed and benefited from these learning sessions. Moses's eyes were now closed, but he had a smile on his face. Abraham imagined he was dreaming of his youth and his many past experiences. He quietly left the room and sought out his mother. He had smelt the wonderful aroma of her freshly baked cakes and decided he was hungry.

As he entered the kitchen, he saw that his mother had company. Aunty Rachel and Shoshanah were seated and eating.

"I know why you are called Shoshanah." Abraham was pleased with his discovery. "You are named after my grandmother. Isn't that right, Mummy?"

"Yes, you are quite right. Shoshanah was a very wonderful, very beautiful woman who married your grandfather a few years after his first wife, your father's mother, died during childbirth. Shoshanah is also a very beautiful girl," Jamilah said as she looked at Shoshanah.

"You are fortunate to be named after such a wonderful person, Shoshanah," said Jamilah as Rachel cuddled Shoshanah. "Your grandmother would have been so proud of you and so pleased that you were given her name." Rachel and Shoshanah smiled lovingly at each other.

Abraham and Shoshanah consumed several cakes and sat quietly whilst Jamilah and Rachel continued talking.

"I have not seen Miriam and Uziel recently," remarked Jamilah. "I suppose they are busy with their baby."

"I helped Miriam recently. Uziel was in Morocco on business, but they are all well," responded Rachel. "However, I think that Miriam would like to return to Acre. She was very happy in Palestine. But it is now more dangerous there, and a new Crusade is imminent."

Their peaceful chatter was interrupted by a commotion outside, followed by a firm knock on the door.

Jamilah's maidservant opened the door to find Micah, the husband of a friend of the family and a congregant from the synagogue. Micah had a son, Eli, of a similar age to Abraham, and the two boys often played together. Micah was welcomed and entered the room.

"Micah, what is the matter?" asked Jamilah.

"Eli is unwell. His skin is yellow, and he is sleeping most of the day. I know Rabbi Moses is not seeing patients at present, but my wife and I do not know whom to turn to." Micah was shaking with anxiety.

"We have seen a doctor who does not know what the problem is. Because of the yellow skin, he suggested segula, but I was hoping for Rabbi Moses's opinion."

Moses had awakened from his light slumber and walked into the room. Micah explained his reason for being there, and Moses offered his sympathy.

"Your son is known to me. I see him playing with Abraham in school and in the synagogue. He is a handsome, bright boy." Moses was obviously concerned. He feared the worst. He turned towards Jamilah with a questioning and appealing demeanour.

"I am enjoying a period of rest and am not ..."

"I am sure it will be acceptable to make an exception in this situation," Jamilah interrupted. Moses looked again towards Jamilah and smiled.

"I will listen to my wife's considerate words and see Eli. I will give you my opinion following my examination of him." Moses seemed relieved. Jamilah knew he was thankful that he had her agreement.

As Moses walked with Micah to his house in silence, he considered his options for the treatment of Eli, assuming he was suffering from jaundice. In most cases the outcome for jaundice was poor and few treatments seemed to help. He was adamantly against the concept of segula, a pigeon strapped on the navel of the patient to allow transfer of the jaundice so that the pigeon dies and the patient recovers. It was ridiculous. It had no logical or scientific basis. What had he always advocated: "Treat disease by the scientific method and not by guesswork, superstition, or rule of thumb."

He would only offer treatments which had some logical basis. He abhorred segula. Using pigeons to transfer disease was like wearing amulets to ward off danger, totally illogical and based on superstition rather than science.

Micah's wife opened the door and was relieved to see Moses. "Oh, thank you, dear doctor, for coming. I am so worried about Eli. He is so ill."

Moses agreed. Eli was lying on his bed and hardly moving. He had a high fever, his skin was deeply jaundiced, and his breathing was shallow. There was a bowl by his bed containing vomit, and his upper abdomen was tender on palpation. Moses was certain of the diagnosis. Eli had a severe malady of the liver.

"Eli has an excess of black and yellow bile, which is collecting in his liver and skin and causing the malady," explained Moses to Eli's distraught parents.

"We must hope that the malady gets better by itself, as it sometimes does. Bloodletting sometimes helps to remove the yellow bile. This should be tried. He must also be given large quantities of boiled water, fruits which are sweet, and aromatic herbs. I also advise pulverised earthworms soaked in vinegar to remove the yellowness. Water of palm trees and a potion of roots with Alexandrian gum and liquid alum powdered with a garden crocus and mixed with beets should be drunk at least three times a day. He must not be given meat or poultry."

Moses had studied the natural history of liver disease and knew that some patients recovered without any treatment, but many did not. He was not surprised that the pigeons died during segula because they were strapped so tightly to the patient's abdomen that they suffocated. Moses often wondered where this practice originated. The idea of transference of disease and sin is mentioned in the Talmud, and he assumed that this was its basis. But sin and disease are not equated, and he saw no rational or scientific reason for the use of segula. However, if all else were to fail, perhaps it should be attempted so that Eli's parents could be reassured that everything had been tried.

"If he fails to improve in the next few days, then as a last resort we can try segula," Moses explained to Micah. "If no orthodox remedies work, we can try unorthodox ones."

Micah and his wife had full confidence in Moses and were reassured.

"We are most grateful, Rabbi Moses, and we will pray for his recovery."

Moses was nevertheless concerned. The prognosis despite bloodletting was poor, but it was important to try everything possible to heal the child.

"Micah, when the disease is stronger than the natural resistance of the patient, medicine is of no use. When the patient's resistance is stronger than the disease, the physician is of no use. When the disease and the patient's resistance are equally balanced, the physician is needed to help tilt the balance in the patient's favour. With God's help, we will try to shift the balance in Eli's direction. But you are right: praying to the Almighty for recovery is also important, as well as relying on the physician."

Eli, however, failed to improve. His skin became ever more yellow. He went into a coma. Segula was tried as a last resort, but to no avail. After five days of loving care, he died peacefully in his parents' arms.

Moses was very upset. The death of Eli affected him badly and triggered another bout of depression.

31

Moses recovered from his latest period of poor health and returned to work after a three-month break. However, he looked far from well. His beard was completely grey, and he walked slowly and with a stoop. Every so often he needed to stop, seemingly to catch his breath. The pressures over the last few years had accumulated and taken their toll on his fragile health.

He was required, because of his esteemed position, to attend the ceremonial accession of al-Aziz as sultan of Egypt. When he arrived at the palace, there were hundreds of guests lined up in the courtyards. Food was present in abundance. A musician was playing an Arab lute, and everyone seemed in a happy relaxed mood. The courtyard was lined by thornless lote-trees and clustered plantains, which in this particularly sweltering summer provided much-needed shade. Water was gushing from numerous elaborate fountains.

Everyone was dressed in luxury linen, silk, or brocade, often embroidered with gold or silver threads. Al-Aziz did not wear a crown but an elaborately wrapped turban. His eunuch bodyguards also wore turbans with a tail left hanging down the back.

Moses watched, in his view, the unnecessary pomp and ceremony with a degree of contempt. So much money being wasted on unnecessary frivolity at a time when many resources were required to improve the quality of life for the citizens. However, he maintained an agreeable countenance since he was the official representative of the Jewish community at the ceremony and did not wish to convey a bad impression.

He offered his congratulations to al-Aziz, both on a personal level and in his role as nagid on behalf of the entire Jewish population.

"I also give you the Jewish blessing which is traditionally given to a head of state: 'Blessed are You, Lord our God, King of the Universe, who has given of his glory to human beings.'"

"You are most kind, Rabbi Maimonides. I have much to be grateful to you for. You are a remarkable man. My father held you in the highest regard and always regarded Jews as his cousins. I do also. The Jews are fortunate to have you as *ra'is yahud*, their nagid. May you live a long and healthy life to continue your good work." Al-Aziz was overtly genuine in his praise.

"I thank you most sincerely on behalf of the entire Jewish population," Moses responded. He came away from the ceremony reassured that Jewish interests would always be honoured and respected by the present regime.

He returned home, his representative duties completed. He was feeling a little stronger but was constantly tired. He had returned to his demanding work schedule two weeks previously but realised that he lacked energy. He was cheered in the knowledge, nevertheless, that during his enforced break he had managed to write many of the medical treatises that he had promised: his treatises on asthma, on poisons, on cohabitation, on hygiene and sanitation, and on haemorrhoids. At present he was working on the aphorisms of Hippocrates and Galen, which he found to be a challenge but nevertheless most interesting. He included occasional criticisms of Hippocrates and Galen. For example, Hippocrates was quoted as saying, "A boy is born from the right ovary and a girl from the left." Moses considered this assertion to be ridiculous. "A man would have to be either prophet or genius to know this," he wrote.

He approved of other comments attributed to Hippocrates, especially his credo on the art of medicine: "Life is short, and the art long, the occasion fleeting, experience fallacious, and judgement difficult. The physician must also make the patient, the attendants, and the externals cooperate."

Two additional medical works were also occupying Moses's mind, and he was determined to complete them: a clinical compendium of diseases which he called *Aphorisms of Moses* (*Pirkei Moses* in Hebrew) and a medication manual, *A Glossary of Drug Names*. Both were to become standard medical textbooks for decades.

The *Aphorisms* proved to be a time-consuming exercise. Moses had been conscious for many years of the lack of a comprehensive textbook which described the clinical manifestations and treatment of recognised common diseases. He aimed to rectify this. His book consisted of fifteen hundred aphorisms arranged in twenty-five chapters, each of which dealt with a different area of medicine. He included descriptions of anatomy, physiology, and pathology, as well as both symptoms and diagnosis. For each disease entity, he described the most appropriate and efficacious therapy and the indications for and against active treatment. He documented important principles of disease management, especially those that applied to surgical treatment.

The reason he undertook to write a glossary of drug names was because of the lack of a suitable pharmacopeia which could be used by physicians. In the *Glossary* he listed, in alphabetical order, some two thousand agents and their indications for use. The majority were of botanical origin, but some were of mineral or animal derivation. Only medications which he was convinced were efficacious were included, such as mouse excrement pulverised in vinegar for alopecia, brain of a camel prepared in vinegar for epilepsy, and earthworms pulverised and imbibed to cleanse the body of a patient with jaundice.

His final medical treatise was a short account of the treatment of fits. He followed Galen in stating that fits are due to thick, cold, viscous humours which can be liquefied by physical exercise and a bland diet. Sometimes fits occur because of excessive alcohol intake, in which case they are caused by an excess of black bile. In children, however, fits reduce in number as the child gets older because the white, moist, cold humour improves in quality, in which case waiting and merely encouraging physical exercise and a bland diet is enough. His advice for avoiding fits entailed regular laxatives, exercise, bathing, and abstinence from wine.

An immense amount of meticulous work was required to codify both the *Glossary* and the *Aphorisms,* but again Moses's extraordinary ability to gather and classify vast quantities of factual material and organise it into a logical order understandable to the reader was demonstrated. He was able to do this for his medical writings as well as for philosophical and religious writings.

The incident when it occurred was frightening. Moses was in his library busily writing. He got up and walked around the room, contemplating a section on tumours that he had written in his *Aphorisms*. Was he justified in advocating cauterisation as a treatment for large cancers that were ulcerating? If the outcome was so poor, why inflict the associated pain? He suddenly felt weak. The room was circulating. He collapsed to the floor. Jamilah heard the crash and rushed in. She was horrified. He was lying on the floor, shaking uncontrollably. She held his head, and he slowly stirred. He stood up with her help. Jamilah fetched some water.

"Do not fret, dear Jamilah. I am now recovered. It was only a faint. I now feel well."

Jamilah was not so sure. Moses's hands were shaking. He was pale. She helped him to the bedroom, where he lay down. His colour returned. He stood and walked to the balcony. He looked upwards to the sky. It was already night; the stars were shimmering above.

He knew that the price he was required to pay for his arduous life was a gradual deterioration of his own health.

32

Miriam looked distressed when she asked to speak with Jamilah in confidence. When they were sitting comfortably, Miriam described her worry. She needed advice.

"I do not wish to ask Moses. He has only recently improved from his weariness and stress." Jamilah was troubled by Miriam's request. "I am worried about his health. Mentioning this might make him ill again. I do not want this." Miriam needed to confide in someone, and Jamilah was an obvious choice. She had thought carefully about this before reluctantly approaching Jamilah.

"Moses will hear about it soon. Delaying this will not relieve him of the strain," replied Miriam. "I need his help and will speak to him myself if you will not." Miriam seemed desperate. Jamilah realised that Miriam was correct: her husband would hear of the problem from others, and it would be better if she approached him herself. But she could not hide her trepidation.

"You are correct. I will talk to him when he returns from the ceremony." Jamilah agreed that it was her responsibility to approach her husband. But regrettably it was not the only disturbing news that she would have to give him. She had prepared herself to discuss with Moses her own predicament but now decided to postpone it. Moses could not deal with two problems at the same time.

Most recently Moses had concentrated his efforts on overseeing the building of a new synagogue in the centre of Fustat. This had been his ambition for many years, and eventually he had managed to secure generously large donations for it come to fruition. The Jewish population had increased in size because of Moses's popularity, which had attracted increasing numbers of worshippers. His previous synagogue, Knessiyat Ilshmiyin, had become too small and cramped for praying on busy occasions such as the Sabbath and holy days. He was pleased with the new build. It was light and airy, and the seating was comfortable. He named the synagogue Beit Knesset Elyiahu Hanavi after one of the greatest prophets of Jewish history, Elijah.

The initiative had an uplifting effect on Moses's mental health. His attitude and persona were far more positive. He continued to receive hostile comments from Samuel ben Ali but felt able to handle them. He was also cheered by Abraham, who was developing into an admirable young man with undoubted potential. He had matured ever since his bar mitzvah three years previously, and his level of scholarship was admirable.

Moses stood patiently in the lobby of the synagogue as the guests arrived. He welcomed each individually and thanked them for attending. He felt very proud, but if it had been his choice, he would have forgone any formal ceremony. The community, however, insisted that a formal celebration take place and that as nagid it was his responsibility to thank the many donors who had contributed to the building fund.

At the opening Moses took the opportunity to deliver an educational discourse on Elijah the prophet. He described how Elijah had performed a miracle for a widow and her son who were on the brink of starvation. Elijah also demonstrated to the many idol-worshippers that the Almighty is the only true God. Elijah became one of the few prophets who was taken to heaven without dying. He is known as the "angel of the covenant", and according to Jewish tradition is present at each circumcision when a new Jewish soul is brought into the world. The entirely male audience was captivated by Moses's talk.

He returned home after the ceremony and was pleased to see Jamilah with Rachel and Miriam, but the tense atmosphere was obvious. All three women seemed dejected. Miriam and Rachel stood as he entered and excused themselves, about to depart. Miriam embraced Jamilah before leaving.

"My dear Jamilah, you look worried. What ails you?" asked a concerned Moses once the two women had gone. Jamilah was hesitant and obviously reluctant to answer. She was convinced that she could not tell him about both concerns; that would be too much. She would only speak about Miriam's worry and leave her personal problem for another day.

"Dear husband, Miriam has asked me to inform you of a disturbing situation. She desperately needs your help and advice."

"Please do not be worried about confiding in me. I know you are reluctant because of my melancholic disposition and weariness, but I am available for help whenever it is needed by the family."

Moses anticipated a serious situation. Jamilah was overly apprehensive, and her usual air of confidence and control seemed to have evaporated. This was unlike Jamilah. Moses sat down and awaited unpleasant news.

"It is about my dear brother, Uziel. There has been a serious problem with his business."

Moses listened carefully. He had heard that there were problems with the flax supply from India and its rising cost. Flax was harvested in India by a specialist flax harvester before exporting the fibres to Egypt, where it was converted to linen for clothes and fabrics, with the linseed oil being used as medication. It is a heavily worker-dependent manual exercise. The plant is pulled up with its roots so that the whole length of the plant fibre can be used. But the length and quality of the fibres are weather dependent.

"Uziel's supplier in India demanded payment before delivery of a recent consignment so that he could pay his workers. Recent inclement weather resulted in a poor harvest and a shortage with an increase in the price of flax. Uziel agreed to pay the high price, but his partner, a trustworthy Muslim, was against the idea and said they should wait. But because Uziel had already received payment for the flax from his customers, he felt that ethically he must deliver the goods to his customers at the agreed low price. The business is now left with huge debts because the supplier's price has risen sharply. As a consequence he is bankrupt, and Mustapha, his partner, blames Uziel and insists on financial retribution through a sharia court of law."

Moses could see the developing scenario and understood the concern. He remained quiet for a while as he collected his thoughts. Uziel was an honest ethical businessman as well as a knowledgeable rabbi. He would have been aware of his responsibilities in honouring a deal which he had made with his clients, and despite the fact that the deal would inevitably be financially disastrous through no fault of his own—he was not in a position to influence the weather—he would be committed by Jewish law to act honestly and fairly and adhere to the low price agreed with his clients. Failing to supply the goods at the agreed relatively low price would have affected the integrity of his customers' business, which was Halachically unacceptable.

"My dear Jamilah, Uziel's actions are entirely in accordance with Jewish ethical practice and law." Moses was pleased that Uziel had not tried to extract a better deal from his customers, having initially made a binding agreement on the price.

"It is unfortunate that he has found himself in this predicament. In Chapter 5 of the *Mishneh Torah* I discuss business ethics in detail. A man must be scrupulous in his business conduct. He must obligate himself in matters of buying and selling so that he stands by his word and does not change it. He should not take away business from his fellow man or bring grief to any man. The general rule is that he be amongst the oppressed and not the oppressors. The Torah states that a man who performs all these actions and their like will be regarded by the Almighty as 'my servant Israel, in whom I will be glorified'." Jamilah seemed reassured but still concerned.

"Do not fret. I will speak with Uziel. He has acted correctly. I will endeavour to redeem his losses."

The following day he met with Uziel, who was naturally worried. The threat of facing a sharia court with its potential outcome was not very pleasant. Uziel repeated the sequence of events that Moses had already heard from Jamilah.

"Your conduct has been entirely consistent with Jewish teaching," Moses said. "As a community, we have a responsibility to assist your dilemma. I will consult with my council and, if necessary, with al-Aziz himself."

"You are most kind." Uziel's worried countenance seemed to lift with the reassuring words from Moses. "I am worried not only for myself and my family but also for Mustapha. We have enjoyed a wonderful working arrangement, and he is an honest partner. He warned against the deal with India, but I ignored him. He must be compensated. I hope he and I can reform the business together."

Moses chaired the committee which raised money for the release of captive Jewish hostages. The fund was large and had not been used for several years because the incidence of kidnapping had been reduced almost to zero thanks to much tighter security and a sympathetic Islamic regime which abhorred such activity. Moses convinced the committee that Uziel had been a hostage to fortune and had rigidly followed Halacha in his business dealings. They agreed and approved the request for financial assistance to support Uziel's business. In addition, al-Aziz, with the support of el-Fadil, decided that the issue was not a matter for the sharia court. Mustapha was content and rejoined Uziel in their business partnership. Trade in flax subsequently returned to normal and prospered. Uziel was, in due course, able to pay back his debts from his personal account.

"Because you were honest in your business dealings, the Almighty has rewarded you. I was merely his messenger," explained Moses as Uziel expressed his immense gratitude.

A distinguished judge who lived in Alexandria brought to the attention of Samuel ben Ali that he could not find the source for one of the decisions Moses had documented within the *Mishneh Torah*. It was an important matter relating to a marital issue. Before informing ben Ali, he had brought this to the attention of Moses, who spent several days trying to identify where, within the corpus of Jewish law, he had obtained the primary information but was unable to find it. Moses was crestfallen. He realised that he should have documented all his source material within the *Mishneh Torah* whilst he was writing it, but he had failed to do so. It was a clear signal to Moses that his astounding memory and ability to recall information was beginning to abandon him. He must now review the entire fourteen volumes of the *Mishneh Torah* and document where all the source material could be found.

But did he have the time, and was he capable of this enormous task at his age? He needed assistance. Abraham offered his services. In addition, Moses approached his student Joseph, who was delighted and honoured to help. Accordingly, in a very structured fashion, they set about documenting all the sources as an appendix to the *Mishneh Torah*.

But ben Ali was not satisfied and maintained his criticism, accusing Moses of fabrication. He insisted that all Moses's responsa should be regarded as null and void and that only ben Ali's own views should be accepted. Moses was shocked by this latest attack and realised that only when the full list of sources was published would the accusations cease.

33

Jamilah decided it was now time to mention her personal problem to her husband. "Moshe, I have noticed an unusual swelling in my breast. What could it be?"

Moses examined Jamilah's breast, following which he looked gloomy. Jamilah admitted to having felt an unusual lumpiness in her left breast six months earlier but said she had ignored it as being the result of natural changes which occur in the breast of a woman of her age. She did not tell her husband that another reason for the delay was that she did not wish to burden him with an additional family problem at a time when he was dealing with Uziel's financial difficulties. However, the lumpiness had now become more noticeable and was causing discomfort.

"I can also feel a lump in my armpit which has become larger. I also have pain in my hip when I walk."

"My dear Jamilah, you should have told me earlier. The black bile in your body is excessive and has accumulated in your breast, armpit, and probably hip." Moses tried to look confident and portray a positive demeanour, but Jamilah's expression was one of acceptance and despair.

Moses had immediately recognised the condition. He had seen women with breast cancer previously, and the outcomes were not usually favourable. Tumours did indeed develop from a superfluity of black bile; the problem was that if the superfluity descended into the depths of the body and pressed into the mouths of the vessels, the tumour gained added momentum and the prognosis was poor. Moses feared that this was the situation with Jamilah. Surgery would not be justified given the lateness and the extent of black bile accumulation. He initiated a course of bloodletting and purgation to express the black humour. He prescribed all the accepted medications such as camphor, musk, violet, and cantharides. All proved ineffective. What is more, he was concerned that bloodletting and purgation were making the situation worse and decided that Hippocrates's dictum *Primum non nocere,* "First do no harm," was relevant. The treatments were detrimental and reducing Jamilah's quality of life, making her feel more ill than the disease itself, in addition to being ineffective. He decided to discontinue all treatments, which greatly pleased Jamilah.

Throughout the ordeal of therapy, Jamilah maintained a cheerful disposition. Everyone was attentive. Miriam and Rachel were always available for comfort and to deal with daily chores. Even Abraham assisted to the best of his ability. Moses spent increasing amounts of time reciting psalms and praying in the synagogue. Nothing seemed to help other than opium, which effectively relieved the pain.

"Do not fret, my dear Moshe and Abraham. I feel the end is arriving, but I have no fear. God has been good to me. I have been so proud to be your wife, Moshe, and your mother, Abraham. I have tried to be a good wife and mother, but if I have failed, I plead for your forgiveness." Moses struggled to keep his composure lest Jamilah be upset.

"The Almighty was good to me also when your father, may his soul rest in peace, introduced me to you," responded Moses. "You are the perfect wife. I will honour and respect you forever. Without your support I would not have been able to achieve my ambitions. Your learning and understanding have been astonishing. I thank you so much."

He struggled with his emotions, and his hands began shaking uncontrollably. The shaking was a problem that he had noticed for some months and which had prevented him from writing. He now had a secretary to dictate his responsa to the numerous requests which he still received.

Each day Moses sat with Jamilah and they reminisced on their marriage. Abraham joined them whenever he was free to do so. She seemed content and mercifully without pain, or at least she never complained. Whenever she was with her family, she maintained a cheerful disposition. Her appetite gradually lessened, and towards the end she could only tolerate sips of water.

Jamilah was eventually bed-bound. She seemed to sleep for longer and longer periods and had difficulty in communicating. On one sunny afternoon, surrounded by her family, she slipped into a coma and two hours later died serenely. Moses remarked, "Her soul has joined the angels, and she is now at peace."

Moses was badly affected by Jamilah's death. Physically he became frailer and weaker. Any form of exertion resulted in breathlessness. His shaking progressed. His previously phenomenal mental agility and level of concentration deteriorated. He often cried, even in public, whenever the memory of Jamilah flooded back. He was incapable of enjoying food and avoided company.

As soon as the traditional period of mourning for Jamilah ended, Moses insisted on returning to his medical practice despite strong advice to the contrary from Abraham, who feared for his father's health. Bouts of depression returned, as did the episodes of chest pain. He continued to supervise the documentation of source references for the *Mishneh Torah* but left much of the actual writing to Joseph and Abraham.

Moses accepted that his own days were also now limited. He regularly recalled past events in his life and worried that he had not achieved all that God had expected him to do. Was he satisfied with what he had accomplished? Should he have contributed more to society? He thought of his religious and philosophical writings, his medical contributions, and his work as nagid. He still received Halachic queries, but his responses were briefer and briefer, often appearing as only a few words appended to the bottom of the letter bearing the query.

He was once again discussing his early life with Abraham, the forced exodus from his homes in Cordoba and in Fez, and the visit to Jerusalem and to Hebron to see the holy sites, when he stopped and remained quiet for a few moments.

"Tiberias … Tiberias," he muttered as he suddenly remembered. Now was the time to inform Abraham.

"My dear son." He seemed more animated. "When the time comes for my soul to be returned to its Maker, I would desire for my body to be buried in Tiberias overlooking the Sea of Galilee, where Rabbi Yohanan ben Zakkai is also buried." This was important to Moses. He had been reflecting on it for many years, ever since he and his father had visited Tiberias on their return to Acre from Jerusalem.

"Dear father, do not be worried. I will ensure that when the time comes, your request will be honoured." Moses seemed content, confident his wish would be respected.

He was so proud of his son, Abraham; how well Jamilah had guided his progress whilst he himself had been consumed with work. As with the generations before him, Abraham was studying to become a rabbi, but in addition he had expressed a desire to follow his father as a physician. This also pleased Moses.

Moses was almost seventy. It had been a year since his beloved Jamilah had died. He still attended the palace whenever requested to do so, but now he found the journey difficult. It was mid-December. The morning was chilly. Al-Afdal had asked to see him yet again. Al-Afdal had inherited Damascus but none of the rest of his father's territories. Despite this, he spent much of his time in Egypt, enjoying the many comforts within the sultan's palace. Moses slowly mounted his mule. Abraham assisted whilst at the same time pleading with his father to rest and to explain to the palace that he was unwell. As usual, Moses refused and made his way.

At the palace, Moses dismounted and slowly walked with a recently acquired shuffling gait to al-Afdal's inner court. He spent over an hour explaining, once again, the causes for the sexual difficulties that al-Afdal was experiencing and strongly re-emphasised moderation. He again described the foods which were known to be of benefit since they heated the body and the foods to be avoided since they cooled the body. The aphrodisiac plants and medications were prescribed as previously. Moses suggested that al-Afdal peruse the treatise he had written for him and hoped he would take heed this time of the advice therein.

When Maimonides left the palace, al-Afdal appeared content. Moses was less cheerful. He was tired and lacked energy. As he walked along the marble-lined corridor towards his mule, he needed to rest frequently because of breathlessness. Fortunately for him there were regularly spaced benches facing the large ornate fountains which he was able to make use of. He eventually arrived at the courtyard, where his mule was busily munching hay. He mounted the mule and headed towards his home. The mule was so familiar with the route that very little guidance was required.

As he dismounted, Moses was aware of a gripping pain in his chest. He had experienced similar discomfort previously, but this time it was more acute. He felt sweaty. The pain seemed to move down his left arm again. The realisation that something serious was occurring prompted him to sit on a nearby bench. After a few minutes, the pain eased. He led the mule to the stables and then entered his house. He walked slowly into the large living room and rested on his personal upholstered chair.

"I feel weary," he murmured to himself. Images of his father, his stepmother, his wife, and his son flashed vividly before him. He pictured the yeshiva where he had studied, his friends, and his dear brother, David. He pictured his childhood house in Juderia, the Jewish quarter of Cordoba, an area that he still regarded as home. The gripping chest pain returned, and he struggled to breathe. He was dying. He spoke directly to the Almighty:

"Dear God, you provided me in life with wondrous and extraordinary abilities. I hope I have used them worthily and fulfilled all that you had expected of me. If not, please forgive me."

Throughout his life he had harboured misgivings that he was failing to achieve his full potential in the service of the Almighty. Speaking these final words aloud provided comfort.

He recited the Shema prayer quietly and closed his eyes.

Abraham had spent the morning studying at his yeshiva but was unable to commit to total concentration. He was worried about his father. During a particularly difficult discussion involving a question of Halacha raised by his deeply religious elderly teacher, he suddenly felt cold and indeed could not prevent a shiver and a cold sweat.

"My father is ill. I can feel his distress. He needs me. I must return home," he muttered incoherently to himself and his teacher.

He apologised and left the room in a state of heightened anxiety, physically unhinged by this weird premonition about his father. He hurried home. His father's mule was in the stable. He rushed into the house. His father was slumped in a chair, no longer breathing but at peace with himself. He said a quiet prayer and kissed his father's head. He could almost hear the angels in heaven shouting, "Hazak! Hazak! V'nit'haziek! Be strong! Be strong! And may we be strengthened!"

The synagogue was filled with worshippers anxious to pay

their respects. It was the custom to read from the Torah and the Prophets whenever an important person died. A chapter from Yehoshua was chanted, "Moses my servant has died. Now arise and pass over the Jordan and all this nation, to the land that I give to the children of Israel."

A passage from Samuel was read: "The glory of Israel has gone into exile. The glory has left Israel, for the ark of God has been taken."

The Jews of Fustat mourned for three days.

The Muslim population also mourned, led by al-Aziz and el-Fadil. Moses's reputation as a physician was recognised by Muslim as well as Jewish physicians. A famous Arab poet and physician, Alsaid ibn Sina Almulk, said of Moses that he was the leading man of his time in the art of healing. He expressed this in poetry:

Galen's art heals only the body,

But Abu Amram's the body and the soul.

With his wisdom he could heal the sickness of ignorance.

His knowledge has made him the physician of the century.

With his wisdom, he could heal the sickness of ignorance.

Were he to attend the moon,

He would free her of spots when she is full,

He would heal her of the periodic defects,

And at the time of her weakness save her from
waning.

When the news of Moses's death reached Jerusalem some
eight days later, the Jews fasted in memory of a great rabbi.
Moses's body was taken through the Sinai and Negev and buried
in Tiberias as he had requested. There are three tombstones. The
original is inscribed with, "Here is buried our rabbi, Moses ben
Maimon, the choicest of humankind." A second tombstone says,
"The Rambam, the strong hand, the teacher of the perplexed".

The third tombstone reads, "From Moses to Moses, there
never arose a man like Moses."

Epilogue

Abraham had lost both his parents within a year. He was inconsolable. His dear mother had been ill over a period of months, in obvious discomfort, and his father had died suddenly. He had time with his mother before she died but was denied the opportunity to be with his father at the end. He bitterly regretted this. He had so much he wanted to tell him and so much to thank him for.

Although Abraham was only eighteen when his father died, he was regarded as the foremost scholar in the community. He had a brilliant intellect and was modest, well-mannered, and very popular. With no dissent he was appointed by al-Aziz as nagid to succeed his father.

Abraham considered that despite being nagid, his first responsibility was to defend his father's writings against all the critics. He worked conscientiously but struggled to complete the sources for the *Mishneh Torah*. Even with Joseph's assistance, the task was, without the guiding hand of his father, beyond their combined ability. He could do no more.

Ben Ali continued with his scathing denigration and denunciation of Moses's writings, concentrating specifically on the issue of resurrection. Even though Moses had written several explanatory letters providing his views on the topic, these were insufficient for Samuel ben Ali, who persisted with malicious assertions that Moses had not accepted the fundamental religious Jewish doctrine of resurrection. This was blatantly untrue, but the evil propaganda spread to Jewish communities elsewhere. In Montpelier in France, Moses's books were publicly burnt by religious Jews to show their disfavour with his alleged beliefs.

Abraham worked tirelessly and forcibly to convince the people that his father had accepted the concept of resurrection. He stated repeatedly that his father considered resurrection to be a generally accepted belief, unproven but believed by a broad consensus and worthy of consent. All who adhere to the religion are obligated to believe in it. But it is unproven and therefore falls short of being a philosophic truth.

Abraham wrote an important book, *Milhamoth Hashem*, in which he answered in a clear and comprehensive manner all the criticisms that had been made of his father's philosophical doctrines in the *Guide*. He felt this was necessary mainly because of the burning of his father's books in Montpelier. He also wrote important commentaries on the *Mishneh Torah* and Talmud, both of which were well-received.

In time the controversy faded and people began to favour Moses's explanations over the negative criticisms. Abraham felt vindicated. Both the *Mishneh Torah* and especially the *Guide* were accepted as works of true brilliance. The *Guide* was repeatedly cited by numerous Christian philosophers and theologians and was translated into Spanish, Italian, French, German, Hungarian, English, Yiddish, and modern Hebrew. It is the medieval Jewish work with the largest number of translations to its name. Thomas Aquinas, the central figure of medieval Christian philosophy, also quoted extensively from the *Guide* in his demonstrations of the existence of God and in his analysis of the creation of the world, divine attributes, and prophecy.

Miriam and Uziel had three children and lived a comfortable

life in Fustat, where Uziel's business continued to thrive. He eventually sold his share of the business to Mustapha, and at the age of fifty he became a full-time communal rabbi. Rachel did not remarry. She never fully recovered from David's death. Shoshanah took care of her mother as Rachel's health faded. She never married. Abraham, like his father, studied medicine and, in addition to being nagid, became a respected physician.

The impact and consequences of Maimonides's medical practice and writings were impressive and far-reaching. Most of Moses's medical texts were translated into Hebrew and Latin and were referred to and quoted for decades. The fundamental principles he advocated in dealing with patients, in applying common sense, in providing unstinting devotion, in relying on evidence of therapeutic efficacy, and in careful clinical observation remain at the very heart of a physician's practice. His ten medical treatises may not be as original as his theological and philosophical works, but they demonstrate his instinctive ability to systemise, clarify, and organise large amounts of information in a way that provides invaluable reference for physicians to act upon. Because of this, his books acted as standard medical textbooks and were referred to for generations.

The reciprocity of mind and body and the importance of achieving a healthy mind in a healthy body was an original concept and became accepted dogma amongst physicians. His obsessional thoughts about hygiene and a good diet, physical exercise, dwellings in pleasant surroundings, and even music and poetry to create happiness and a cheerful mood were all considered by future generations to be important for a healthy lifestyle. These concepts were adopted widely with a concomitant improvement in living standards, a legacy to Moses's brilliant mind, his accurate scientific observations, his common sense, and his logical thinking.

Moses's attitude towards medicine was based on his

formidable religious background and knowledge, which regarded the maintenance of health and life as a basic commandment from the Almighty. This approach remains as his lasting testament. Multitudes of physicians have taken inspiration from this ideology as well as from Moses's remarkable achievements. One cannot fail to be impressed that a single individual could have accomplished so much.

In conclusion, Moses's attitude towards his work and life can best be summed up by the following quotation taken from the *Mishneh Torah*:

> If a person undertakes to study Torah, forgo gainful employment, and support himself through charity, that man profanes the divine name, shows contempt for the Torah, extinguishes the light of religion, brings evil upon himself, and removes his life from the world to come. For it is forbidden to derive benefit from the Torah in this world. Torah unaccompanied by labour will in the end be rendered as nought. It leads to sin, and the man will eventually rob his fellow creatures.

Mishneh Torah, H. Talmud Torah 3:10

Nobody can accuse Moses ben Maimon of failing to adhere to his own firmly held belief of the importance of Torah learning whilst at the same time contributing to the well-being of his fellow man.

NOTES ON FROM MOSES TO MOSES

There have been dozens, if not hundreds, of books written on the theological, philosophical and medical writings of Moses ben Maimon, most being of the highest scholastic content. Whereas Maimonides's concepts and beliefs have been subjected to detailed critique and form the basis of much Talmudic study, far less is known about his life. It is true to say that his various journeys are well-documented, although there is controversy about the actual dates, but remarkably little is known about his family and his everyday life.

In writing this book, it was my intention to weave a fictional account around the little that is factually known about Maimonides's everyday family life. Accordingly, the book is historical fiction with fabricated names and events.

Moses's father, Rabbi Maimon ben Yosef, was an erudite and learned dayan. Little is known of him, other than his being the father of the Rambam. He authored a commentary in Arabic on the Torah as well as books on Jewish ritual and festival law. All the events in this book which include him are purely fictional.

It is known that he was remarried after his first wife died in childbirth, but to whom?

Moses's exploits in the yeshiva in Lucena are pure fiction, although it is known that he did study with Rabbi Migash, as indeed did his father before him.

Much is documented about Cordoba in the eleventh and twelfth centuries. Menocal (2002) has written extensively on the topic, and her wonderful book *Ornament of the World* provides a graphic account of life in that city. In Cordoba, Muslims, Christians, and Jews created an exemplary culture of tolerance, one which modern-day society could learn a great deal from. All the different religions flourished economically, and certainly the Maimons enjoyed a high standard of living. Moses invariably signed his letters throughout his life as "Moses son of Maimon the Spaniard", a clear indication of a lifelong love of and commitment to his beloved Cordoba.

Sadly, invasion by the Almohads changed all that. How many Jews converted to Islam so that they could remain in Cordoba is not known, but many undoubtedly did. However, the Maimons did not and were therefore forced to leave their wonderful home and lifestyle in Cordoba and spend many years in forced exile. The adventures described during their travels are all entirely fictitious. There is no mention in Maimonides's writings of a sister who accompanied them; Miriam is also a figment of my imagination.

Likewise, the exploits in Fez are imaginary. It is not known where Maimonides learnt his medicine, but he did live for some years in Fez, where the Karaouine School, a famous academic institute, was based and where medicine was taught by distinguished Arab physicians. Whether Maimonides converted to Islam has always been a controversial issue. If he did, it would have been a "pseudo-conversion" as a ruse to enter the Karaouine institution. However, strong evidence for this does not exist. There is a suggestion from the literature that at one stage of his life he was in danger because of an allegation of false conversion against him, which was the reason for his rapid exit from Fez.

The Maimon family undoubtedly visited Palestine, as it was named at the time. Moses describes his visit to Jerusalem and his prayers at the Wailing Wall as being deeply spiritual. The family also visited the Cave of Machpelah in Hebron. It is thought that Rabbi Maimon died in Palestine, although there is no indication of where he is buried. The situation in Palestine at that time for the Jews was depressing. They were forbidden from living in Jerusalem, and the level of Judaic observance was pitifully meagre.

In Alexandria there was a long-standing dispute with the Karaite population and a suggestion, albeit not proven, that Maimonides tried to intervene, unsuccessfully. There is documented evidence to confirm that Maimonides had a lifelong disdain for Karaitism, which he regarded almost as blasphemy.

In Fustat he was appointed as nagid and did serve the palace as a court physician to Saladin. However, all the exploits I describe in this role are purely fictional and figments of my imagination. The adjudication that he made regarding the case of Yehoshua who "lay" with a boy has been taken from an actual documented case when Maimonides was nagid. Readers may be confused and surprised by the outcome, as indeed was I. But perhaps one should be careful about applying modern-day standards to events of eight hundred years ago.

Maimonides, as physician to the palace, was highly regarded by Saladin, whom he met on several occasions. There is evidence to suggest that Maimonides's *Treatise on Poisons* was written at the direct request of Saladin, who was concerned by the large number of deaths amongst his soldiers from scorpion bites and snakebites. The exploits I have described with el-Fadil and al-Afdal are purely fictional.

What is not fictional is the brilliance of his three major texts, the *Commentary on the Mishna*, the *Mishneh Torah*, and the *Guide of the Perplexed.* Only a genius could have written such erudite discourses which remain relevant eight hundred years later. In the *Commentary* he identifies the thirteen principles of faith which are accepted and included as a recognised part of the Jewish prayer book. They are recited as a liturgical hymn on Friday night and during festival services (Yigdal) and as Ani Ma'amin after morning prayers.

The *Mishneh Torah* took Maimonides nine years to complete. It was written in fourteen volumes. The numerical value of the Hebrew word for "hand" is fourteen, so the text was referred to as *Yad ha-hazachah* or "The mighty hand".

All ten medical treatises written by Maimonides, often in response to requests or queries posed by various patrons, are informative and served as comprehensive texts for the Middle Ages.

Maimonides's ten medical texts, all written in Arabic, are as follows:

- *Extracts from Galen*

  This volume consists of extracts of Aelius Galen's most important pronouncements. Two Arabic manuscripts remain extant today.

- *Commentary on the Aphorisms of Hippocrates*

  This volume consists of comments and criticisms of Hippocrates. It was translated into Hebrew by Samuel ibn Tibbon.

- *Medical Aphorisms of Moses (Pirke Moses)*

  This text is made up of fifteen hundred aphorisms dealing with different areas of medicine. A complete

Arabic original version exists in the Gotha library in Germany.

- *Treatise on Haemorrhoids*

  This was written for a member of Saladin's family. Details of both prevention and treatment are documented.

- *Treatise on Cohabitation (Sexual Intercourse)*

  Written for al-Afdal, this work provides advice and advocates moderation.

- *Treatise on Asthma*

  This work was written at the request of a patient with breathing difficulties. Medications and environmental issues are discussed.

- *Treatise on Poisons and Their Antidotes*

  This book was written in response to a direct request from Saladin. Several Arabic, Hebrew, and Latin manuscripts are extant. It became the authoritative textbook on toxicology and was used throughout Europe and the Near East. It was widely referred to for many hundreds of years.

- *Regimen of Health (Regimen Sanitatis)*

  In this text, the environment and health are discussed, as are psychosomatic issues. This work became very popular, and many translations and original manuscripts are extant.

- *Discourse on the Explanation of Fits*

  This work includes a description of the symptoms, the causes, and treatment of fits. Many translations are available.

- *Glossary of Drug Names*

  This is a pharmacopoeia consisting of 405 short paragraphs containing names of drugs. There is an extant manuscript in the Hagia Sophia library in Istanbul.

Nothing is known about Maimonides's wife, not even her name, which is surprising considering that he wrote so much during their marriage. Apart from Abraham, did he have other children? Another unanswered question. I have woven a fictitious account of his married life. There is a suggestion that Maimonides had a second marriage after his first wife died in Alexandria, but I could find no convincing evidence to support this. Much is documented about his brilliant son, Abraham, who succeeded him as nagid in Fustat and became a physician.

The vicious criticisms of Maimonides's work, mainly from Samuel ben Ali (sometimes referred to as Shmuel ben Eli), are well-documented, as indeed are Maimonides's responses to the allegations.

Throughout his life, Maimonides lived in Arab countries, and Arabic was his first language. He and his family lived for many years under difficult conditions because of the Almohads and were *dhimmis*. However, they remained steadfast in practising their religion despite the persecution.

I have tried to highlight Maimonides's writings with my probably naive interpretation of what might have been his thought processes and illustrate this with quotations from his theological, philosophical, and medical writings.

I hope the reader will forgive any inappropriate meanderings but accept the book as an attempt to add a human dimension to a man whom I have had the utmost regard for over the last twenty years and one who can only be described as a genius, in the same category as the great thinkers of the many centuries who followed him.

The esteem to which the Rambam is generally held as a physician can be demonstrated by the so-called "Oath of Maimonides", which although attributed to him, was probably written decades after his death. However, it reads as though it could have been his work, as it encapsulates many of his principles in treating patients and emphasises the importance of continuing education and lifelong learning as a prime requirement for a physician;

> The eternal providence has appointed me to watch over the life and health of Thy creatures. May the love of my art actuate me at all times, may neither avarice nor miserliness, nor thirst for glory or for a great reputation engage my mind, for the enemies of truth and philanthropy could easily deceive me and make me forgetful of my lofty aim of doing good to Thy children.
>
> May I never see in the patient anything but a fellow creature in pain.
>
> Grant me strength, time and opportunity always to correct what I have acquired, always to extend its domain, for knowledge is immense and the spirit of man can extend indefinitely to enrich itself daily with new requirements.

Today he can discover his errors of yesterday and tomorrow he can obtain a new light on what he thinks himself sure of today. Oh, God, Thou has appointed me to watch over the life and death of Thy creatures; here am I ready for my vocation and now I turn unto my calling.

Finally, for Maimonides, medicine, health, and religion are closely linked to the well-being of both the body and soul. Two quotations from Maimonides's theological writings, not his medical ones, illustrate this, and I consider them to be as pertinent today as when they were written over eight hundred years ago:

> The art of medicine, although it treats only the body plays a very large role in acquiring both the ethical virtues and knowledge of God, and hence in attaining true happiness and wellbeing. Learning and studying medicine is an important form of divine worship. ... For through medicine we calibrate our bodily actions so that they become genuinely human actions, actions that render the body a tool for the acquisition of the virtues and scientific truths.

> Maimonides, *Shemonah Perakim*, chapter 5

> I guarantee that all who obey the rules of diet and hygiene which I have laid down will stay free of disease until they die at an advanced age without ever needing a physician, while

their bodies will be healthy and remain so throughout their lives.

Maimonides, *Mishneh Torah*, Hilchot De'ot
4:20

According to Maimonides, a healthy body is desirable not only for itself but also as a platform upon which the soul can strive towards its proper perfection.

Rabbi Moses ben Maimon is buried in Tiberias on the western shore of the Sea of Galilee in Israel. His tomb is one of the most important pilgrimage sites in Israel. It is also the burial place of Rabbi Isaiah Horowitz and Rabbi Yohanan ben Zakkai.

On the wall of Maimonides's metal-topped shrine is the quotation "From Moses to Moses there were none like Moses."

BIBLIOGRAPHY

Arbel, I., *Maimonides: A Spiritual Biography* (New York: Crossroad Publishing Company, 2001).

Blau, J., and S. C. Reif, *Genizah Research after Ninety Years* (Cambridge: Cambridge University Press, 1992).

Buijs, J. A., *Maimonides: A Collection of Critical Essays* (Notre Dame, IN: University of Notre Dame Press, 1988).

Collins, K., S. Kottek, and F. Rosner, *Moses Maimonides and His Practice of Medicine* (Haifa: Maimonides Research institute, 2013).

Davidson, D. A., *Moses Maimonides: The Man and His Works* (Oxford: Oxford University Press, 2005).

Friedlander, M., *Moses Maimonides: The Guide for the Perplexed* (New York: Dover Publications, 1981).

Hourani, G. F., *Arab Seafaring in the Indian Ocean in Ancient and Medieval Times* (Princeton, NJ: Princeton University Press, 1995).

Leibowitz, Y., *The Faith of Maimonides* (Tel Aviv: MOD Books, 1989).

Lerner, R., *Maimonides' Empire of Light* (Chicago: University of Chicago Press, 2000).

Levy, Y., and S. Carmy, *The Legacy of Maimonides: Religion, Reason, and Community* (New York: Yashar Books, 2006).

Menocal, M. R., *The Ornament of the World*) New York: Little, Brown and Company, 2002).

Nuland, S. B., *Maimonides* (New York: Schocken, 2005).

Reif, S. C., *A Jewish Archive from Old Cairo* (Surrey: Curzon Press, 2000).

Reif, S. C., *The Cambridge Genizah Collections* (Cambridge: Cambridge University Press, 2002).

Rosner, F., *Sex Ethics in the Writings of Moses Maimonides* (New York: Bloch Publishing Company, 1974).

Rosner, F., *The Medical Legacy of Moses Maimonides* (Hoboken, NJ: KTAV Publishing House, 1998).

Rosner, F., *Medical Encyclopaedia of Moses Maimonides* (Northvale, NJ: Jason Aronson, 1998).

Rosner, F., and S. Muntner, "The Surgical Aphorisms of Moses Maimonides", *American Journal of Surgery*, 119 (1970): 718–25.

Rosner, F., and S. Samuel, *Moses Maimonides: Physician, Scientist, and Philosopher* (Northvale, NJ: Jason Aronson, 1993).

Stitskin, L. D., *Letters of Maimonides* (New York: Yeshiva University Press, 1977).

Seeskin, K., *Maimonides: A Guide for Today's Perplexed* (Springfield, NJ: Behrman House, 1991).

Seeskin, K., *The Cambridge Companion to Maimonides* (Cambridge: Cambridge University Press, 2005).

Shulman, Y. D., *The Rambam: The Story of Rabbi Moses ben Maimon* (Lakewood, NJ: CIS Publishers, 1994).

Twersky, I., *A Maimonides Reader* (Springfield, NJ: Behrman House, 1972).

Weiss, R. L., and C. Butterworth, *Ethical Writings of Maimonides* (New York: Dover Publications, 1975).

Yelling, D., and I. Abrahams, *Maimonides: His Life and Works* (New York: Heron Press, 1972).

Zeitlin, S., *Maimonides: A Biography* (New York: Bloch Publishing Co., 1955).

Printed in the United States
By Bookmasters